GENA SHOWALTER

THE DARKEST SURRENDER

Lords of the Underworld

HQN™

Recycling programs
for this product may
not exist in your area.

ISBN-13: 978-0-373-77581-1

THE DARKEST SURRENDER

To Donna Glass, a real-life Bianka Skyhawk. Your support and enthusiasm for the Lords of the Underworld thrills me more than I can ever say. Thank you, thank you, a thousand times thank you! (Did I mention I'm thankful?) And from all of the warriors currently residing in the Budapest fortress: you're welcome to come over anytime. Gideon adds: And I hope like hell you don't! Also, Lysander says there's a cloud with your name on it—next to his.

THE DARKEST SURRENDER

PROLOGUE

Fifteen hundred years ago...
Or
A million years ago...
(Just depends on who you ask.)

FOR THE FIRST TIME EVER, the bi-century Harpy Games ended with more participants dead than alive, and every single one of the survivors knew fourteen-year-old Kaia Skyhawk was to blame.

The day began innocently enough. With the morning sun shining brightly, Kaia strolled through the overcrowded camp hand in hand with her beloved twin sister, Bianka. Tents of every size littered the area, and multiple fires crackled to ward off the early-morning chill. The scents of filched biscuits and honey coated the air, making her mouth water.

Forever cursed by the gods, Harpies could only eat what they stole or earned. If they ate anything else, they sickened horribly. So Kaia's breakfast had been a meager affair: a stale rice cake and half a flagon of water, both of which she'd pilfered from a human's saddle.

Maybe she'd appropriate a biscuit from a member of a rival clan, she mused, then shook her head. No, she'd just have to remain semi-hungry. Her kind didn't live by many rules, but the ones they had, they revered. Such as: never fall asleep where humans could find you, never reveal a weakness to *anyone* and, most importantly, never thieve a single morsel of food from one of your own race, even if you hated her.

"Kaia?" her sister said, her tone curious.

"Yes?"

"Am I the prettiest girl here?"

"Of course." Kaia didn't even have to look around to confirm that fact. Bianka was the prettiest girl in the *entire world*. Sometimes she forgot, though, and had to be reminded.

While Kaia had a disgusting mop of red hair and unremarkable gray-gold eyes, Bianka had luxurious black hair, shimmering amber eyes and was the image of their exalted mother, Tabitha the Vicious.

"Thank you," Bianka said, grinning with satisfaction. "And I think you're the strongest. By far."

Kaia never tired of hearing her sister's praise. The more powerful a Harpy was, the more respect she earned. From everyone. More than anything, Kaia craved respect. "Stronger, even, than…" She studied the Harpies in the area, searching for someone to compare herself to.

Those who were old enough to participate in the traditional tests of might and cunning bustled about, preparing for the one remaining event—Last Immortal Standing. Swords whistled as they were tugged from sheaths. Metal ground against stone as daggers were sharpened.

Finally, Kaia spotted a contender for her comparison. "Am I stronger, even, than her?" she asked, pointing to a brute of a woman with bulging muscles and thick crisscrossing scars adorning her arms.

The injuries that had left those scars must have been severe indeed; immortality caused their race to heal quickly and efficiently, rarely allowing any evidence of hard living to show.

"No question," Bianka said loyally. "I bet she'd run and hide if you decided to challenge her."

"No doubt you're right." Actually, who *wouldn't* run from her? Kaia trained harder than anyone and had even felled her own instructor. Twice.

She didn't want to boast, but she'd always trained harder than any other Harpy in their clan. When everyone else stopped for the day, she continued until sweat ran down her chest in rivulets, until her muscles trembled from the strain…until her bones could no longer support her weight.

One day, perhaps even one day soon, her mother would be proud of her. Why, just a few nights ago, Tabitha had slapped her on the shoulder and said her dagger throwing skills had almost improved. *Almost improved.* No sweeter praise had ever left Tabitha's mouth.

"Come on," Bianka said, tugging at her. "If we don't hurry, we won't have time to wash in the river, and I really want to look my best when I watch our clan destroy the competition. Again."

Just thinking of the prizes her mother would collect caused Kaia's small body to puff up with pride.

The Harpy Games had begun thousands of years ago as a way for clans to "discuss" their grievances without causing a war—well, without causing any *more* wars—as well as allowing allied clans to showcase their superiority, even against each other. Elders from each of the twenty tribes met and agreed on the competitions and awards.

This time around, each winner of the four battles earned one hundred gold pieces. The Skyhawks had already earned two hundred of those pieces. The Eagleshields had won one.

"Out of your head…that's a good girl," Bianka said as she quickened her steps, forcing Kaia to quicken hers in turn. "You daydream too much."

"Do not."

"Do, too."

"Not!"

A sigh from her sister, an admission of defeat.

Kaia grinned. The two of them drew a bit of notice from nearby Harpies, and she made sure to stroke the Skyhawk warrior medallion hanging from her neck. Her mother had gifted her with hers a few months ago, and she treasured the symbol of her strength almost as much as she treasured her twin.

Most everyone who met her gaze nodded in deference, even if she belonged to a rival clan. Those who didn't…no Harpy would dare attack another while on neutral ground, so Kaia didn't worry about possible conflict. Actually, she wouldn't have worried anyway. She was as brave as she was strong.

At the very edge of camp, nestled in a grove of trees, she noticed something strange and halted. "Those men," she said, pointing to a group of bare-chested males. Some roamed freely, a few were tied to posts and one was chained. To her knowledge, males were never allowed to enter or even watch the games. "What are they doing over there?"

Bianka stopped and followed the line of her finger. "They're consorts. And slaves."

"I know that. Hence the reason I asked what they're doing over there and not who they are."

"They're meeting needs, silly."

Kaia's brow scrunched in confusion. "What kind of needs?" Their mother had always stressed the importance of taking care of yourself first, your family second and everyone else not at all.

Bianka considered her response carefully, then shrugged and said, "Doing laundry, bathing feet, fetching weapons. You know, menial things we're too important to do."

What she took away from that? If you owned a consort or slave, you'd never have to do laundry again. "I want one," Kaia announced, and the tiny wings protruding from her back fluttered wildly.

Like all Harpies, she wore a half top that covered her breasts—though hers were tragically nonexistent at the moment—but remained open in back to accommodate the small arch of her wings, the source of her superior strength.

"And you know what Mother always says," she added.

"Oh, yes. A kind word will win you a smile, but who in their right mind wants to win a smile?"

"Not that."

Bianka pursed her lips. "You can't really kill a human with kindness. You have to use a sword."

"Not that, either."

Exasperated, her sister tossed her arms in the air. "Then what?"

"If you don't take the treasures and the males you want, you'll never *get* the treasures and the males you want."

"Oh." Bianka's eyes widened as her attention returned to the men. "So which one do you want?"

Kaia tapped a fingertip against her chin as she studied the candidates. Each of the men wore a loincloth, and each hard body was streaked with dirt and sweat, but none of the men were cut or bruised as she was, indicating they'd proven themselves on the battlefield. Or at least, had tried to do so.

No, not true, she realized a second later. The one in chains was covered in battle marks, and his dark eyes were definitely defiant. He was a fighter. "Him," she said, motioning with a tilt of her chin. "Who owns him?"

Bianka looked him over, trembled. "Juliette the Eradicator."

Juliette Eagleshield, an ally as well as a coldhearted beauty trained by Tabitha Skyhawk herself.

Conquering a male the Eradicator had failed to tame would be… "Even better."

"I don't know about this, Kye. We were warned not to speak to any of the men."

"*I* wasn't warned."

"Oh, yes, you were. I know this because you were standing right beside me when Mother delivered the warning. You must have been daydreaming again."

She refused to be swayed from her chosen path. "New rule—if a daughter doesn't hear a warning, she doesn't have to heed it."

Bianka remained unconvinced. "He reeks of danger."

"We love danger."

"We also love to breathe. And I think he'd rather chop us into pieces than bathe our feet. Not to mention what Juliette will do to us if we succeed in taking him."

"Trust me. Juliette isn't as strong as I am, or she wouldn't have had to chain him." Sure, Juliette was known for her willingness to slay anyone at any time, no matter their age or gender, but Kaia would soon be known as the girl who had one-upped her.

Her sister thought that rationale over for a moment, then nodded. "Very true."

"I'll just explain the punishment he'll receive if he disobeys me, and I promise you, he won't disobey me." Simple, easy. Her mother was going to be *so* proud.

Tabitha wasn't proud of many people, only those who proved to be her equal. So…in other words, she wasn't yet proud of anyone. Maybe that was why every Harpy wanted to be her and every male wanted to win her. Her strength was unparalleled, her beauty unmatched. Her wisdom, limitless. All trembled at the mere mention of her name. (If they didn't, they should.) All respected her. And all admired her.

One day, all will admire me.

"H-how are you going to sneak him away?" Bianka asked. "Where are you going to hide him?"

Hmm, good questions. But as she pondered the answers, indignation filled her. Why should she sneak him away? Why should she hide him? If she did, no one would know what she'd done. No one would write stories depicting her strength and daring.

More than she wanted a slave to do her bidding, she wanted those stories. *Needed* those stories. Because she and Bianka were twins, they were constantly teased about sharing what had been meant for one. Beauty, strength, anything, everything. As if they each had only half of what they should.

I'm enough, damn it! And I will *prove it.*

She would take the man here, now, in front of everyone.

Nearly bursting with urgency, Kaia turned to her sister and cupped her wind-pinkened cheeks. Worry consumed Bianka's delicate features, but that didn't stop Kaia from saying, "Allow no one to pass this point. I'll only be a moment."

"But—"

"Please. For me, *please.*"

Unable to resist, her sister sighed. "Oh, all right."

"Thank you!" Kaia kissed her right on the mouth then marched away before the sweet-tempered darling could change her mind. She palmed a dagger. The men pretended not to notice her as she shoved her way past them, and not a single protest was uttered. Good. Already they feared her.

When she reached the object of her young desire, she posed as she'd seen her mother pose a thousand times before. Hip cocked to the side, a fist resting on top, the blade of the dagger pointing outward.

The man sat on a stump, his elbows propped on his scabbed knees. His head was slightly bent, his inky hair falling over his forehead.

"You," she said in the human tongue. "Look at me."

Through the tangled locks, his dark gaze lifted and leveled on her. He was handsome, she supposed. Each of his features appeared to be chiseled from stone. He had a blade of a nose, sharpened cheekbones, thin but red lips and a stubborn chin.

Up close, she realized his chains were wrapped around his wrists and only his wrists, a metal link stretching between the two. Nothing bound him to a post. Either Juliette had no idea how to properly restrain a captive or the man was weaker than Kaia had assumed.

Disappointing, but she wouldn't change her mind now.

"You're mine," she told him boldly. "Your previous mistress might try and fight me for you, but I'll defeat her."

"Is that so?" His voice was deep and husky, seemingly layered with thunder and lightning. She repressed a shudder. "What's your name, little girl?"

Her teeth gritted together, her momentary apprehension forgotten. She wasn't a little girl! "I'm called Kaia the... Strongest. Yes, yes. That's what I'm called." Titles were important among the Harpies, chosen by the tribe leaders, and while Kaia had yet to receive hers, she was absolutely certain her mother would approve of her choice.

"And what exactly do you plan to do with me, Kaia the Strongest?"

"I'm going to force you to meet all my needs, of course."

He arched a brow. "Such as?"

"Doing my chores. *All* of my chores. And if you don't do them, I'll punish you. With my dagger." She wiggled the weapon in question, the silver blade glinting lethally in the sunlight. "I'm quite cruel, you know. I've killed humans dead before. *Really* dead. So dead they even hurt afterward."

He didn't flinch at the weapon or at her implied threat, and she fought a wave of frustration. Then she consoled herself with the knowledge that most humans had no true concept of a Harpy's skills. Clearly, he was one of the uninformed. Because he himself couldn't lift a thousand-pound boulder, he probably couldn't fathom anyone else doing so.

"When shall I begin these new duties?" he asked.

"Now."

"Very well, then." She had expected an argument, but he unfolded his big body from the stump. Gods, he was tall, forcing her to look up...up...up.

She wasn't intimidated, though. While training, she'd fought beings a lot taller than him and won. Well, maybe they'd only been a little bit taller. Fine, they'd all been shorter. She wasn't sure anyone was as tall as this man. No wonder Juliette had claimed him.

Kaia grinned. Her first solo raid, in broad daylight no less, and she would be leaving with a prize among prizes. She'd chosen well. Her mother would find no fault with the man, and might even want him for herself. Maybe after Kaia finished with him, she would gift him to Tabitha.

Tabitha would smile at her, thank her and tell her what a wonderful daughter she was. Finally. Kaia's heart skipped a beat.

"Don't just stand there." Before the male had time to reply, she rushed behind him, wings flapping frantically, and pushed him. "Move."

He stumbled forward, but quickly managed to catch himself. With his head held high, he marched the distance. Just before he reached the edge of the enclosure, however, he stopped abruptly.

"Move," she repeated, giving him another push.

He remained in place, not even twisting to face her. "I can't. This clearing has been encircled with Harpy blood, and the chains prevent me from leaving without suffering severe pain."

Her gaze narrowed on the muscled width of his tanned back. "I'm not a fool. I won't remove your chains." Plus, she wanted him docile while she paraded him through camp, not vying for freedom. When Juliette discovered what she'd done, a challenge would be issued. Kaia would need her attention focused, not divided.

"Removing my chains isn't necessary." Not by tone or deed did he reveal a hint of his emotions. "Simply add your blood to the circle already there, then smear a drop on the chains, and you can lead me across without any problems."

Ah, yes. She'd heard of blood-chains before. They trapped the wearer within the confines of the circle, however wide or small that circle was, and only a Harpy's blood could negate the restriction. *Any* Harpy's. "Good idea. I'm glad I thought of it."

She surveyed the Harpy camp. No one had noticed her, but Bianka was nervously shifting from one foot to the other, looking from Kaia to the camp, the camp to Kaia, her gaze pleading.

With swift precision, Kaia used her dagger to slice her palm. The sharp sting barely registered. After adding her blood to the crimson ring on the ground, she smoothed her weeping flesh over the cool links of metal between the man's wrists. That done, she raced behind him a second time and pushed.

He stumbled past the circle, paused to shake his head, stretch his spine, flex his shoulders. No matter how hard she pushed this time, she couldn't budge him. Then he turned back and grinned at her. Before she could reason out what was happening, he had his hands wrapped around her neck, her feet lifted off the ground.

Her eyes widened as he choked the life out of her with a power no human should have possessed.

Despite her lack of air, fogging brain and burning throat, realization struck. He *wasn't* human.

Hatred suddenly poured from him, his dark eyes swirling hypnotically. "Foolish Harpy. I might not be able to break these chains, but that circle was the only thing preventing me from rampaging through the camp. Now, all of you will die for the insult delivered to me."

Die? Hell, no! *You have a dagger. Use it!* She tried to stab him. Laughing cruelly, he batted her hand away.

In the background, she heard Bianka shriek. Heard footsteps pound as her sister hurriedly closed the distance. *No,* she tried to shout. *Stay back.* Then her thoughts fragmented as the man choked harder, tighter.

A black wave swept her into a sea of nothingness.

No, not nothingness. Screams echoed...so many screams... Grunts, groans and growls. The slide of metal against flesh, the pop of breaking bones, the sickening sound of wings being ripped from their slits. The nightmarish symphony lasted hours, perhaps days, before at last quieting.

"Kaia." Callused hands wrapped around her upper arms and shook her. "Awaken. Now."

She knew that voice... Kaia fought her way from the sea, her eyelids fluttering open. A moment passed before her mind cleared and the darkened haze faded. Through a sliver of moonlight, she saw a blood-soaked, scowling Tabitha Skyhawk looming over her.

"Look what you've done, daughter." Never had her mother's timbre lashed so harshly—and that was saying something.

Though she wanted to refuse, she sat up, grimaced as

pain lanced through her neck to attack the rest of her, and shifted her gaze, studying the camp. Bile rose. Harpies and…other things floated in rivers of scarlet. Weapons lay on the ground, useless. Strips of cloth from decimated tents had caught on tree branches and now waved in the wind, a sad parody of white flags.

"B-Bianka?" she managed to gasp, her voice raw.

"Your sister is alive. Barely."

Kaia pushed to shaky legs and met her mother's amber eyes. "Mother, I—"

"Silence! You were told not to enter this area, and yet you disobeyed. And then, *then* you tried to steal another woman's consort without gaining my permission."

She wanted to lie, to preserve her dream of the coming accolades. She found she could not. Not to her beloved mother. "Yes." Tears stung her eyes, that dream quickly flaming to ash inside her. "I did."

"Do you see the destruction behind me?"

"Yes," she repeated softly.

Tabitha showed her no mercy. "You alone are responsible for the travesty this day."

"I'm sorry." Her head fell, chin resting against her sternum. "So sorry."

"Keep your sorries. They cannot undo the anguish you have caused."

Oh, gods. There was *hatred* in her mother's voice now. True, undiluted hatred.

"You have brought shame to our clan," Tabitha said, ripping the medallion from Kaia's neck. "This, you do not deserve. A true warrior saves her sisters. She does not endanger them. And so by this selfish act you have earned your title. From this moment on, you will be known as Kaia the Disappointment."

With that, Tabitha turned and walked away. Her

boots splashed in the blood, the sound echoing crudely in Kaia's ears.

She fell to her knees and sobbed like a child for the first time in her life.

CHAPTER ONE

Present day

"I WANT HIM."

"Where have I heard that before? Oh, yeah. The day of the Unfortunate Incident, something you made me swear never to discuss, even upon threat of death. And I won't discuss it now, so don't get your panties in a twist. I just thought you were more careful with your affections nowadays."

Kaia Skyhawk peered over at her twin—Bianka the Heavenly Hills Ho, as Kaia had recently dubbed her. A name her precious sis deserved. Girl had nailed an angel. A freaking angel. 'Course, in return Bianka had dubbed her Kaia: Bed-warmer of the Underworld for getting down and dirty with Paris, the biggest man-whore in existence.

The title didn't sting nearly as much as her last one. Fine, her current one. Harpies had long memories, and shouts of "Look, everyone, it's the Disappointment" still happened anytime she ran into another of her race.

Anyway. Bianka was as ravishingly gorgeous as ever, a dark fall of hair cascading down her back, her amber eyes bright. And just then she was flipping through a rack of designer dresses, a mix of determination and concern radiating from her.

"That happened, like, a million years ago," Kaia said, "and Strider is the first man I've...damn it, he's just the first man I've wanted, *truly* wanted," she added before her sister could comment on her "boyfriends" throughout the centuries, "since. Or ever."

"Actually, *that,* as you called it, happened a mere fifteen hundred years ago, but *we aren't discussing it.* So what about Kane, keeper of Disaster, huh? I thought you once had a moment with him? A shock to your senses or something like that."

"Nothing but static."

A snort full of amusement. "Try again."

"I don't know. Maybe his demon sensed a kindred spirit in me and reached out, hoping to fan the flames of a romance. That doesn't mean Kane and I are destined to be together. I'm not attracted to him."

"Better, and okay, Kane's out. Maybe you need to look elsewhere for a boyfriend. Like, say, the heavens. I can set you up with an angel." Bianka held up a flowing swath of blue material with sequined flower appliqués sewn into the top and layer after layer of lacy ruffles at the bottom. "What do you think of this one?"

Ignoring the dress, Kaia pressed on. "No setups. I want Strider."

"He's no good for you."

He's perfect for me. "One, he doesn't belong to another Harpy. Two, he isn't psychotic. Well," she added with a few seconds of afterthought, "he isn't psychotic all of the time. And three, he's...he's my consort, I know it." There. She'd said the words out loud to someone other than herself and the brain-damaged man in question.

My consort.

Consorts, as Kaia now knew, were extremely hard to find and utterly cherished because of that. Actually, they were necessary. Harpies were volatile by nature, dangerous and, when annoyed, lethal to the entire world. Consorts calmed them. Consorts appeased them.

If only you could select your consort from a catalog and be done with it. Instead, instinct picked for you, and your body followed suit. Wouldn't have been so bad, except each Harpy was granted one consort during her seemingly endless life. Only one. You lost him, and you suffered eternally. If you didn't kill yourself outright.

That Kaia had once tried to steal Juliette's, that Juliette had been without her male all this time, not knowing whether he lived or had died, hating him for what he'd done but needing him anyway, that Juliette still loathed Kaia and had promised retribution—retribution the bitch still clearly planned to achieve—shamed her. But then, what could she say to defend herself? Nothing!

She had disobeyed. *She* had set the man free. *She* had unleashed his fury upon an unsuspecting community.

Every year Kaia mailed Juliette a fruit basket with a "sorry about your consort" card, and every year the basket was returned with rotten apple cores, black banana peels and a picture of Juliette flipping her off with "Die, Whore, Die" written in blood somewhere.

Only reason Juliette hadn't yet attacked was out of respect for Tabitha, who was still a force to be reckoned with among allies and enemies alike.

Don't think about the past. You'll start spiraling.

She'd think about her consort. Strider. Barbaric, slutty, idiotic Strider. He was an immortal warrior who'd long ago stolen and opened Pandora's box to "teach those asshole gods a lesson" for daring to pick a "mere woman" to guard such a "dumb relic," and because of his rampant senselessness, he and the friends who'd helped him—the infamous and deliciously frightening for everyone but a Harpy Lords of the Underworld—had been cursed, forever forced to carry the demons they'd set free inside themselves.

Strider, the beautiful moron, was possessed by the

demon of Defeat. He couldn't lose a single challenge without suffering debilitating pain. Of course, that made him determined to win *everything*, even something as silly as Rock Band. Which she refused to ever again play with him because she'd totally nailed the Fender, then the drums, then the mic and he'd spazzed out and yelled at her before passing out and twitching with pain.

So melodramatic.

Anyway, his determination made him stupid, egotistical, stupid, an all-around asshat and stupid! But there was no man more handsome, no man more fierce.

No man who wanted less to do with her.

Had she mentioned he was stupid?

"Well?" Bianka shook the dress in Kaia's face, forcefully claiming her attention. "Opinion, please. And sometime today."

Focus. "Don't kill the messenger, but that thing will make you look like a cracked-out prom queen who has no plans to sleep with her boyfriend when the big dance ends—because she doesn't have a boyfriend. She's too weird. Sorry."

Bianka merely shrugged, unperturbed. "Hey, cracked-out prom queens might be weird, but they're hot."

"If *hot* is a synonym for *destined to die alone,* you're right. So go ahead. Buy the dress, and I'll buy you a hundred cats to keep you company while you spend the rest of eternity trying to figure where your relationship with the angel went wrong, never really understanding that the problems started *this very night.*"

"Do you know *anything* about me? Hello, I like dogs. But fine, whatever." Red lips pursing, her twin snapped the hanger back onto the rack and continued her search for "the perfect gown" to wear when she broke a bit of bad news to *her* consort, Lysander.

Poor Bianka. She hadn't just nailed an angel, she'd

bound herself to one. Forever. Lysander lived and worked in the heavens and was so boring Kaia would rather shove bamboo splints under other people's fingernails than spend time with him. Okay, bad example. She actually enjoyed shoving bamboo splints under other people's nails.

There was something so *best-musical-ever* when people screamed and begged for mercy, and she could listen to a good musical all day.

"Kaia?" Bianka said. "What the hell are you sighing about?"

"Musicals."

"Musicals? Seriously? When I'm dying for help? Will you just listen to me for once?"

"In a minute. Geez. I really like this thought train." Or rather, she'd liked the station stop before the musicals. A male this boring needed an equally tedious nickname… like…Pope Lysander the First. That's right. He was an elite warrior with wings of gold and yeah, he was a demon slayer extraordinaire, and okay, that was sexy as hell, but he was also morally upstanding. Like over the edge OCD about it. Kaia shuddered with distaste. He was slowly but surely sucking the fun right out of her once delightful sister.

In fact, Lysander's aversion to blatant shoplifting was the reason they had abandoned Budapest, returned to Alaska and broken into Anchorage's Fifth Avenue Mall at night rather than taking what they desired in broad daylight. As usual. Too many prying eyes.

To be honest, Kaia was kind of embarrassed about the concession. She would have told *her* man to take his request to "please don't steal in front of humans, it gives them ideas" and stuff it up his ass. Also, she despised the lack of thrill, *needed* it to soothe her darker side, but whatever. She loved her sister. More than that, she owed Bianka a debt she could never hope to repay.

They might not ever discuss the Unfortunate Incident, but Kaia had never forgotten it. (See? A Harpy with a long memory.) Every day she remembered how Bianka had writhed in a pool of her own blood, her eyes glassy with pain. How moans of anguish had parted mutilated lips.

Bianka sighed. "Okay, let's get your problems out of the way so we can concentrate on me. Tell me why you picked Strider as your heartmate. I know you're dying to extol his virtues."

For a moment, Kaia could only blink at her sister, certain she'd misheard. "Are you freaking kidding me? Heartmate? Did you just say *heartmate?*"

Bianka snickered. "I did, and I almost gagged. Lysander's influence, you know. Anyway, Strider's such a tool. And a challenge." Another snicker echoed. "Get it? A challenge…he can't lose one…but he sure as hell acts like one."

Kaia rolled her eyes. "I think you've been hanging with the angels too much. Your IQ has dropped."

"What? That was funny." Square-tipped nails painted bright blue drummed against the metal rack between them. "And by the way, the angels aren't that bad."

"Whatever you need to tell yourself, my love."

Bianka blew her a kiss full of fang. "All's I'm saying is that Strider's gonna be a handful—and not the good kind. He's—actually, wait. I recant. He's too big to be anything but a good handful. Or more. But he's also gonna be a bad one. Wait. That doesn't ring true, either. How should I put this? He's going to—"

"I get it already! He's got a huge package, and he's irritating as hell. What's your point?"

"Glad you're finally up to speed. It's sad, really, that you need so much explanation." The sparkle in her sister's eyes dimmed. "Anyway, you told him how you felt about him and he rejected you. He'll be annoyed by any further contact you initiate, and an annoyed demon-possessed warrior is a global disaster waiting to happen."

"I know." If she had realized his importance to her sooner, she wouldn't have slept with his friend Paris, the keeper of Promiscuity. Otherwise known as Paris the Sexorcist, a male so sensual he could make your head spin. And if she hadn't slept with the Sexorcist, Strider the Stupid wouldn't have rejected her.

Maybe.

Or maybe he would have. Because to her consternation—yes, consternation, and not an all-consuming, organ-flaming rage—he kinda sorta desired another woman. Haidee, a pretty female who belonged to his friend, Amun, keeper of Secrets.

At least Haidee was off-limits, and Kaia didn't have to worry about Strider getting handsie. Honor among evil demons, and all that.

But damn it, just the thought of his *gaze* on another woman caused Kaia's nails to elongate and sharpen, her fangs to sprout and her blood to boil. *Mine,* every cell in her body cried. She would kill anyone who made a play for him, as well as anyone *he* made a play for; she wouldn't be able to help herself. Her dark side would take over, driving her to protect what was hers.

"Seriously, he's lucky to be alive, and not just because I want to chop off his man parts and feed them to zoo animals while he watches," Bianka continued. "Any man who can't recognize your worth deserves a good torturing."

"I know." Not because Kaia was anything special—though she was, kind of, maybe…damn it, she used to be—but because no one could reject a Harpy without suffering severe consequences.

Actually, most Harpies would have taken Strider despite his wishes. So maybe *she* was the stupid one for allowing him to push her away. She just wanted him willing. She *needed* him willing. To abscond with him was to defeat him, and to defeat him was to hurt him.

She couldn't bring herself to hurt him. Even at the expense of her sanity.

"You're too good for him, anyway," Bianka said, loyal as always.

"I know," she repeated once more, lying this time. She would only ever be a disgrace to her clan. He deserved better.

Her sister sighed. "But you still want him." A statement of fact, not a question.

"Yeah."

"So what are you going to do to win him?"

"Nothing," she said, fighting a wave of depression. "I chased after him once." And he'd found her lacking. "I'm not going to do it again."

"Maybe—"

"No. A few weeks ago, I challenged him to kick more Hunter ass than me." Hunters, the enemy out to destroy all things demon. The fanatics who loved to go after innocents who dared get in their way. The pre-dead humans who would meet the tips of her claws if they approached Strider again.

Well, if they dared approach him with a weapon in hand. She might let them crawl toward him to apologize for the trouble they'd caused throughout the centuries. Torturing the Lords—only *she* was allowed to do so. Blowing up buildings—yawn. Could they be any more B-movie? *Sooo* irritating. Decapitating the keeper of Distrust—okay, that one was a little more than irritating, considering Strider was still messed up about it and everything.

Speaking of Distrust's murder, Haidee had helped carry it out. Yep, *that* Haidee. The one Strider desired.

Kaia didn't understand it. If he could want Haidee despite her crimes, why couldn't he want Kaia?

"I wanted to help him kill the men who were after him. I wanted him to see how capable I was," she added. "I wanted him to admire my skill. But did he? *Noooo.* He was pissed. He raged about all the pain I was going to cause him. So I let him win. Freaking *let* him. You know I *never* throw a fight." That smacked of weakness, and too many people viewed her as weak already. "And how did he thank me? By telling me to get lost." Hu-mil-i-ating. "Now, let's change the subject." Before she threw a temper tantrum and razed the mall to the ground. "What look are you going for?" she asked, flipping through the racks herself.

"Slutty yet sophisticated," her sister said, allowing the change without comment.

"Good choice." She rubbed her tongue against the roof of her mouth as she studied the colorful array of garments. "Think dressing up will help your sitch?"

"Gods, I hope so. I plan to let Lysander rip the garment off me, make love to me in the dirtiest way possible, and then, while he's trying to catch his breath, drop the big, bad bombshell on him and run like hell."

Something Kaia would have loved to do with Strider—the dirty loving part, anyway—but he wouldn't give a shit about anything she told him. As he'd already proven. "What are you going to say to Lysandy, anyway? Exactly."

Bianka shrugged her seemingly delicate shoulders. "Exactly…I don't know."

"Try me. Pretend I'm your disgustingly in love angel consort, and confess."

"Okay." A sigh, a straightening of her spine, then lovely amber eyes were staring over at Kaia with trepidation. "All right. Here goes." A pause. A gulp. "Darling, I, uh, have something to tell you."

"What is it?" Kaia said in her deepest voice. She propped her elbows on the bar, the hanger hooks digging into her skin. "Tell me quickly because I need to spread my happy fairy dust and wave my magic wand when—"

"He doesn't spread happy fairy dust! He's a killer, damn it." The indignation drained as quickly as it had formed. "But as for that magic wand…" Bianka shivered, smirked. "It's *really* big. Probably bigger than Strider's."

Kaia just blinked at her, waiting.

Her sister inhaled deeply, exhaled slowly. "Fine. Continuing. Darling, for the first time in forever, my family has been invited to participate in the Harpy Games. Why for the first time in forever, you ask. Well, funny story. You see, my twin sister did the *dumbest* thing and—"

"I'm sure you're exaggerating about that part," she interjected, still using that deep voice to mimic Lysander. "Your twin is the strongest, most intelligent female I've ever met. Now tell me something *important*."

"Anyway," Bianka went on smoothly. "I'm not sure why we've been invited, but a gold embossed card demanding our attendance came via Harpy Express a few days ago. We can't refuse without bringing intense shame to our entire clan. We would be labeled cowards, and as you know, I'm no coward. So…I'm leaving in one week, and I'll be gone for four. Oh, and each of the four agreed upon events involves bloodshed, possible limb removal and definite torture. See ya." She gave a pinkie wave, stilled, then waited for Kaia's response.

Kaia nodded. "I like it. Firm, informative and unwavering. He'll have no choice but to let you go without a fuss."

Some of Bianka's worry melted away. "You really think so?"

"Gods, no. I don't, not at all. He's gonna flip his lid. For real. You've met him, right? Protective to the extreme." Lucky girl. "So what about this one?" She held up a barely there confection with thin silver chains connecting the sides.

"I think it's great. Perfect, actually. I also think you're a brat."

She flashed an unrepentant grin. "You love me anyway."

"Like you said, my IQ has dropped." Bianka chewed on her bottom lip. "Okay, so. Here's how I think it will go after I confess. First, he'll try to stop me."

"You got that right."

"Then, when he realizes he can't, he'll insist on going with me."

"Right again. Are you good with that?" Everyone would make fun of her for hitching herself to a do-gooder. Even their mother. *Especially* their mother. Tabitha hated angels more than most, since she'd always thought their youngest half sister's father was an angel and had blamed the man for Gwen's supposed weaknesses.

"Yeah." Bianka smiled dreamily. "I'm good with that. I don't like to be without him, and really, I will slaughter anyone who speaks ill of him, so that'll add spice to my days."

"Not to mention weed out the competition because I will help you with those slaughterings." How she wished she could take Strider with her.

Actually, no, she thought next. Thank the gods he wasn't going with her. She was reviled among the Harpy clans. She would die of mortification if he saw her own kind turn their backs on her, and she would fall into that shame spiral if he ever heard her despised nickname.

A soldier like Strider prized strength. She knew because she was a soldier like Strider.

Of course, her next thought struck hard and cut deep—Haidee was strong. The bitch. Though (mostly) human, the girl had managed to defeat death time and time again, coming back to life to fight the Lords. Until she'd fallen in love with Amun.

If I didn't adore Amun so much, I'd send that female back to the grave—for the last damn time! No one caught Strider's notice without suffering unbearably.

Maybe before Kaia left for the games she'd ensure the girl acquired a raging case of head lice or something. No one would be hurt, Strider would be repulsed and Kaia would feel like she'd accomplished some sort of revenge. Win-win.

"Are you listening to me or have I lost you to the thought train again?" Bianka asked, exasperated.

She pulled herself out of her head. "Yes, I'm listening. You were talking about something...of great consequence."

"You *were* listening," her sister said, hand fluttering over her heart. "Anyway, thank you for offering to help punish everyone who insults Lysander. You're my favorite enabler in the world, Kye."

"You, too, Bee." Things would work out for Bianka. Lysander would support her no matter what, and the Harpies would see how intractable he could be and back down. Kaia, though... No, things would not be working out for her.

"Mother Dearest is gonna be there," Bianka said, trying for a casualness neither of them felt for this particular topic, "and she's gonna hate him, isn't she?"

"For sure. But then, she has lousy taste in men. Take our father, for instance. A Phoenix shifter, aka the worst of the worst in terms of immortal races. They're always pillaging and burning stuff to the ground. Seriously, you have to be a real nutbag to hook up with one of them. Which means, what? Mother is a real nutbag. I'd be worried if she *liked* Lysander."

What would Tabitha think of Strider, though?

Bianka gave a low, warm chuckle. "You're right. She does, and she is."

"And you know what else? She can suck it, for all I care." Brave words, yet, on the inside Kaia was still a little girl, desperate for her mother's approval. "But, maybe, I don't know, maybe she'll finally bury the hatchet with me." Gods, was that needy tone really hers?

Bianka leaned across the rack and patted her shoulder. "Hate to break it to you, sister mine, but the only way she'll bury a hatchet is if she gets to bury it in your back."

She tried not to sag with regret. "So true." And she wouldn't care. She *wouldn't*. Really. But why, why, why did no one but her sisters consider her good enough?

One mistake, just one—when she'd been a child, no less—and her mother had written her off. One mistake, just one, and Strider wouldn't commit to her. Wasn't like she'd cheated on him. They'd both been single for years, and hadn't even been on a date together. They hadn't kissed. Hadn't really even talked. And the night she slept with Paris? She hadn't known she would one day want Strider sexually. Or at all.

He should have recognized her appeal from the very beginning and tried to seduce her. So, really, when you thought about it, the blame could totally be laid at his door. Or maybe at his demon's. Defeat had yet to realize that losing her was far worse than losing a challenge. Otherwise, Strider would suffer *without* her.

She wanted him to suffer without her.

The demon was bonded to Strider and essential to his survival, so…maybe she could do something to win the evil fiend over. *If* she decided to make another play for Strider. Which she wouldn't. As she'd told her sister, he'd lost his chance. Besides, approaching him now would make her seem desperate. Which she was.

Gods, this was depressing. And infuriating! Opposition was to be crushed, always, but how was she to fight a man she also wanted to protect?

"What are you thinking about now?" Bianka asked. "Your eyes are almost completely black, so I know your Harpy is close to taking over and—"

"Hey. Hey, you! What are you doing in here?" someone shouted.

Forcing herself to breathe deep and calm down, she threw a quick look over her shoulder. Great. Mall security had arrived. "I'm fine, swear. Meet you back at the house?" she said, tossing the chosen dress at her sister.

"Yeah," Bianka said, catching the garment and stuffing it down her T-shirt for safekeeping. "Love you."

"Love you, too."

They sprinted off in different directions.

"Stop! I'll shoot!"

Kaia's red hair practically glowed in the dark, making her the easier target, so the guard—who didn't shoot, the liar—chased after her as he radioed for backup. The fact that she'd flipped him off before taking that first corner had nothing to do with it.

Most of the store lights were switched off, and the rest of the mall offered very little illumination. Not that it mattered to her superior Harpy eyesight. Her gaze expertly cut through the shadows as she dodged and darted her way toward the exit. Unfortunately, the human knew the area better than she did and managed to keep up with her.

Time to kick things to the next level.

Her wings fluttered…readying…but just before she could blaze into hyperspeed, the guard did the unthinkable and tasered her. *Tasered. Her.* Not a liar, after all. Kaia fell to her face, oxygen instantly turning to lightning in her lungs. She was mere inches from the doorway, yet her spasming muscles prevented her from completing her escape.

She could have jerked the clamps from her back. She could have twisted, pitched one of the many daggers strapped to her and ended her pain. Ended the human. But this was her hometown, and she didn't like to kill the locals. Or rather, she didn't like to kill more than one a day and she'd already hit her limit.

A lie, but she'd go with it.

Plus, why kill the guard when she hadn't truly given the chase her all, knowing deep down that he could provide what she'd secretly craved: a reason to call Strider.

After all, someone would have to bail her out of jail.

CHAPTER TWO

STRIDER WAITED IN THE LOBBY of the Anchorage Police Department, his friend Paris at his side. They'd already posted Kaia's bail and were now waiting for her to be released into their custody. *Come on, Red. Hurry.* He was currently on the receiving end of several once-overs from the male cops—fun fact, he'd had less invasive body cavity searches—as well as a few very thorough eye-fuckings from the females. Paris was, too.

They were armed, yeah. Strider wouldn't visit a church in heaven without a few blades stashed *somewhere*— especially now that he knew heaven was guarded by freaking giant-ass angels—much less stroll into a building filled to bursting with guns and humans who knew how to use them. But, so far, no one had commented. Not that they could see his arsenal, hidden beneath his jacket, T-shirt and jeans as it was.

"Why did we have to be the ones to do this, again?" Paris asked. At six-foot-eight with an all-muscle frame, the keeper of Promiscuity was, to put it mildly, a big guy. Three inches taller than Strider, the bastard, but—and that was a huge *but*—not nearly as powerful.

Considering how many times they'd thrown down, the comparison wasn't merely an opinion but a solid fact.

"I owed her a favor," he said, careful not to reveal any emotion. Like the fact that he'd rather be locked in his enemy's dungeon, torture on the day's menu, than here.

Like the fact that he didn't want to see Kaia again. Ever. Like the fact that he didn't want *Paris* to see Kaia again. For way longer than ever. "She called it in."

"What favor?"

"None of your damn business." He didn't even like to think about it. And talk about it? Hell, no. Too embarrassing. Like being caught out in public with your pants down.

Wait. Bad example. "Pants down" was a good look for him. A *really* good look.

Ego check. He'd told himself he was going to stop patting himself on the back for all his wonderful qualities. After all, it wasn't fair to the citizens of the world. They couldn't help being inferior to him in every way.

"Well, I don't owe her anything." Paris flicked him a glance, ocean-blue eyes glinting. Tension radiated from him. Tragically, uh, *fortunately,* that didn't affect his handsomeness. He had a head of hair most women would kill to own, a mass of differing shades of brown, from the darkest of midnight to the sweetest of honey, and a face most women would kill just to glimpse.

Kaia had probably fisted that hair. Had probably smothered that face with kisses.

Strider's jaw clenched. "You slept with her. Do you really need a reminder of that?"

"No, no reminder. But when you think about it, that means *she* owes *me.* And now you owe me, too, summoning me the way you did, interrupting my quest to demand I help you." Acid filled those words. Not because of Strider, but because of the "quest."

Sienna, the woman Paris desired above all others, was trapped in the heavens, a slave to the god king. Worse still, she was now possessed by the demon of Wrath. Paris hoped to find her, save her and punish everyone who had hurt her.

Strider pressed his tongue to the roof of his mouth, remaining silent. Paris had found his "one and only," as the stupid shithead was now fond of saying—and sounding like a pussy—yet had still slept with Kaia. A man with a one and only shouldn't screw around, in Strider's humble opinion. Yeah, yeah. Paris couldn't help himself. Because of his demon, he had to sleep with a different person every day or he weakened…died.

A petty part of Strider almost wished his friend had chosen the weakening path rather than touching the Harpy.

Of course, the thought caused guilt to eat at him. Kaia was not Strider's one and only, if such a thing even existed for him. She was too competitive, too strong and too wily to cause him anything but misery. And yes, he got the irony. He was that same way with *everyone*. But he *was* attracted to her, and as possessive as he was and had always been, he didn't like the thought of her sleeping with anyone else.

Especially since he had to be the best at everything he did. Because of *his* demon, he had to win, even in bed. And as Paris had more experience than anyone he knew, there was no way Strider could compete in that arena.

Maybe he could have ignored his other reasons for rejecting Kaia's recent and numerous come-and-strip-me glances, but he couldn't ignore that one. Not even once. Because once a man tasted the forbidden fruit, he would go back for more. He wouldn't be able to help himself, the tether on his sanity already broken. So Strider would keep going back, and every time he touched her, tasted her, peeled her panties away with his teeth, he would later experience agony in its purest form.

Yes, Strider was damn good in the sack. Not that he was going to pat himself on the back. He didn't do that anymore, he reminded himself. Okay, fine. He'd make an exception because of the extreme superiority of his talent. He was far better than "good." He was flipping amazing.

But he never took on a fight he wasn't sure he could win. Nothing was worth the physical and mental torment that accompanied a loss, and Paris was probably better than "flipping amazing."

Fine. No probably about it, if the moans Strider had heard from the many hotel rooms Paris had rented throughout the centuries could be believed.

Now, the pleasure that came with a win...sweet gods above. There was nothing like it, not even sex. Strider was addicted to the rush the same way Paris was addicted to ambrosia, the drug of choice for immortals. In fact, he'd stab a dear friend in the throat before letting him—or her—trounce him in something as minor as a spelling bee.

The best way to spell victory? K-I-L-L.

"Anyway," Paris said, drawing him back to the present. "What did Kaia do for you that you'd willingly indenture yourself to me?"

"I already told you. It's none of your damn business."

"Yeah, but I figured if I kept asking, you'd cave."

"You were wrong. News flash, I'm a little more stubborn than most. And by the way, I didn't indenture myself to you. In exchange for your help tonight, I agreed to go to Titania with you to hunt for Sienna." Titania. Dumbass name. But Cronus, the egomaniacal god king, had renamed Olympus to piss off the now incarcerated Greeks who had once reigned there.

Took a real set of titanium cojones to name a location after yourself. Or maybe Cronus was simply overcompensating for something.

Not that Strider and his beloved cock, which he'd modestly nicknamed Stridey-Monster, knew anything about that. They were perfect in every way.

Ego check. Damn it. How many would he need in one day?

"Dude, you totally indentured yourself. You also agreed

to kidnap that shithead William and take him with us," Paris said.

"I also agreed to kidnap that shithead William and take him with us, yes." A fact that still pissed him off. William, a sex-addicted immortal who *wanted* to sleep with Kaia. Unfortunately, Willy was also the only person who could actually spot Sienna, being as how Sienna was dead and he had that whole I-see-dead-people thing going on.

Also, it helped that the guy could now flash. For whatever reason, the abilities the gods had once stripped him of were now returning.

Anyway. Something Strider and his cohorts had recently learned was that "dead" didn't necessarily mean "gone forever." Not for humans and certainly not for immortals. Far from it, in fact. Souls could be captured, manipulated…abused. Sienna was of the abused variety, and Paris was desperate to save her.

The besotted warrior shifted from one booted foot to the other. Behind the counter, a female groaned as if the movement was torture—for her. "You agreed to help me knowing you'd have to find Sienna, no matter how long it takes, or you'll hurt. Bad."

As far as Strider was concerned, the longer it took them, the better. The more distance between him and Kaia, the better. He had to prove to himself that he could walk away and forget about her.

He'd done it before. Only problem was, now he knew her better and the attraction was stronger.

"You've been in the heavens for weeks and made no progress," he said. "You needed me."

"Yeah, but you didn't need me. Not for something as simple as this."

Actually, he did. He needed to see Paris and Kaia together. Needed to remind himself why he couldn't have her, why he had to stop thinking about her all the damn time. Why she was bad news. Preferably before his demon decided they had to have her—or else.

Besides, Strider had needed to escape Budapest, his home not-really-sweet home, as well as put some distance between himself, Amun and Amun's new girlfriend, Haidee. Strider had laid his semi-best moves on her, but she'd wanted nothing to do with him. Sure, he'd also insulted her at every turn and threatened to decapitate her, but give a guy a damn break. He'd had excellent reasons.

Haidee had once been a Hunter, had killed his best friend, Baden, keeper of Distrust, and had attempted to savage his home.

Yet still he'd desired her. And now, every time he looked at her, he was reminded of his failure. His loss. The ensuing pain. But...and here was the kicker. He'd never had a problem resisting her. He'd kept his mouth, hands and favorite appendage to himself without any difficulty.

Kaia, however, wouldn't be extended the same courtesy if they spent any alone time together. Already his mouth watered for a taste, his hands itched for a touch and his favorite appendage stood at embarrassing attention.

Oh, yes. He had to get as far, far away from the whole situation as possible.

"Stridey-Man. You here with me or what?"

He blinked into focus. Paris. Police station. Humans with guns. Winking in and out was stupid. He blamed Kaia for his lax concentration—another reason to avoid her. "I don't want to talk about it," was all he said.

Paris opened his mouth to respond, but closed it with a snap when they heard the welcome sound of high heels clacking down the nearest hallway. Then Kaia was rounding the corner, silky red hair hanging down her back in complete disarray, gray-gold eyes bright and wicked body swaying with a seductive beat Strider prayed only he could hear.

No. He didn't want to hear it, so he wouldn't pray that he alone could. But if anyone else heard it, he'd rip out their goddamn eardrums. Because Kaia was, despite everything, his friend. They'd fought enemies together, bled for each other. Hell, they'd joked and laughed together. So yeah, they were friends, and he didn't like his friends being harassed. And that was the only reason, damn it. He'd do the same thing for Paris. Who'd better not hear that beat!

"Don't you go getting into any more trouble, you hear," the officer escorting her said with open affection, and Strider wanted to kill the guy for so blatantly harassing her—or speaking to her at all. "We love ya, but we don't want to see you here again."

Calm down. You're not dating her, and you're not going to date her. Or kiss her. All over. The cop's flirting doesn't matter.

"As if I'd let myself get caught a fourth time," she replied with a grin that was all about the charm.

A grin that caused Strider's chest to constrict. No one should have lips so plump and red, or teeth so straight and white. Didn't help that she wore pink knee-high snakeskin boots, a micromini jean skirt and a white tank top that clearly showcased the white lace bra underneath.

Miracle of miracles, she was wearing a bra today.

She stopped short when she spied him, her smile fading. He wasn't sure what he'd expected from her, but he did know that reticence wasn't it.

Her gaze moved to Paris, and the smile returned. As did the constricting in Strider's chest. "Hey, stranger. What are you doing here?"

"I'm not sure exactly." Paris threw him a quick frown. "Not that I'm unhappy to see you, you understand."

"Yeah. You, too. And thanks for the pick up. Appreciate it."

"Anytime. Just hopefully not anytime in the near future."

She chuckled, the sound warm and rich and its undertones so erotic that it stroked over his skin. "Can't promise."

Neither said anything romantic, yet both of their voices grated on him. Maybe because he'd needed them to goo-it-up with each other so that his hormones would get the "not going there" message.

He had a feeling he would have been annoyed no matter what.

Like her smile, her chuckle shut down when she switched her attention to Strider. "So," she said. "You." As if she'd just spotted an oozing culture of flesh-eating bacteria on the bottom of her shoe.

The unfriendliness isn't a challenge, he informed his demon as the stupid shit perked up.

There was no reply. Truth was, Defeat was intimidated by Kaia and didn't often wish to draw her notice.

And really, the only time Defeat deigned to speak to Strider was when his competitive spirit was engaged. "Competitive spirit" being a nice way of saying Strider's ass had been glued to the chopping block. He much preferred the little bastard to stay at the back of his mind, a dark, silent presence easily ignored.

"I expected you to send someone, not show up yourself," Kaia added, rocking back on her heels.

"After the message you left me?" He snorted. "Hardly."

"Are you whining? Because I hear a whiny schoolboy tone."

She does not amuse me. "I don't whine."

He'd listened to that message a thousand times and knew every word, every hitch in her breath by heart. Beep. *Strider. Hey. It's Kaia. You know, the girl who saved your life a few weeks ago? The same girl you stomped all over afterward? Well, it's payback time. Why don't you get your lazy ass out of bed and come bail me out of jail before I decide to break out and use your face to test the stilettos on my boots.* Beep.

Animosity was good, and he seriously hoped she maintained a tight grip on it, despite the fact that he'd had to move heaven and earth to get here. Heaven—phoning Paris and convincing the warrior to drop everything up there, have Lysander bring him home, and come with Strider. Earth—phoning Lucien and convincing the warrior to drop everything and use his flashing ability to get them from Budapest to Alaska in a mere blink of time. Neither of which had been an easy task.

In fact, he would rather have had his tongue removed with a dull, rusty butter knife. Both men had asked questions. Lots and lots of questions he hadn't wanted to answer.

And yeah, Strider now owed the keeper of Death a favor, too. They were piling up, all because of the deceptively delicate-looking, utterly curvy stunner in front of him—who clearly wanted his head on a pike.

"Would have been nice if you'd given me some direction. Torin had to search every—" Strider stopped himself before he publicly admitted that Torin, the keeper of Disease, could hack into every database known to man. A skill like that was better kept under wraps. "He just had to search for you. Cost us some time."

"So?"

"So. That's all you have to say for your appalling behavior?" Thank gods she was doing as he'd hoped and holding tight to that animosity of hers. Yeah, thank gods. "You could have called Bianka. Word is, she's here in Anchorage with you." Not that she'd taken *his* call. "Instead, you waste my time with this shit."

"So?"

Damn it! Would it have killed her to show him a little gratitude? He could have stayed home, left her rotting. Instead, she'd metaphorically batted her lashes at him and he'd jumped like a girl with a rope. Frustrating woman.

He'd done her wrong, yes, and unlike Haidee, she hadn't deserved it. *Thought you weren't gonna ponder that.* The memories came, anyway.

A group of Hunters had been riding his tail for days, but he'd been too wrapped up in his pity party over losing Haidee to Amun to notice or care. Kaia had stepped in and saved the day, preventing a disastrous ambush. And gods almighty, she was sexy when she fought.

He hadn't seen that particular fight, but he'd seen several before it—and the one after it—and had even practiced battle-moves with her. He could very well imagine the lethal dance she'd performed that night.

Then had come the battle after, when she'd challenged him to a round of Who Can Slaughter More Hunters. He'd been royally pissed because one, she could slaughter more Hunters, no question, and two, he'd had other things to do. Like take his first vacation in centuries. Still, the challenge had been issued, his demon had accepted, and Strider'd had to drop everything or suffer a loss.

To his shock, she had let him win. Harpy that she was, she could rip through an entire army in seconds—all without breaking a sweat or a nail—but rather than render the final blows, she'd piled up her still-breathing conquests and given them to Strider. *Then* she'd taken off.

He hadn't heard from her again until she'd left that message.

Yeah, he needed to apologize.

"Not to point out how lame you are or anything," Kaia said to him, buffing her nails on her shirt, "but I once had to bail Bianka out of jail twelve times in one day. I didn't complain a single time."

Not amused, he reminded himself. "Have I ever told you how much I hate when people exaggerate?"

"I swear!" She stomped her foot. "I honestly didn't complain."

Really not amused. I won't laugh. "Not what I was calling you on."

"Oh, well." The indignation drained from her. "I never exaggerate. *Ever.*"

His throat got tight as he swallowed back a laugh—of exasperation, not amusement, he assured himself. "You're exaggerating now."

"And you're still whining, you crybaby!"

Gods, she was lovely when she was pissed. Her eyes glittered more gold than gray, as if flames danced through her irises, and her cheeks flushed the color of a rare, exotic rose. That glorious mane of red hair practically lifted from her scalp, as if she'd stuck her finger into a socket. Energy crackled around her.

"Wow," Paris said, glancing around. "This is a lot of fun."

"Have I ever told you how much I hate sarcasm?" Strider asked him.

Kaia drew in a measured breath, her gaze remaining on Strider. "Lookit, all your crybaby bawling aside, I'm not paying you back and I'm not showing up for my hearing." Her chin flew into the air, all snotty attitude and refusal to forgive. "So there."

Goodbye, non-amusement. Screw an apology. Defeat was humming now, gearing up to fight, intimidated by her or not. Strider popped his jaw but didn't say another word. He just turned on his heel and stomped out of the building before things got ugly, forcing Paris and Kaia to follow. Together. Maybe they'd do him a solid and hold hands.

He heard them clomping behind him, chattering

steadily, and jerked his sunglasses from his jacket pocket. He slid the metal frames up his nose. Despite the chill in the air, the sun was bright, glaring. Down the steps he stomped, then he stopped, whipped around.

No hand-holding, but definite we've-seen-each-other-naked sparks. Their heads were pressed together, their tones low, intimate. They were probably reminiscing about the thousands of orgasms they'd shared.

This was exactly what he'd wanted, needed. A reminder.

A reminder that Paris had once ripped the clothes from Kaia's body. Had once tossed her down on his bed, watching her lush breasts jiggle as she bounced. Had grabbed her knees and pried them apart. Had stared into the hottest, wettest slice of heaven ever to grace the earth. Had bent his head, licked, tasted, feasted, hearing feminine cries of surrender and passion ringing in his ears, soft yet firm legs pressing into his back. Maybe even stilettos. And then, when the hunger had become too much for him, Paris had surged up and sunk into a core so tight, so exquisite, he would never be the same.

Kaia had wrapped herself around the warrior. Had screamed his name. Had scratched him and bitten him and begged him for more.

Paris's face suddenly morphed into Strider's, and it was Strider who slammed into that lithe little body, in and out, over and over again. Hard and fast as he grunted and groaned, desperate for more.

Fantasy...overload...

His hands curled into fists. Damn this, and damn Paris and Kaia. Because, if he were being honest, he was as furious with Paris as he was aroused by Kaia. And he was so damn aroused just then he had to fit his T-shirt over the waist of his slacks to hide the growing evidence. Paris should have resisted Kaia; he desired someone else, and Kaia deserved better than to be second place.

Why couldn't Kaia see that?

Any moment now, Strider would stop wanting to rip them apart, stop wanting to grind Paris's face into the concrete and afterward, suck the air right out of Kaia's lungs. Any moment, he'd want to slap his boy on the back for a job well done and start thinking about Kaia as a pretty girl he counted as a friend but not a potential lover.

Yes. Any moment.

CHAPTER THREE

"GET LOST, WOULD YOU," Kaia whispered fiercely to Paris as they descended the steps that led to her freedom…and Strider. "You're like a bad rash that keeps coming back."

He laughed, a booming sound that still managed to hold traces of pain.

"Seriously. This is the most attention Strider has paid me in *forever,* and you're ruining everything. Beat it before I beat *you.*"

Paris stopped and gripped her arm, forcing her to stop, as well. Sympathy had replaced his amusement, highlighted now by the golden rays stroking him with the care and concern of a lover. Such a beautiful man. Even the elements had trouble resisting him.

"Listen up, sweetheart, because I'm about to give you a lifesaving tip. Be a good girl, and don't poke at the bear today. He's on edge already."

Her eyes narrowed, dark lashes fusing together to keep Paris and only Paris in the crosshairs. "I thought you were the smart one, giving in to my wiles as easily as you did, but, hello. Sometimes the bear needs poking or he'll never come out of hibernation."

One corner of his mouth twitched. "Oh, yeah? Well, think about this. What's the first thing a bear out of hibernation does?"

Duh. "He eats. And to be honest, I'm really looking forward to that."

"Yeah, yeah, I know. That can be fun." Leaning down, mouth still twitching, Paris whispered, "But you know what else? Bears torture. Bears *love* to torture, Kye. They're mean. When a human gets in a bear's way, especially after a long sleep, the end result is never pretty. Let this one acclimate to your...what did you call your smart-ass mouth? Wiles."

"First, I'm not exactly human," she said, raising her chin. "And here's a news flash for you, my little man candy. I'm stronger than you are. Stronger than *he* is. Stronger than all of you put together. I can handle anything he dishes out."

"For fuck's sake," Strider suddenly snarled. "Enough already. We need to leave, Paris, so you can stop making out with our fugitive."

Our, he'd said. Not *your*. Such sweet progress. Trying not to smile, Kaia stepped away from Paris and slowly turned to face Strider, some of her annoyance with him cooling out. Breath snagged in her throat. Paris was beautiful, yes, but Strider...Strider was magnificent.

Her first glimpse in weeks had been of him standing in the station's lobby, stark white walls surrounding him, and her knees had almost buckled. His finger-combed pale hair had been in complete disarray, sticking out in spikes. His navy blue eyes had swept over her, lingering in all the right places, and her stomach had quivered.

Now, at this second glimpse... He was tall, towering over her even though she stood several steps up and wore high heels. He had a delicious muscle mass that couldn't be hidden underneath the long leather jacket, tight black shirt and denim. And gods, his face. His oh-so-innocent, yet oh-so-wicked fallen angel face.

At first, she hadn't recognized that face for the luscious contradiction it was. She had seen only the innocence, and had continued searching for someone with the qualities she'd always found most attractive: brooding, dangerous and temporary.

That's why Paris had snagged her attention.

He mourned the loss of his human female. Brooding— check. He was an ambrosia addict who could kill without hesitation. Dangerous—check. He was a sure thing, a one-time-only event, and wouldn't cling. Temporary—check. Afterward, though, she'd snuck out of his bed—a Harpy always left after the main event—hollow and empty.

Which was probably why she'd gone back for seconds a few weeks later. She'd wanted to feel what she'd felt while they were together. Fulfilled. Satisfied. But he'd turned her down, physically unable to give her a repeat, and pushed her out of his room. Yeah, he could have pleasured her and taken nothing for himself, but that would have been a pity-session and wasn't something she could tolerate.

So, because she'd worn a robe and only a robe to his second seduction, she'd left in a robe and only a robe— and, distracted as she'd been, she'd smacked into Strider in the hallway.

That's when she first saw the devil in his eyes.

In that moment, she felt as if a switch had been thrown inside her. She'd made a mistake going after Paris. The man in front of her was everything she'd ever wanted and more.

His hair had been wet and plastered to his temples, darkening the strands. He'd had a white towel wrapped around his neck and no shirt to hide a stomach that boasted rope after rope of bronze strength. She'd watched, fascinated, as little droplets of sweat had traveled his golden happy trail before disappearing into paradise. A paradise she'd wanted to visit. With her tongue.

His shorts had hung low on his waist, revealing the jagged edges of the sapphire butterfly tattoo on his right hip. The moisture in her mouth had dried. Clearly, he'd just come from a workout. A very intense workout. Breath had still sawed in and out of his lips. Lips, she had realized, that promised untold pleasure when they curled in sinful amusement.

"Nice outfit," he'd said, navy gaze blazing a slow journey from the top of her rumpled head to the purple polish on her toenails, lingering on her pearled nipples and between her quivering thighs.

"All's I could find," she'd replied in an uncertain voice, thinking this might turn out to be the immortal version of a walk of shame. *How can I fix this?*

"Lucky robe, then. It'd look better without the belt, though."

Okay, maybe I don't have to fix anything. For the first time in their acquaintance, desire had layered his tone. That desire affected her far more strongly than the once-over had. "Yeah?"

"Oh, yeah. So, you looking for someone in particular?"

"That depends." Sultry arousal sweeping through her, she stepped closer to him. "What does *someone* have in mind?"

Behind her, hinges squeaked as a door opened. "Kaia?" Paris suddenly said, and she turned, her stomach rolling. He tossed a pair of fluffy pink slippers at her. "You forgot these. I'd keep 'em, but they aren't my size."

"Oh." They plopped to the floor right in front of her. "Thanks."

"You're welcome. Strider. Hey, man," Paris called.

"Hey," he replied tightly. "Interesting night?"

"None of your business."

As Paris disappeared inside his room, Kaia wheeled back around. Now Strider's expression was guarded, closed off.

"Interesting night?" he asked, directing the question at her this time.

She gulped. "Not really. Nothing happened. This time," she forced herself to add. If he did anything with her tonight, and found out the truth about Paris later, he'd hate her. So, full disclosure. Except—

"See ya around, Kaia." Strider skirted around her, wandering off rather than teasing her about what she'd done. Or asking her what had really happened. Or caring on any level.

Clearly, nothing would have come of her sudden attraction to him even if Paris hadn't interrupted.

"—some goddamn attention to me!" Strider was snarling now. "Not that *I* want it, you understand. You're pissing off my demon."

Pissing off his demon? She wanted to *seduce* his demon. Right? Or had she written the two off as she'd told Bianka?

She blinked, focusing, and studied him anew. His fury had very nearly sharpened his features into deadly blades, and her knees *did* buckle. *So damn magnificent.* A savage, a brute. Paris caught her before she hit the pavement and held her up.

Oh, gods. Weakness? Here? Now? Her cheeks flamed with embarrassment.

Strider took a menacing step toward her, then froze in place. "Paris, dude, let her go," he snarled, and Paris immediately obeyed. Navy eyes snapped to her, more animal than man. "When did you last eat, Kaia?"

Thank the gods. He thought her weakness stemmed from a lack of nourishment, not the irresistible sight of him. She shrugged, happy she remained on her feet under her own steam. "Don't know."

As she had chosen not to steal or earn one of the bowls of slop given to the residents of Cell Block B, and as she'd been in the slammer for two days…well, she was starved.

Fine. She could have eaten. Bianka had come to the rescue, as always, eager to bust her out and feed her. She'd shooed her sister away with a stern warning—followed by a figurative bitch slap—not to return. Otherwise, Kaia would ensure the nickname Heavenly Hills Ho spread and stuck. Forever.

"Damn it, Kaia. You're shaky on your feet and you can't concentrate worth a damn." His gaze shot to Paris. "Phone Lucien for pickup. I'll meet you in Buda. I want to feed her, and then we can—"

Paris was shaking his head. "I'll phone Lucien for pickup, but I'm not waiting for you in Buda. When you finish your business, if that's what the kids are calling it these days, have Lucien or Lysander bring you to the heavens. Either one will know where I am."

Strider gave a stiff nod.

Paris ruffled the top of Kaia's head before striding off and disappearing around a corner, leaving her alone with the warrior of her dreams. Exactly what she'd furtively hoped and prayed for as she'd shoved Bianka out of the cell and locked herself back inside.

They stared at each other for a long while, neither moving, neither speaking. Tension spreading, thickening. His warrior nature had never been more evident. He stood with his arms at his sides, his hands inches away from the now-visible butt of his guns, and his legs braced apart, ready to spring into action. Against her? Or anyone who thought to hurt her?

Finally, she could stand the silence no longer. "You're going to the heavens?"

He nodded, his skin like polished gold in the sunlight. The vibe of animal savagery left him, and he actually relaxed. She liked this side of him, too.

"Why?" What she really wanted to ask: How long will you be gone? Are you meeting a woman? An angel? His friend Aeron had fallen in love with a goody-goody with wings. Why not Strider, too?

I'll kill the bitch.

"Sure you want to know?" he asked. "It involves Paris and another woman. A woman he wants."

Relief bombarded her. "Sweet! Gossip." Grinning, she rubbed her hands together. "Give me."

He ran his tongue over his teeth. "I *never* repeat gossip, Kaia."

"Oh," she muttered, shoulders sagging with disappointment.

"You didn't let me finish. I never repeat gossip, so listen closely." He was fighting a smile, and the knowledge delighted her. "The woman Paris loves...hates, whatever. He wants her, like I said, and she's being held prisoner up there."

Sooo. Strider was going to war to aid his bro, not to give some wide-eyed, ripe-for-the-plucking winger a booty call. Her relief tripled. "I could, I don't know, help you help him. I have connections up there—" not necessarily a lie "—and I—"

"No!" he shouted, then more calmly stated, "No. Thank you, though. But... Do you really not care that the man you desire now desires someone else?"

"Wait. Who says I desire him?"

"You don't?"

"No."

His expression didn't change, but he did clear his throat. "Not that it would have mattered either way, you understand. But as I was saying, he's already spoken to Lysander about getting a little angelic help, and gotten a no-can-do."

"Of course Lysander won't help him. He'd help Bianka, though, and Bianka would help me."

"Nope. Sorry."

Stubborn brute. He was so desperate to get rid of her, he wouldn't even consider using her. Another rejection; how quaint.

Motions stiff, he waved her over. "Come on. Let's take care of your hunger."

All I want is a few nibbles of you. "Don't worry about me. I can take care of myself."

"I know, but I'll stay until you're fed. I want to make sure you aren't arrested again."

Her Harpy squawked inside her head, a command to prove to Strider just how capable she was, just how worthy. *Are you?* "Fine. Oh, and here's a truth missile for the demon who always wants to win. I doubt you can keep up," she taunted, more out of habit than anything.

He huffed out a breath, and she figured this was round two of pissed-off mode.

"Lead the way," he snapped before she could apologize.

Okay, so maybe she shouldn't have pushed so hard. *My bad.* "I will." She didn't take him hunting, though. Not yet. She took him to the cabin she and Bianka shared a good distance from civilization. Thankfully, her sister was nowhere to be found. "Feel free to look around. I need to shower and change."

"Kaia," he began, following her down the hall. "I'm kind of pressed for time here and because of what you said, I need to keep up with you and—"

She shut her bedroom door in his stunned face, heard him snarl low in his throat and grinned. The grin vanished as a thought occurred to her. There was plenty of stolen food in the kitchen. If he noticed, there'd be no good reason for her to take him hunting.

Have to risk it. I smell. Kaia hurried through a shower, grateful as the grime and total body makeup that had caked her washed away. She almost raced from her room after changing into a glittery pink T-shirt that read Strangers Have the Best Candy and short jean shorts, but caught a glimpse of herself in her full-length mirror. Outfit was fine, but not her hair. The red mass was sopping wet and practically glued to her head and arms, making her resemble a drowned clown.

Back to the bathroom she raced for a crucial blow-dry. She thought about applying another layer of makeup to her exposed skin, wanting Strider to want her for *her,* not any other reason, but discarded the idea. Let Strider see. Let Strider crave. Right now, she'd take him however she could get him. Later, they could work on their reasons why.

If she decided to give him another chance.

Finally, she raced from the bedroom. In record time, too. Just under twenty (forty) minutes.

A trail of fragrant steam followed her as she strode down the hall. No Strider in the living room, where she kept her life-size hula dancer lamp and the castle she'd built from empty beer cans. He must be looking around. She wondered what he thought of her place, her things, and tried to see the room through his eyes.

Besides the coffee table, which was carved to resemble a hunched over wooden Sumo wrestler with a sheet of glass perched on top, and the chair with arms that were actually painted to look like humans legs that stretched to the floor, the furniture was beautiful, pieces she and Bianka had stolen throughout the centuries.

History was a scent that clung to almost every polished piece. Okay, maybe not the white rug with two yellow pillows sewn at one end, so that the whole thing looked like eggs in a frying pan. Or the hamburger beanbag chair, complete with lettuce, tomato and mustard layers, but that was it.

And okay, maybe the couch and love seat had been chosen for comfort more than anything else, and were no more than a decade old. She'd crashed a frat party a few years ago and had liked the way the overstuffed cushions had conformed to her body. Plus, they were a pretty tawny color, almost the same as Bianka's eyes, so she'd made sure to leave with them. No one had tried to stop her, either. Maybe because she'd carried each one over her head. By herself.

Colorful vases decorated the tabletops, interspersed with personalized bobblehead dolls and the occasional stuffed squirrel in a crazy outfit. Weapons and artwork hung on the walls right beside the homemade plaques congratulating her on a job well done. Her fave: the one for giving Bianka the best birthday present ever—the tongue of the man who'd called her a "mean, ugly hag."

There were also photos of her and her family. Bianka, as well as their younger sis, Gwen, and their older half sis, Taliyah. Kaia partying hard at clubs, Bianka winning beauty pageants, Gwen trying to hide from the camera, and Taliyah standing proudly over her kills. Mercenary that she was, she had a lot of kills.

In the kitchen—Kaia skidded to a halt, her heart banging frantically against her ribs. Strider. Gorgeous, sexy Strider. He sat at the pool table she'd plucked from his fortress her very first visit there and now used in the breakfast nook. Food was scattered in every direction, from bags of chips to cheese slices to candy bars.

He wasn't looking at her, hadn't even glanced at her, but he *had* stiffened when she'd stepped inside. "I figured that, since these things were here, they were acceptable for you to eat. Which means I more than kept up with you. I outwitted and surpassed you."

"Thanks," she said dryly. How disappointing. The one time she wanted her man to forget he had a brain, he remembered.

She leaned against the door frame and crossed her arms over her chest. Her stomach tightened, threatening to growl, but she remained in place, waiting. Only when he'd gotten a good once-over would she move.

"Kaia. Eat."

"In a minute. I'm enjoying the view. You should give it a try."

He tensed. "There's a note from your sister on the fridge. She said she's in the heavens with Lysander, and she'll see you in four days for the games."

"'Kay."

"What games? Never mind," he rushed out before she could reply. "Don't tell me. I don't want to know. What perfume are you wearing? I don't like it."

Asshat. "I'm not wearing any perfume." And she knew he loved it. He had a weakness for cinnamon, something she'd noticed while stalking, uh, hanging out with him.

Within hours of learning that little tidbit, she'd stocked up on cinnamon-scented soap, shampoo and conditioner.

"Stop…enjoying the view and come eat," he said through clenched teeth.

He'd closed the blinds over the only window and flipped on the overhead light. Natural sunlight complemented her skin the best, but— Oh, who was she kidding, acting all modest? *Any* light complemented her skin.

"Kaia. Come. Eat. Now."

Gods, she adored that authoritative tone. She shouldn't. She should hate it—barbarians weren't supposed to be attractive to modern women—but still, she shivered. "Make me." *Please.*

Finally his gaze skidded over to her. He was on his feet a second later, his chair sliding behind him. His mouth floundered open and closed, and his pupils dilated. He licked his lips. He reached out to grip the edge of the table, his nostrils flaring as he fought to breathe. "You… Your… Shit!"

Every pulse point hammering, she twirled. She knew what he saw—rainbow shards dancing hypnotically over every inch of visible flesh, the blush of health and vitality…the promise of seduction. "You like?"

As if in a trance, he moved around the table and stepped toward her. Closed the distance...stopped just before he reached her and cursed. He spun, giving her his back, and tangled a hand through his hair.

"I've gotta go." His voice was hoarse, the words pushed through a river of broken glass.

What? No! "You just got here." And he'd been so close to making a move on her. Just the thought caused her nipples to bead and moisture to pool between her legs.

"I told you, I promised Paris I'd help him. I have to help him. Yeah, that's what I have to do."

Would she ever overcome his determination to resist her? 'Cause yeah, she wanted him, wanted to give him another chance. And another. However many he needed to get this right. "Strider, I—"

"No. *No.* I told you before, I'm just getting over a bad relationship, and I never hook up with anyone who's dated one of my friends."

Oh, really? "That bad relationship wouldn't happen to be with Haidee, would it? The woman who didn't want you? The woman who, what? Is *dating one of your friends.*"

Silence. Such thick, awful silence.

He wasn't going to defend himself. Wasn't even going to try to explain his illogical choices and reasons. Well, he'd forgiven Haidee for killing Baden. Why couldn't he forgive Kaia for sleeping with Paris?

"You're not innocent, Strider. You've nailed more tail than you can count. In fact, last time I saw you, you'd just eaten peach body lotion off a stripper." Kaia had decided then and there that peaches were the most disgusting fruit *ever,* and the world would be a better place without them.

She'd already written to her congressman, demanding that all orchards be burned to the ground.

"I never said I was innocent. I just said—"

"I know. You can't date anyone your friends have dated. You're also a liar. But maybe…I don't know, maybe you could sleep with one of my friends and we could call it even." Oh, gods.

First, how desperate did she sound? Unbearably! She'd known this would happen if she made another play for him. And yet, she'd done it anyway. Like Pavlov's dogs, she drooled every time she spotted Strider, abandoning her pride for any scrap he'd toss her way.

Second, thinking of this man with someone else had her claws elongating and her Harpy screeching. Her wings flapped to the same staccato rhythm as her heart, causing her shirt to lift and fall, lift and fall.

If she wasn't careful, her Harpy would take over, control her actions. Her vision would go black, and a need for blood would consume her. She would stalk the night, hurting anyone who got in her way.

Only Strider would be able to calm her down, but he didn't know that. Even if he *did* know it, he clearly didn't want the responsibility. He was doing everything in his power to push her away.

"I won't be sleeping with one of your friends," he said flatly.

The hottest threads of tension drained from her. "Good. That's good. All of my friends are ugly hags, anyway." They were gorgeous, every one of them, but if he'd taken her up on the offer, she would have cut them loose in a heartbeat and gotten new ones. Repulsive ones.

"Kaia. There's nothing you can say to change my mind. I like you, I do. You're beautiful and smart and funny as hell. You're strong and courageous, too, but nothing's ever going to happen between us. I'm sorry, I really am. I'm not meaning to be an asshole here, just truthful. We're just not good for each other. Not a good match. I'm sorry," he repeated.

They weren't good for each other? What he really meant was *she* wasn't good enough for *him*. After she had chased him, lost a fight to protect him, threw herself at him time and time again, she wasn't a *good match* for him. And he...was...sorry...

Suddenly she wanted to claw *his* face. Drink *his* blood. *Don't forget the upcoming games.* Hurting him would hurt her, and she needed to be at her best.

She drew in a deep breath, held it, held, her lungs burning, blistering, before she slowly released every molecule, singeing her throat, her nose. She might have thought Strider deserved something, someone, better, but *she* deserved better than this. Right?

He finished lamely, "I hope you understand," completely unaware of the havoc he'd created. Or maybe he just didn't care.

He needed to learn the proper etiquette for dealing with his Harpy.

She needed to teach him.

She should close the distance between them and trace her fingertips all over him before he had time to dart away, all the while pressing her curves against him. Anything to arouse him. Anything to force him to see her as more than the beautiful, smart and funny girl who had nailed the keeper of Promiscuity. Then, as he begged for release, she should walk away.

He wouldn't be harmed, but he would leave with a better understanding of how rotten denunciation felt.

Kaia couldn't bring herself to take a single step, however. She might just find herself on the receiving end of rejection and failure yet again. He might push her away before she could make her move. And really, a thousand other rejections and failures awaited her in the coming weeks.

So much for giving him countless chances.

"I do understand," she whispered. "Just…have fun on your trip, okay." A dismissal. "I plan to have lots of fun on mine." A lie. Although she did plan to hold her head up high and kick as much ass as she could. So much ass, in fact, that her clan would have to rethink her title.

Kaia the Disappointment no longer. Maybe she'd become Kaia the Stompalicious. Or Kaia the KillYouDead-atron.

"So…you're going on a trip?" he asked, and he sounded relieved.

Do not react. "Yep. I sure am."

Still he didn't face her. "Where? When?"

Don't you dare react. "In four days, I leave for—oops, never mind." She moved around him and sat at the table. "You don't want to know, remember?" Doing her best to appear nonchalant, even smug, all while the bastard ripped her heart out of her chest and danced on the pieces, she opened a bag of chips.

"You're right. Just…be careful, and I'll see you—just be careful, okay?"

He'd stopped himself from saying *later. I'll see you later.* Because he had no plans to see her again. Ever.

"I will," she said, as she fought tears for the second time in her life. She deserved this, she supposed. Punishment for the Unfortunate Incident, for Paris, hell, for all the rejections *she* had dished out over the centuries. "You, too." Much as she currently despised him, she wanted him healthy, whole.

"I will." He strode out of the kitchen, out of her home, out of her *life,* the front door banging ominously shut behind him.

CHAPTER FOUR

THE NEXT DAY, STRIDER SPENT his morning roaming the Budapest fortress, checking on his friends. Anything to distract himself from thoughts of Kaia and how sad she'd sounded just before he'd left her. Not to mention how he'd longed to pull her into his arms, hold her, comfort her. Devour her.

Not going there.

Legion, a spoiled full-on demon minion turned spoiled human with a porn-star body turned tortured prisoner of Lucifer turned subdued, silent bed-bound damsel in distress, rolled to her side, facing away from him when he entered her bedroom.

Physically, she had healed from her hellish captivity. Mentally...she might never heal. She'd spent several weeks being passed from one demon High Lord to another, raped, beaten and gods knew what else. No one knew because she refused to talk about it.

"Hey, there, princess." Strider eased beside her on the bed and patted her shoulder. She flinched, jerking from the touch. He sighed, removed his hand.

He didn't like visiting her. Oh, he liked her as a person, for the most part, and ached for the trials she had endured, but he was afraid Defeat would view her emotional distance as a challenge and force him to push her for more. More she wasn't ready to give.

She needed help, and her closest friend, Aeron, and his

joy-bringing angel, Olivia, were trying, but so far Legion hadn't responded positively to anyone. She wasn't eating properly, and was slowly but surely wasting away. Strider knew there was a guardian angel keeping watch over her, even though he'd never gotten a peek at the guy. What he did know: the invisible bastard wasn't doing his job.

Yeah, Legion had been a selfish pain in the ass before, but she didn't deserve this. And actually, Strider had liked her better the other way.

"What happened to you has happened to a few of the guys here, did you know that? A few times to Kane, in fact. Since he's possessed by Disaster, he's like a magnet for that kind of thing. And I'm not gossiping or sharing private info. When we lived in New York, he ran a support group to help others. Maybe you should, I don't know, talk to him or something."

Silence.

Her blond hair was tangled and matted, her skin sickly with a grayish cast. Underneath the thick white fabric of her nightgown, he could tell her shoulders were frail.

"One time Paris and I even—wait. That *is* gossiping. Never mind. You'll have to ask Paris if you want to know that little tidbit."

Silence. From her and his demon. Most definitely she presented a challenge, and yet, Defeat was letting the indifference slide.

He tucked the covers higher, just under her chin, and saw a glistening teardrop slither down her cheek.

Okay, then. "I just wanted to check on you, but I know you're not comfortable with me so I'll go," he said gently. She couldn't relax with him here, and he didn't want to make things worse for her.

More silence. He released another sigh as he stood. "Call me if you need anything. All right? Anything at all. I'm happy to help."

Again, no response from either Legion or his demon. He wondered what was up with his—distracted? hiding? uncaring?—companion as he strode to his next stop. Amun's room.

Despite the fact that he and Amun—and hell, even he and Haidee—were on good enough terms, he'd avoided contact for over a week. Just seeing her caused little sparks of pain to dance through his chest. Not because he still wanted her, but because he'd lost her, could never have her, and his demon couldn't forget what they'd endured because of her dismissal.

Haidee opened the door, and he studied her out of habit. She was average height, her pale hair streaked with pink. One of her eyebrows was pierced, and one of her arms sleeved in tattoos. Dressed in a Hello Kitty T-shirt and ripped jeans, she would be carded at any bar.

When she saw him, she frowned and moved out of the way, allowing him inside. Despite that frown, she appeared lit up from the inside out, pulse after pulse of…he grimaced. What the hell *was* that?

If he were fed the muzzle of a .40 and told to guess or die, Strider would have said love in its purest form seeped from her pores. Almost hurt to look at her, she was so radiant.

Shit. "Are you pregnant?"

"No." A secret smile curved her lips. Well, well. Picking up Amun's all-things-are-a-mystery vibe already. "What's up?"

Strider rubbed a hand over his heart, expecting more of those flickers of pain, especially with that glow blasting at his corneas, but…nothing. Not even a skip in the organ's beat. Okay, fine. Whatever. He could roll.

His gaze swept through the room. Haidee had taken over the decorating, so the place was no longer like vanilla ice cream—plain, unadorned and completely lacking a personality.

Haidee favored contemporary styles with a Japanese flair. He tried not to cringe. Lanternlike lights hung from the ceiling. The walls were now brown and orange, each color staggered to form a boxed pattern. Bonsai trees seemed to grow from every corner, and white shag carpets stretched under three glass nightstands. White carpet. Had she not seen the amount of dirt a warrior's boots could track in? The comforter on the bed was white, too, with beaded orange pillows.

If she'd tried this shit in his room, they woulda had a serious beef. A man needed to feel comfortable in his surroundings or he couldn't relax. This wasn't comfortable.

Only once had Strider "lived" with a woman, and only because she'd challenged him to move in. *I know I can make you happy if you come home to me every night. Can you make me happy, though? I guess we'll find out.*

After a few weeks of cohabitating, he'd willingly accepted defeat. He could not make her happy because he didn't *want* to make her happy.

He thought back to Kaia's house and *her* decorating flare. Now there was a woman who knew how to make a place comfy and fun. Seriously, she'd had a toilet painted to resemble an open mouth. *I want.*

Haidee cleared her throat. "Strider?"

He turned to face her. "What?" Her expression was expectant, all soft and gooey with whatever pulsed from her, and he recalled that he'd come to her, not the other way around. "Yeah, uh. Where's Amun?"

"Cronus summoned him to the heavens."

"Why?"

Another secret smile. "Don't know yet."

"How long's he been gone?"

"Three hours, nine minutes and forty-eight seconds.

Not that I'm watching the clock or anything. Can I help you with something?"

"Nah." He'd just wanted to see the guy, he supposed. After everything Strider had done to him…trying to keep Amun and Haidee apart… Guilt, man, how it ate at him sometimes. "I'll just, uh, catch him later."

Her brow furrowed with confusion. And concern? Yeah. That was concern. "You sure?"

He shouldn't have been surprised, but…she'd killed Baden, keeper of Distrust. She'd tried to kill Strider. And she'd had very good reason for both. Long, long ago, they'd helped slaughter her family, destroy her life. Hell, because of a demon, she'd been killed time and time again.

Each time she'd come back, she'd remembered only her hate, knew only about the deaths of those she'd once loved. Sought only vengeance. Made sense, since she'd been possessed by a piece of the demon of Hate. And maybe that was another reason Strider had wanted her. That piece of Hate had caused other people to dislike themselves and even her. Strider had gotten over that quickly, had *defeated* that, which was why he suspected being with her had been a bit of a rush for both him and his own demon.

That she now adored Amun, that she now supported the Lords and their cause, well, it was a miracle Strider needed to stop questioning.

"Yeah. I'm sure." He leaned over and kissed her on the cheek. Never before had he initiated contact that didn't involve knives. "See you around, Haidee."

Her mouth fell open, and she sputtered. "Yeah. See ya," she said weakly. He'd never been quite that nice to her, either.

He must be softening in his old age.

Next he found himself standing in the doorway of Sabin's bedroom, eating handful after handful of Red Hots. He had a stash of his favorite candy hidden in every corner of the fortress. He watched his friend toss all kinds of shit into a suitcase. His wife, Gwen, bustled around him, making a halfhearted attempt to fold the mountain of clothes Sabin had wadded into balls, stack the weapons he had only partially sheathed and remove the bullhorn from the case for a third time.

Once, the Harpies had called her Gwendolyn the Timid. Strider didn't know what they called her now, but the moniker certainly didn't fit anymore. The little firecracker had come into her own and kicked even Kaia's ass, locking her in the dungeon below to prevent her from peeling Sabin's skin from his body and wearing it as a victory coat.

Kaia.

His heart skipped a stupid beat, making him feel like a schoolboy with a crush. Something he'd never been. Zeus had created him fully formed, a weapon ready to be unleashed upon anyone who threatened the former god king and those he loved. Even then, before Strider had been given his demon, he had liked to win, railroading anyone who got in his way.

What joy could be found in defeat? None.

His demon grunted in agreement.

Strider refocused on his surroundings before the little shit began pushing him around. As he continued to watch Gwen, he noted how much she resembled her older sister.

Kaia.

Here we go again. Gwen had a thick mass of blond hair streaked with red—the same shade of red as Kaia's. If he were being honest, though, Kaia's was prettier. Wavier, silkier. And while Gwen's eyes were a startling mix of gray and gold, just like Kaia's, Kaia's were still lovelier. On her, the gray veered toward liquid silver and the gold, well, the gold flickered like fireflies.

What are you? A wuss? Stop weaving poetry.

Anyway. When Kaia's Harpy took over, her eyes went

completely black, death swimming in their depths. But, if he were still being honest, even that was sexy.

Gwen and Kaia shared the same button nose, the same cherub cheeks. Same stubborn chin. Yet somehow Kaia was sin incarnate and Gwen was innocence walking. Made no sense. Even still, the resemblance affected him, heating him up.

He willed his body to remain unaffected. Sabin would fuss if Strider sported a hard-on around his precious. And of course, "fuss" meant Strider would find his intestines wrapped around his neck, breathing a thing of the past.

Bring it, he thought.

Defeat chuckled, startling him.

On edge, he waited for a challenge to be issued. It never came. Sweet gods above, he'd have to be more careful. No more close calls.

What was he doing here, anyway? He should be in the heavens with Paris. He should be in Nebraska with William, torturing the family who had abused Gilly, a human they'd befriended. He should be out there killing Hunters. He should be in Rome, bargaining with the Unspoken Ones—monsters who were chained inside an ancient temple, desperate for freedom.

He'd given them one of the four godly artifacts needed to find and destroy Pandora's box. A relic the Hunters were searching for, as well.

The Unspoken Ones had the Paring Rod and the Cloak of Invisibility, and the Lords had the Cage of Compulsion and the All-Seeing Eye. So. Lords 2. Hunters 0. Boo-yah.

Unspoken Ones weren't interested in the actual artifacts, though. They were interested in what they could *trade* for the artifacts. Whoever presented them with the head of the current god king (minus his body) would earn the Paring Rod in return, leaving only the Cloak to claim.

The Cloak Strider had once owned but had exchanged for Haidee.

At the time, he hadn't minded making the exchange because he'd been pretty damn confident the Unspoken Ones would keep the thing to bargain with him later. Still was. He'd have to pay through the nose, he was sure, but that was better than allowing Haidee to escape him and reveal his secrets to her Hunter friends.

And he'd meant to go back long before now, but losing her to Amun had knocked Strider on his ass for over a week, his demon a writhing, seething cauldron of pain.

Maybe that was why he'd been unable to let go of the idea of being with Haidee, he mused now. The echoes of that pain. Maybe that was why he still resisted Kaia.

Don't think about her anymore, you nutcase. You'll start foaming at the mouth. He resisted her because she would ultimately trample his pride, his well-being and probably even his will to live.

Did he really need another reminder of that?

He forced his thoughts back to the artifacts. Strider had vowed to recapture the Cloak. And he would. Soon. Because whoever found Pandora's box first would win the war, and more than he wanted Kaia, not that he was thinking about her, he wanted to win the war against the Hunters.

Talk about the ultimate victory. The pleasure he would feel…gods, he could only imagine. Better than sex, drugs or rocking hos.

Anyway. Instead of all of that, he realized he'd purposely cleared his plate this morning, visiting everyone, making amends just so he could leave and… Shit! Not good. This was not good at all.

Just so he could leave and check on Kaia. He had to make sure she was okay. Even if that meant putting his obligations on hold again.

Dude. You can't do that. And he wouldn't. No damn way. Now that he'd realized his intention, he could put a stop to it.

"Why the hell are you just standing there?" Sabin suddenly lashed out. "State your business and leave, Stridey-Man. You're turning Gwen into a raving lunatic."

"*You're* turning *me* into a raving lunatic!" she growled, removing the bullhorn from the suitcase yet again. "We don't need all this stuff."

"How do you know?" Sabin demanded. He scrubbed a hand through his dark hair, the gold in his eyes lighter than usual. "You've never participated in the Harpy Games before. And goddamn it, you shouldn't have to participate in them now!"

"You heard Bianka. Every single one of Tabitha Skyhawk's daughters have been summoned. And even if we hadn't, even if only a handful of clan members had been summoned, I would still be going. They're my family."

"Well, you're now part of *my* family."

"Actually, *you're* part of *my* family, and as I'm the General, the Captain and the Commander, you go where I go. And I'm going!"

"Fuck." Sabin plopped onto the edge of the bed and put his head between his knees.

"That bad, huh?" Strider asked, doing his best to sound casual. *I'm not dying of curiosity. Really.*

Kaia had tried to hide her fear yesterday, but she hadn't quite managed it. He had mentioned her trip, and she had trembled, paled. He shouldn't have noticed. He'd had his back to her. Except there'd been a crack in her curtains, allowing him to study her reflection in the windowpane. And oh, had he studied.

She had sparkled like a diamond, drawing his eye automatically, and he'd been so eager to touch her that his body had been on fire.

Harpy skin...there was nothing more exquisite. Nothing. Funny, though, that he'd never wanted to stroke and taste Gwen, Bianka or Taliyah the way he'd wanted to stroke and taste Kaia.

Not that he was thinking about her anymore.

Defeat uttered another of those chuckles, and Strider tensed. When the little shit made no reply, accepted no challenge, he relaxed somewhat. Damn it. What the hell was going on with his demon?

Gwen chewed on her bottom lip. "Bianka told me the games are so violent that half the participants end up dead or praying for death. And once, about fifteen hundred years ago, far more than half died. Like, nearly all of them."

Strider straightened, his blood chilling. "What? Why?"

"She didn't tell me more than that, so don't look at me like you'll cut my throat if I don't fess up. Anyway, she wasn't exaggerating," Gwen continued. "Oh, wait. She did tell me a bit more. Apparently the Skyhawks haven't been allowed to participate in centuries because of something Kaia did, not that anyone will tell me what. No one in our clan has ever spoken of it, and I was never really around other clanswomen. They've always shunned us. But now, suddenly, they're welcoming us back with open arms. It's weird, and I don't like it, but I'm not sending my sisters into hostile territory alone."

Strider's mind snagged on one detail only. Kaia had caused the turmoil. What had the gorgeous troublemaker done?

"Oh, and one other thing. Bianka thinks this is a trap." Gwen angled Sabin's head up and sank into his lap. Automatically the warrior wrapped his arms around her, holding her tight. "She thinks the Skyhawks, Kaia especially, will be targets, everyone out for revenge."

Kaia...a target for every Harpy with a grudge... Now

his blood heated for a different reason, the need to rage an inferno inside him. "Men are allowed to go?"

"Consorts and slaves, yes, and they're more than allowed, they're encouraged. Blood is medicine to Harpies, and those consorts and slaves help the injured participants heal."

"Does Kaia have a…slave?" He croaked the question. On one hand, he wanted her to have one, to be safe. On the other, he already wanted to murder the ugly prick.

Defeat snarled, no trace of amusement in the sound. Or his usual fear.

This isn't a challenge, buddy. Or was his demon upset by the thought of someone besides Strider hurting Kaia?

In a sick, twisted way, that kind of made sense. His sense of possessiveness was highly developed, with his enemies especially, but even with friends. Kaia was a bit of both.

Thankfully, Defeat offered no reply. Strider didn't need the added complication of fighting Kaia and/or anyone who challenged her. She wasn't his responsibility. She wasn't his problem.

"No," Gwen finally said, sadness creeping into her tone. "Kaia doesn't have a slave."

Relief, so much relief. "We'll find her one, then." Fury, so much fury.

"No." Those strawberry-blond tresses slapped her face as she shook her head. "She thinks *you* are her consort."

Yeah, once upon a time Kaia had said something like that to him. He'd believed that she believed, but he'd also believed she was mistaken, that she was letting simple attraction confuse her. Not that there was anything simple about her attraction to him. She wanted the best of the best for herself, and he couldn't blame—

Ego check. He massaged the back of his neck with his free hand. Rephrasing: she wanted someone strong, capable and handsome. Shit. *Ego check,* he thought again. She'd wanted someone *somewhat* handsome.

No. That didn't work. When a fact was a fact, there was no getting around it. She'd wanted someone extremely handsome, and he fit the bill. But...

Paris was handsomer.

Handsomer wasn't even a word, damn it. Was it? Yeah, it probably was, and had most likely been coined *because* of Paris. "So?" he said with more force than he'd intended.

"So, she won't take anyone else," Sabin blurted. "Harpies are territorial, possessive and stubborn as hell. Meaning, they're just like you and can't compromise worth shit."

Gwen frowned. "Hey!"

"Sorry, baby, but it's true." Then, "Kaia will take you or no one," he said to Strider. "That's just the way it's sliced."

"Which is why..." Gwen inhaled deeply, exhaled slowly, her gaze locking on Strider with menace. "You know I love you, right?"

He gave a stiff nod. Shit, shit, shit. Him or no one. A blessing and a curse. He didn't have time for this. He didn't want this. He couldn't spend any more time with her. Had already said goodbye to her.

A goodbye that had come close to rousing his demon. With every step he'd taken from Kaia's home, Defeat had prowled through his head, wanting to act, to pin her and take her—victory would be so damn sweet—but not allowing himself to do so. Loss would be so damn painful.

Strider had never been happier that the demons of Pandora's box were afraid of the Harpies. And with good reason. They were descendants of Lucifer, the master of all things demonic.

Plus, Defeat had seen Kaia fight. No matter what weapon she used—gun, blade, claws, fangs—she blazed through her opponents faster than the eye could track. Nice qualities in a date, sure, and definite aphrodisiacs.

If your very existence didn't depend on your victories, as his did.

Strider finished off the last of his candy, and chucked the empty box into the trash bin beside Sabin's desk. *Swish.* Two points!

Defeat purred his approval, little sparks of satisfaction shooting through Strider's veins.

"—listening to me?" Gwen asked.

"Yeah, sure," he lied, gaze quickly finding her. She was no longer perched on Sabin's lap. Now she stood a few inches from Strider, her legs braced apart, her hands fisted at her sides. He recognized that pose. "But, uh, give me a refresher. You were saying…"

She rolled her eyes. "I was telling you that you only have two days to take care of any pressing business you might have. Because even though I love you, I'm going to make sure you attend the games. Kaia needs you, and you *will* be there for her. Or else."

His attention flicked to Sabin, all what-are-you-going-to-do-about-this. Sympathy filled every curve and hollow of the man's face, but there was no hint of determination or ire. Okay, so. His fearless leader would be doing nothing. Perfect.

He glared at Gwen. "Don't even think about challenging me," he snapped. "I won't hesitate to retaliate." Of course, one little scratch on the girl and Sabin would attack him. He'd have to go berserker on his boss, but two victories for the price of one? Bring it.

"As if I would ever use your demon against you," she replied, startling him. "God, I can't believe you think so little of me." She truly sounded offended. Just as he opened his mouth to apologize to her, she said, "I'm only planning to beat the crap out of you, tie you up and have Lucien flash you to where the first meeting is being held. Jeez! Cut me some slack."

"Only" planning, she'd said. He pursed his lips. "You do realize that beating the crap out of me and tying me up would be, what? Using my demon against me. The loss would destroy me."

"Oh." Her features fell. "I hadn't thought that far ahead." Then she raised her chin, reminding him of Kaia all over again. "I'll still do it, though. Just make this easier on yourself and agree to go with her. Please."

"Begging doesn't work on me. Neither does crying, just so you know." Once upon a time when he'd done the dating thing, he'd learned that begging and crying were forms of feminine warfare. Women wanted something, and they did anything to get it.

Admirable, but it hadn't taken him long to harden his heart against such wiles. Or to decide that long-term relationships simply weren't for him. As easily as he'd learned about his partners' ploys, they'd learned about his.

He had to win, and they always tried to use that to their advantage. How many times had he heard some variation of, "Bet you can't spend the whole day with me and like it?" Countless.

"Well?" Gwen demanded. "Yes or no? Easy way or hard way?"

"How long?" he gritted out.

"Four weeks," she replied, clearly hopeful.

She could have said "eternity," so emphatic was his reaction. Four weeks. Four damn weeks with Kaia. Feeding her, protecting her, guarding her with his body if the opportunity presented itself.

His cock twitched with eagerness. *This isn't something to look forward to, you idiot.* He'd guard her with his body if *circumstances demanded.* But even with the rephrase, this had trouble written all over it. Getting in and getting out as swiftly as possible was his M.O. now, and one that worked for him. No one had time to learn his quirks—or use them against him.

Kaia, though, she already knew, and she never hesitated to challenge him. Part of him liked the thrill of that, yeah. You couldn't win if you never entered the game, and she was all about the game. On the flip side, you couldn't lose, either.

"What about our war with the Hunters?" he asked Sabin. If there was anyone who liked winning as much as Strider, it was Sabin. Dude would have sold his mom on eBay just to fund a battle. If he'd had a mom, that is.

"I've already talked to Cronus," Sabin replied. "Galen is currently out for the count, too injured to cause trouble, and Rhea is missing."

Galen, the immortal warrior possessed by the demon of Hope—also, ironically, leader of the Hunters. Rhea, the biggest bitch of a god queen ever to control half the heavens. Both topped his long list of enemies.

"Missing? Still?" He'd known she had disappeared, but he'd kinda figured she'd gone into hiding, since her husband had discovered her most recent treachery against him—convincing her sister to act as his mistress and spy on him—and wanted to punish her. "Is foul play expected?" Not many beings could successfully abduct a goddess.

"Yeah, though Cronus won't share any deets."

Maybe because he didn't have any. That might explain why Cronus had summoned Amun. No one was better at obtaining answers than the keeper of Secrets. "This is the perfect time to strike the Hunters, then," he forced himself to say.

"No, actually, it's not." Sabin cocked a brow. "Remember that girl we saw, the one who accepted the demon of Distrust into her body?"

"No, Sab. I forgot," he said dryly. They'd both been in

the Temple of the Unspoken Ones, and watched as the beings manipulated the air to reveal what was happening an entire continent away.

Galen had somehow found the unfindable. The lost demon of Distrust, crazed and worked into a frenzy. He'd then trapped Distrust inside a room and convinced the beast to possess someone else. A female, a Hunter.

Though they'd made inquiries, they'd never learned anything more about the girl. Not her location, not her condition.

"Attitude." Sabin tsked under his tongue. "Anyway, Cronus has decided he wants her. He's got Amun looking into it."

Ah. So that's why Amun had been summoned. Rhea be damned, he supposed. But if Sabin knew this, that meant Haidee had known. Which meant she hadn't wanted to share the information with Strider. A little punishment, he was sure, and he couldn't blame her.

"What does the girl have to do with us kicking some Hunter ass now?" he asked.

"The Hunters will be scrambling to keep her hidden and too busy to attack us."

"So you hope. But again, if that's the case, there's no better time to strike."

"*If* we can find them. Without Amun, we have to rely on our lame-ass detective skills."

Hardly. "We've got Ashlyn." Maddox, the keeper of Violence, had married a woman with the ability to stand in one location and listen to all the conversations that had ever taken place there. *No one* could hide from her.

"Haven't you heard? She's currently bedbound. The twins she's carrying had a sudden growth spurt. She's so big, she needs help getting to the bathroom. Maddox thinks she'll deliver soon."

Poor bastard was probably going crazy with worry.

Ashlyn was (mostly) human, and therefore as delicate and fragile as a glass vase. Nothing like Kaia, who could— *Do not go there.* "I don't know about you, but I'm a damn good detective."

Sabin shrugged. "Okay, think of it this way. I had a choice to make. Take advantage of our advantage, or take care of my wife. Guess which one I picked?"

When had Sabin become such a pussy?

"At least we don't have to worry about our boys being hurt because we left them behind."

As if they'd have to worry about that, anyway. The "boys" were as competent as Strider. Not to mention the fact that they were possessed by baddies like Pain, Disease and Misery. They were all but feral and had no need of babysitters, battle forthcoming or not.

"Well, I still can't go. I have plans," Strider said. *And I can't waver, that's all there is to it.* "I promised Paris I'd help him in the heavens."

"Help him later," Gwen said, butting back in to the conversation. "Kaia needs you now."

His body reacted instantly, skin prickling with awareness—*Kaia needs you*—cells awakening—*Kaia needs you*—shaft thickening, hardening—*Kaia needs you...needs you to touch her, strip her, fill her up.*

"I'll think about it," he said raggedly, then strode into the hall and headed to his own bedroom before Gwen could threaten him a second time. Once there, he shut himself in and moved to the room's center, gaze locked on his walls, mind buzzing.

He and Kaia had the same decorating tastes. Weapons had covered her walls the same way they covered his. He wondered if, like his, each piece in her collection belonged to the humans and immortals she had defeated over the centuries.

Kaia. Defeat. Two words that had become synonymous to him.

Harpies were all about survival of the fittest, and that he could dig. Because of Gwen, he knew that sleeping in front of humans—or anyone but their consort, for that matter—was forbidden. He knew they were not allowed to reveal a single weakness to anyone—even their consorts. And they were never, ever to steal from their sisters. If they broke any of those rules, they were punished.

Damn it, what the hell was he going to do about her? She could take care of herself against anyone except another Harpy. Plus, Kaia would need every advantage she could get. Like, first and foremost, resting. She would need to rest between games, whatever those games might be. She thought Strider was her consort, so she would only rest with him at her side.

Second, she would need someone to ensure she ate properly. Look how she'd allowed herself to waste away in jail.

Third, she would need someone to guard her back if she stole anything, and knowing her, she would steal a lot of somethings. Preferably someone who didn't have to guard her—or his—own back, as well.

Half the participants usually died, Gwen had said. Half. Harpies showed no mercy, took no prisoners. For whatever reason, Kaia would have a bull's-eye on her back.

If he did this, if he went with her...he would have to find a way to steel himself against her appeal. Because, no matter what, he couldn't sleep with her. Not just because of Paris, but because she would view any intimate contact as a commitment, as a Harpy/consort bond. A *forever* kind of bond. No way was he signing on for a lifetime sentence.

Could he resist her, though?

Better question: Could he protect her? If her enemies learned who he was, they could use his demon against her.

They could challenge him to hurt her. They could challenge him to destroy her.

Win? Defeat said, raspy voice drifting through Strider's head.

Shit. *I stopped myself from going there, so you do the same. Please.*

Win, the demon repeated, a demand this time. A demand that held a tinge of fear.

Too late, he thought. Defeat had gone there, and there'd be no backing off. *Win, against any Harpies who try to hurt Kaia?*

WIN.

Yep. Against the Harpies who tried to hurt Kaia. *Why? She isn't your favorite person. Why have me protect her?*

Win, win, win.

Why he'd expected an answer, he didn't know. Unlike some of the other demons, his had a very limited vocabulary. Guaranteed, he'd gotten the short end of the stick. But...maybe Defeat recalled just how good a victory over Kaia felt, and wanted more. If she died, he couldn't have more. Or maybe, possessive as even the demon was, Kaia was their personal battlefield, and others weren't allowed to play there. Ever.

What he did know? He was going to the Harpy Games.

CHAPTER FIVE

KAIA LOVED WATCHING MOVIES, but right now, she felt like she had the starring role in a horror flick called *Slumber Party Massacre*. Only instead of a sleeping bag and a teddy bear, she carried a hatchet—call her sentimental—and a serrated blade.

She strode with her sisters down a long, dark hallway, seemingly alone, weapons clutched in their hands, too. Weapons were also hanging from their waists and rising from their backs. If the Bad Guy truly had been watching from the shadows, waiting to strike, he probably would have seen them moving in slow motion, their hair blowing in the breeze. Also, scary music would have been playing in the background.

Too bad this wasn't Hollywood.

Taliyah was in the middle. She was the oldest among them by far, as well as the strongest, the deadliest. Tall, slender, pale from head to toe, she looked like an elegant ice queen—and had a personality to match. Emotions were not something Taliyah allowed herself to experience. While Kaia had always striven to be like their mother, Taliyah had opted to be the opposite. Logical, level-headed, a planner.

Bianka and Kaia flanked her sides, with Gwen on Kaia's left. At one end of the Estrogen Brigade was Sabin, at the other was Lysander. Typically at events such as these, consorts were supposed to trail a few feet behind, but these men were hardly archetypal. They were equals. Beloved. Determined to protect.

Each of the women radiated a white-hot tension that blended perfectly with Kaia's own. All thanks to the very stupid Strider. He wasn't going to support her. Earlier today Gwen had led her to believe…had made her think…hope…crave…oh, well. Strider hadn't shown up, even though she and her sisters had waited outside for half an hour and were now late to the meeting.

Stupid, *stupid* Strider.

Doomed, *doomed* Kaia.

Well, she had finally written him off and admitted that she was better off without him. He was rejection, humiliation and heartbreak wrapped in a pretty package. She could find another pretty package without all the extras, thank you.

At least Bianka and Gwen would be well-guarded, and that eased her stress somewhat. But if anyone so much as threatened them because of what Kaia had once done, she would turn the *Slumber Party Massacre* into *Blood, Bath and Beyond,* a documentary by Kaia Skyhawk.

And if anyone teased Bianka about dating an angel, well, they, too, would have a starring role in that documentary. Sadly, she had a feeling there were going to be a lot of starring roles.

At first glance, Lysander looked every inch the do-gooder. His hair gleamed as if the strands were gold silk. His skin was just as pale with only the faintest hint of rose. He wore a long white robe, his golden wings tucked in, the tops arching over his shoulders. He had no visible weapons. But then, he didn't need them. He could create a sword of fire from nothing but air. Only after a second glance would the Harpies realize he was a warrior through and through, muscled and brawny, with a ruthless determination to protect what was his.

By then, it'd be too late.

Sabin, well, everyone would know what he was the moment they spotted him: a badass lacking any type of moral compass. He had brown hair and ocher eyes, his features a study of harsh planes and sharp angles. More weapons spilled from his six-foot-seven frame than an entire human army could carry, and his every step reminded her of a dying heartbeat. *Thump.* Pause, pause. *Thump.* But, uh, what was with the bullhorn in his hand?

There'd be no teasing Gwen about him, but her little sis would probably have to beat the ladies off him. Sabin was everything Harpies admired. Wicked, ungoverned by society's rules and way beyond dangerous.

A danger readily apparent, even though he wore a T-shirt that said I'm Not a Gynecologist, but I'll Take a Look.

Kaia wanted to buy one of those for Strider.

Finally they reached the doors to the auditorium of the elementary school. Yes, an elementary school. In "Brew City," Wisconsin.

Only this morning had the texts gone out, informing everyone where to go for Game Orientation, and the location had puzzled her. A million years ago, orientation had been held in a wide-open field several miles from civilization. Sure, times had changed. But an elementary school? Really?

After expressing his own puzzlement, Lucien, keeper of Death, had flashed her and Gwen, dropping them off at the school's front doors. Lysander had flown Bianka in, and Taliyah had simply materialized from what looked to be a thick, dark mist. Girl had developed a new ability, apparently, but when questioned, had refused to give up the deets. Like what the ever-loving hell could she do? Kaia had never, in all her centuries, seen anyone step from a misty doorway of their own creation.

Wasn't fair, either. Taliyah already had a kick-ass ability. She could shape-shift. Not that she ever used the ability. But now she could do this, too, yet Kaia couldn't do *anything* cool.

Pouter! Kaia stopped when she reached the auditorium doors. They were closed, a murmur of voices drifting through the tiny crack between the metal slats. A tremor slid down her spine, vibrating into her limbs.

Taliyah stopped, too. She sheathed her weapons and placed a firm hand on Kaia's shoulder, her crystalline gaze pointed. "You know I'm with you, no matter what. Right?"

Her heart swelled with love as she shoved the hatchet and blade into their holsters. "Yeah, I know." Her mother might have written her off, but her sisters never had. They supported her. Through anything, everything.

"Good. Then let's do this."

Taliyah pushed open the double doors, the hinges squeaking in protest. Without the barrier, the murmurs became full-blown conversations. Conversations that died as all eyes swung to the newest entrants.

Kaia searched the sea of faces she hadn't seen in centuries, but didn't spot her mother. Or any other Skyhawk for that matter, despite the fact that there were close to a hundred females watching her through narrowed eyes. She raised her chin. Several of the ladies reached for sword or dagger hilts, but none so much as stepped toward her.

All that hate-filled attention should have intimidated her, she supposed. However, Kaia found herself delighting in it. She was strong, stronger than ever, and she *would* prove herself. Finally.

Finally they would know she was worthy.

Tabitha could take her "almost improved" and shove it up her—

"Well, well. Look who decided to join us, everyone. Kaia the Disappointment. And company, of course." The familiar voice echoed from the walls. Juliette the Eradicator. "What a surprise. We thought you'd opted not to enter, which would have been a very smart move on your part. But then, you've only got half a brain, isn't that right?"

Annnd here were the twins-only-got-half jokes again.

Juliette went on, "I feel obligated to warn you that you will lose, and you will not have fun when you do. Or survive. Not that I'd know anything about that. I've taken home the gold in the last eight games. But I guess *you* wouldn't know that, seeing how you weren't invited to them."

Bianka growled, Taliyah tensed and Kaia gritted her teeth as she faced her nemesis.

Juliette stood in the center of the stage. Tall, toned and stunning, she had shoulder-length black hair and eyes of the purest lavender. She wore a tank top and a short skirt that revealed the tattoos inked into her legs. Ancient godly symbols that bespoke revenge. Loosely translated, each one meant "the redheaded bitch must suffer." Nice.

"Pretty soon, you'll have to kiss your gold goodbye," Kaia told her. "It's mine this time around."

Juliette grinned slowly, smugly. "Actually, no. No, I won't. In case you didn't know, I won't be participating this year. I'm running things. In other words, I'm top dog. The elders met, decided, and I am now the be-all and end-all."

That so did not bode well for Kaia's victory. As the woman who called the shots, Juliette would decide who broke the rules and who didn't, and in the end, she would tabulate the final scores. No wonder Kaia had been invited to participate. Nothing was stacked in her favor.

"Well, you're definitely a dog," she managed to say through her apprehension. How many times over the centuries had she apologized to Juliette? Innumerable. How many fruit baskets had she sent? Hundreds. What more could she do? Nothing. And she was sick of trying when *this* was the result.

Rage flickered in those lavender eyes, but Juliette offered no retort. "Your men must sit with the others." Motions jerky, she pointed to the back of the auditorium, where a large group of men perched side by side in the balcony, mere spectators.

"Actually, our men stay with us. And that is not something we will discuss." Taliyah stalked forward, every inch the predator. "Now, you may continue with the meeting." The command was not lost despite the polite delivery.

"I will," Juliette huffed. "Have no worries on that front." She launched into a speech about proper behavior before, during and after the games.

Ignoring her, Kaia "and company" followed her oldest sis. They stopped to the right of the stage, beside another clan. The Eagleshields. Juliette's family. Her chin lifted another notch. Every member stepped back, away from her, as if she had a contagious disease they didn't want to catch, and a blush heated her cheeks.

No, not every member widened the distance, she realized a second later. Neeka the Unwanted had stood alone on the group's fringes and now stepped forward, closer to the Skyhawks. She was grinning.

"Taliyah." Neeka inclined her head respectfully. She was deaf, having been stabbed in the ears during a raid. She'd been a child and hadn't healed from her wounds, and her own mother had later tried to slay her for daring to live with such an infirmity.

The woman must have trained at the Tabitha Skyhawk school of Mothering.

The two females embraced, patting each other on the back once, twice. When they parted, Neeka looked at Kaia. Shockingly, her grin of pearly whites remained in place. She had hair on the softer side of jet and rich brown eyes.

A few freckles dotted her nose, darker than her mocha skin, the only "flaws" in an otherwise too-perfect face.

"All grown up now," Neeka said in a perfectly modulated, very soft tone.

"Yep." She waited for the insults to start flying.

None were forthcoming. "I hope you're as lethal as gossip claims."

Wait. What? "Probably more so," she said modestly. Well, modestly *for her.*

The grin widened. Clearly, Neeka had taught herself how to read lips. "Good. That'll make the next few weeks bearable. So, tell me. About a year ago, someone mentioned you hung a human outside a sixty-story building. By his hair. That true?"

"Well, yeah." And she wasn't sorry. "Gwennie was missing, and he was the last one to see her." She shrugged. "I wanted answers."

"Rock on. What about—"

"Enough," Juliette snapped. "You are wasting our time with your exaggerations when you should be *listening* to *me.*"

Exaggerations. Please. Rather than defend herself—and look as though she protested too much—Kaia repeated what had been said. Juliette was behind Neeka, so the poor girl had no idea everyone now watched them, quietly waiting for their cooperation.

The admonishment didn't send Neeka back to her clan. She remained beside Taliyah. Odd. What was—

From the other side of the spacious room, another set of double doors opened. And then Kaia was staring across the distance—at her mother. Tabitha the Vicious. Juliette quieted as gasps of awe abounded.

A legend had just arrived.

Kaia's stomach knotted, and she gulped. She'd known this moment would come, had thought she was prepared for it. But… Oh, gods. Her knees knocked together, and she had to press her weight into her heels to steady herself.

Damn it, her sudden case of nerves needed *some* outlet. Her skin prickled as though little bugs with white-hot legs were crawling all over her.

Over a year had passed since she'd last spoken to her mother, and that final conversation had not been pleasant.

I don't know why I've stuck by you as long as I have, Tabitha had said. *I push and I push and I push, yet you've done nothing to redeem yourself. You remain in Alaska, fighting with humans, stealing from humans, playing with humans.*

Kaia had gaped. *I didn't realize I needed to prove myself to you. I'm your daughter. Shouldn't you love me no matter what?*

You have me confused with your sisters. And look where their indulgence has gotten you. Nowhere. The other clans, they still hate you. I have guarded you, protected you all this time, never allowing them to act against you, but that ends today. My *indulgence has gotten you nowhere, as well.*

Their definition of *indulgence* varied greatly. And, to be honest, that variation cut her so deeply she didn't think she'd ever heal. *Mother—*

No. Say no more. We are done here.

Footsteps had echoed as her mother walked away. For good. There'd been no phone calls, no letters, no emails or texts. Kaia had simply ceased to exist. Juliette still hadn't attacked her, so she had assumed her mother had continued to "protect" her despite that fact.

Maybe she'd assumed wrong.

Maybe that's why she now found herself in this place.

And yet, even knowing Tabitha might want her hurt and broken, her gaze drank her mother in, her first glimpse in all these months, unbidden though it was, and gods,

Tabitha was lovely. Though she'd lived for millennia and given birth to four (beautiful) daughters now past legal drinking age—*waaaay* past—she appeared to be no more than twenty-five. Beautifully tanned skin, a silky mass of black hair, amber-brown eyes, and the delicate features of a china doll.

A few times over the years, she'd dyed her hair red and Kaia had thought, hoped, that meant... But no.

"Tabitha Skyhawk," Juliette said, her tone reverent. She inclined her head in greeting. "Welcome."

"*That's* your mother?" Sabin suddenly demanded of Gwen. "I mean, you told me she hated you and that's why she stays away, but that woman looks like she only hates broken nails and stocking runs."

"She's only my mom by birth, so don't hold it against me," Gwen replied. "And I assure you, she'd break your face without a thought to her nails."

Gwen had always been the sensitive one, the one in need of safeguarding. Yet she hadn't cried the day Tabitha had called her unworthy. She had simply shrugged and moved on. Not once had she looked back.

"She can't be all bad," Sabin said. "Not with those legs."

Men. "She has the heart of a child, you know. Yeah, it's in a box beside her bed." *And guess what? It's mine!*

After the Unfortunate Incident, Kaia had dogged Tabitha for *centuries,* desperate, willing to do anything, battle anyone, to earn back her mother's respect and love. She had failed, time and time again. Finally she'd realized the fruitlessness of her efforts and turned her attentions to the humans. An act that had once again earned Tabitha's castigation.

You remain in Alaska, fighting with humans, stealing from humans, playing with humans. The words ran through Kaia's mind a second time. Among humans, she was a prize among prizes, thought to be lovely, courageous and fun. *Of course* she'd played with them.

You're over the rejection, remember? You don't care.

Her mother entered the room the rest of the way, nine Harpies filing in behind her. When the doors shut with a soft whisk, the group stopped and surveyed the room, the occupants. All ten gazes zoomed past her without even the slightest pause, as if she were invisible.

Look at me, she thought frantically. *Mother, please.* For those few, pregnant seconds, she felt like a needy little girl again. Of course, those golden eyes never returned to her. Worse, they landed on Juliette and sparked with pride. Pride. Why?

Did it matter? A bitter laugh welled in Kaia's throat. Then she noticed the matching medallions hanging from each of their necks, and the laugh escaped on a choke. Small wooden discs, intricate wings carved into the centers, the precious symbol of Skyhawk strength. Kaia had always been fine with the fact that her mother had trained Juliette, as well as other members of allied clans. But giving someone other than a Skyhawk a medal? Oh, that burned!

Another memory surfaced. Suddenly she felt the scrape of leather against her nape as *her* necklace was ripped from her.

"Our flight was delayed," Tabitha explained, her hard voice echoing from the domed ceiling. "We apologize."

Even so stiffly uttered…an apology? From Tabitha the Vicious? That was a first. Was Kaia dreaming? Had she entered some sort of parallel universe and just didn't know it? No, she couldn't have. If so, Tabitha would have smiled at her. She hadn't.

So the apology *had* happened.

Her knees started knocking again, and there was no stopping them.

"Sorry I'm late," a husky male voice said from behind her.

And back to the dream theory. No way Strider was here and apologizing. That would mean he was her lifeline—a line to more than just insanity. Kaia whipped around, certain there would be no change in her surroundings. To her eternal shock, her eyes supported her ears.

Strider was here in all his warrior glory.

A smile from Mother Dearest or not, she *had* entered a parallel universe. There could be no other explanation. Could there? "What are you doing here?" The scent of cinnamon wafted from him, and as she inhaled—panted, really—her heart skidded into an uncontrollable beat.

"Thank gods," Sabin muttered. "Gwen almost had my balls for breakfast when she heard I'd let you leave the fortress this morning."

Gwen blushed. "Sabin! Now isn't the time to spill our bedroom secrets."

Bianka chuckled behind her hand. "I don't think that's what he meant, Gwennie-bo-Bennie."

As she spoke, Lysander inserted himself between her and the two demon-possessed immortals. He might have agreed to a truce with the Lords of the Underworld, but that didn't mean he liked them. And as he'd cut off their good buddy Aeron's head, the Lords weren't his biggest fans, either, and he clearly didn't want them taking out their dislike on Bianka. As if they would. Demon-possessed or not, the warriors treated the Skyhawk girls like family. Irritating cousins who'd overstayed their welcome, but family nonetheless.

Another round of gasps suddenly echoed. The men had finally been noticed, *really* noticed as more than blood donors and carnival ponies, and murmurs of "angel" and "lords" arose. The first was filled with amusement, as Kaia had feared, the second with jealousy.

Jealousy. For her. She tried not to puff up like a peacock.

She failed.

"What are you doing here?" she repeated in a low whisper. To Strider. Who was here. Here, with her.

"Ask me tomorrow, and I might have thought up an answer," he replied dryly.

Once again, she found her heart swelling. Not with love, not this time, but with equal measures of lust, joy and relief. He was sexier than ever in a bloodstained white T-shirt and ripped-up jeans. Dirt streaked his fallen angel face and his blond hair was plastered to his scalp and dripping with sweat.

"I would have been here sooner," he added, "but my final perimeter check at the fortress proved fruitful."

"Hunters?"

"Yeah. Bastards. Always trying something sneaky."

"You killed them all?"

His blue eyes glittered, revealing hints of the victorious demon inside him. "Every last one."

That's my man. "Good girl." Yes, she had just called him a girl. And he was here. He really was here. She couldn't get over that amazing fact. Did that mean he'd realized they belonged together? Had he forgiven her for sleeping with Paris? She fought the urge to throw her arms around him, to hug him tight and never let go.

He must have read the questions and desires in her eyes because he said, "Just don't get the wrong idea," spoiling everything. "You needed a medicine cabinet, so here I am. As soon as the games are over, I'm gone. I don't tell you that to be rude, but to be honest." Gentle, so gentle. "Okay?"

"Yeah, sure. Th-thanks." Not wanting him to witness the withering of her joy, she turned back around. *I will not cry.* Her mother hadn't broken her (for the most part); he wouldn't, either (not again).

Once more she was the center of attention, every gaze fastened on her. She raised her chin exactly as she had the first time, refusing to reveal her upset.

"So what'd I miss?" he asked.

"See the rocking brunette over there?" Sabin pointed to Tabitha. "That's their mother."

"*That's* their mom?" Strider gasped out.

Kaia's hands curled into fists, her sharpening nails cutting past skin. Warm—too warm—trickles of blood slid between her knuckles before dripping onto the floor. "If you aren't careful, I'm going to…" There was no threat mean enough. "Just…don't compliment her."

"Don't challenge me, Red. You won't like the results."

Red. From anyone else, that would have been a term of endearment. From Strider, it was a curse. "Why? You planning on spanking me?"

"I'll leave." The words were firmly stated.

She pressed her lips into a mutinous line. His absence was the one thing she wasn't willing to risk. Whether she liked him or not—currently *not.* He might be a pain in her ass, he might be stubborn and sometimes hateful, but he was the best chance she had of winning this thing, and she knew it. With Juliette in charge, she needed someone's head on a swivel, watching her back 25/8.

"My mom's not my favorite person, okay?" She twisted without looking at him and whispered, "Now can you please act like you're into me, just for a little while?"

At last Tabitha deigned to acknowledge their group. Her gaze moved over the men, and only the men, her mouth curling in distaste. All the while, she stroked the hilt of the blade hanging from her waist.

"First, I didn't compliment her. Second, she looks like she eats other people's hopes and dreams for breakfast, and not just because they're tasty. That's not attractive. Third, *you* look like you *sprung* from other people's hopes and dreams. I couldn't—can't—believe you're related."

How…sweet. Kaia was completely blown away. Damn him! First he delivered a nasty blow, announcing he wasn't sticking around. Then he complimented her. How was she supposed to maintain emotional distance from him when he said things like that?

"Wait. What? Who said that?" Strider growled before she could form a reply.

"You did," she replied, "and I know what you're going to say next. You sounded like a pansy." She hated to snipe at him, but her sanity was at stake.

Strider snapped his teeth at her.

"Who said what, then?" she asked on a sigh.

His dark gaze roved their little group, then returned to her mother, a muscle ticking in his jaw. "Never mind. Doesn't matter."

O-kay. Consorts. You couldn't live with them, but you couldn't cut out their tongues without earning a lifetime of hateful glares, either.

"Now that everyone's here, let's get back to business, shall we?" Juliette said. "The games have always been an important part of our lives, allowing us to righteously punish those who have wronged us—" of course she peered at Kaia when she said that "—as well as prove how strong we've become to those we adore. So here's to doing what we do best. Kicking ass!"

Cheers erupted.

"If you'll each check your messages, you'll find the team rosters," Juliette announced, her voice dripping with satisfaction, her attention momentarily fixed on Strider.

And that's when Kaia realized the cold, hard truth. Rage nearly sent her flying onto that stage. *Steady, calm. That's what Juliette wants.* What else she wanted? Strider.

Clearly the bitch had been waiting for the day Kaia found her own consort, most likely planning to take him away the same way Kaia had once taken hers.

Fan-fucking-tastic. How had word already leaked when she and Strider weren't officially an item? And damn it all, an uncommitted Strider would be easy prey. The rage mutated into fear, and bile rose in her throat, threatening to spill out.

Strider and Juliette…Juliette, who hadn't slept with Paris…twined together, naked, writhing, moaning, begging…

Oh, gods. *Concentrate on the here and now.* Everything else could be dealt with later. Maybe. If she continued down that thought path, she would attack someone— namely Juliette and Strider—or break down. Neither was an acceptable option.

Trembling, Kaia withdrew her phone from her back pocket, scrolled and quickly found a text. Only, she wasn't listed on Team Skyhawk. Her sisters weren't, either. "I don't understand."

"Mother claims she no longer has any daughters," Taliyah said. "Which means we cannot compete as Skyhawks. I had to petition the council to start a new clan. Once that was taken care of, we were in."

No reaction. She would give no reaction. She wasn't dying inside. She *wasn't.* "Then what's our new team name?" The answer appeared on her screen before she could finish. Team Kaia. Her sisters, as well as Neeka and a few others, were competing on Team Kaia.

For a moment, her surroundings faded, as did her hurt, and she basked in her sisters' unflinching support. They loved her. No matter what, they loved her. They accepted her. They thought she was good enough, just as she was. Then the world spun back into focus, and she had to blink against the burn of tears.

Damn it. How many times would she have to battle the urge to sob today?

"The first competition begins bright and early tomorrow morning," Juliette went on. "Afterward, everyone will be notified of exactly where the next competition is taking place. As you know, we no longer host the games in one location because previous contestants rigged and sabotaged them ahead of time." Even though Kaia hadn't been responsible—hello, she hadn't been invited—Juliette tossed the words at her.

Whatever. Her spine snapped straighter, as though anchored in place by steel rods.

Strider's hand settled on her lower back, warm and steady, comforting. Sizzling. Sweet heaven, her surroundings faded once again, until only the two of them existed. She imagined his mouth replacing his hand, his tongue licking, trailing lower. A gasp escaped her.

Get yourself under control. If she got "the wrong idea" about something as innocent as a pat, he'd take off, as promised. Like she could blame him. Had the situation been reversed, she would have done the same.

Deep down, they were just alike. Warriors honed on the field of battle, sharp as a dagger, cynical, willing to do anything for their friends. And on some level, they *were* friends. Had been since the first. He might not want to be here, but he didn't want her to get hurt, either. So he'd come; he would help her. But he wouldn't let her push for more. As long as she maintained an emotional distance, he would stay. Would be her "medicine cabinet."

As pissed off and hurting as she was, she was also grateful.

"Something else is also new this year," Juliette continued, pulling Kaia from her thoughts. "The prize. This time around, the winners will not receive silver and gold after each competition."

"What?" someone shouted.

"That's why we're here!" another growled.

Juliette held up her hands, a command for silence. A command that was instantly obeyed. "This year, we have something better."

Amid questioning murmurs, the curtain at the side of the stage parted. And then—Kaia's mouth dropped open. No way. No damn way. The "slave" she'd tried to acquire all those centuries ago, the one who'd wreaked such havoc on the Harpy clans, strode to Juliette's side. He was chained at the wrists, just as before. He was more muscled now, his dark hair longer, but his features were still sharp, stubborn.

"Dear gods. Is that *him?*" Bianka gasped out.

"Yeah," she managed to squeak. No one had told her that Juliette had found him. *When* had she found him? Where? "That's him."

"Him who?" Strider demanded.

At first, Kaia thought she detected a note of jealousy in his tone, and it was such a loverlike response she wanted to kiss him deep and dirty. Strip him down to nothing more than skin and a smile. She wanted to ride him hard, fast and forever. *All mine.* Then common sense punched her right in the jaw. He might be jealous, but not in any way that mattered. Strider had decided to help her, and his demon would allow no one to interfere. Especially not another warrior.

Part of her resented that. The other part of her *really* resented that. "Laying it on a little thick, aren't you, *Meds?* He's no one you need to concern yourself with."

"Kaia," he snapped.

"Hush it, would you?" She couldn't tell him the truth. Still didn't want him to know of her past foolishness, when he already thought so little of her. "You're making me look bad in front of my team."

"Kaia."

"Fine. I'll explain later," she lied.

A tense pause. Then, "You'd better."

"Or else?"

"Yeah."

Her nemesis—the man she'd searched for over the years, determined to punish for what he'd done to her sister, but had never found—now held a long, thin spear. Its thicker, oblong tips were comprised of glass, something glowing and twirling inside them.

Power, so much power, radiated from that spear.

Juliette claimed the weapon without a word of thanks. The man—his name, she had long ago learned, was Lazarus, though she and Bianka had nicknamed him The Tampon for being such a douche—spun on his booted heels. His dark gaze moved over the crowd…searching…before snagging on Kaia. He stopped, stared.

Oxygen froze in her lungs, making it impossible to breathe. No damn reaction, she thought. Not here, not now. Later, though, she would seek him out. She would hurt him as she'd always wanted.

Slowly he grinned. So handsome…so coldly evil. She hissed, her fangs popping free of her gums. *You're dead, cowboy.* He belonged to Juliette, yes, and everyone clearly blamed Kaia rather than him for what he had done to their loved ones. And yeah, they blamed her with good reason. Had she done as she'd been told, he wouldn't have had the strength to harm anyone. But *he* had been the one to rip through flesh, with his teeth, his claws. *He* had been the one to render those deathblows.

He would be the one to pay—by Kaia's hand.

Every time she had sent a fruit basket to Juliette, she had referenced the past—but in her mind, she had offered the apology because of what she planned do in the future. She was going to kill him. No one hurt her sisters. No one.

"Forget later. Him, the fuck, who?" Strider demanded again.

Before she could think up a reply, the Tampon kicked back into gear, exited the stage, and was once again hidden behind the curtain. Smart of him. She wasn't sure how much longer she could have refrained from flying at him.

When she went for him, it would be in private. No one there to save him.

"Later," she repeated.

"This," Juliette said, drawing everyone's attention to the spear in her hands, "is very, very precious. Far more so than silver or gold." Her lavender gaze locked on Kaia. "I'm sure you've sensed its power, but what you don't know? That power can be transferred to *you*. You can wield it, control it. You'll be stronger than you ever imagined. You'll be invincible."

Murmurs abounded.

If what Juliette claimed was true, why hadn't she transferred the powers to herself? Why hadn't she struck at Kaia already? Why was she so willing, so eager to give the thing away?

Juliette flashed an indulgent smile. "Throughout the centuries, the gods have called this mighty weapon the Paring Rod. I, however, have a better name for it. First prize."

Strider stiffened.

Sabin cursed.

Both men would have leapt on the stage if Taliyah and Neeka hadn't held them back. The action proved unnecessary, however, because the weapon disappeared in a blink, in Juliette's hand one minute, gone the next.

"What the hell?" Kaia, Gwen and Bianka asked in unison.

Kaia peeled her sister's hands off her man and cupped his cheeks, forcing him to focus on her. "What's going on?"

"First prize," Strider gritted out. "It's the fourth artifact. The one we need to help us find and destroy Pandora's
box."

"Which means first prize," Sabin finished bleakly, "has
the power to wipe us out. Forever."

CHAPTER SIX

HOW THE HOLY HELL HAD this happened?

Strider paced the length of the dingy motel room, the ice in his veins making his movements sluggish. His boots hammered into the shaggy brown carpet, creating a well-worn path.

Kaia was perched on top of the TV, watching him, her expression concerned. Her long, smooth legs were crossed at the ankles and swinging, banging into the screen every other second. A little faster, and she would have matched the *thump, thump* beat of his heart.

Sabin and Gwen sat at the edge of one of the double beds, and Bianka and Lysander sat at the edge of the other. Taliyah had taken off with a pretty black girl, and neither had said a word about where they were going or how long they'd be gone.

"The Unspoken Ones claimed to have the Paring Rod," he croaked. Someone had to get the conversation/raging argument started.

"Clearly, they lied." Sabin propped his elbows on his knees, head falling into his upraised hands.

Yeah. Clearly. Shit. Shit, shit, shit. "This is bad. Really bad."

He should have known, should have suspected at the very least. Instead, a few weeks ago Strider had visited their temple. He hadn't minded giving the monstrous beings the Cloak because he'd thought they had another artifact already. Why not one more? He'd thought they would guard both relics until he could return and bargain, buying both.

He'd thought wrong.

What a cluster! If the Unspoken Ones had possessed the Rod, they wouldn't have given it to Juliette. Not without payment, and that payment would not have come in the form of cash or jewels. They wanted only Cronus's head.

Since the god king still lived, no exchange had been made. Which meant the Unspoken Ones were completely untrustworthy, and there was no telling what they would do with the Cloak if Strider failed to deliver that head.

Win, Defeat growled. No question, just a flat-out acceptance for the challenge presented.

There would be no squabbling on his part. Even though they now had two open objectives. The Cloak, and Kaia. *I know. I will.*

First, he had to steal the Paring Rod. Sabin hadn't lied. If it ended up in the wrong hands—and by "wrong," he meant any hands but his own—Pandora's box could be found, and he and his friends destroyed. Their demons would be ripped from their bodies and sucked back inside.

Great in theory, but man and beast were connected in a hard-core, can't-live-without-you kind of way. Apart, the men would instantly kick the bucket and the demons would go bat-shit crazy.

Urgency rushed through him. Strider stopped in the center of the room and faced Kaia. "We have to steal it."

Her mouth fell open, red and lush and oh-so-tempting. "Uh, what now?"

"Forget the games and help me steal the Rod." He gritted his teeth like a good little soldier and added, "Please." Sometimes a guy needed a wingman, and now was one of those times. He had no idea how Harpy minds worked or where that Juliette person was likely to hide her treasure.

Kaia was his inside source. His only way in.

Her pupils dilated—with anger. Great. Exactly what he didn't need. The little lady in a temper, unafraid to use it. Then she ran her tongue over her teeth, and a bolt of lust shot straight through him, melting the ice and leaving a smoldering inferno behind, making him long to stoke that temper higher.

At a time like this? Really?

No time is the wrong time, his libido piped up. *She might attack, but at least her hands will be all over you.*

He could have kicked his own horny ass.

"Not just no, but hell, no," she said, chin lifted stubbornly.

Dread replaced his urgency. He knew that look. He'd seen it before, directed at the roomful of Harpies. Their gazes had flayed her alive, for some reason, but she hadn't backed down.

"And you aren't stealing it, either," she added.

As if. "Are you trying to punish me, Red?" He'd made the fatal mistake of being honest with her, of telling her he was here to help her but not to romance her. He'd known better, too. Never show a woman your cards. "Because if that's the case—"

"Oh, my gods. Are you *that* egotistical?" Those silver-gold eyes sharpened like daggers, cutting him up inside. He didn't like her angry (for the most part), and he didn't like her hurt. Just then, she appeared to be both. "Not everything is about you, Strider."

"I know that. Believe me, I ego check all the time. So tell me, what's the problem? I seem to recall a certain red-headed Harpy once saying she'd do *anything,* as long as it was immoral and the price was right. So do it. Name your price, and do it."

"There is no price," she snapped. "Not for this."

"Are you afraid?" A low blow, yeah, but he was desperate.

She hopped off the TV, teeth bared and sharpening into something far more dangerous than one of those daggers, black bleeding into her eyes and overshadowing all hint of color.

"You're gonna get it now," Bianka sang, and Lysander pressed his hand over her mouth, preventing her from saying anything else.

"Idiot," Sabin muttered. "I'm not even gonna assist you. You deserve what's about to happen."

"I'm afraid of nothing." Two voices layered Kaia's words, and both were raspy, menacing...slashing. In and out she breathed, each inhalation labored, each exhalation ragged. "You're very lucky my Harpy is adamantly opposed to harming you, or you'd be in pieces right now. And if you try to steal the Rod on your own, *after* I told you not to, I will challenge you to contests you cannot possibly hope to win. Forever."

He wanted to shake her. Wanted to kiss her—but only to shut her the hell up, of course. Damn it, she skirted the edge of challenge even then. Defeat prowled from one side of his skull to the other, practically foaming at the mouth for a go at her. Only fear of losing kept the demon from accepting.

You're the one who demanded we come here. You're the one who decided to take down anyone who attacked her. Yeah, Strider had been leaning in that direction himself. Yeah, he kinda wanted to gut and decapitate her opposition before they could strike a single blow against her. However, he understood his own motives—attraction, and an overdeveloped sense of possession. Defeat's motives? Not so much. *Why are you doing this?*

Win, was all the beast said. As always.

"Got it?" Kaia demanded when he offered no response.

Disappointment rocked him. She *was* trying to punish him, and he'd kind of expected better of her. They might snipe and snap at each other, they might be hopelessly fascinated by each other, but they were also friends. Or so he'd thought. Friends helped friends.

Case in point: he was in Wisconsin when he should have been in any of a thousand other places.

He spun around and glared at Bianka. He didn't mind thieving on his own. Usually. However, Harpies were a different breed of animal than anyone or thing he'd dealt with before. They could move faster than the eye could track. They could rip through a man's trachea with only their teeth. Hell, they could rip through an entire army in seconds.

There was no line they wouldn't cross, no deed too vile. If he went for the Rod and they caught him, they would kill him. But without the Rod, he was dead, anyway. So, no contest. He was going for it.

"What about you?" he threw at Bianka.

"Tone, warrior," Lysander said, his voice so mild Strider almost couldn't detect the power behind it. Almost.

That's not a challenge, he told his demon, refusing to repeat himself to Kaia's twin. Thankfully—or not—Defeat was still too focused on Kaia, the Cloak and the Rod. If Strider failed to obtain the latter two, and soon, he would lose the battle. He would hurt. Yet he couldn't leave Kaia without hurting, either.

Bianka shoved Lysander's hand away from her mouth. "Sorry, big boy, but I can't help you."

"Why?"

She shrugged, all innocence. "If you want me to list reasons, I'll list reasons. I can't guarantee they'll be truthful, though."

He faced Gwen. "And you?"

"S-sorry?" she said, sounding confused. She glanced

at Kaia, who shook her head. He knew because he was watching her reflection in the picture over the nightstand between the beds. "I can't," she finished more firmly.

Okay, something was going on here. Kaia wasn't afraid. No matter what he'd said, he knew that. Girl was too brave for her own good. She'd stood in a roomful of Harpies, and even though they'd regarded her as if she were a slab of ribs and they were dedicated vegetarians, she'd kept her head high, daring them to try and take a bite.

The only time he'd ever seen her lose her cool, trembling with an emotion he hadn't been able to name, was when she'd looked at her mother. Her very hot, clearly murderous mother, who might have spoken inside his head. He still wasn't sure.

As the freakishly young-looking, dead-eyed brunette had perused his body, judging him, taking his measure, he'd heard a cold, emotionless and yet very feminine voice whisper, *Kaia will die before the final game begins.*

Like hell. Nothing else had been said, and no one else had heard the threat. And shit, maybe he had an overactive imagination. Either way, he didn't care. He was here, he'd do what he'd promised, but damn it, Kaia was going to bend a little in this matter.

"Get lost," he told the couples on the beds.

Knowing Strider as well as he did, Sabin gathered Gwen without protest and hustled her out the door. Their knowing gazes locked until the last possible moment. They'd move mountains to obtain that Rod, with or without the approval of the Skyhawks. First, though, they'd do what they could to obtain answers. Even if that meant splitting up and being without backup.

Thanks to a soft, "I'll be fine," from Kaia, Bianka and Lysander followed close on Sabin's heels, shutting the door behind them with a soft *click.* The angel didn't know him, or what he was capable of, but must have recognized the danger he posed.

"Why?" he demanded, swinging around.

Kaia didn't pretend to misunderstand. "They'll say I had no confidence in my abilities. They'll call me a coward."

"So?" She was willing to risk his life for her ego? "A little ridicule never killed anyone."

She flicked the long length of that curling red hair over one shoulder, the picture of feminine pique. At least the black had faded from her eyes, a sign her Harpy was under control. "Lookit, you're here, and much as I hate to admit this, you'll find out anyway, so I might as well tell you."

A heavy pause. "Go on."

She gulped. "A long time ago, during the Harpy Games, I tried to steal…something from another…clan."

Oh, really? "Why the hesitation?"

"Anyway," she continued, ignoring him, her cheeks flushing prettily. "My actions resulted in a massacre. Half the Harpy population was wiped out, and I have never been forgiven."

He knew what that meant. They had ostracized her. And if anyone understood the sting of rejection, it was Strider.

When the gods had chosen Pandora to guard *dim-Ouniak,* the box containing the evil spirits that managed to escape the depths of hell, he had allowed pride to rule him. How dare they pick her, a female, when he had never lost a battle? Anyone Zeus had wanted eliminated, Strider had eliminated.

He'd wanted to prove himself worthy, which was why he'd helped steal and open that box. Of course, he'd had every intention of recapturing the demons after they'd caused a little havoc. He would have been all "See what I can do? See what your precious Pandora *can't?*" But the box disappeared, and the havoc had been far more than a little. He'd never encountered its like, before or since.

Not even when Defeat was first shoved into his body and the urge to hurt, maim and destroy consumed him. Yet that hadn't been enough of a punishment for the Greeks. They'd kicked him out of the only home he'd ever known and never acknowledged him again.

So, rejection, unforgivingness, yeah, he knew them intimately. But he couldn't let anything, even Kaia's potential downfall, stop him from obtaining that Rod. Too much was at stake.

"If I take something else...they'll kill me, Strider. *After* they ensure I feel every bit of pain they have felt."

She believed what she said. The truth glistened in her eyes as surely as a sheen of tears. "I'll protect you."

"Don't make me state the obvious about what you can and can't do," she said with a bitter laugh. "I could run, sure, but what kind of life is that? And what if they go after my sisters when they're unable to find and punish me?"

Good point, and one he couldn't—wouldn't—shake her from. He tried another route. "No one has to know you took it. We'll get in and get out, no problem."

Sad, she shook her head. "Wouldn't matter if I left evidence behind or not. If the Rod goes missing, they'll blame me no matter what."

"So?" he said again. He had to harden his heart.

"You know nothing about Harpy justice, Strider. There is no trial. There is no innocent until proven guilty. If I'm suspected, I will be hunted, I will be tortured and as I said, I will be killed."

"I'll protect you," he repeated, and that was the truth.

She arched an auburn brow. "You're going to make me state the obvious, but okay. You can't."

That isn't a challenge. "I can."

"You'll protect me from an army of Harpies who

wouldn't hesitate to hurt everyone you love to get to me? An army of Harpies who would help the Hunters if it meant punishing me?"

Shit. "What do you propose I do then, huh?" He stalked to her, gripped her upper arms—she felt so fragile, so vulnerable—finally shaking her as he'd wanted to do for so long. Every movement wafted her scent to his nose, cinnamon and sugar, a feast for his senses. His mouth watered, his blood heated. "What? Tell me."

Her heartbroken expression never wavered. "What you originally came here to do. Act as my consort. I will fight, and I will win the Rod. Honorably."

"I thought you didn't do honorably."

She peered up at him through narrowing eyes, indignation at last replacing sorrow. When her lashes fused together, he was strangely glad to see the silver swirling underneath, no hint of gold. "In this and only this, I do. Too much is at stake," she added, mirroring his thoughts. "Not just for me, but for my sisters."

Win.

The Rod? *Dude, I'm working on it. A little space would be nice.*

Win!

I know, damn you! "What if I… Shit." He released Kaia to scrub a hand down his face. As many battles as he'd fought during his long life, he could sniff out a dead end before he turned the corner and spied the brick wall. They were at an impasse, and he knew it. She wouldn't budge—unless he changed the stakes.

"Do this for me, and I'll sleep with you. Okay?"

For a moment, she gave no reaction. Then a squawk parted her lips and she batted him away from her. And by "batted" he meant that she used so much force, he actually spun around, unable to stop himself.

"How magnanimous of you." An instant later, she was

in front of him again. She shoved him, hard, and he stumbled backward until the backs of his knees hit the edge of the bed. "To offer up your body when you so clearly have no desire for me. To lower your standards and whore yourself. To use me, no matter how badly I'll suffer in the end."

Her words were like arrows, direct hits, and he cringed, but he offered no reply. Not yet. As he collapsed and bounced on the mattress, he focused on his demon. *This isn't a challenge to dominate her sexually, you get me?*

Win!

Strider pressed his tongue to the roof of his mouth. He thought the demon was still focused on the Rod, but he couldn't be sure. So, when Kaia jumped on top of him, straddling his waist, he twisted, tossing her down and pinning her with his weight. And gods, that felt *good*. She fit him perfectly, her breasts soft against his chest, the apex of her thighs offering an exquisite cradle to the thickness of his shaft.

The scent of cinnamon continued to waft from her, enveloping him, hazing his thoughts. Heat, so much heat, pulsed from her soft, luscious skin, branding him.

WIN.

Bastard. "This is life and death, Kaia."

She was panting as she tangled her hands in his hair, nails biting into his scalp. "For me, too."

"Would you do it for…Paris?" he asked, hating himself. "No."

No hesitation from her, and that eased the tightness in his chest. A tightness he hadn't even been aware of until just that moment. "Kaia."

"Strider."

"I—I never said I didn't desire you." He wasn't sure what he'd meant to say, he only knew that wasn't it, that the words had slipped out without his consent. "I do. How could I not?"

She nibbled on her bottom lip. "Are you saying you agree to be my consort?"

"No." He wouldn't lie about that. Not to her. And not because she'd rip him to pieces when she discovered the truth. "I can't give you forever."

The nibbling increased in intensity, leaving a bead of blood in the center of her mouth. "Because we're not a good match?"

Of course she would remember every insult he'd ever thrown at her. "Yes."

"Then what *can* you give me?"

"Here. Now." Something his body craved more with every second that passed.

"In exchange for my aid in the theft of the Paring Rod." A statement, not a question.

"Yes." Maybe even without it. So badly he wanted to arch into her, rub against her, stoke her passions until she begged him to finish her off.

She ran the pink tip of her tongue over her teeth. Teeth sharpening into a mouthful of daggers, but gods, that tongue was pretty. "You'll have to convince me," she said huskily, even as she drew his head down…down…until his lips hovered just above hers. "Give me a taste of what you're offering."

WIN, WIN, WIN.

A challenge. Intentional or not. And this time, he had no trouble interpreting what his demon expected, needed. Strider had to kiss her, and he had to convince her, or he would hurt.

He waited for fury to fill him, but as he stared down at her, breathing her in, all he wanted to do was give her that taste.

He removed her nails from his scalp and flattened her

hands over her head, forcing her back to bow, her body to slide against his. Her nipples were hard, just waiting for his mouth.

"Don't say another goddamn word," he commanded, and then he finally, *finally* went in for the kill.

CHAPTER SEVEN

KAIA FELT AS IF SHE'D BEEN waiting for this moment forever. And in a way, she had. At long last, she lay in her consort's embrace, and he was meeting her needs. Her wildest, most sensual needs. Strider's lips pressed against hers, his tongue thrusting inside her mouth, hot, decadent, his taste filling her up, consuming her. She'd never loved cinnamon more. Sweet and tangy with just a little spice.

The weight of his muscled body pinned her to the mattress, and the weapons strapped all over him pressed into bone, probably bruising. As if she cared. What were a few bruises when one of Strider's big hands held her head tilted to the side to deepen their connection?

What were a few bruises when her breasts rasped against his chest with her every inhalation, and her aching nipples rubbed at him, sparking the desire inside her to a hotter degree?

She spread her legs, allowing his lower half to fall more firmly against hers. His erection—so big, so long, so perfectly thick—hit her just right, and she gasped. Hotter, hotter, *sooo* much hotter.

"Strider," she moaned.

"Kaia."

Her name on his lips…heaven and hell, sweet and torturous. A siren's song. "More."

"How do you like it?"

"However you give it." Her nails had already length-

ened into claws, and she dug them into his back, accidentally cutting past his shirt and into skin. He groaned, and
their teeth scraped together. His fingers clenched on her
jaw. "Sorry," she panted. She squeezed his hips with her
knees, just in case he thought to leave her.

"Don't be sorry," he growled. "Just do it again." He
sucked on her bottom lip, hard, causing sizzling goose
bumps to sprout from head to toe.

More erotic, freeing words had never been spoken. As
a Harpy, she was stronger and more vicious than almost
all other immortals. She'd always had to temper her passions and hold back. Even with Paris.

She didn't think she'd have to hold back with Strider—
and wouldn't. Whatever she dished, he could take. Hell,
he would revel in. He was too strong, too determined for
anything less. And really, he might look like an angel, but
he was far wickeder than any other Lord. The best kind
of wicked, at that. Devilish. Gentle and easy weren't his
style.

He found humor in the strangest things. If he discovered
one of his friends chained to a female's bed (cough Lucien
cough), he took pictures and emailed them to everyone he
knew. How cool was that?

A man like that would never ask her to stop stealing.
He might even join her on her obligatory forays, keeping
her dark side happy without causing too much damage.
More than that, he knew triumph and loss better than any
other. He would revel in her every accomplishment, good,
bad or ugly. He would be the first to tell her when she'd
screwed up, but he wouldn't write her off.

Or maybe the man she pictured in her mind was pure
fantasy. The one on top of her thought to barter with her,
his body in exchange for her cooperation. That pissed her
off royally—but not enough to stop this tasting.

He was her drug of choice, she mused, and she was already addicted to him.

"Kaia! Pay some fucking attention to what's happening here," he snarled.

Startled back to her senses, she blinked up at him. He was panting, sweating—perhaps more than he should—his features tight with strain. He must have been calling for her for quite a while. And damn, she'd stopped kissing him to ponder his virtues and follies, she realized. A travesty she would rectify immediately.

"I'm here." She wrapped her legs around him and locked her ankles, arching up. More contact with his erection, more gasping from her. So delicious. So perfect. So freaking hot.

"Good girl." His tongue found its way back inside her mouth, and they dueled, fighting for dominance.

She let him win, submitting, allowing him to take the lead, urging her toward complete satisfaction. Or maybe insanity. Her mind fogged with desire, her blood heated to blistering and her Harpy sang with approval.

This was everything she had been dreaming of, fantasizing about, craving with every fiber of her being. Her man, feasting on her, grinding against her. She would never get enough of him, would always want more. Always need more. Her nerve endings caught fire, the ever-growing blaze nearly too much, the ache between her legs fierce.

She had to lock this deal up tight. Love him within an inch of his life, bind them together, and never, never, allow him to escape her. Never allow any of the other Harpies near him. He was hers. Would always be hers.

You can't think like that. He's a warrior, used to control. You try to bind him, and he'll run. This has to be a partnership, not a Harpytatorship. Yes, okay. She could do that. Work with him. Anything to keep him with her, to kiss him again, to have him, all of him.

Question—could *he* work with her?

"Damn it, Kaia." He removed his hand from her jaw and cupped one of her breasts, squeezing. "What the hell is going on in that head of yours?"

"You, us, together. Yes," she moaned, pressing herself into the touch. Hot, she was so hot, and only growing hotter. "More."

"Good, okay, yes. Harder?"

"Harder. Please." She lifted her hips off the mattress, the springs squeaking, and moved herself against him. Steam might even have risen from her pores, surrounding them both, thickening the air. "More. All."

"Damn, your mouth is a firestorm. Burns. And yeah, baby doll, I'll give you—" He sucked in another breath, stiffened, cursed. Cursed so violently she was surprised her ears hadn't started bleeding. "All right. Yes. We'll do this. You and me. I'll give you more, all."

His voice was…odd, she thought distantly. No longer layered with arousal, but as stiff as his body now was, and formal. Almost robotic. Why? What had changed? She mourned the loss.

He fit their lips back together and the kiss continued. She rubbed her core up and down his length, unable to stop herself, never loosening her grip around his waist. He settled against her, his skin slick with sweat. She fell back to the bed, but all the while she fought through the now cooling lust-fog, determined to figure out what was going on with him.

His tongue moved in and out of her mouth, mimicking sex. His hand squeezed her breast every few seconds. He swirled his hips at the same time, brushing against her clitoris. It was a dance, each movement fitting the rhythm of the next. His technique was flawless. Soon he would make her come.

Technique, she thought then. Yes, that's exactly what this was. A technique. He was hard where it counted, yes, but also where it didn't, his muscles petrified into stone. He wasn't moaning in surrender. How could he? Every swish of his tongue was calculated, as if he were thinking about what to do rather than allowing instinct to guide him. As if he had absolute control and wasn't even close to losing it.

Which meant he wasn't enjoying what he was doing. He was simply performing, driving her need higher and higher, manipulating her. Giving her what she wanted, but not taking what he needed.

He had somehow managed to detach himself.

"What do you like?" he asked. "Tell me, and I'll do it."

She could have been anyone, and it wouldn't have mattered to him. And when it was over, he would have taken her, had her, but she would have been one of a thousand others, unimportant and temporary. An easy conquest. A means to an end.

No. *No!* She would not be Kaia the Disappointment. Not with him. She would not be content with the scraps of his affections and call it good. She would have all or nothing. Settling was for the weak.

She was not weak.

But even knowing what he was doing, even hurting as she was—again—and even as desperate as she was for release, she couldn't bring herself to harm him physically. Not by her hand, and not by using his demon. He had to win this contest of wills *without* smothering her pride anymore than he already had. Somehow, someway.

She cut off a bitter laugh. Once again she would be throwing a fight. This time, however, the prize was far more important. His body...and his heart? No, not his heart. That, he would never offer. Not to her. The same determination that had sculpted him into such a fierce warrior and lover had turned him into an emotional recluse.

Cooling…cooling… "Strider?"

A swipe of his tongue, a squeeze of his hand. "Tell me," he said, ignoring her. "Your mouth, the heat is gone."

"Sorry."

"Don't be. Either way, I like it. But why the change?"

Enough of this. Besides, she didn't know. She'd never heated up like that before. "I don't…I don't think you can stop." Gods, saying the words, letting them raze her throat, left her trembling with frustration.

He froze above her, beads of sweat still dripping from him. In fact, his shirt was soaked, sticking to his chest. "What did you just say?"

"I don't think you can stop kissing me, stop touching me."

With more of those black curses ringing from him, he jolted away from her, off the bed and to his feet. He remained at the edge of the mattress, glaring down at her as she eased to a sitting position. She struggled to breathe, her lungs still cooling…cooling.

"Damn it, Kaia."

She flashed her fangs at him. "That isn't my name."

That gave him pause. "What? Kaia? I happen to know otherwise."

"No. *Damn it, Kaia* isn't my name."

His eyelids narrowed even as the corners of his lips twitched. "Whatever."

That's all he had to say to her? After everything they'd just done?

"Will you steal the Paring Rod for me or not?" he asked.

Apparently so.

Did he feel nothing for her? No hint of true passion? She licked her lips, and she was heartened to note his gaze followed the movement. "Not. But," she added before his demon could punish him for failing to convince her. And yes, she knew that was one of the reasons he was pushing her so hard for this. At least, she hoped. Made it easier to forgive him, to excuse him, for reducing their electrifying kiss to a bargaining chip. "We'll compromise."

He shook his head, once, and very stiffly. "No."

"Yes."

"No."

"Yes. Compromise doesn't cause you physical pain."

His lashes fused together, shielding the navy of his eyes. "It doesn't help me, either."

She lifted her chin. "Do you want to hear my proposal or not? If not, there's the door."

"Gods almighty, I hate when your chin goes up." He popped his jaw. "Fine. Talk."

"I will fight in the games. If at any point," she rushed to add, "I'm disqualified or I think my team cannot bring home the gold, I will risk my life and my future to steal the Rod for you."

Silent, he crossed his arms over his chest.

She knew exactly what he was thinking. "Also, you can't do anything to aid a disqualification. Not for me or for any member of my team."

Oh, yes. That's exactly what he'd been thinking. Suddenly fury sizzled and snapped off his skin like tiny flickers of lightning. His eyes lit up, twin red lasers, a skeletal mask flashing over his features. "What if, while you're playing your games, someone else manages to steal it?"

His demon really was pulling his strings. She sympathized. She hated when her Harpy took over. "Not possible. You could call every warrior and god you know, but the lot of you still wouldn't be able to find it, much less grab it. And no, that wasn't a dare. Just a truth. Harpies are a suspicious and possessive race, and we take extreme measures to guard what we consider ours. Believe me, Juliette will let *no one* near the Rod."

Several minutes passed before he relaxed. He couldn't fight the Harpies on his own—not successfully—and he had to know it. "Very well. We have a deal." She opened her mouth to respond. "But you listen to me, little girl," he added darkly.

Little girl. Exactly what Lazarus had called her, all those centuries ago. Shadows shimmered through her line of vision, the only color a crimson bull's-eye on Strider's chest. *Calm, steady.*

Don't interfere, she told her Harpy.

"You've claimed I'm your consort, and that consorts are precious. You've also claimed you'll do anything to protect yours."

She snapped her teeth at him. "I never said that." Not out loud.

"Fine. Maybe Gwen told me. Thing is, it's true."

And he planned to use the knowledge against her? "Well, look at you, Mr. Smartie Pants." She clapped her hands. "Congratulations. You know I can't hurt you. But hey, what does that matter? I can always pay someone else to do my dirty work."

A muscle ticked below his eye. "You're willing to let an artifact that can kill me remain in the hands of your enemy," he said, ignoring her threat. "That woman, Juliette, the one with the boyfriend you still haven't told me about, isn't going to give you the Rod. Whether you win or not, she hates you and will hardly reward you."

Kaia fisted the comforter, nearly ripping the material. "How do you know she hates me?" He'd only caught the tail end of the meeting, and Juliette hadn't spoken to her directly after his arrival.

"I have eyes, Kaia. Every time she looked at you, she wanted to carve your face with her dagger. What'd you do to her, anyway? And don't tell me she just hasn't forgiven you for what you did to the clans. Her beef with you is personal. No one else looked at you the way she did."

Floundering, she blinked up at him. He was too observant for his own good. "What makes you think *I* did anything to *her*?"

"Come on. You must think I'm stupid, answering my question with a question and assuming I won't notice and will let the matter drop."

"Well, now that you mention it…"

"Funny." He held out his hand and waved his fingers in her direction. "Come here."

Unable to resist a chance to touch him, any chance, she reached up. The moment she met his grip, he hefted her to her feet until only a whisper separated them. He peered down at her, his body heat snaking around her and squeezing like a boa.

Tension crackled between them so hotly she imagined she could almost feel the flames. His lips were swollen, red and still wet from her kiss. His eyelids went to half-mast, as if he'd slipped into a dream and wouldn't emerge.

If he looked this sumptuous turned on, how would he look sated?

Mind, out of gutter. This was clearly another attempt to distract her, to win her over to his side. She had to remain strong. "Well?"

"Did you make a play for her man?" he demanded. O-kay. Obviously he'd emerged from the dream.

Her cheeks flushed with color and that was all the answer he required.

He released her to scrub his hand down his face. "Damn it, Kaia."

Without his touch, her skin cooled. She would not admit to her own stupidity, even acute stupidity committed so long ago. She would not admit she'd sought to prove herself worthy to a mother who would never love her, and that she'd failed on every level.

"I saw him, I wanted him and I took him. End of story." The truth muddied by his own suppositions. Strider would never find his way to the surface, and that was for the best.

"And she found out?" His voice snapped like a whip.

Yep. He was lost in the mire of her omissions. "She did." Kaia nodded, her head bobbling. "That's exactly right."

"How?"

Her eyes widened. Why wouldn't he let this go? "Excuse me?"

"How did she find out?"

"Oh, uh, she walked in on us," Kaia said, gaze falling to the floor. Realizing what she'd done, she forced her attention back up. There were two things a girl needed when telling a lie. The first, confidence. You could convince anyone of anything as long as you believed it yourself. The second, details. The more details you supplied, the more credible the story. "We were in the middle of the act. Very hot and heavy. I wasn't at all distracted with him."

Strider was quiet for a moment. Then he said smoothly, "Is that so?"

Perhaps he wasn't as blinded by the mud as she'd thought. What had given her away? Well, it didn't matter, really. He could suspect the truth all he wanted, but he'd never know for sure. And hell, there might be another way to convince him of what she wanted.

She glared up at him. "Yes, that's so. I had him flat on his back atop a pile of furs." She pictured Strider in just such a position, and her desire reignited, adding a smoky note to her voice. "He was naked...I was naked. I straddled his waist, and gods, he was beautiful, so lost to passion. To me."

Strider whipped around, as if he could no longer bear to face her. There. Done, she thought. He was utterly convinced of her slutty nature. Her shoulders sagged just a little. Part of her wished he would have continued resisting.

Better this way, she reminded herself. He'd already considered her promiscuous. Adding weak and dumb to the equation would have hampered her future progress with him.

Not that she'd really made any today.

SHE WAS LYING, STRIDER thought, suddenly needing every ounce of strength he possessed to stop himself from grinning. Damn if she wasn't ten times sexier as she spun her web of deceit. Maybe because she'd almost had him. *Would* have had him, if she hadn't glanced down at her feet. So telling, that glance. When Kaia believed something wholeheartedly, her confidence was like a shining star. She did nothing to signal a back down.

Defeat liked that they'd figured out her game and was shooting little sparks of pleasure through his bloodstream. A victory he hadn't anticipated, yet one that was as delicious as ambrosia-laced wine. Almost as delicious as Kaia's kiss.

Don't think about that right now.

He couldn't help himself. Hell's fire, that kiss…the woman was passion incarnate, so sensually giving he could have gorged himself on her forever and still found himself hungry. Her tongue had thrust just right, her nails had scraped just right, and her legs had wrapped around him better than just right.

She'd just…fit him. Fit his body perfectly. Every curve, every plane, every indentation. Two puzzle pieces locking together. And they'd still had their clothes on! If he ever stripped her, he'd— No. No, no, no. He couldn't venture down that road again. The kiss had been a mistake.

A damn exquisite mistake, but one that could have done serious damage to his cause.

Already his mind was muddled by her.

And unfortunately, he couldn't blame her skin this time. What was bared, she'd dulled with makeup, making her look like any other human. No, not true. She'd never look like a human, no matter what she did. Her features were too dazzling, too flawless.

She'd never kiss like a human, either. She was too bold, too lush, too damn eager.

Too mine, he'd thought midway through, wanting to give her "all" as she'd said. Wanting to give her *everything.* Only then had he realized how lost he was, simply enjoying her, not even trying to please her. Just taking, giving and taking some more. There was nothing more dangerous for him. He *had* to please her, more than Paris had, or he would suffer.

Reining in his own desires had been the most difficult battle of his life, but he'd done it. He'd won. And oh, Defeat had loved him for it, sparking the same sense of pleasure that raced through him now. Which had made it all the more difficult to hold back, to measure each of his caresses, every single lick.

Except one moment she'd wanted all, everything, and he'd been willing to supply it, to take her over the edge, and the next she'd wanted him to stop. He recognized a challenge when he heard one, and 'I bet you can't stop' was one-hundred-percent, raise-the-red-flag challenge.

What he hadn't known—still didn't know—was *why* she'd done it.

Didn't matter, he supposed. What was done was done, and there was no going back. He had to forget the kiss and concentrate on the journey ahead. On the games, the Rod and ultimate victory. He had to forget the color that bloomed in her cheeks, the breath that sawed in and out of her nose, the flecks of fury that had detonated in her eyes every time he'd spoken. Had to forget the fact that she was gorgeous when her emotions were roused, that she lit up like a firecracker, and he wanted so desperately to be burned.

Kaia cleared her throat. "Strider," she began.

He held up his hand in a bid for silence. "Look, here's how it's gonna be. You don't trust me, and I don't trust you, but we are going to work together. So, you're going to tell me about tomorrow's battle, and then we're going to scout the competition."

Or rather, she would scout. He would search for the Rod. Much as he understood her plight, her pain, that understanding didn't change the facts. No artifact, no box.

So, he *would* find and steal that Rod. Even at the expense of Kaia's pride. He wouldn't like himself afterward, he was sure, because victory required a betrayal of her trust, but nothing would sway him from this course.

"Got it?" he demanded, already fighting a wave of guilt.

A pause, heavy and unsure. Then she whispered, "Yes. All right. We'll work together."

"Good." He cleared his expression and spun back around. He made sure to glare at her for good measure. "Now, start talking."

CHAPTER EIGHT

WILLIAM THE EVER RANDY, honorary Lord of the Underworld and a man so physically perfect he'd once been voted Most Beautiful Immortal of All Time—so what that he'd been the only judge of that particular competition; he would swear on what remained of his soul that the scores hadn't been fixed—stood in the living room of a human residence.

Strider the Reneger should be here with him. *I must be rubbing off on him.* Strider had promised to be here with him. Instead the lucky bastard was spending time with the very Harpy William often dreamed of seducing.

William had been with vampires, humans, witches, shape-shifters and goddesses, but he'd never been with a Harpy. He wanted to be with a Harpy. *Whine, pout.*

Maybe, when he finished here, he would give Strider a wee bit of competition for Kaia's affections. The warrior liked to compete, after all, and William was *such* a giver, always thinking of others rather than himself.

That giving nature was the very reason he was here.

"Here" was an average home, with average rooms in serious need of a decorator. Beige furniture, beige walls and beige carpet, as if the owners were afraid of color. Oh, and had he mentioned the half-empty vodka bottles that were hidden inside vents, behind books and even in hidden cutouts in the mattresses?

This mundane, prisonlike alcoholic's paradise was where his Little Gilly Gumdrop had grown up.

Gilly, a.k.a. Gillian Shaw. Human, brown-eyed, too sensual for her own good. At seventeen, she had known more horror and terror than most immortals experienced in an eternity. All because of the owners of this home in Nowhere, Nebraska.

William didn't have many friends, so he took care of the ones he had. Sure, he liked the Lords of the Underworld well enough. They were fun to torture and damn entertaining to watch as they fell in love, one by one, like flies meeting the swinging net of a swatter. Case in point— Strider. Until William intervened, of course. Surely Kaia would at last succumb to his delightful wiles and forget all about the keeper of Defeat.

The entertainment alone was worth the price of his ticket into their Budapest Fortress: allowing the freaking (minor) goddess of Anarchy to hold William's most treasured possession for ransom. He lay awake nights dreaming of ways to retrieve that possession, a book written in code that foretold how to save him from the curses the gods had heaped upon him. But he wasn't going to think about that right now.

He was only going to think about his Gilly. He'd met her months ago, when the keeper of Pain's woman brought her to the fortress, and he'd been instantly smitten. Not in a sexual way, she was too young for that—he would remind himself a thousand times if necessary—but in a white-knight kind of way.

She'd looked at him, and she'd seen a gorgeous immortal warrior who could give her body untold pleasure. Of course. Everyone did. She'd also seen a gorgeous immortal warrior who could slay her dragons.

He wanted to slay her dragons. He *would* slay her dragons.

A few times over the past several months, he'd returned to the fortress injured from battle. Gilly had taken care of him, always tender, sweet, ensuring he ate something, was tucked into bed and comfortable. She wasn't intimidated by him. She laughed with him, joked with him, and when he pissed her off, she stayed and fought with him, rather than running away to hide from his temper.

She knew, soul deep, that he would never hurt her. Even if he didn't always know it himself. There was a darkness inside him, a churning darkness sprung from the vilest pits of hell. A darkness he'd never loved more than he did at this moment.

Hardly anyone noticed his evil side. They saw the irreverent scamp he projected. And no, that image wasn't a lie. William was irreverent to the bone, but there was more to him, and somehow Gilly saw that part, too.

And still she accepted him. Had never asked him to change. Had only thought to enjoy his company, to protect him. *No one* had ever tried to protect him before.

Now, he would protect her. Her family had hurt her in the worst possible way. Therefore, her family would die in the worst possible way. Vengeance was its own form of safeguarding, after all. Sure, time had passed and she'd had no recent contact with them. That didn't change the fact that they'd hurt her in the most terrible way, forced her to brave the streets on her own—and that they could do it again, to someone else. He'd wanted to do this for a long time, and that hadn't changed. In fact, the need had only grown stronger.

William walked around the room, lifting knickknacks, discarding them and smiling when they shattered on the floor. Gilly's mother and stepfather were currently at work, and her stepbrothers no longer lived here, so he didn't worry about noise control. When he finished that little exercise, he studied the pictures on the mantle over the fireplace.

There were none of Gilly.

Obviously they'd written her out of their lives. No afterthought, no concern for what had befallen her once she'd left.

What he did see: a thirtysomething bleached blonde with silicone-enhanced breasts and an average-looking thirtysomething male.

Stomach clenching, William thumped the man's face. The bastard was going to pay for every illicit touch, every ounce of shame inflicted. The mother would pay for allowing it to happen. The brothers would pay for failing to save her.

Her family had given her no option but to run away at the age of fifteen. Fifteen. On her own, surviving as best she could, for over a year before Danika had found her and brought her to Budapest. But because of what had been done to her, because of what she'd had to do merely to eat, she no longer valued herself. She saw herself as used, dirty, unworthy. She'd never said as much, but he knew. When she stayed at the Lords' fortress, she slept in the bedroom next to his, and he'd heard the way she cried out at night. He knew nightmares plagued her.

Her family would pay for every single one of those dark dreams, too.

His ears suddenly twitched, picking up the sound of the garage door sliding open. He grinned. Oh, goodie. The first contestant of Hurt, Suffer and Die was home.

When he'd first arrived, he had dropped his bag of "toys" on the floor and now bent to pick it up. Oh, yes, he'd never loved his darkness more.

This was going to be fun.

KANE, KEEPER OF THE DEMON of Disaster, strode down the long, winding corridor inside the unfamiliar heavenly palace where he now found himself. The walls were straight up weird, comprised of thousands upon thousands of threads braided and strewn together. Thick and colorful threads with animated scenes playing across them, as if the people he saw were truly living and breathing right in front of him, and he had only to reach out to touch them. It was the most awe-inspiring sight he'd ever beheld— and was that Strider and Kaia crawling along a moonlit hill, females sneaking up on them, weapons trained on their skulls?

He stopped and narrowed his gaze on them, his hands fisting. A head-exploding ache tore through his temples. Only when he peered straight ahead and forced the image of what he'd seen out of his mind did the ache lessen.

In and out he breathed. His thoughts fogged, then cleared. Then he couldn't recall what he'd been upset about in the first place. Oh, well. In, out. In, out. Clearer and clearer. The air carried the sweet scent of ambrosia, he realized. To keep visitors pliant?

If only that kind of thing worked on him. But the goddesses who lived here could have pumped gasoline through the vents, and it wouldn't have affected him. His demon loved all things devious, clandestine and potentially life-threatening. And maybe, just maybe, that love would prevent the bastard from cracking the floor Kane stood upon or from unraveling the ceiling above him, the need for calamity sated for just a little while.

A guy could hope, anyway.

Kane jumped back into motion. He had a purpose, didn't he? Oh, yeah. The Moirai had summoned him. Why the hell had they summoned him?

Whatever the reason, he'd smile like a good little boy. He did *not* want to piss off the Moirai, and in his current what-the-fuck-is-happening state of mind, he had to be extra careful. They were neither Greek nor Titan—he didn't know what they were—and yet, neither godly race had ever raised a hand against the three females who lived here, and they never would. Because the Moirai were the weavers of Fate. They spun and they wove, and the scenes they created happened. Always.

No one approached them without a summons. Not even Cronus, the god king. And in all of Kane's centuries, he had never met anyone who had received one. Until today. He, Disaster, was the lucky recipient.

He'd just returned from town, having spent the entire night searching for Hunters. Finding none—Strider must have killed them all before he left, the greedy bastard—he'd fallen straight into bed, still wearing his weapons, leather and boots. Before he could switch off his lamp, a glowing string had unfurled from his ceiling, a yellowed scroll hanging from the end.

He'd read the parchment, as confused then as he was now. A cross between a wedding invitation and a prescription medicine wrapper, the thing had been written in ancient Greek.

You are cordially invited to the Temple of the Fates. Failure to appear could result in decapitation or death.

Decapitation or death? Really? Then, an instant later, his surroundings had faded and he'd been standing inside this temple, those walls of thread all around him. He'd kicked into gear, thinking any hesitation on his part would result in that decapitation. Or death.

So while he knew *where* he was, what he didn't know was why. Why him? Why now?

Guess he'd find out.

The wall tapestries seemed to go on forever, but finally—unfortunately?—he reached the end of the line and entered a...weaving room? Three women, hags really, sat on wooden stoops, hunched over, long white hair frizzing over their shoulders. All three wore white robes, pristine and unwrinkled.

The one with hands spotted by age—Klotho, he knew from the legends surrounding them—spun the threads. The one with gnarled fingers, Lachesis, wove the strands together, and the one with pupil-less eyes, Atropos, snipped the ends.

Kane pressed his lips together, silent. He waited to be acknowledged, respectful of a power far greater than his own. And perhaps that's why they had picked him, he thought then. None of the other Lords would have treated them with the deference they deserved and punishment would have had to be issued.

If they only knew the truth. He might know how to dish the respect, but really, he was the group's biggest screwup. The one who couldn't do anything right. The one left behind because he had a tendency to cause more harm than good. He never dropped his smile, though. Not here, and not around his friends. He didn't want them to know the truth. He didn't want them to know that, inside, he was just one big, steaming pile of mess.

For the most part, he operated on autopilot. When his demon became too much for him—the need to let go, the desire to obliterate, forget, pretend, filling him up—he… did things. Destroyed things.

Sabin, keeper of Doubt and the warrior Kane would have followed straight into hell, knew. But Sabin was the only one who did, and, not surprisingly, Sabin approved of his violence, even helped him channel it. Before taking off with his wife, Sabin had left him a little present. Part of him was eager to go back, to do what needed doing. The other part of him was content to remain here, waiting. He'd ignored that present to head into town, after all, thinking to resist the temptation. He'd even planned to nap upon his return. Anything to save his soul from further damage. But how much longer would he have lasted?

He stood there, waiting to be acknowledged, for an hour, perhaps two. Usually inactivity provoked his demon to act, creating some disaster or another. Maybe it was the ambrosia as he'd hoped, or maybe the demon was as afraid of the hags as everyone else in the heavens, but Disaster behaved, not even humming in the back of Kane's mind, though that sound rarely ever faded.

"Why are you here, boy?" Klotho finally asked, her voice a cackle of smoke. She never looked up from her task.

Uh, what now? "I received your summons. My lady," he added. Gods, he was such an ass-kisser. But a guy had to do what a guy had to do. He was wearing his cup, yeah, but that didn't mean he should hang a sign on his nuts, requesting someone kick him there.

"Summon you? Why, that was thousands of years ago," Lachesis replied. "I'm sure of it."

"Sure of it," Atropos echoed. "Yet you never came."

"And so your summons was revoked."

"You may leave the way you came."

He could only gape at them. They'd summoned him *thousands* of years ago? Why hadn't they decapitated him, then, for his failure to appear? "I mean no disrespect, but I only just now received your kind invitation."

"Not our fault."

"You probably weren't paying attention."

"Perhaps you'll learn to pay attention."

"You may leave the way you came."

Reverence was one thing. Not having his curiosity assuaged was quite another. Besides, if they'd brought him here to impart words of wisdom that could save him and his friends, or to issue words of warning, he damn well wanted to hear those words. Therefore, he wasn't leaving without them.

"May I purchase the information from you?" he asked.

"What information?"

"Who said anything about information?"

"You're a dotty one, aren't you?"

"You may leave the way you came."

He flicked his tongue against one of his incisors. "If you didn't wish to inform me of something, all those thousands of years ago—" he was careful to keep his ire out of his tone "—then why did you summon me in the first place?" The same question, asked in a roundabout way. *Come on, take the bait. Tell me.*

"Klotho, do you recall the last time someone tried to talk circles around us?"

"Oh, yes, Lachesis. We wove her into the never-ending." *The never-ending what?*

"Perhaps she's learned her lesson."

"Perhaps she hasn't yet learned her lesson."

"*She* didn't leave the way she came."

"Who is 'she'?" he asked, standing his ground. A stupid move, perhaps, but he couldn't leave the way he'd come, so what choice did he have? Flashing himself from one location to another with only a thought wasn't an ability he possessed.

"She? She is your girl, of course," Atropos said.

He blinked. "My girl, what?"

"The one in the never-ending."

"No, no," Klotho said. "She's not his. The other one is. Or is it the other way around?"

"Mayhap they both are his," Lachesis countered.

"She's mine? *They're* mine?" he gasped out. His what? Lovers? If so, no thanks. Been there, destroyed too many because of that. His women suffered, always. His demon made sure of it. Kane was better off alone.

"Of course she's yours, though not the one in the never-ending. She belongs to no one. Unless she does, in fact, belong to you."

The three cackled.

"Good one, sister mine. I'll have to remember that for the warrior's next summons."

"Who does or doesn't belong to me?" he asked, gaze darting from one hag to the other. *Next summons?*

"Irresponsibility, of course."

"Irresponsibility," he echoed. As in, the keeper of Irresponsibility? Kane knew the immortal was out there. There'd been more demons in Pandora's box than naughty warriors, so the gods, desperate to contain the leftovers, had given them to the prisoners of Tartarus. Irresponsibility was one such leftover.

He'd even looked for…her. Shit. He'd always assumed the keeper was a man. His mistake, and one he wouldn't make again. He and his friends wanted all demon-possessed immortals on their side. Which meant finding them *before* the Hunters did.

After all, Galen, keeper of Hope and the Hunters' leader, could convince anyone of anything. And the last thing the Lords needed was for him to convince their brethren to destroy them.

"Didn't I just say that?" one of them asked.

"You just said that."

"You're not too bright, are you, boy?"

"How do I get her out of the never-ending?" he asked, ignoring the question. He might not want a girlfriend, but he wanted to find this female demon-keeper. What could she do? What powers did she wield? "What *is* the never-ending, anyway?"

"How does he not know the answers to these questions?"

"Didn't we tell him these answers already?"

"Perhaps our time line is off again," Klotho said.

Again? How often did that happen? Better question—what were the consequences when it was off?

"Should we rewind?"

"Should we leap forward?"

Dear gods. Neither option seemed wise.

"Yes," they said in unison, shaking the tapestry they were working on. A moment passed in silence, then another.

Then, "What are you doing here, boy?"

Kane found himself blinking again. Nothing had changed. Not his surroundings, not the women. Everything was the same as when he'd first entered the room, yet they'd forgotten he was here?

Had they rewound? Had they fast-forwarded? Shit. If so, what did that mean for him? "You summoned me," he croaked out.

"Yes, yes. We summoned you."

"Only this morn, too. Good of you to come so quickly."

"Impressive."

They must have rewound thousands of goddamn years. When he left this temple, would he return to ancient Greece? His stomach clenched.

"Such a worrier, you are."

Could they read his thoughts then, as well as manipulate time? He really should have taken their advice and left the way he'd come. This was…this was as messed up as he was.

"As if we would disrupt the fabric of time for you."

"You will return the way you came."

Thank the gods. "You mentioned a female."

"I didn't mention a female. Did you mention a female?"

"Not me. I don't mention a female to the keeper of Disaster for thousands of years."

"Perhaps our time line is off again."

Again, they shook the tapestry in their hands. He waited it out through several heartbeats of silence, his mouth dry, his knees knocking.

"I—I think I'll leave the way I came," Kane said, backing away inch by inch. He couldn't take any more of this. They simply weren't capable of giving him a straight answer, their minds unable to differentiate between the past and the future. "I thank you for inviting me, though, and for your hospitality. If you could just point the way out…"

Atropos, her eyes so white they resembled a blanket of snow, lifted her head from her scissors and seemed, impossibly, to be peering over at him. "Finally, you present yourself to us. After all this time, we had given up."

He massaged the back of his neck. Did everyone who was summoned go through this? "Yes, finally." He backed up one step, two. "I apologize for your wait and I thank you again for your time, but I really must—"

"Quiet." Lachesis glanced up, as well, though her gnarled fingers never stilled. "We always know what happens, but never why it happens. You have made us wonder and wonder, and we would at last like an answer."

"An answer to what?" he asked, pausing, unsure he wanted to know.

The third hag, Klotho, did not follow the others' lead and glance at him. She simply said, "We want to know why you began the Apocalypse," and continued spinning her threads without a care.

CHAPTER NINE

"LET ME GET THIS STRAIGHT," Kaia whispered fiercely. "When you said scout the competition, you actually meant *scout the competition?*"

Strider cast her a quick glance as they used their elbows to pull the weight of their bodies along the twig- and dirt-laden ground. The moon was high and full, but with the canopy of leaves above them, its golden light skimmed the branches, never quite reaching them. No prob, though, because he'd trained his eyes to cut through darkness and zero in on the details that mattered.

Except tonight, he was concentrating on all the details that *didn't* matter.

Unimportant: Kaia looked sexier than ever. His own personal GI Jane doll—the X-rated edition. She'd painted her face black and green to better blend into the night, and wore a black bandanna over her mass of red waves. Her short shorts had *Booty Camp* stamped across the ass.

Strider kept envisioning the vigorous de rigueur training at such a camp. The hands-on instructing. The type of discipline dished out to the attendees who misbehaved.

Hello, Stridey-Monster.

Just what he needed—his dick as hard as a steel pipe and rubbing against the ground, leaving a telltale trail. That damn kiss had ruined everything. Had he kept his tongue to himself, he could have continued thinking of Kaia as a friend and only a friend. Now, he just wanted to convince her that blow jobs were a mandatory part of their arrangement.

Don't you dare speak up, he told his demon.

Silence.

Whew. "You're damn straight I meant we'd scout them," he finally said. A sharp stone scraped his stomach and he welcomed the sting. Helped clear his perspective. A discussion about goals—good. Fantasizing about his companion—bad. So, so wonderfully bad. "What'd you think I meant?"

"Well, duh. I thought you wanted to hobble them."

Wait just a sec. "So it's okay to bust your opponent's kneecap before a competition, but it's not okay to steal the grand prize for your...your...consort?" He almost couldn't say the word. Doing so made their arrangement seem permanent, rather than temporary.

She stopped to gape at him. "I can't believe you just asked that. Busted kneecaps are expected among my kind. Even encouraged."

"I thought you'd never participated in the Harpy Games before?"

"True, but I watched my mother when she did."

"Fine," he grumbled. "You can do some hobbling." Meanwhile, he'd stick to his original plan. While she decreased the number of her competitors, he would study the Harpy campsite. Layout, sentry placement, response times. "Use your hands, though, because knifing them seems a bit harsh." Actually, he just didn't want to accidentally track the blood inside the tents, leaving evidence of his intentions behind.

"Say no more. I came prepared for a little nonslashing action." She slid one of her elegant hands down her... panties? She did. Sweet heaven, she did. Right in the center, where she was probably warm and wet, ready for his mouth, his cock. "I've got something I think you might like."

Hell, yeah, she did. Stridey-Monster got real uncomfortable real fast, and yep, there was definite snakelike trailage behind him. Then Kaia shocked him by sliding her hand back up and holding out her palm. In the middle rested a small silver bar.

Disappointed and surprised, he frowned. "What's that?"

"Watch." She gripped one end and flicked her wrist. Snap. The bar grew several inches. Another flick, another few inches, until the damn thing resembled an oversize police baton. Or Stridey-Monster.

"I want one of those," he said.

Her eyes glittered with relish. "I know, *right*. But hands to yourself, demon boy. This one's mine. Now, come on." She skidded back into motion.

"Hey. I'm your consort. What's yours is mine, Harpy girl." And what'dya know? Saying the title hadn't been such a chore that time.

He crawled after her. Finally they reached the edge of the makeshift camp, as evidenced by the fire crackling in the heart of the grounds. In his early days here on earth, his hunting of Hunters had very often led him to camps just like this one. Multiple tents, boulders acting as chairs, and fowl roasting over the flames. Only, there'd always been soldiers patrolling the area.

"No one's here," he whispered.

"I know," Kaia replied. She sighed, despondent.

The occupants had left in a hurry. The scuff of their boots in the dirt was evidence of that, as though they'd been moving too swiftly to pick up their feet. The fowl was burned, charring more and more with every second that passed, plumes of black smoke wafting toward the sky. There was a water bottle lying flat, liquid gushing from it.

"I heard them abandoning ship," she added, "but I hoped there would be a few stragglers. Doesn't anyone defend their turf anymore?"

She'd heard them? When he, a trained soldier, hadn't heard a goddamn thing? No need for an ego check. He sucked. *Don't forget Mission One. The Rod—and not the one in your pants.* "I'll give the place an inspection. You stay here and act as lookout."

"No way. I'll give the place an inspection. You stay here."

"Damn it, Kaia. You better—*umph.*" Something hard wrapped around his ankles and jerked, sliding him backward. He twisted midway, sitting up despite his momentum, and shoved.

There was a pained, feminine grunt as his assailant stumbled and he was released.

Win, Defeat suddenly said, speaking up for the first time since they'd left the motel.

Did. For the moment, at least. Female warriors surrounded him, glaring down at him. Each held some type of weapon, from machetes to axes to Neolithic daggers.

Well, well. Slowly he stood, palms up and out, all innocence—all lie. "Evening, ladies. Something we can do for you?"

Kaia settled into a crouch and squawked. A squawk he recognized. Her Harpy had just taken over. From the thought of him being injured? Or because another woman had put her hands on him? Either way, she was seeing the world through a haze of red and black, a need for blood thickening her tongue.

"Mine," she said in a low, dual-layered voice. That was the only warning she gave before she attacked.

As she twirled that bat with a grace and purpose that astonished him, Defeat gave a whimper rather than another demand for victory. She moved like a dancer. A lethal, psychotic dancer who hoped to spend the rest of her life in prison. *My kinda woman.* Metal slammed against bone, the latter crackling. More grunts, a few groans.

And then the battle was *really* on.

He caught a glimpse of Kaia's expression as she spun. Cold, merciless. Red flickers joined the black in her eyes. Like flames. True, crackling flames. He could feel their heat, causing sweat to bead over his skin. An azure glow even emanated from her skin. Not a Harpy glow, with those lovely rainbow shards trapped beneath the surface, but the hottest lick of fire.

He remembered their kiss—again—and the way she'd burned him, how hot she'd been. A living furnace. It had turned him on, made him feel on top of his game. Now he wondered...

Was she exhibiting some sort of power?

Her claws slashed and her teeth cut. Bodies moved so quickly around her, his gaze couldn't quite track them, but every few seconds Kaia would be thrown backward, as if someone had slammed into her. A heartbeat later, that someone would howl in pain—because they'd been burned?

Win, Defeat growled, fear momentarily forgotten.

Great. *Give me a minute.* There were a few things he needed to figure out. Namely, how to insert himself into the fray without running into Kaia's fists.

Win!

The answer slid into place. Strider withdrew Jose, his Sig Sauer, from the waist of his pants. He'd come prepared, too, knowing he'd have to take out anyone who got in his way. Now, he just wanted to murder anyone who tried to "hobble" Kaia. That's what friends did for each other.

He fired a single shot into the air. *Boom.* Gasps, the rustle of clothing, the stomp of boots. Then, silence.

"Back the hell up," he snarled, lowering his aim. "Now.

And before you start wondering if I have the balls to splatter your brains across the trees, let me put your minds at ease. I do."

Kaia stilled, panting and blood-splattered. The women quickly backed away from her. As fast as these winged stunners could move, they could have charged him, attempted to kill him. They didn't. Either they realized he'd take a few of them out before they managed to reach him, as promised, or they feared his demon.

Defeat hummed his approval, tiny sparks of pleasure warming Strider's chest. More sparks than usual, considering he hadn't exactly won yet. Then Strider recalled the very first challenge his demon had accepted regarding Kaia and these women.

Anyone who tried to hurt her had to suffer. *Nice.*

"You," he said to Kaia. "Come closer."

She, too, obeyed. He brushed his free hand down her arm, a caress meant to calm, to comfort. But, shit! Touching her was like touching melted steel. Blisters immediately formed on the pads of his fingers. Did he care? Hardly. What was a little pain when her well-being was at stake?

Eventually the raspy fury of her breathing decreased and the black faded from her eyes, the flickering flames dying. Her skin cooled.

"First-class work out there, baby doll," he said.

"Anytime, sugar muffin." Though the words were raw and ragged, she spoke with only one vocal inflection. Her Harpy had been contained.

He shifted his gaze. He and Kaia were still surrounded, but now the circle had grown even wider and he could make out individual features. Harpy after Harpy scowled at him. Dread poured through him as he moved in front of Kaia. His protectiveness probably bothered her, but he wasn't going to let her take the lead in this. These were her people, and as her sister Gwen had once proven, family had a hard time killing family.

Strider never had a hard time killing anyone. Call it a gift.

Kaia moved to his side and threw the baton at…her mother's feet. He wanted to curse.

"Hello, Tabitha," she said evenly.

The dark-haired beauty stepped forward, her expression blank as she pondered him rather than her daughter. "Put the gun away, demon. For all your crowing, we all know you won't use it."

Kaia moaned. "You shouldn't have said that."

Grinning pleasantly, Strider angled the line of the barrel and squeezed the trigger. *Boom.* A high-pitched, disbelieving scream. He'd nailed the Harpy beside her. Blood spurted from a gaping thigh wound. The now-injured female hopped up and down before her strength drained and she fell to the ground.

Win! Defeat giggled like a schoolgirl.

More sparks of pleasure erupted in his chest as he notched a brow. "You were saying?"

Tabitha peered at Kaia and cursed, then switched her attention to her trembling clanswoman and shrugged. "You merely grazed her, missing everything of importance."

"Did I? Well, then, let me try again." Once more he squeezed the trigger. This time, the bullet grazed *Tabitha's* thigh. She wore ankle-length black pants, and the material concealed the evidence of what he'd done. Nothing could hide the coppery tang saturating the air, however.

A slight baring of her pearly whites was the only indication she gave that she'd been hit.

"Oh, damn," he said. "Missed everything of importance again. I might have to keep practicing. Who's next?"

Gasps of outrage abounded.

Tabitha held up her hand for silence. Even the night

birds obeyed, their chirps evaporating like mist. "*Of course* it would be you who fell for the old campfire trick," she said to Kaia. "I'm not surprised."

"That makes two of us. You fell for the old your-enemy-has-fallen-for-the-old-campfire-trick trick." She settled two fingers in her mouth and whistled, loud and high-pitched.

Suddenly leaves rattled above him. He watched, wide-eyed, as Sabin, Lysander, Taliyah, Bianka, the Harpy called Neeka and several other females he didn't recognize revealed themselves. They were high up in the trees, arrows notched and pointed at the competition.

Defeat started humming again.

What are you so happy about? They'd been there all this time and he hadn't known. They could have slaughtered him before he'd even realized he was under attack. And he'd thought himself so skilled, so…undefeatable. Well, there was no need for *any* ego checks today. He more than sucked. He blew chunks.

No reason to blame himself, though. Kaia and her Booty Camp had ruined his concentration.

"This is a first," Tabitha gritted out. Murmurs of admiration circled her, mixed with a few snorts of disbelief and several gasps of fury. "Now I *am* surprised."

"How?" His jagged tone matched her mother's.

Kaia didn't pretend to misunderstand. "I texted them before we left the motel."

Good thinking, but he hadn't known that, either, which meant he more than blew chunks. "And you couldn't have clued me in?"

"No." So simply stated, as if the thought had never entered her mind. "So, Mother Dearest," she said, tuning him out. "Are you regretting your choice to cut your daughters from your team?"

"No," Tabitha said, as flatly as Kaia had and with no hesitation.

Ouch. Kaia stiffened, but only for a moment. He didn't dare glance over at her, didn't dare wrap his arm around her waist and offer any more comfort. Now wasn't the time. But later…yeah, later, despite his raging bodily needs and the danger to his self-control. Comforting her was part of his consort duties, and for the next four weeks, he *was* her consort. In all the ways that mattered.

Sex didn't matter.

At least, that's what he was going to tell himself. Over and over again, until he believed it. Or until a backlog of semen poisoned and killed him. He could plan to sneak off and indulge in a few one-night stands, he supposed, but he knew he wouldn't. And not just because Kaia would permanently maim any females he so much as flirted with, but because, well, he didn't want anyone else.

He'd tasted Kaia's sweetness, had felt the wickedness of her curves pressed against him, and knew no mortal woman could compare. But he'd get over this infatuation, of that he had no doubt. Even Haidee hadn't held his attention for long.

Haidee. Huh. He hadn't thought about her much today, though she had consumed his brain for weeks. Classic Strider. Over the centuries, he'd been a major contender for the World's Shortest Attention Span.

"Do you truly think you can win the games?" Tabitha asked Kaia.

"Yes."

"Against *me?*"

"I hate to repeat myself, but yes."

That's my girl. Well, his girl for now.

"Juliette might have won the last eight games, but that's because I wasn't allowed to fight. As you know, I've never lost," Tabitha said, stroking the medallion that hung from her neck.

Again, Kaia stiffened, a wave of hurt blasting from her. A wave quickly suppressed. Did the necklace hold some significance? He made a mental note to ask Gwen, as he was certain Kaia wouldn't give him a straight answer. She never did.

"There's a reason you've never lost. You've never fought me," Kaia replied haughtily.

She is going to be killed.

The feminine voice stampeded through his head. Tabitha's voice. The same voice he'd heard during orientation. Her attention hadn't transferred to him, but he knew. "Like hell," he muttered.

Kaia threw him a disbelieving, offended look. "It's true."

"I know that, baby doll. Wasn't talking to you."

"Oh. Well. Okay."

Win! There was a tremor in Defeat's tone, but still, the little bastard wasn't going to back down. They'd decided to aid Kaia, and they would. She would not be killed.

She is going to be killed—and there is nothing you can do to help her.

"Stop it," he commanded, gaze narrowing on the woman responsible.

Tabitha blinked innocently. "Why is your consort speaking to me without my having addressed him first?" she asked Kaia. "Have you not taught him the proper order of things?"

So the little man wasn't supposed to speak to the womenfolk without an invitation? Screw that. "Just stay out of my head, Harpy, or I'll make sure you regret it. By the way, how's the leg?"

She hissed at him.

Win!

I know, Strider reassured the demon. *I told you. I won't let anything happen to Kaia.*

Kaia blinked, too, only she appeared shocked. She didn't question her mother, though, and he wondered if she remained quiet because she knew her mother wouldn't answer or because questioning her mother would have revealed ignorance and ignorance would have been perceived as weakness.

Harpies, man. Life seemed to be one big chess match for them. Ridiculous, if you asked him. And yeah, he got the irony. But he *had* to turn everything he did into a contest of wits and might. They didn't, nor did they suffer afterward. They just did it for funsies.

"Don't concern yourself with my man," Kaia finally said, her chin lifting.

My man. He kinda liked the sound of that.

His jaw clenched. This was pretend and he couldn't let himself confuse pretend with reality.

"I'm surprised you won a fearsome Lord of the Underworld," Tabitha said.

"I'm not," Kaia replied with a shrug. "I'm pretty much made of awesome."

Still not a flicker of emotion crossed Tabitha's face. Not pride, nor disappointment. "I guess we'll find out *exactly* what you're made of tomorrow, when the games truly begin."

CHAPTER TEN

PARIS, THE KEEPER OF Promiscuity—or Sex, as Paris called the demon—clutched two standard-issue daggers as he slinked through the back-alley shadows. Standard issue *sucked*. Sure, they sliced and diced just fine, but up here, with gods, goddesses, vampires and fallen angels, slicing and dicing wasn't enough.

Whatever. Keep going.

Never ceased to amaze him how similar the immortal world was to the human one. In this heavenly metropolis, there were bars, shops, restaurants and hotels. Not to mention drugs and those who sold them. Whatever you wanted, you could get.

Speaking of, I'll want some ambrosia. Soon. Already he was shaky from withdrawal.

No time to imbibe now. He couldn't be late.

Couldn't afford to so much as talk to anyone. One look at his face, one inhalation of his scent, and people—no matter their species or gender—threw themselves at him.

Perhaps he should have let them, he thought next. Sex derived strength from anything erotic, and Paris hadn't yet supplied that crucial daily dose. But then, he hated sleeping with people he didn't actually desire and tried to limit himself. And he'd get today's influx of strength just as soon as he met with the goddess of weaponry.

The female owned crystal daggers that could morph into *any* type of weapon the holder desired. He could have them, she'd said, *for a price.* No one ever wanted money from him, so he'd agreed to give her what she did want. Him. He'd whore himself, and that was fine. Whatever. He'd done so a thousand times before and would probably have to do so a thousand more. Eventually he'd get over the guilt and humiliation.

He needed those crystal blades to rescue the female he *did* want. Sienna.

His Sienna. Killed because of his actions, only to be brought back in soul form. A soul he could not see or hear. Yet.

Cronus, the god king, had enslaved her and paired her with the demon of Wrath. To keep Paris away from her, Cronus had then trapped her in another realm. He would pay for that. *After* Paris saved her. And he would. He had a three-part plan.

1. Obtain the crystal daggers.
2. Find Arca, former messenger goddess. Rumor was, she knew where Cronus hid his greatest treasures.
3. Find Viola, minor goddess of the Afterlife. Rumor was, she could teach *anyone* to see the dead.

Boom, done. Simple, easy. Yeah. Right. Seduction was the only thing easy for him.

Whatever he had to do, though, he would do. For centuries, Paris had dreamed of being with a woman more than once. Because of his demon, his body failed to respond to a lover after one release. So his relationships lasted only the one night. Except with Sienna. He'd had her, and then he'd immediately gotten hard for her again. In that moment, he'd known they belonged together—despite the obstacles that stood between them.

She was a Hunter, his enemy. She had tricked him,

drugged him and helped imprison him. Whatever. She'd also helped him escape, and that's when she died. Shot down by her own people while in Paris's arms.

He'd relived that nightmare over and over again, thinking of all the things he could have, *should have,* done differently. Thinking about her final words of hate, her wish that he had been the one to die. She'd blamed him for what had happened, and rightly so.

Yet still her soul had come back for him. Had escaped its heavenly prison and found him. For help? Revenge? He didn't know and didn't care. All he knew was that Cronus had carted her away before he'd gotten a chance to speak with her. She had to be terrified, confused and desperate.

He could soothe her. He just had to find her.

Want, his demon said, drawing him out of his mind.

Dread flooded him. That command could mean only one thing.

Paris focused, and sure enough at the end of the alley loomed a trio of ugly bruisers. Fallen angels, he would guess, who, for whatever reason, had given over to their dark sides. They couldn't be gods, even minor ones, because no power pulsed from them.

He had only to pass them and turn right, and he'd reach the goddess's street.

When they spotted him, they grinned greedily.

I want, his demon said.

You'll get yours soon enough.

Ignoring him, Sex blasted his special fragrance from Paris's pores. Soon the scent of chocolate and expensive champagne thickened the air. From experience, he knew that every time the men breathed in, desire would flood them. Desire for Paris and Paris alone, even if they didn't swing that way.

Damn you! he growled.

I want!

His dread intensified as their grins faded and they began licking their lips.

"You want by, you'll get on your knees."

"We each get a turn."

"And I'll be first," the biggest one said.

Paris slowed, but didn't stop and didn't change direction. Fallen angels were, in essence, little more than human. He could plow through them, no problem.

Hurt...kill... A soft whisper, a dark urge, one that had filled his mind more and more lately. Not from his demon, but from deep inside *him.* He wasn't sure why it happened, or what had caused it, but every time, he'd given in. Now would be no different. He would reach the goddess, and these men weren't going to deter him. He would plow through them, true, but he'd make it hurt—would kill—when he did.

In unison, the trio said, "Knees. Now."

"Actually," Paris replied. "The only thing going down will be you."

He tossed both of his daggers in quick succession. The tip of one sank deep into the jugular of the guy on the right. The tip of the other embedded in a wall of golden brick, missing its mark.

Sex whimpered, racing to hide in a far corner of his mind. His demon was a lover, not a fighter.

The two remaining men watched, wide-eyed, as their friend collapsed, twitching as death approached.

Hurt...kill... Having run even as he'd thrown, Paris barreled into them, his arms spread, knocking both of them to the ground. They pulled themselves out of their sexual stupors and rolled him to his back, their fists hammering at him.

Vessels burst in one of his eyes, limiting his line of sight. His nose popped out of place. His jaw separated.

The pain intensified with every blow, but still he fought. And fought dirty, going for groins, throats and kidneys.

Hurt...

Kill...

The dark compulsions rose...rose...consumed. With a roar, he brought his legs up and kicked. Both men flew backward. He leapt at the one closest to him, pinning the guy's shoulders to the concrete with his knees. One punch, two, three. Blood splattered.

He hit and hit and hit, until the guy's head lolled to the side, his swollen eyes open but glazed. Only then did he realize the other guy had jumped on his back and had been punching him in the head that entire time.

Paris reached back, gripped a fistful of shirt and jerked. Guy soared over his shoulders and landed on top of his buddy, losing his breath. As Paris grabbed for the blade in his ankle holster, his opponent gathered his wits and swung a meaty fist, knocking him into the wall. Temple against brick, and brick won. Dazed, the blade was batted out of his hand.

A booted foot slammed into his trachea, pushing him to his back and holding him down.

The pressure increased as the guy unsheathed a dagger of his own, bent down and stabbed Paris in the stomach. An agonizing lance of pain. A searing hiss of air through his teeth.

"That should keep you docile." Looming over him, panting raggedly, scowling, the guy unzipped his pants.

"Not a smart move," Paris managed to croak out. Though instinct demanded he wrap his fingers around the guy's ankle and shove, he inched his hand behind him, toward the hilt of his remaining blade. "You want to keep that thing, don't you?"

"Shut your mouth. Had you played nice, I would have let you go after I finished with you. Now..."

Finally the boot lifted from Paris's neck, then the guy was crouched between his legs, working at *his* zipper. *Distracted. Good.* Using the last of his strength, Paris swung his arm up. Another dagger found solace in a jugular.

Blood gurgled from the guy's mouth, shock and pain glazing his eyes. Paris ripped the blade free, but that wouldn't save him. Crimson continued to flow, and he slumped over, on top of Paris, motionless…dead.

Weak but determined, Paris pushed the weight away and lumbered to shaky legs. He gave himself a once-over. His clothes were ripped, stained and soaked in blood, his skin abraded, bruised and sliced. The goddess might turn him away the moment she saw him.

Probably not a bad idea. She expected pleasure, and right now he was too pathetic to see to hers. On the flip side, he needed sex to heal. But if he used her to heal, taking his own pleasure while unable to see to hers, he wouldn't be able to sleep with her a second time in exchange for the crystal daggers.

Okay. Change of plans. Next female he spotted, he'd seduce, unleashing his demon, nothing held back. The thought sickened him, but whatever. Then he'd head to the goddess's palace. He'd be late, but he could charm her out of any pique that tardiness might cause. Another sickening thought.

Get over yourself. He'd chosen to travel this path. He would live with the emotional fallout.

Resolute, Paris stumbled out of the alley.

SIENNA BLACKSTONE HUDDLED in the corner, enveloped by tormenting shadows. Her wings—those ever-growing black wings, courtesy of the demon now inside her—pulled at tendons and bone she hadn't known she had, shooting aches all through her body.

Cronus had brought her here—wherever "here" was. A

dilapidated castle guarded by gargoyles that came to life. Those gargoyles could see and hear her—unlike Paris, the warrior she'd hoped to find—and they ensured she remained exactly where she was. And when she actually fought her way through their fangs, horns, claws and tails, some kind of clear shield prevented her from stepping into the outside world.

At first, she'd been terrified. Someone should have told her death would be a thousand times more horrifying than life. Over the ensuing weeks, she'd had to learn to adapt to all these supernatural creatures. Though she'd known demons existed and had once hated them, everything else was new to her. And now all she wanted was to get out of here so she could reach one of those demons. Hold him. Help him. But…

She could leave only when she vowed to obey Cronus in all things. A condition she didn't understand.

Why did he so desperately want her obedience? Her aid? What did he expect her to do for him? He'd never said. But in his desperate bid for control of her, he'd even taken her to spy on her former colleagues. Hunters. God, the things they'd done…

She was disgusted, and she was angry. She'd once hurt an innocent man—for them. She had struck when Paris was at his weakest—for them. She would have helped them kill the warrior if he hadn't escaped with her. She had blamed him for her death, thinking he'd used her body as a shield. She had hated him for that. Now, she only hated herself.

No, that wasn't true. She hated the Hunters and everything they represented.

Before she died—again—she was taking them down. Actually, she would help Paris take them down. Somehow, some way, she would leave this castle. She would find him once more. She would tell him everything she knew about his enemy. Every secret hideout, every battle plan, every strategy she'd ever heard whispered about. And if he still couldn't see or hear her, she would tell someone who could, like his dark-haired friend. And then…then she was gifting Paris's other friend, Aeron, with Wrath.

Doing so would finally end her. Forever.

That wouldn't make up for the wrongs she'd done, she doubted anything could, but it was a start.

You just have to find a way out….

A sigh left her. She wasn't chained, and she knew Cronus kept other prisoners here. They screamed and ranted and raved constantly. Unlike her, they didn't have the run of the entire castle. They were limited to the bedrooms on an upper floor. The few times Sienna convinced herself to drag her winged self up the stairs, the demon inside her had gone insane, flashing all kinds of hateful images through her head. Images of blood, torture and death.

The people upstairs…they were warriors, demon-possessed like her. She didn't hate them, didn't want to hurt them. She wanted to help them—but her demon wanted to punish them. Always punish.

You can't help them down here.

I can't hurt them, either.

Arguing with herself. She laughed. She'd always forced herself to be demure, even somber. She'd always quashed any hint of temper and sarcasm. The fear of injuring somebody's feelings, the shame of disappointing her loved ones had been too much. After her younger sister's abduction, she'd had to be a rock. Causing more emotional turmoil would have destroyed her.

Well, no longer. She was strong. She was capable. She was needed.

She could overcome her demon and aid the beings upstairs. She could.

For Paris.

CHAPTER ELEVEN

THE NEXT MORNING DAWNED bright and early. Too bright, too early. Kaia had stayed awake all night, her mind too active to snooze. So when she spotted the big orange glow of the sun, she glared and flipped it the bird.

"Go away, you bastard!"

Strider lounged on "their" bed, watching her with an amused glint in his eyes. He'd slept, sprawled out over every inch of the mattress. She'd paced.

"Who're you talking to?" he asked in a sleep-rumbling voice.

A sleep-rumbling voice that turned her on. Damn him, everything about him turned her on. *Be proactive. Nip this in the bud.* "Maybe I was talking to you," she snapped, stomping to the bed, grabbing a pillow and beating his chest with it.

He didn't bother raising his arms to protect himself. "Has anyone ever told you what a bundle of joy you are in the morning?"

Bang. "No." *Bang.*

"Will you just sit down for a sec?" He ripped the pillow out of her hands and tossed it to the floor. "Geez. I need— I mean, *you* need a breather from all your worries."

"I don't have any worries," she said, plopping beside him. Lysander had taken them all up to the heavens and given them each a room in his cloud, where no other Harpy could reach them. She and Strider had shared, and no one, not even Lysander, could breech its perimeter unless they both gave permission.

Never had she encountered such a kick-ass security system. Even better, misty walls of baby-blue acted as TV screens, revealing anything she requested to see. Her mother? Done. Juliette? Gag.

The absolute best? Kaia had only to say, "I want a dagger," and one would magically appear in her palm.

No wonder Bianka had decided to shack up with a goody-goody. And really, Bianka would just have to take one for the team and do a little more of that shacking to convince Lysander to buy Kaia one of these. You know, so they could spend quality sis-time together. They were twins, after all, and Bianka needed her.

"You started stressing the moment you got that text," Strider said. "Five minutes after we got here!"

That text. Ugh. Her stomach cramped as worry flooded her. Not that she'd admit it. The first Harpy Game, Tag, would begin in two hours.

Team captains were too valuable to lose so early in the games and never competed in the first event. Instead, the four strongest, most violent members were chosen, and the captain merely prayed they survived.

But though she was captain, Kaia had to compete.

Last night, thanks to the cloud walls, she'd kept watch on her motel room. One after the other, Harpies from every other team had snuck inside, hoping to brutalize her. As if she would stay in a room she'd rented under her own name. Please. But that's how stupid they thought she was. Worse, they would continue to come after her unless they were taught to fear her.

That, she had learned from her mother.

And so today she would teach them to fear her.

The other three going in? Taliyah, Neeka—who Kaia had never seen fight, but Taliyah had recommended her, and Kaia trusted her older sis—and Gwen. Bianka was still pouting, but bottom line, Bianka was too damn sweet.

Once, she'd BBQed another Harpy who'd trashed her appearance. Cool, right? Well, as the girl screamed and writhed, a guilty Bianka had raced off to fetch a glass of water for her. Who did that? Marshmallows, that's who.

"If you won't sit still, at least tell Papa Stridey what's bothering you."

There was that rumbling voice again, caressing her, seeping past her skin to fuse with her cells, becoming a part of her. It was clear the bud remained un-nipped. "I'm thinking that only prison rules are going to apply."

A laugh burst from him. "What does *that* mean? That you shouldn't drop the soap? What, does round one involve multiple showerheads?"

"Would you be serious?"

He snorted. "You telling someone to be serious. Weird. But..." He sat up, his features lighting with interest. The sheet fell to his waist, revealing row after row of muscled strength. "Tell me round one involves multiple shower-heads."

Her lips twitched, even as her mouth watered for a taste of him. "No, you pervert. No showerheads. I have to kill the biggest and the baddest my first day on the inside. That way, all the others will leave me alone."

"Smart. How can I help?"

"By sitting in the stands and looking pretty."

"A given. But what can I do to help you win? That's why I'm here, right?"

As if she'd forget. He wasn't here because he loved her, needed her, wanted to make something work between them. He was here to help her win that damn Paring Rod.

He didn't know about the Rod when he arrived. He likes you. You know that. Yeah, he liked her. Just not enough. She sighed.

"Just...I don't know, cheer me on." Hearing him might strengthen her. It might also distract her, but they would find out together.

"I can do that. You're fun to watch."

Her heart skipped a beat. "Yeah?"

"Oh, yeah."

His voice had dropped, huskier than before, all kinds of innuendo in his tone. Her nipples tightened, and she had to jump to her feet and turn away from him to prevent him from seeing the evidence of her arousal.

He'd watched her last night, when her Harpy had simply reacted to the threat around him, determined to protect him at all costs. He'd also watched her when she... She shuddered, remembering.

Something had happened to her while she'd fought her mother's soldiers. Something that had never happened before. She had burned. With rage, yes, but also with actual, literal flames. They had licked inside her, searing her cells, her organs, and leaving only ash. Or so she'd thought. Yet when she had stilled, she hadn't noticed a single smear of soot on her skin.

Now suspicions danced through her mind, adding to the already turbulent waters.

Phoenix blood flowed through her veins, half of her genetic makeup. She'd met her father once, when he abducted her and Bianka, whisking them to the Land of Cinder. He—and all his kind, really—were utterly heartless, completely detached from emotion, as if any softer side was burned away in their constant fires. Not even her mother could compare, and that was saying something.

Not only were they emotionally callous, they were physically formidable, too. Poison leaked from the Phoenixes' fangs and claws. Their wings, which looked as smooth and delicate as the clouds around her, were actually tongues of blue flame. A single brush from those flames, and an entire building could be razed.

There was a bright side, though. When a Phoenix burned something—or someone—the resulting soot was powerful enough to bring the dead back to life.

Her dad had hoped his baby girls would be more Phoenix than Harpy, but the opposite had proven true, and he'd released them. After torturing them with his poison, of course. He'd scratched their biceps, just a tiny scrape for each of them, and they'd felt as if they'd been injected with a mix of acid, broken glass and Napalm. They had writhed and screamed for days.

A true Phoenix wouldn't have hurt like that, would have been immune to the toxin, which was why Kaia had never thought she'd develop Phoenix-like tendencies. But yesterday's burning…could she have developed an immunity, and in turn taken on their abilities?

"Yo, Kye. We need to beat feet," Bianka suddenly called from the other side of the door.

Kaia blinked, realized she still stood beside the bed, but now Strider towered beside her. She hadn't heard him move, but there he was, his heat already wrapped around her, his scent strong and sweet in her nose.

He gripped her forearms, his head tilting to the side thoughtfully. "Where were you that time?"

"Nowhere," she answered automatically. Her standard reply when someone other than her sisters asked her a question like that.

Did she lose herself in her thoughts that often? *If I weren't so entertaining, maybe I wouldn't*—

"Kaia!" Strider rolled his blues, and she noticed the pupils had gobbled up his gorgeous irises. He'd also loosened his grip, was now caressing the length of her arms with his fingertips. "We're really going to have to work on your lying, baby doll."

Did he…could he…desire her? "Here's an idea. You want the truth from me, you'll have to buy it." With kisses. Or orgasms. *Whatever.* Yes, he'd already offered to buy her artifact-stealing services with sex, and yes, that had pissed her off. But he hadn't truly wanted her then. He might want her now, and that changed everything. Not about the Paring Rod, of course, but about *them.*

His lips curved into a wicked smile. "Who said I wanted the truth?" He stopped the caressing only long enough to tweak her nose. "You're cute when you lie."

She popped her jaw. Puppies and goldfish were "cute." *I'm hot, damn it.* "I lie amazingly well. Just ask everyone I know! They've never been able to tell."

"Actually, I'm probably the only one who can tell you're full of shit. I'm observant like that."

"And humble, too. Meanwhile, you need to work on your man-sluttiness." She rolled her shoulders, lifting her forearms and thereby his hands, causing his knuckles to brush the sides of her breasts. Dear gods, that felt good, lighting her up inside.

He flashed his teeth, as if he'd experienced a jolt of pain, and his nostrils flared with the force of his breathing. "And just how will we work on that sluttiness, hmm? In bed?"

He did, she thought, dazed. He desired her. Why else would he mention a bedding when she'd been hinting that he was *too* slutty? "I like the way your mind works. We should—"

"Kye?" Bianka called, cutting her off. "You in there? I know you're in there. *Come. On.*"

"Yeah, Bee. I'm here, but I need a minute," she screeched. She never removed her gaze from Strider. "We'll continue this later. Okay?" *Please.* She needed his touch, his intensity. His everything.

"Uh, no, we won't." One step, two, he backed away

from her. His arms dropped to his sides, contact severed completely. "We're gonna keep this thing platonic."

Her eyes narrowed to tiny slits, his beautiful face the only thing in sight. "Platonic? When you've had your tongue down my throat?"

His eyes narrowed, too. "Fine. We'll continue this later."

"Really?" Happiness burst through her—followed by dread. "I'm supposed to believe you changed your mind—" she snapped her fingers "—that easily? What's your game?"

"No game. Your argument was solid."

Happiness was renewed, and gods, look how beautiful the sun suddenly was, so big and bright above their cloud. "Well, all right, then. Later." She tried not to smile as she skipped to the door and greeted her sister.

STRIDER HADN'T KNOWN what to expect at the first competition and after the whole elementary school thing, he'd prepared himself for anything, everything. Or so he'd thought. Just then, he found himself drowning in shock and the ceaseless, excited buzzing of his demon. The little shit had never encountered so fervent a swell of competitive spirit and was currently bouncing around like a kid on a steady caffeine shooter diet.

Strider sat in the bleachers of a high school basketball court, about a hundred other guys surrounding him. All were strangers except for Sabin, who occupied the seat on his left, and Lysander, who occupied the seat on his right. Most were human, though some were clearly immortal. He spotted the telltale pale skin of a vampire, the dark aura of a warlock and the reptilian grace of a snake shape-shifter. Unfortunately, he didn't see the "him" Kaia had supposedly slept with.

On the other side were the Harpies. While the men were quiet and subdued, the females were rowdy. They were jumping up and down on the steps, throwing pop-corn and even cups of soda at the court. They wore tiny, tight T-shirts that ended just under the bra line—for those who were wearing bras. And shorts so short he spotted his favorite place on a woman—the sensual curve where bottom met leg—more than once. Yeah, he spied the center of paradise, too.

"The Falconways are going down!" someone called.

"You wish, Eagleshield. But then, you've always liked a woman on her knees."

"Please! You couldn't satisfy a nymph if you were cranked on Viagra."

"Viagra only works on men, you idiot."

"Hello, you and your clanswomen have mustaches, so why not dicks, too?"

Snickers, boos and hisses blended together.

"And I thought my Bianka was...enthusiastic," Lysander said. "I would never have guessed she was actually considered sedate among her kind."

Sabin snorted. "Come on. If you aren't revved by the lesbian jokes, you're gay."

Lysander's dark gaze swung to Strider. "Are *you* revved by this?"

Angels, man. "I've been on low simmer since we walked through the doors. In fact, I didn't need the jokes to crank my chain." What he didn't mention: it was all because of Kaia.

His "talk" with her—one he'd tried to postpone forever, but had swiftly realized the futility of postponing as she batted gloriously long lashes at him, all kinds of desire in her eyes—would happen sooner than even she had planned.

He'd stood in front of her, breathing her in, absorbing her body heat, peering down at that pin-up face, and he'd wanted his mouth on her, all over her. One more taste. One more, and he'd force himself to return to the friend zone.

"Lysander!" an eager female voice called from across the court. "Lysander! Over here!"

Strider searched the raucous crowd for Bianka. He found her at the top of the bleachers, waving a candy bar in the air and grinning like a loon. Her silky black hair was divided into pigtails that bounced against her arms. Cute, until you noticed the smoking hot Catholic schoolgirl uniform she wore. "Cute" mutated into "heart attack waiting to happen." A white button-up top was knotted under her breasts, a tie hanging between them. The short plaid skirt left a huge gap between her thighs and her knee-high socks.

Made him wish Kaia had opted to cheer her team to victory rather than fight. In that getup, she'd look better than a heart attack waiting to happen. She'd kill him on the spot.

No, he was glad she'd chosen to fight. He planned to use the needed separation from her to spy on the Eagleshields, maybe search their belongings. In fact, as soon as Tag began, he was out of here. And he wouldn't feel guilty about that. Every man for himself.

What if Kaia's hurt? By her own admission, she would be throwing down with "prison rules."

A flash of red in his eyes, his fingers clenching on his legs. Kaia was a damn good fighter, he reminded himself. If he trusted anyone on her team to succeed, it was her.

"Lysander!" Bianka called again. "Look up, baby. I'm over here!"

"There are too many. I can't find—Bianka?" Lysander's jaw dropped.

Guess he hadn't seen her since they'd left the heavens. Then, she had worn a scarlet robe.

"Lysander, did you see this?" Bianka turned and lifted

her shirt, showing him—and everyone else—the panties she wore. They were neon-green with the words *Property of Lysandy* scripted across the ass.

Lysander stood, as if to fly over to her, then caught himself and plopped back down. "Sweet Deity."

"Your woman wears underwear out in public," Sabin said. "Must be nice. How'd you manage that little miracle?"

"Only the Deity knows."

Great. Now Strider couldn't stop wondering about Kaia. What kind of panties did she—or did she not—wear?

The girl beside Bianka must have complained about the high-pitched tenor of her voice, because Bianka's grin faded and she leveled the girl with a scowl. An argument ensued. Then, of course, the two leapt at each other in a tangle of flailing limbs.

"She is magnificent, isn't she?" Lysander asked no one in particular.

"Sure," Sabin said, distracted now. He was stroking the bullhorn at his feet. "So where are *our* girls?"

Our girls. Strider liked the sound of that. He shouldn't like the sound of that. "Don't know."

Do you truly think Kaia can bring home the victory?

The insidious voice filled Strider's head. Male. Familiar.

She might be killed...

Oh, hell, no. "Sabin," he growled. This time, he didn't have to wonder about the speaker. As the keeper of Doubt, Sabin fed off the insecurities of those around him.

"Sorry," his leader replied.

"Get your demon under control."

"Believe me, I'm trying. I don't want him going after anyone on Team Kaia."

Win. She must win.

And there was Strider's demon, who—wait just a sec.

She must win? Defeat had never cared about a victory other than Strider's before. Why Kaia? Why now? Because her triumph was (perhaps) linked to the Paring Rod? Because the demon knew—and feared—the consequences of her failure? Because, she was…his? Their personal playground? He'd wondered before…

Can't think like that. He wouldn't do what needed doing.

To Defeat, he said, *First, I plan to obtain the Paring Rod before the games end. Second, she'll win.* If she didn't… he speculated about the likelihood of Defeat hurting him, even though the loss was not his own. Strider wouldn't have protected her, as the challenge he'd already accepted demanded. So…

Likelihood high, he decided. He should have talked her out of this. Whatever happened next was his fault.

For once the prospect of the pain he might suffer held no sway. He simply didn't like the thought of *Kaia* being harmed.

"Lysander!" Bianka called, once again drawing Strider's notice. Her fight with the other Harpy had ended with the poor woman draped over the back of the bleachers, unconscious. "Did you like them or what?"

Lysander's expression softened. "I did, my love. I liked them. I like everything you wear."

Pathetic, Strider thought. Just because a guy was in love didn't mean he had to pussy up.

Oh, look, there was Kaia! Strider jumped to his feet, waving at her to get her attention. He planned to tell her to be careful, but she was too focused on the happenings in front of her as she strode from the double doors leading into the gym. Her teammates flanked her sides. They wore matching uniforms of bloodred leather, the half tops crisscrossing in back to reveal their wings, the shorts fringed at the hem to allow for easier movements.

Kaia's red curls were pulled back in a ponytail that

swung left and right. No elbow or kneepads safeguarded her. Damn it, he wished she'd worn pads. If the girls fought on that planked floor, they were going to lose some skin, and he liked her skin how it was.

Win!

I know. I heard you the first time, asshole.

The Harpies in the stands noticed the incoming team and started booing. A frown pulled at Kaia's lips, but she gave no other indication that she cared. Popcorn rained down, showering them, a few kernels even popping members of Team Kaia in the eye.

"Hey, Millicent," Bianka screamed down at one of the popcorn launchers. "I see you've set aside this special time to humiliate yourself in public. Your aim sucks!"

A pretty blonde whipped around, hands fisted on her hips. "Hey, there, twin-half number one. Or is it two? I can never remember. You're both just too insignificant. If I throw a stick, will you leave to fetch it?"

"I am not a dog, you bitch." Bianka propped her hands on her hips. "At least, your dad doesn't think so. This morning he told me I'm the hottest chili pepper he's ever had. You know, as I crawled out of his bed."

There was an audible gasp among the crowd, and Strider could only blink. The "dad" thing was worthy of such horror?

"My father's dead, you heartless mutt," the one named Millicent gritted out.

"Oh," Bianka said, her shoulder sagging. Then she brightened. "Your mom thinks I'm chili-pepper hot. She told me so this morning when I crawled out of her bed!"

The gasps turned to snickers. Millicent flew up the steps to tackle Bianka. *Ding, ding.* Another fight was on.

Strider found himself grinning. "Do you think she realizes what she just implied?"

"Yes," Lysander said on a sigh.

"Fingers crossed she and the woman she's pounding stop fighting and start kissing," Sabin said. "That happens, and someone better cue the bow-chicka-wow-wow."

Lysander straightened, clearly intrigued. "I see what you mean about engines being revved."

Suddenly the Harpies who were booing erupted into deafening cheers, and Strider forgot everything else as he turned his head to find out why. His jaw clenched. Tabitha and her crew had just entered the court.

They wore half tops and fringed shorts, too, only theirs were blue. Then another team stalked in behind them, wearing purple. Another team in pink. Another team in yellow. Damn. How many teams were there? Another in green. Another in black.

His mouth dried up when he noticed that some of the women were bigger than he was. More muscled, taller, and hell, he would not have been surprised to see beans and franks. Although some of the contestants were as seemingly delicate as Kaia.

The women formed a large circle on the court, leaving the center empty. The one called Juliette, the brunette who'd run the orientation, stepped forward and held up her hands. Finally the crowd quieted.

"If you're like me, you've been waiting for this moment for a long time," she called, and had to stop when cheers once again rang out. Only when they faded did she add, "And so, let's not waste a moment. First rule, you don't talk about Tag. Second rule, *you don't talk about Tag.*"

More cheers.

Grinning, Juliette said, "Just kidding. Now for the real rules. Only one member of each team is allowed in the ring at any given time. When that member wants out," more boos rippled, faded, "all she has to do is tag one of her teammates. If she can reach one."

Annnd...even more cheers exploded through the gym.

"If someone is too injured to continue, she must tap out for good. But think carefully before you go that route, ladies, because even if you heal, you can't go back in."

"I didn't pay to see cowards," someone shouted.

Juliette nodded her agreement. "For those of you who have never before played this type of game, you should know that the competition doesn't end until only one team remains. Here's a hint—fight dirty."

"Eagleshields are gonna kick ass," someone else called.

Juliette's grin acquired a dark, evil edge as she focused on Kaia. "Good luck, everyone. You're going to need it." With that, she strode off, disappearing from view as the contestants swallowed her up.

Kaia tossed Strider a quick glance. So. She'd known where he was, had been as aware of him as he was of her. He nodded in encouragement, even as the bottom dropped out of his stomach. The females surrounding Kaia were eyeing her like she was a juicy filet and they'd just ended a week-long fast. He should be down there, shielding her, not sitting up here, doing nothing.

"Don't worry," Sabin said, patting him on the back. "Gwen won't let anything happen to her."

"I'm not worried," he gritted out. No way would he let Sabin, Doubt himself, have more confidence in his woman's abilities than Strider had in his. Just no way. "*Kaia* will protect *Gwen*."

Boss man blinked at him, incredulous. "You want to argue about that? Really?"

Yes, damn it, he did.

Win.

Always. "Just shut the hell up and watch the game," he said. "I'll let you know before I head to the other side and start my spying."

CHAPTER TWELVE

I WILL NOT FAIL. I WILL not fail. I will not freaking fail. The mantra blazed through Kaia's mind as she settled into position.

Neeka was the first in the "ring" for Team Kaia. Shoulders squared, head high, the girl strode to the center of the court, alongside the first from every other team. Soon, twelve Harpies stood there, facing off, waiting for the whistle to blow. The rest of the combatants waited on the sidelines like Kaia, crouched, one hand extended.

"We've got this," Gwen muttered beside her.

"I know," she said, glad there wasn't a tremor in her voice. Strider was up in the stands, looking edible in a T-shirt with an ironed-on tie, and ripped jeans. The only glance she'd allowed herself had been a mistake. He was a distraction she couldn't afford, but she'd had to assure herself that he was up there, that he hadn't abandoned her. She only prayed he witnessed her victory, not her defeat.

I will not fail. Too much was at stake. Her reputation. Strider's respect. Hell, his life.

Not that he'd agreed to her terms. He'd never flat-out said he'd wait for her to win the Rod and keep his thieving hands to himself. She'd realized that only an hour ago as she'd prepared for Tag. She'd needed a distraction from her the-world-is-at-stake panic and had replayed her every conversation with Strider.

Was he planning to search for the Rod during the game?

Most likely. She wondered if he didn't trust her to bring home the gold, or if he was simply too impatient to wait.

Don't think about that now. Concentrate.

I will not fail.

"Wait till you see Neeka fight," Taliyah said, almost... grinning? Surely not. Taliyah never grinned. Or scowled. Or yelled.

"If she's so good, why'd her clan let her go?" Kaia asked.

"'Cause she's deaf and they're idiots. Plus, she was voted Most Likely to Go Off the Deep End and Kill Everyone Around Her."

And she was now on Kaia's side? "Sweet!"

The shrill screech of the whistle sounded, echoing from the walls and blasting Kaia's ears.

Game on.

Immediately the girls in the center of the court leapt into action. Kaia stiffened, watching. They attacked each other, claws and fangs bared, and within seconds bodies were slamming into the wall of waiting onlookers. Blood sprayed, warm and rich. Her Harpy caught the coppery odor of it and squawked for a taste.

Calm, she would remain calm. The only people she could harm were the ones in the ring. Hurting anyone outside it would result in a disqualification. If her Harpy took over, she would hurt *everyone*.

Each team could be disqualified from one event, and one event only, and still qualify for the grand prize. If that happened, though, you had to hope and pray you had a good showing at the other three events, earning at least third place each time, or you wouldn't stand a chance.

An unholy shriek drew her attention, and she found herself concentrating on Neeka. The sweet-looking beauty... dear gods. Neeka jumped up and hovered over the battling girls Matrix-style, slow motion, arms outstretched, knees drawn up, gaze quickly roving, taking stock, before picking her prey and dropping in a blink. She landed atop a wide set of shoulders, her hands wrapping around the attached head and twisting. Bone snapped, and the poor girl collapsed.

Ouch! Neck injuries were the worst.

Neeka grinned in satisfaction—just as a muscle-stacked brunette slammed into her, knocking her down. Neeka's head cracked on the floor, blood quickly pooling around her. She was dazed, unable to rise, and her opponent used her unstable condition to her advantage, punching and punching and punching, fists raining like poisoned hail.

Shit. If Neeka were knocked unconscious, no one from Team Kaia would be able to enter the ring anytime soon. Or at all. They had to be tagged in.

Several others noticed that Neeka was down and swarmed her helpless, prone body, pummeling her senseless.

"Come on, Neeka!" Bianka shouted from the stands. Kaia would have recognized her twin's beloved voice anywhere, amid any kind of noise. She only prayed Neeka could somehow discern the praise since she couldn't hear it. "Show 'em your titanium balls!"

"Kill her!" someone else shouted. "And hack off those balls of hers!"

"How about I kill you instead, hater?" Bianka snapped back. Then there was the stomp of feet, a pained *hmph*.

Kaia didn't switch her attention, though she knew her twin had just attacked whoever had spoken.

Somehow, Neeka collected her wits. Bodies flew in every direction as she once again Matrixed over the combatants. This time she didn't attack, but dove for Gwen, slapping their palms together.

Gwen darted into the ring, and Kaia breathed a sigh of relief. "Good job," she said. She would've patted Neeka on the back, but feared knocking the poor, shaking thing to her knees.

"They punched out a tooth!" Neeka slurred past cut, swollen lips.

"You'll have a chance at revenge," Taliyah assured her.

What Juliette hadn't explained to the crowd was that every team member had to enter the fray at least three times. If someone failed to do so because they were, say, dead, that team was considered out, disqualified. And to be declared the winner, every member of your team had to be conscious by the final round.

Apparently, this particular game had been played at the last three bi-century competitions. Rumor was, Tag could churn on for days, but even then, there were no breaks allowed. Not to drink or heal or use the bathroom.

Rumor also was, the winner was sometimes declared simply by waiting to see who woke up first.

As the fight continued, other team members tagged in and out. Like the first group had done to Neeka, the new ones swarmed Gwen en masse. She was fast, though, dodging with the speed of a bullet.

"You can do it, baby!" Sabin's proud voice boomed through the gym, louder than everyone else.

Bullhorn, Kaia thought.

The member of Team Skyhawk managed to grab Gwen's arm as she passed, swinging her in the opposite direction. Gwen used the action to her advantage, knocking down several of her opponents bowling-ball style. Practically vibrating with the need to retaliate, the fallen jumped up and turned on her. When they realized who they had in their sights, they dove on her. For a moment, all Kaia could see was her sister's flailing legs.

Sparks of rage heated Kaia. And guess who played dirty, leaping in there and going for Gwen's wings? That same member of Team Skyhawk. Worse, the bitch was laughing. The sparks grew...spread...

"Get off her!" Sabin shouted now. "Or I swear to the gods—there you go, baby! Yeah! That's the way."

Gwen roared with pain and rage as she kicked a few of the girls off her.

"That just happened," Sabin blasted arrogantly.

Of course, the girls came back for more.

Kaia had never felt so helpless.

Another roar, and then Gwen was clawing her way out. Tension had whitened her face, making the blood splattered there stark and obscene in comparison. She managed to fight her way to the sidelines and tag Taliyah, who sprang in with a vengeance.

First person she attacked was her mother's soldier, tossing the girl to the ground and grinding her face into the wooden planks.

"You okay?" Kaia asked Gwen.

"They...broke my...wing," her sister panted.

Oh, *shit*. Kaia's hopes plummeted, her body cooling down. A Harpy's wings were the source of her strength. When those wings were disabled, she weakened unbearably. Gwen would have to go back in and fight at least two more times, but how effective would she be when she would hit and move as feebly as a human?

Before the question formed completely, Kaia had begun to strategize. They were warriors; they could deal. Gwen would go in a second time toward the end of the match, remaining in the ring for only a few seconds, and then tag out. Then, when every other team had been disabled, Gwen could go in for her third and final time. Boom, done. Easy.

Win.

Kaia blinked in astonishment. Okay, that hadn't been *her* inner voice, but a man's. Familiar, and yet...not. Only one person—or creature?—craved victory as much as she did. Automatically, she looked up. Strider was no longer situated between the pale-faced Sabin and the stoic Lysander. He wasn't in the stands at all.

Red flickered in her line of vision as she returned her attention to the battle. The wolves had descended on Taliyah in unison, pinning her in as they punched and kicked her to the ground. Only, they couldn't hold her down. She was there, the center of their fury one moment, but gone the next, a cloud of black smoke in her place.

Confused, the combatants looked around. Another cloud of smoke appeared behind them, and Taliyah stepped from its center. She twisted, giving herself an unstoppable momentum, and lashed out. Heads banged together, and bodies fell.

When those who were standing realized what was happening, they once again descended on the tall, slender Taliyah. And once again, Kaia's older sister disappeared in a cloud of smoke, reappearing elsewhere.

The same scene repeated itself over and over again. Taliyah was merciless, slashing and biting before dancing away. But the Harpies she felled soon made their way to their feet and tagged in another team member.

Like Kaia, the ones on the sidelines had been watching her, and they'd learned to anticipate her moves, to watch for the smoke. So the next time Taliyah appeared, they were waiting for her. A fist immediately met her jaw, propelling her backward. No one approached her, because they knew. And yep, when she righted herself, she disappeared as expected. Another fist met her jaw when she reappeared, once again sending her flying.

She shook her head, probably seeing stars. They didn't jump her this time, either. They simply waited.

Taliyah's ice-blue gaze sought Kaia.

My turn, she thought, eagerly holding out her hand. *Come on.*

Taliyah raced forward, enduring pummeling fists and jackhammering boots to reach—Neeka.

For a moment, Kaia stood frozen with shock. Then reality slammed into her like a strong right hook, and she snarled with affront. "What the hell, Tal!"

"Better this way," was all her panting sister said.

What, her sis doubted her skills? Oh, that cut. "You know I have to go in three times."

"Yeah, but it'll be better if you go in at the end."

When everyone was bruised and battered and at their weakest. Oh, that cut *deeper*. "Gwen's wings are damaged. *She* needs to go in at the end, not me."

"She will. She'll just go in before you."

This time, she wasn't cut. She was destroyed. Her family loved her, yes, but like her mother—like Strider—they had no faith in her. "You're not the leader of this team. You gave that right to *me*."

"Do you see what they're doing to us, baby sister? Warring teams are working together to destroy us. But you, you they're going to try and massacre."

"I know." She raised her chin. "I'm prepared."

Win.

There was that deep, raspy voice again. Not Strider, not his demon as she'd hoped. How could it be, when the warrior was nowhere to be seen? But...who did that leave?

Taliyah sighed. "All right. Fine. You want in next, you'll go in next. But the loss will be on your shoulders."

The loss. As if defeat was a given.

Tears burned Kaia's eyes as she concentrated on the fight. The swelling in Neeka's face had gone down, so her vision was no longer obscured. Still, every single one of her opponents knew she was deaf and opted to use the infirmity against her. They called out instructions to each other, outlining a demolition she couldn't hear—or defend herself against.

"You take the left and I'll take the right."

"I've got middle."

"I've got rear."

Neeka lifted herself into the air.

"Grab her ankle!"

The girl in the middle did as commanded, swinging Neeka around and tossing her away from her teammates, ensuring there would be no tagging out. Breath gushed from her parted, bleeding lips when she landed. Someone was there, waiting, and kicked her in the stomach. She curled into a ball, trying to suck in a breath.

The red dotting Kaia's gaze darkened to black. To her knowledge, opposing teams had never worked together before. That they were, that Kaia's demise was the goal that united them...that they still hated her so much...she felt scraped raw inside.

She'd been a kid when she'd inadvertently destroyed their families, for gods' sake.

Well, she wasn't a kid anymore, and it was past time these women learned she wouldn't lie down and take their shit. As her determination increased, the black dots wove together, nearly obscuring her vision completely, leaving only the haze of body heat.

Calm down before you forget where you are and what you can and cannot do.

Inhale deeply...exhale sharply... That didn't help. Kaia pictured Strider, his fall of blond hair, those navy blue eyes, that wicked smile. Finally the black faded, and her sight returned to normal. She watched as Neeka battled her way from the midst of the violence and scrambled toward Taliyah.

As promised, her sister kept her hands at her sides. Kaia reached out and gently tapped Neeka's obviously broken fingers. The girl collapsed on the sidelines as Kaia stepped into the ring. As one, everyone stilled and glared over at her. They were bleeding, sweating, panting. And clearly, they'd been waiting for her.

"My sister died because of you."

"I lost a daughter."

"We never sought revenge against you out of respect for your mother, but she has at last disavowed you."

No reaction. The burn started up in her chest again, but she willed it away. Locked it up tight. No going Harpy. Or whatever else. "Good. Now let's see what I can do to each of you."

"I have a feeling I'll be *disappointed* in your skill."

They chuckled, and her cheeks flushed. And then, as one, they turned and tagged in a new team member. She recognized the woman on her mother's team. Had once trained with her.

Like Kaia, these women had yet to fight. They were at full strength and utterly determined to use it. Against her face, no doubt.

You're strong. You can take them.

Win!

Yes. She would.

That was her last thought before her opponents descended. Kaia ducked and spun, going low and slashing. Someone managed to nail her in the temple with a hard rasp of knuckles, but that didn't stop her claws from slicing into several Achilles tendons. Grunts of pain sounded, and then the crash of knees hitting wood.

"That's the way!" Strider shouted.

He was here. He was still here. Dizzy pleasure rushed through her, but she didn't have time to stop and focus. The Harpies again rushed her. This time, she allowed them to surround her, arching her spine as they punched, swinging her elbows forward and backward, kicking, every motion fluidly blending into the next.

WIN!

"Pluck out their eyes!" Bianka screamed.

The dance never slowed, even though she did not remain unscathed. She was punched—everywhere. She was kicked—everywhere. Soon her muscles were knotted and bruised, her limbs shaking. Strider was up there, watching, and the knowledge kept her strong. A few times, the burn tried to work free of its cage, but she maintained a sturdy enough grip to keep it hidden.

With an elbow to the trachea, she finally took out one of her opponents for good. That left ten more to go. Then another one went down as Kaia took a page from Neeka's book and broke a neck.

This enraged the nine remaining, and they attacked with greater fervor.

Kaia darted out of the center of the horde, intending to run and gain enough momentum to leap and kick someone's teeth into her brain. But she was grabbed her by the hair and jerked backward. She crashed into a hard wall before multiple fists battered at her.

"Come on!" Strider roared. "You're better than this. Fight!"

"Eat their tongues for dinner!" Bianka shouted.

Though she fought with all of her might, they managed to pin her with embarrassing ease, holding her arms and legs to the floor. Those who didn't have a grip on her rose above her and rained down their damage. She felt bones breaking, organs rupturing.

They laughed. Then, thankfully, she couldn't see their smug expressions, the world around her fading to black. And not the good kind of black that might have saved her. Before her Harpy could come out of the shadows swinging, before the burn could spring from the cage, she was flipped over, her wings receiving equal punishment.

So much pain…agony…loss…failure…

"Damn it, Kaia!" Strider.

"No! *Noooo!*" Bianka.

"Snap out of it." Taliyah.

"Just move, Kye. Just get to me." Gwen.

Win! Win!

A warm flood in her throat, spilling out her mouth. Maybe blood filled her ears, as well, because the noise level dulled...dulled...until there was only silence. Then a fist hammered into her temple, again and again, and she was no longer aware of the silence.

Only oblivion, such sweet oblivion.

CHAPTER THIRTEEN

STRIDER WAS READY TO COMMIT cold-blooded murder. He'd start with Sabin and Lysander, who tried to force him to remain in his seat. They might not realize it, but their actions challenged his demon and Strider face-planted them both. They released him, but rather than bolt for the basketball court, he stayed put. Barely.

He'd tried to leave once before this, determined to reach the Eagleshields on the other side. Then Kaia had been tagged into the ring. He'd found himself racing back to his seat.

If he allowed himself to act, he would slaughter his way through those women. Game over. No first prize awarded—and if he failed to find the Paring Rod himself, he would need Kaia to win. Also, Kaia would be humiliated by his interference. But just then, he didn't really give a flying fuck about first prize or humiliation.

Was Kaia okay?

She'd gone limp, and an eternity seemed to pass as she was beaten. And beaten some more. Thankfully, the Harpies soon lost interest in her unconscious form and turned on each other. When Strider saw her, he nearly leapt from his seat again. Blood covered every inch of her face. Her clothes were ripped, and just as bloody. Her hands were swollen, her chest motionless.

Sabin straightened and dusted the dirty popcorn from

his shoulders. "She'll be okay," he said. "Look at Bianka over there. She's pissed, not frightened."

Funny that the keeper of Doubt was trying to reassure him, but Strider obeyed. He looked. Bianka paced the top of the bleachers, and everyone around her had long since moved out of her way. She stomped so hard the wood was probably cracked underneath her.

He scrubbed a hand—a trembling hand!—down his face, his attention returning to Kaia, where it remained for yet another eternity. She needed to drink from him. He wanted her to drink from him. She just had to move, just had to finish this.

Come on, baby doll. You can do it.

Her team could still pull through and win. And even if they didn't... No. He wouldn't let himself contemplate that. What mattered, surprisingly, was Kaia. She'd been doing so well, fighting with a skill that had aroused him. Yeah. He'd watched her while sporting a hard-on. Then they'd gang-banged her.

What the hell had she done to warrant such hatred?

Next time they were alone, she would tell him. No more lies, either. No matter how sexy she was while she spun them.

Finally, movement. She twitched. Every muscle in his body tensed. No one noticed her as she blinked open her eyes. He knew the exact moment clarity struck her because her teeth flashed in a crimson snarl. But broken as she currently was, there was nothing she could do to hurt those who had hurt her. So she did the next best thing. She crawled to Taliyah.

"Come on, baby doll," he muttered, his thoughts forming into words and grinding past the knot in his throat. "You can do it."

Win. Defeat had been shouting for victory long before Kaia entered the match.

Yeah, she will. Gods, he'd never been prouder of another living being. Not even his friends, who had fought Hunters at his side, watching his back. Because when they'd gone down, they'd been out for the count. Not Kaia, though. She continued on.

Kaia's hand inched up, her face contorting in a grimace. Someone screamed and scrambled toward her, intent on stopping her from tagging out, but at last her hand connected with her sister's and the pale-haired Harpy jumped in with a fury.

Seconds later, screeches of pain erupted, a symphony of abuse. Bodies flew—and didn't get up. Until a panting, blood-splattered Taliyah was the only one standing in the ring. She tagged in Gwen, who simply hobbled around kicking everyone who was down. Gwen tagged in Neeka, who did the same. Neeka retagged Gwen, who entered for a third time.

When Gwen finished, she tagged in Kaia, who managed to crawl a few more inches and kick one of the fallen in the stomach. The action, though, must have aggravated some of her more serious internal injuries because she lost consciousness for a bit.

"Come on, Kaia!" Strider shouted.

"You can do it," Sabin screeched through that bullhorn, and damn if Strider didn't wish he had one of his own.

The other Harpies began to rouse. The one Kaia had kicked came to with a jolt, jarring Kaia awake in the process.

"Damn it, Kaia! You're the best. Show them!" Strider wanted to vomit as she was once again attacked. Somehow, someway, she finally managed to crawl her way to Taliyah and tag her in.

He thought they'd do it. Thought they'd win. But in the end, when Kaia went in a third time, she was pinned and beaten so badly she passed out for good, knocking her

team out of the competition. Even worse, it was Team Skyhawk that claimed first and Team Eagleshield that claimed
second.

SOMETHING WARM SLID DOWN Kaia's throat. So delicious,
she thought, swallowing weakly. More, she needed more,
but she didn't have the strength to swallow a second time.
Until that warmth hit her stomach. It quickly moved
through the rest of her, chasing away the cold heaviness
of her limbs, energizing her.

She pried her eyelids apart. Strider loomed over her, she
saw, his wrist poised over her mouth. Blood dripped onto
her now closed lips and slid down her cheeks. He reached
down with his free hand, about to force her mouth to part.
When he realized she had awoken, he froze.

Her lips parted of their own volition, another mouthful
of warmth sliding into her stomach and filling her up.

"That's it," he said, pressing his wrist into the opening
she provided. "That's a good girl."

Her fangs extended, and she bit. She sucked and sucked
and sucked, drinking in the healing powers of his blood.
He tasted like rich, aged wine sprinkled with dark chocolate and honey. No one had ever tasted this good.

As she savored, she studied him. He sat beside her, his
hip touching hers. Lines of tension branched from his eyes
and mouth, and his skin was pallid. Unsure how much
blood he could afford to lose, she forced herself to stop
drinking from him.

He arched a brow. "That enough?"

No, but it would have to be. She nodded. The action
heralded a wave of dizziness, and she grimaced. In and out
she breathed, slow, measured. Finally, her mind calmed,
leaving her alone with her thoughts.

She recalled entering the ring, kicking ass—and then
getting her ass kicked. After that...damn, damn, damn.

She was lying in an unfamiliar bed in an unfamiliar room. That meant…damn, damn, damn.

"Where are my sisters?" Wow. Speaking *hurt*. Someone must have punched the hell out of her trachea.

"Bianka went back to the heavens with Lysander because I was about to permanently hinder her ability to breathe. She hovers. And Gwen is somewhere with Sabin, drinking his blood, I'm sure, and healing." Strider's voice was cold, distant. "Taliyah and the others, I don't know."

"But all my girls were alive after the competition?"

"Yeah. All of them."

"And they weren't on the verge of dying?"

"No."

Relief speared her. All right. Okay. They were alive, healing. She could deal with anything else. Maybe. "Who—who won?"

He ran his tongue over his teeth. "Your mother. You guys didn't place."

Because of me, she thought, her chest hollowing out. Because she'd passed out, which was almost as bad as a disqualification.

Her eyes burned, so she closed them. Damn it. She needed a moment alone, needed time to compose herself. Or sob. Strider had just seen her at her worst. She couldn't break down now and further blacken his opinion of her.

More than that, she had to look hideous. In fact, she needed to cover every mirror in the vicinity with a mourning shroud before she saw herself and considered committing suicide. "Be a good consort and go fetch me a bottle of water so I can steal it from you. I'm thirsty."

"Drink your tears, crybaby."

Her eyelids popped open and she gaped at him. The urge to cry vanished completely. "How can you treat me like this! Where's your compassion? I'm obviously dying."

"Please. You've got a few paltry wounds."

Paltry? Paltry! She glanced down at herself. Her clothes had been cut away, leaving her bare. Only she still looked dressed. Her skin was slashed and tattered in places, with black and blue bruises branching in every direction. "These are the worst wounds you've ever seen, you bastard, and you know it."

His lips quirked at the corners. "Nah. I once had a paper cut between my index finger and thumb. You don't know the meaning of pain until you've experienced something like that."

He. Was. Amused. "You are five seconds away from a dagger through the heart." Huffing and puffing, she pulled the covers up to her chin. Every movement caused a ripple of agony. Worth it, though. Being naked in front of Strider—no problem. Being naked and injured? Hell, no!

"Watch your tone, okay? My demon is acting up." Even as he spoke, he gently tucked the soft material around her.

Some of her anger drained. "What do you mean, acting up?"

"He's eager for a fight."

"Why?" She knew she shouldn't say anything else, knew Strider would be pissed, wouldn't understand, but it was for his own good. "I doubt you can tell me in a way I'll understand."

The long length of his lashes fused together, anger suddenly pulsing from him. "He was cheering for you. He watched you lose. That upset him. He didn't hurt me, but now he needs to win something. Got it?"

"Yes." His demon had cheered for her? Really? Was that the voice she'd heard, as she'd first suspected? "Thank you."

"This is not something to smile about."

She was smiling? Oh, yeah. She was. She smoothed her features. "Fine. I'll behave. Now, don't you feel better?"

A moment passed before the tension she'd sensed in

him drained. He'd won. A little skirmish, yes, but he'd still won, granting his demon some sort of victory and hopefully calming him.

"You did that on purpose," he said, thoughtful.

"So?"

"So. You're sweet." Tenderly he swept the hair from her brow. "We're going to talk. If you're feeling up to it," he added.

His body heat cocooned her more surely than the blanket. "Why wouldn't I feel up to it? Paltry wounds, remember?" As her dry tone echoed, she began to understand something else about Strider. He'd shown her no sympathy earlier because he'd realized how close she teetered to the edge of a breakdown. Any softness would have sent her over, and she would have collapsed.

She would have resented him for that collapse, would have worried about the consequences. Now, she didn't have to. She could simply enjoy him.

"*Are* you okay?" he asked softly. "Be honest."

"I'm fine."

"Do you need anything else?"

"A naked rubdown."

His pupils expanded, gobbling up his irises. "Besides that."

"Besides this, besides that," she mocked, forcing herself to glare at him. "Lookit, I can tell you're sincerely slightly concerned about my physical well-being, but if you don't get me some water like I already told you I needed, I will personally—"

"Clearly, you're feeling up to a talk." His lips twitched into a full-fledged smile this time.

There. Much better. He hadn't wanted her to collapse, and she hadn't wanted him to torture himself about her condition.

"Therefore…" He held up a glistening bottle and waved

it in her face. A few droplets of condensation splashed onto her chest, and she gasped. "I can admit that I've got what you want, and exploit you."

The sudden dryness of her mouth made her gums ache. She'd been lying before, about being thirsty, but now, seeing that bottle, she wanted. Had to have. Would die if she didn't. "Give me."

"Uh-uh-uh. You want this," he said in a singsong voice, "you'll have to earn it. So I'll be asking you some questions, and you'll be giving me the answers. And, just so you know, I also have a hamburger and a chocolate shake to pay you with."

She licked her lips, hating him and loving him at the same time. This was exactly why she never spilled Harpy secrets. They could be used against her. But because of Gwen, Strider knew Kaia truly had to earn her food. If he asked a question, and she accepted payment for her answer, she couldn't lie to him. Otherwise, she would sicken, just as she would if she ate something she'd prepared for herself.

Once again he waved the water bottle. "Deal?"

"Deal," she gritted out, no longer having to fake the resurgence of anger. He would want to know about the next competition. She knew it. She—

"Tell me why the Harpies hate you so much."

Was wrong. She sagged against the mattress and peered up at the ceiling. Water damage had darkened several panels. They were in another cheap motel, then. Were probably still in Wisconsin.

"I'm waiting, baby doll."

"The answer's not important."

"I'll be the judge of that."

She sighed. "The man…Juliette's man. The one you saw the day of orientation. When I was fourteen, I wanted him to be my slave, to do my laundry, that kind of thing, so I tried to steal him and prove my worth. My strength." As she spoke, she began to tremble. If she told him the rest, the truth, he would leave her. Just like most of her clan had left her.

How could he not? He'd just watched her lose. To hear that she'd always been a failure, that she would probably never be more…

Did she really want the bottle of water *that* much?

"And?" he insisted.

Better to lose him now, she rationalized. He was only staying for the Rod, anyway, and if he left, she wouldn't have to worry about the next competition. About losing in front of him again.

"Instead," she finished, "I set him free and he almost killed me. He *would* have killed me if not for Bianka. She pulled him off me and he turned on her. Then, of course, he turned on everyone else. More Harpies were lost that day than any other day in our history. Even during the Great Turf Wars, when we battled other species."

Strider frowned. "If he hurt so many, why isn't *he* blamed for what happened? No one looked at *him* with hate in their eyes. No one went for *his* throat."

That was his reaction? Why hadn't he run? "Juliette had him contained. I unleashed him. Had I stayed away, he wouldn't have had the chance to do anything."

"All right, then answer me this. If he's so dangerous, why has Juliette kept him around?"

"A Harpy will forgive her consort for almost anything," she grumbled.

A moment of silence. "What is Juliette's consort, anyway?" he asked, opting not to comment on her "forgive almost anything" revelation. Why? She'd just given him an eternal hall pass. "Not a human, that's for sure."

"I don't know what he is. I'd never encountered anyone like him, and haven't since."

His lips pursed. "So you didn't sleep with him?"

"I was fourteen. What do you think?" At his blank look, she scowled. "Wait. Don't answer that."

"Gods, you're huffy. I know you didn't sleep with him. I just wanted to hear you say so." He traced a fingertip along her jaw, gentle, so gentle. "And thank you. For the truth this time."

Do not melt. He hadn't exactly declared himself. "Thank you? That's all you have to say to me?"

"Yeah. What? Did you expect a limerick?"

No. She'd expected a lecture and a goodbye. "Because of what I did, they named me Kaia the Disappointment." There. Now he knew everything. Now he knew the person he'd put his trust and faith in—well, sort of—might not be able to deliver.

"What is it with Harpies and name-calling?" he asked, again surprising her.

Every time someone called her KtD, she died a little inside, but Strider acted as if it were no big deal. She didn't know whether to laugh or to cry. "I wouldn't worry about us and our name-calling. We haven't given you one yet."

Something dangerous flickered in his eyes, there one moment, gone the next. "Like I care what you call me." His voice was flat, emotionless, offering no hint as to what she'd seen.

He was *such* an asshole sometimes. *Well, I'll see your "don't care" and raise you a "what do you think about this?"* "Just so you know, we call Paris the Sexorcist."

Strider's nostrils flared as he sucked in a sharp breath. Silence gripped them for so long, she started to feel guilty. Then he said stiffly, "You've earned your first payment." He twisted the cap off the water, slid a warm hand under her neck and lifted. Her lips met the cold cascade of liquid and she forgot all about the guilt.

She gulped like crazy, and gods, each drop tasted better than the last. When she finished, Strider crunched the plastic and tossed it over his shoulder. He eased her back down and released her. She pursed her lips to stop herself from begging for more contact.

He leaned toward the nightstand and claimed a section of the hamburger he'd already cut into fours. Her stomach churned, growled.

"Guess I don't have to ask if you're hungry," he remarked with a grin.

Em-barr-ass-ing, but at least he'd lost that emotionless edge and was still determined to talk with her. A miracle of miracles. She wouldn't complain again.

"If you want this, you'll have to tell me if you honestly think you can win the next competition. Not to mention the next and the next. Because, after this last round, I like the thought of stealing the Rod more and more."

There was a trace of remorse in his voice, and she knew bone-deep that he meant to steal the Paring Rod no matter what she said. If he could. What she didn't know, however, was why he cared about her opinion concerning the next of the games right now.

He must have read the question in her eyes because he said gruffly, "I don't want you hurt like this again."

An ache bloomed in her chest. She would answer him. Not for the hamburger, but because of his concern. "I—" Shit. Honestly? She'd thought she would be able to win round one, that knowing the other teams would come after her would give her an advantage. Yet they had converged on her and she'd been helpless.

Next time, they would make another play for her, for every member of her team. There was just no way around it. And she couldn't whine about fairness because, had the situation been reversed, she would have done the same thing to whoever had hurt her family.

Family. The single word echoed in her mind, and she

remembered Taliyah's doubt. All her life, she'd only ever wanted to be admired. Loved. Respected. All her life, she'd only ever let everyone down. She *was* Kaia the Disappointment.

"I'm sorry I lost," she whispered.

His expression gentled, and his fingers found their way back to her brow, caressing. "You didn't let me down. No one could have pulled a victory out of their hat with that kind of opposition."

Comforting, but deep down she knew *he* would have found a way. He always did.

"You worried me, though," he added, the gruffness returning. "I won't lie about that."

Spoken like a true consort, and longing filled her. She wanted that, wanted him. Now, always. So. For him, she *would* find a way. "Yes," she finally answered. "I can win the next competition."

Cold, hard, merciless. That's how she would have to be. And she would. She would prove her worth, as she'd always wanted to do. No one would stop her.

The assassin-like thoughts were ruined when she yawned.

Strider fed her the hamburger, then asked her inane, easily answered questions so that she could have the shake as payment. When she finished, he said, "Rest now. I've got big plans for you later."

Her gaze snapped to the apex of his thighs, to the semi-erection he currently sported.

A laugh boomed from him. "Dirty-minded Harpy."

"You said big. I just assumed..." Hoped...

"Sleep," he ordered, grinning.

"Well, was that what you meant or not?" Her eyelids fluttered closed, but she was grinning, too.

"You'll just have to wait and find out."

CHAPTER FOURTEEN

THERE WAS A SLIGHT CHANCE William had kinda sorta perhaps gone slightly a wee bit too far. He would, of course, be the first to admit he *might* have made the tiniest of mistakes. Mistake or not—mostly not—he couldn't be held responsible, he thought as he kicked his way through what was left of Gilly's parents.

Bottom line: they'd asked for it. *Literally* asked for it. While he'd "worked," jamming out to "Scotty Doesn't Know" by Lustra, one of his favorite songs because he felt like the lyrics epitomized his life, he'd given his targets adrenaline injections, preventing them from passing out. Of course, he'd also torqued their veins, preventing them from bleeding out.

Fainting and blood loss ruined a good torturing every damn time.

Toward the end, when they'd realized there was no hope for survival, the begging had commenced. Only after they'd confessed to their sins, infuriating him beyond all reason as he learned that the abuse he'd imagined had not come close to the full truth, that Gilly had endured far worse, had he ended them. He almost wished he hadn't. Would have been nice to stretch out the session for a few more days. Oh, well.

Now he had some cleaning up to do.

William turned a full circle, surveying the carnage and trying to decide where to begin. Maybe he should just walk away. There was just too much to do. Then he recalled the way humans liked to freak out, how news stations liked to blast "psychopath on the loose" stories, and figured word would reach Gilly. Not that he wanted to keep her in the dark about what had happened. He'd tell her. One day. In the far future. When she was older. Like…fifty, maybe.

After everything these people—no, these monsters—had done to her, she wouldn't be upset. How could she be? They'd damaged her in the worst of ways when she'd been too young and weak to protect herself. He'd simply returned the favor.

His stomach churned as a thought occurred to him. Maybe she would have liked to kill them herself. To deliver her own vengeance, find closure, that sort of thing. Or, what if he had this all wrong and she had wanted them left alone? Humans were so particular about lines you could and couldn't cross, and gods forbid if you dared leap over one. You were forever labeled wicked and fiendish.

Like William's long-ago good buddy Vlad the Impaler. Talk about getting a bad rap. Behead a few thousand of your enemies, spear their bodies on pikes and display them for the world to see and boom, you were "evil." It was ridiculous!

To humans, torture and death weren't simply a part of the circle of life. The torturing was frowned upon, considered inhumane, and the death of a family member was a reason to mourn. They didn't understand the soul carried on in some capacity or another, that might equaled right, and weakness invited the wrath of your rivals.

"What in all hell did you do?" a male voice suddenly gasped out from behind him.

William spun—and found himself facing a very pale Kane. "What are you doing here? In fact, how'd you get here?"

Kane's hazel eyes never strayed from the wreckage. "I

asked the Fates to send me to you," he said distractedly. "How many people did you take out in here? A hundred?"

"What were you doing with the Fates? No one gets to see them. And why the hell seek *me*?"

"They summoned me, and we'll get to that." He pointed to something on the floor. "What is *that*?"

William didn't bother to look. "Does it matter? Grab a trash bag and start chucking." Why had the Fates summoned Kane? The second the question formed, William dismissed it. He didn't really care. "We've got a lot to do and not a lot of time to do it."

Recruiting the keeper of Disaster wouldn't have been his first choice—they'd never really hung out. And besides, Kane attracted the kind of trouble he'd do best to avoid, for a while at least—but William wasn't going to complain.

"Who are—were—these people?"

"Names are so last season, don't you think? All you need to know is that they offended me."

"Offended you," Kane echoed, still unmoving.

"Yeah."

Kane met his stare. "Their names wouldn't happen to be Gilly's Parents, would they? Because, the way I hear it, you were jonesing for a piece of them. Several pieces, it seems." There was no condemnation in his tone, only acceptance.

The lack of condemnation didn't matter. Never confirm nor deny something you've done, but always threaten those who question you. That had always been William's motto. "You tell anyone about this and I'll personally ensure your pancreas receives the same treatment."

Kane didn't piss his pants in fear. Just blinked over at him.

"Why were you with the Fates, anyway?" He still didn't

care, but he would have discussed something as boring as the weather if it meant changing the subject.

Kane shook his head, those brown, black and gold locks swaying against his cheeks. Without a word, he stomped off to the kitchen. He returned a short while later, two Hefty bags in hand. He gave one to William.

"Thanks."

Quiet, they worked side by side for half an hour.

Kane ruined it with a sigh. "So you asked about the Fates."

"I also asked why you came to see me in particular. I've already lost interest."

"Well, find it again. You'll want to hear this, since it will affect you and all."

Smart move, offering a tidbit of information to entice him. William often used the same tactic. "Spill already."

"They told me...they told me—" Kane released one end of his bag and scrubbed his weary face. "They told me I'd start the Apocalypse."

A nasty little word, *Apocalypse*. William paused. "They what now?"

"You heard me." His hand fell to the collar of his shirt and he jerked at the material. "I'm not gonna repeat myself."

"You're Disaster, so it makes sense, but there's no way you could—" Every muscle in William's body suddenly stiffened as a thought occurred to him. "Oh, hell, no. You will not sleep with her, do you hear me?"

Confusion furrowed Kane's brow. "Sleep with who?"

He didn't need this. "Why did you have the hags send you here, to me?" Each word was more clipped than the last.

"Because I hear you're tight with Lucifer or something. That you created the Four Horsemen. And since those horsemen play a huge role in the end of the world, I just assumed—what? Why do you look like you're about to vomit?"

This was bad. Bad, bad, bad. If the Fates had told Kane he'd start the Apocalypse, then he'd start the Apocalypse. But the fact that Kane had then thought to visit William… that meant the Apocalypse might start sooner than anyone realized. "I am not tight with Lucifer. Would a homie have torn my arm from its socket when I paid a visit to his little underground spa? Huh, huh? No!"

"No, but a brother might. Sibling rivalry, and all that."

"He's not my brother!" The lie slipped out easily, automatically, just as it had slipped out for most of his existence. But this was a Lord of the Underworld. Like he had room to judge. "Fine. He's my brother." And oh, did the admission grate. Sibling rivalry did not begin to explain the hatred between them. "What of it?"

Okay, wait a sec. He'd just realized something. The Harpies were descendants of Lucifer. Lucifer was his brother. Therefore William's little crush on Kaia was—

Fucking gross! The words blasted through him, and he shuddered. Kaia was just going to have to live without the bliss of this touch.

Damn it! His brother ruined *all* his fun.

An overhead lightbulb shorted out, golden sparks spraying around Kane. He paid them no heed. "Nothing. I'm just curious. Are the horsemen good or bad? On our side or someone else's?"

"Don't know." Except that he did.

"Fine. Let's try this another way. You mentioned something about a woman…about me sleeping with her…"

No reaction. "So?"

"So who am I not supposed to sleep with, oh, Prince of Darkness?"

Yep. Sooner than anyone realized. "The only female horseman," he grumbled, something constricting in his chest. "Or horsewoman. Whatever. They don't really concern themselves with gender down there."

"Okay, I'm confused."

William stalked to the one clean recliner in the room and plopped down. How much of a pussy would he be if he put his head between his legs? Then again, he'd be an even bigger pussy if he hyperventilated. "Here it is, flat out. Lucifer and I have different mothers, but we share the same father. Hades."

"Wait. I thought Hades and Lucifer were brothers."

"So do a lot of people, because the pair of them are so fond of spreading the rumor. But here's another big surprise—*they're both liars*. Anyway, you want to hear the rest or should I let you finish telling me everything you don't know?"

Kane's eyes narrowed to slits but he waved a hand through the air.

"I didn't like living down there." Understatement. It had been hell. Ha. William had just made a funny. "I found a way to purge some of the darkness from inside me, and thus the Four Horsemen were created."

"How do I not know this? My demon lived down there, too."

"Hello, Disaster existed on Lucifer's side. We had a little trouble sharing and had to divide the space into different realms. Luci took the fire and the demons, blah, blah, blah and I took purgatory and the souls. Although, his minions would sneak in and steal from me, but I've forgiven him for that." Forgiveness in the form of a curse, he thought with a grin. One Luci would never be able to break.

"What does this have to do with me?" Kane asked.

"I'm getting to that." *What to tell, what to tell.* Hades had chosen to shack up on Lucifer's side. Apparently he viewed William as an embarrassment who lacked a truly "evil" soul.

First, rubbish. No one was more evil than William. Look at what he'd done to these humans. And he wasn't sorry! Second, there was nothing wrong with wanting to break from family tradition and be your own person.

You're digressing. When the Greeks had taken over the heavens, they'd imprisoned the Titans, and Hades, who had helped Zeus claim the throne, was deemed uncontrollable and imprisoned, too. William had used the heavenly distraction to his advantage and finally made his escape.

Not wanting to war for the underworld throne, wanting it all for himself, Lucifer had helped him.

William had spent many glorious centuries after that screwing anything that moved. Even Hera, Zeus's beloved queen. Of course, Zeus ultimately caught him with his pants down, and before he could jump out a heavenly window, William had found himself cursed and locked in yet another prison.

Now he was free, and he could flash to and from different locations once again. Life was sweet!

"William?"

He blinked. "What?"

"You were about to tell me how this has anything to do with me."

"No, I wasn't."

"Damn it, tell me why you think I'm going to sleep with one of your freaking offspring," Kane demanded with a shudder. "'Cause that's just gross. I'm already vomiting in my mouth."

He rested his elbows on his knees and glared. Deep breath in. "For you to start the Apocalypse, you'd have to help free a horseman. And the only reason I can think of for you to help set one of those bastards free is because you'd fallen in love. You're not into men, so that leaves my girl. And the only reason you'd fall in love with her was because you'd slept with her." Deep breath out.

Kane snorted. "What, her girl parts are laced with crack?"

"Basically, yes," he said, deadpan.

At last Kane lost his air of disbelief. "Forewarned is forearmed. I won't visit hell. So, problem solved."

"I like where your head's at, even if it's in Stupid World."

"Hey—"

"Listen. The Fates are not kind. They didn't drop you here out of the goodness of their hearts. They don't have hearts. They saw you begin the Apocalypse, and so they started arranging the dominos in a line. You will now face temptation on every corner and somehow, someway, they will get you into hell."

Before Kane could form a reply, something busted through the window, shattering the glass, rolling between them. They looked at it, then at each other. A grenade.

"Oh, shit," William said, jumping to his feet.

"Fire in the hole," Kane shouted, reaching for him.

They were too late. *Boom!*

Fire licked over him—and about a thousand shards of wood and rock—as intense air pressure sent him flying. Up, up he flew. Down, down he fell. When he landed, he landed on his head, cracking his skull. Kane smashed on top of him, crushing him. The warrior didn't get back up.

Damned Disaster. William knew exactly where to lay the blame for this.

"You...okay...man?" He managed to work the question out of his raw throat.

Something hard slammed into his temple, and darkness swallowed him in one tasty bite. He knew nothing more.

WILLIAM...FLOATED. A second after the thought formed, something cold and hard pressed against his razored back.

Wheels began squeaking, little bumps up and down shooting fire through him, and he realized he'd been laid flat on a gurney, someone carting him away. *Do not groan. Do not cringe.*

"This one looks dead," a masculine voice said. It was unfamiliar. Fiftyish. With the raspy quality of a smoker.

"No, sir. Not yet." Another male, this one young, probably early twenties. "But if you think he's bad, you should see the other one. The demon."

"Now that just won't do. I need them both alive."

"But, sir—"

"Do not question me, son. Do whatever it takes, but keep both these creatures alive."

A pause, an audible gulp. "This one isn't a demon, though. We should—"

"I don't care what the hell he is. He was with the other one inside that bloodbath. He deserves what he gets."

No pause this time. "Yes, sir. I agree, sir."

The gurney hit another bump, a bigger bump, knocking William's head a second time. Just as before, there was no stopping the darkness.

Beep. Beep. Beep.

The slow, rhythmic beep blended with the sound of rushing footsteps and frantic breaths. William blinked open his eyes, and gods, that hurt. It was like he had splinters under his lids and each of those sharp little pieces of wood had scraped at his corneas. When he was finally able to focus, he frowned.

A thick layer of film coated the room and everyone in it. People were rushing all around him, but he couldn't make out their features.

"We're losing him!" someone—a female—shouted.

"His demon—"

"I know! I'm doing my best, but that may not be good enough."

They were talking about Kane. About losing... William tried to raise his arms. He would help save the warrior. Only his wrists were bound to his bed, and he didn't have the strength to break free.

What the hell?

"Doctor, this one's waking up."

"Damn it, I'm not ready to deal with him. Give him another ten cc's. He'll keep until I get this one out of the danger zone."

Something sharp jabbed at his shoulder, and his mind suddenly spun out of control.

"——ALL RIGHT, BIG BOY?"

William fought his way out of the darkness and immediately regretted it. The pain! He ached all over. His skin felt charred, his bones as smooth as pudding and just as soft.

"That's the way. Just a little more."

His lashes parted. For a moment, the world spun. But soon, everything righted itself and he found his gaze settling on a pretty female. Fatigue had drawn her delicate features taut. She wore a white lab coat and had a stethoscope anchored around the back of her neck. Her blond hair was pulled back in a ponytail, and a pair of wire rims sat on her nose.

"You're probably wondering who I am and why you're here."

That would be a big, fat affirmative, though he could guess the answer. The Hunters had made their next move. He remembered hearing the hate in the voices of "sir" and company when they'd discussed the demons.

William's gaze moved to his bound wrists, his bound ankles. They hadn't trusted sturdy rope, but had used thick, heavy chains. Next he took stock of his injuries, and he realized only a miracle was keeping him in one piece. He felt like a box full of tattered Christmas ribbons, his flesh so ripped he could see the equally ripped muscle underneath.

"Well?" the woman prompted.

"Don't care." He had to unlock his jaw to speak, causing his temples to throb. "The man..." No other words would form, his throat simply too raw.

"He's alive," she answered, knowing what he desired.

Thank gods. Relief speared him. He could deal with anything else she said.

"I didn't want to be the one to tell you this, but you have a right to know. Your friend...he's currently being transported to the deepest pits of hell."

Except that.

CHAPTER FIFTEEN

KAIA HAD KNOWN STRIDER possessed a brutal streak, and she'd thought she liked that about him. Now, she was pretty sure that streak was going to get him killed. Because she was freaking going to murder him! Painfully. After she drank him dry, that is.

His "big plans" for her? More blood-drinking. Or so she assumed. An entire day had passed since she'd woken from her nap, but that was *all* he'd let her do.

Of course, she had to ensure he regretted his choice. Had to show him the consequences of teasing her into thinking they'd kiss and touch and, well, make sweet, dirty love until their hearts exploded from the strain.

She didn't need more blood. Earlier her bones had snapped back into place and her cuts had woven back together. She was completely healed, utterly capable of a little ravishing, but every hour on the hour he would cut his wrist and hold the wound over her mouth. Even now, she was suckling, swallowing a delicious mouthful of his rich, warm blood now spiced with the sweetness of cinnamon.

The warmth spread, as it had every time he'd fed her like this, tickling her nerve endings, reminding her of what they *weren't* doing.

"Just a little more," he said, his voice all kinds of husky. His forearm flexed beneath her grip.

Her eyes closed as she savored his decadent flavor, her

murderous thoughts fading. Would she ever get enough of him? No, never, she decided a second later. He'd well and truly addicted her. Not just to his kisses, as she'd already realized, and not just to his blood, but to his presence. His wicked smile, his warped sense of humor.

What would she do if he left her after the games as planned?

Normally she would tell herself she'd find a way to keep him. She would pat herself on the back for her strength and cunning, and bask in the knowledge that she could do anything she wished. Having just survived the ass-beating of a lifetime, she wasn't quite so optimistic. Besides, what hope she *did* have had to be directed at the coming games.

So, by gods, she would hoard a thousand different memories of Strider. Just in case. They'd keep her company during the long, cold winters alone, and sleep beside her during hot, sultry summer nights. No matter where he was or who he was with, she would never be without him.

In order to make those memories, she first had to seduce him. Soon. Forget revenge. Even now her body hummed for him, desperate for deeper contact. If only he would let her drink from his jugular…

She'd asked, repeatedly, and he'd said no, repeatedly. Did he not trust her? Or did he not trust himself? She imagined urging him to the mattress and splaying herself on top of him. Her breasts would mesh into his chest and her core would settle over his straining erection. And yes, he would have an erection. She would make sure of it.

She would rub herself against him as she drank from him. He would moan, his hands settling on her ass to move her faster, harder against him. Soon that wouldn't be enough, for either of them, and he would rip at her clothes. She would rip at his. They would be naked and—

Before she could swallow another mouthful of his

blood, he jerked away, removing her fangs from his vein and severing all contact. "Enough," he said, panting. "You're medicated properly now."

She'd been writhing on the bed, she realized, panting herself. Had been angling toward him, her legs parting, her core desperate for him. Gods, she was already wet, aching.

He stood, walked away. He stopped and turned. Then he faced her, propping himself against the TV stand. She sat up, trembling and hot, enjoying her first full view of him since she'd exited the bathroom a few minutes ago, having showered and changed into the fresh clothes Bianka had brought her. At that time, he'd already positioned himself at the edge of the mattress and had merely motioned her over.

She'd thought…hoped…but no. She'd reached him and rather than throw her down and conquer Kaialand, he'd tossed her down and fed her again.

As she studied him, she lost her breath. His pale hair shagged around his fallen angel face. His lips were red, as if he'd chewed them. A lot. He wore a black T-shirt that read I Heart William.

"William gave it to me," he said with a shrug, noticing where her gaze had lingered.

Just hearing William's name made her snicker inside. The dark-haired charmer had a crush on her, and she couldn't wait until he realized why she'd always turned him down. She'd probably laugh so hard she'd pee herself!

Anyway, she didn't care about Strider's T-shirt, but about the pecs underneath it. They were hard and well-defined, his nipples slightly puckered—definitely lickable. At the shirt's hem, she could see the bulge of his weapons, tucked into dark denim. That denim also covered the bulge of something else she'd really like to see, but whatever.

With only the slightest twinge in her side, she pushed

to her feet. "I need you to be brutally honest right now," she said.

Wariness cloaked his features. "Okay."

"How pretty do I look?"

His gaze dropped, following the line of her body. She wore a red lace halter dress that veed in the middle, all the way to her navel. The hem stopped just below the curve of her ass.

Strider's pupils did that expanding thing, almost always a prelude to touching. "You need to put on a pair of pants." His voice was a croak. And he did not move toward her.

This was one of those times when "almost" sucked the big one. "Duh. As if I'd go out like this. I've got a pair... right..." She looked around. "There." She stalked to the nightstand and lifted the "pants" in question. A scrap of red lace spandex that wouldn't fall below her dress.

With a quick step, step, tug, she shimmied into the material and once again faced off with her consort.

His mouth hung open. "We were just sitting on the bed, together, and you were just drinking from me, your mouth on my skin, and *you didn't have any panties on?*"

"You mean you didn't look?" she said with a pout. No wonder he'd left her so easily.

"No. I wouldn't let myself."

"Why?"

"Damn it, Kaia," he said, ignoring her. "You can't just go around pantiless."

"Which is why I just pulled on a pair. Were you not watching?"

His eyes narrowed to tiny slits. "You said pants. That you were putting on a pair of pants."

"Yeah. *Under*pants."

"Just..." He popped his jaw and extended his arm in her direction, waving his fingers up and down her body. "Where are you going to hide weapons in that thing?"

"Strider, please. Give me and my girls some credit." She spread the deep V, revealing her braless breasts, her nipples flushed and beaded. Small, thin blades were strapped to her sides, just under her armpits. "We've been doing this since well before puberty."

"Sweet Jesus." A strangled sound left him as she adjusted her dress back into place, and she fought a grin. The more he resisted her, the more he was going to find himself the recipient of these little peep shows.

"Come on," he said, voice husky once again.

She closed the distance and twined her fingers with his, happy with the contact. "Want to make out?"

"Sweet Jesus," he repeated. Little beads of sweat popped up on his brow. "We've got plans. Remember? Big plans. We have to be somewhere."

So blood-drinking hadn't been the only thing on his agenda. But then, sex clearly hadn't been added. "Where're we going?" she asked, careful to cut the disappointment from her voice.

"You'll find out." After a quick perimeter check, he tugged her into the cool night air. First thing she realized was that they were still in Wisconsin. She hadn't looked and she hadn't asked. The moon was hidden behind clouds, casting pink and violet shadows in every direction. Snow covered the ground, trees stretching up...up...

"You cold?" Strider asked.

"Nah. This is nothing." Besides, body heat radiated from him, enveloping her. "Any hint of Harpy or Hunter activity since I woke up?" Or hell, even for the two days she'd been down.

"No. We hid you pretty well."

Even still, she kept her guard up. They walked several blocks before he stopped in front of a pickup and released her. Only took him three minutes and eighteen seconds to break in and gun the engine. She did *not* mention that she could have done it in two. His demon might view that as a challenge.

She merely said, "Good job," as he threw the truck into gear and sped down the road. "Now, tell me where we're going because I do not like surprises. Unless they involve a man waiting naked in my bed," she added just to taunt him.

His grip tightened on the wheel and his knuckles leached of color. "I talked to your sister. Taliyah. We've got two days to get you ready for the next competition."

Wait just a sec. "You're going to *train* me?" He thought she was so terrible a fighter she needed a few pointers? Well, why not? she thought with a bitter, inner laugh. She'd *disappointed* him with her loss, and she had no one but herself to blame. That didn't matter. Shock and hurt blasted her like poisoned darts. This was not the kind of memory she'd hoped to hoard.

"No, of course not," he said, and she began to relax. Then he added, "*I'm* not going to train you."

She wanted to rant and rail at his lack of trust and support. She'd vowed to win the next round, hadn't she? Yes, yes, she had. Her mind might have been hazed by pain, but she remembered that.

Kaia held her tongue, though. Victory was as important to Strider as it was to her. He wasn't doing this to be cruel. But damn it, even knowing why he'd set this into motion, the hurt escalated inside her.

I'm good enough just the way I am. A plaintive plea in her head. "Why won't you do the training?" she asked. Gods, was that whiny voice *hers?*

There was a heavy pause before he admitted, "My demon."

What did the pause mean? He was lying? No, she thought next. He wasn't lying. But she doubted his demon was the only reason. "And you're afraid training with me will challenge him?"

"Yeah. It's happened before."

He'd once told her that everything was a challenge with her and that was one of the reasons they couldn't be together. She'd thought he would soon come to see the merit in her challenges. After all, he experienced pleasure every time he won, and if he won multiple times a day because of her...

So far, that mind-set had only backfired on her. He hated the pain that accompanied defeat so much, he viewed every competitor as a threat. The more she pushed him, the more he pushed away from her.

That has to change. So. Okay. She would give him what he wanted, she decided. Peace. Smooth sailing. Utter tranquility. She'd be so easy to be with, he'd have more fun watching grass grow. Maybe then he'd take her to bed.

Why couldn't he like her for the girl she was, though?

Why couldn't anyone?

"Fine," she said on a sigh, hating herself for throwing a pity party. He was with her. He hadn't taken off. Hadn't searched for the Rod while she was too weak to stop him. "That's fine. I'll train with whoever you want."

The truck wound down the city streets, lights flashing over the windshield every few seconds. Kaia propped her booted feet on the dash and leaned as far back as her seat would allow. Her dress hiked up her thighs, revealing the edge of her panties.

He kept his gaze on the road. "I didn't expect you to agree with my plan."

Did he sound...disappointed? Nah. Just wishful thinking on her part. "I aim to please."

"I—" He smashed his lips in a mulish line, shook his head. She didn't press for more—as her new plan for peace dictated—and he didn't offer it. Several minutes ticked by in utter silence. Then, "Why don't I have a nickname?"

That clearly wasn't what he'd wanted to discuss, but she could roll. Smooth sailing, she reminded herself. "Well, you haven't earned one."

"So what do I have to do to earn one?"

"Don't know. Everyone's different. It's a we-know-it-when-we-see-it kind of thing."

Another bout of silence ensued, this one so tense and heavy she couldn't have hacked through it with a sword and chain saw. She had no idea what was swirling through his head.

"I thought you didn't care what we called you," she said, just to shatter the tension.

"I don't," he gritted out. "I was just curious."

"Okay."

"Again with the agreeable attitude. Are you more injured than I realized?"

She busied herself with plucking at her dress, trying not to let the comment get to her. "I'm not always a pain in the ass, you know."

"Stop messing with your clothes," he growled.

She froze, not even daring to breathe. He'd still not glanced her way, yet he'd known what she was doing? He was *that* aware of her?

"Okay. Consider it done." Smooth sailing was already paying off. Fighting a grin, she settled deeper into the seat and dropped her feet onto the floorboard.

About an hour from civilization, they pulled off the highway and into the parking lot of a dilapidated shack sporting a blinking neon sign that read Crazy Abel's. There were a handful of other cars there and two big burly guys stumbling from the front door.

"A bar?" she asked, trying not to pout. "A *human* bar?"

"You get to play before you pay."

Really? Forget pouting. Excitement poured through her. "You should have told me. I would have worn my slutty outfit."

His narrowed gaze swept over her, lingering on her cleavage. He parked—nearly sideswiping another car—and she jumped out, halfway to the entrance before he'd even opened his door. She passed the still stumbling humans, grimacing at the smell of cheap beer and cigarettes. They whistled at her and changed directions to follow her.

"How much?" one asked.

Oh, no, he didn't. She spun around, hands on her hips, teeth bared in a scowl. "What did you say?"

"We'll pay the price, whatever it is, we swear," the other said. "After." Both snickered, then the first patted the second on the back in a job well done, as if he'd just negotiated the deal of a lifetime.

Before she could reply, Strider stalked over and punched them both in the back of the head. At the same time. They propelled forward, but he caught them by the hair before they could hit the ground, used his knees to slam into the back of theirs, and forced them both to kneel before her.

"Apologize," he commanded, and there was so much darkness in his voice she could almost smell the fire and brimstone. "Now."

Kaia's heart fluttered. The men obeyed, babbling and crying. Strider lifted one and tossed him. The human went soaring and crashed into a car, the alarm suddenly screeching. The second man joined him a moment later.

"Thanks," she said, fighting the urge to melt into a shivery puddle at his feet.

"My pleasure."

They entered the bar side by side.

THE WOMAN WAS GOING TO SLAY him with that killer body of hers. Delicious curves were wrapped in a swath of material that might not pass for a bathing suit in some countries. Her skin was luminous, but lacking its multihued shimmer. She must have covered herself with total-body makeup. Not that he'd complain.

Anything that would stop other men from desiring her had his stamp of approval.

Who was he kidding? Men not desire her? That was never going to happen. No matter what she did to her skin, no matter what she wore, men would *always* desire her. The knowledge pissed him off—and filled him with pride.

She considered *Strider* her consort. No one else.

Resisting her was becoming harder. And harder. Literally.

"Hey, who is—Anya? Gideon? Amun? And, like, a thousand others." Kaia had to shout to be heard over the blaring music. She peered up at him with wide silver-gold eyes, soft with an emotion he couldn't name. "How did you get all of them here?"

A man could lose himself in those fathomless depths. "I asked and Lucien flashed." More like he'd demanded and Lucien had dragged his feet. But who cared about details? "They're only here for the night, though."

"Sweet! One night, I can love them. Two, and I always want to kill them."

"Just don't mention," he lowered his voice, "first prize. Okay?" They'd be all over his case about it. What he'd done with the Cloak of Invisibility would be thrown in his face. His motives would be questioned. His smarts. They'd want to stay, want to search for the Paring Rod, steal it.

He and Sabin had already chatted. The others needed to guard the two artifacts they already had. They needed to protect the fortress in Buda. They needed to remain vigilant against Hunter attacks. If, however, the two of them failed to steal the Rod on their own before the final Harpy game kicked off, they would call for reinforcements.

Tonight, while Kaia was distracted with her training, they were going to hunt down the Eagleshields. In fact, that's what Sabin was doing right now. Peering down from the heavens, finding the seemingly unfindable. Boss man should be here any minute to drag him away.

"I won't mention anything about anything, I swear. And thank you!" A huge grin split Kaia's red-painted lips and she clapped. Then she jumped up and planted a scorching kiss on his cheek before dashing away. Her mouth burned his flesh, perhaps imprinting his every cell.

The past few days, all he'd been able to do was think about her. She'd been so pale, so still, so weak, and he'd been so desperate to help her, yet unable to do more than feed her his blood...and crave. Oh, had he craved. *Still* craved.

Something he'd realized, though, was that sleeping with her had to wait until after the games. Right now, he had to remain strong. He couldn't risk being laid flat by losing a challenge. Any challenge. Even one in the bedroom.

Once her well-being no longer depended on him, nothing would keep him out of those microscopic pants. He had to have her. Had to taste her, hear her cry his name. Hell, he planned to gorge himself on the woman, no matter the consequences. And not just once, as he'd thought to limit himself before, but over and over again.

He watched as she threw herself into Amun's arms. The warrior looked tired, and there were bruises under his eyes, but he appeared genuinely happy to see Kaia as he spun her around. Gideon, the punked-out keeper of Lies, grabbed her up and hugged her tight. She threw back her head and laughed before messing up his blue hair and tugging at his eyebrow ring. How carefree she was, how uninhibited.

How mine, he thought darkly, then forced himself to add, *for now, at least.*

Inside his head, Defeat perked up.

Oh, no, you don't. You just stay silent, you little prick. You weren't invited to this party.

A growl rang in his ears, and he recognized the sound as the war cry it was.

You want to win the Paring Rod, right? Or would you rather return to Pandora's box and rot? Because if I fail, Kaia's our only hope. And if she fails, we'll lose the artifact. If we lose the artifact, the Hunters could use it to get their hands on the box, suck you back inside. Eternally trapping you.

Silence.

Yeah. He'd thought so. There was nothing Defeat despised more than his memories of the box, the darkness and isolation. What he didn't mention was that if he managed to steal the Rod, Kaia would hate his damn guts. She'd forgive him, though, as Juliette had forgiven her man for his dark deeds. Right?

"Kye," he heard Gideon say. "I wouldn't like you to meet my hideous husband, Scar." He motioned to the black-haired stunner by his side with a wave of his hand. Since Gideon couldn't speak a word of truth without experiencing debilitating pain, he'd lied. About everything.

"Actually, the name's Scarlet," his wife replied. She was the keeper of Nightmares and when she killed a man in his dreams, he died for real. She was tall, slender and mean as hell. "And in case you're wondering, I don't have a penis."

Why couldn't I have gotten that demon? Nightmares? Talk about cool.

Defeat *harrumphed.*

You're a pain in the ass and you know it.

"I'm Kaia. Or Damn it, Kaia, as Strider likes to call me."

"I do not," Strider growled. He called her baby doll. And she was. Now where the hell was Sabin? He needed out of here *el pronto*.

Kaia ignored him. "Weren't you, like, locked in the Lords' dungeon not that long ago?" she asked Scarlet. "Too dangerous to roam free, untrustworthy, violent in the extreme, blah, blah, blah."

"Yeah. Thankfully, that's what whips this one into a frenzy," Scarlet said, motioning to Gideon with a tilt of her stubborn chin.

Gideon wiggled his dark eyebrows, and Kaia chuckled, warm and husky and...hell. Strider felt his body responding. So not a good time to sport wood.

Kaia was in good hands, he thought, especially since Gideon's were brand-new. Bastard had gotten his old ones cut off by Hunters and had been forced to regrow a pair. At the time, Strider had flipped out about the pain his friend had been forced to endure. Now, he got a good laugh out of it. Anyway, he didn't have to worry about Kaia—or lust after her, which he would continue to do if he stayed here and watched her—so he made his way to the bar, only then noticing the blonde with pink streaks in her hair and tattoos sleeving her arm. Haidee. Shit. Having her and Kaia in the same room probably wasn't a good idea.

She turned, two beers in her hands, and when she spotted him, she nodded in acknowledgment. Still she glowed—and not from pregnancy as he'd first assumed. No way she'd drink a beer if she were. Quite simply, she glowed with love, his second assumption.

Once again, there was no pang in his chest when he looked at her and he'd never been happier about that.

"You shouldn't be here," he said, then told the bartender to bring him a beer.

Hurt flashed in her eyes, quickly masked.

"I wasn't trying to be mean," he admitted. "Just trying to protect you."

Smiling sweetly, she shook her head. "Don't worry about it. Amun just returned from the heavens and there was no way I was going to be parted from him today. Especially when I might be parted from him tomorrow."

How forlorn she sounded. "Why tomorrow?"

"I don't want to talk about it," she grumbled, losing the smile.

He lifted his hand to pat her on the back, to offer comfort. Before contact, he dropped his arm to his side. Even such a token gesture from him might make her uncomfortable, and besides, he realized he shouldn't be offering.

With their violent, turbulent history, any such offering might tick Amun off. And rightly so. Strider could imagine his own reaction if, say, one of his friends had a past with Kaia—cough Paris cough—and the bastard put his hands on her. Hello, rage.

In that moment, he realized he had never truly desired Haidee as a forever after. Desired her, yes, but he'd never felt so strongly about her, or anyone really, that he couldn't pick up and walk away. Without regret. Without remorse. Well, Kaia was a maddening, life-and-death exception. For the time being. He needed her. He wanted her, and when the time was right, he would have her. End of story.

That thought alone consumed him with lust, abolishing every other emotion inside him.

Not now, damn it. I have to let her relax and train with the boys. "By the way," he said to Haidee in an attempt to distract himself. "I know you know why Amun was summoned by Cronus the other day."

"Yeah. So?" Her dejection eased, her features lighting with amusement. "I'm no longer possessed by the demon of Hate, but I still like to torment you every now and then.

Besides, I knew one of your buddies would step in and share the details."

Win.

Great. Contrary female. Now Strider had to win a battle of wills with her. But he supposed he understood why his demon leapt at this chance for victory, small though it would (hopefully) be. Accommodating as Kaia had been during the drive here, the bastard needed to feed.

"What'd he learn? And yes, we are having a prolonged conversation whether you want to or not. I'll follow you around like a puppy on a leash all damn night, if that's what it takes." If that threat didn't scare her into answering, he didn't know what would.

"Nothing." She sighed. "Amun couldn't find her—the girl now possessed by the demon of Distrust. Cronus wants him to return to the heavens tomorrow and try again. Now you have both answers. Happy?"

"A little." He'd won and tiny sparks of pleasure filled his chest. "Tell him—" Strider's eyes widened as a thought struck him. "Have him call me when Cronus is done with him and he's rested up a bit." Amun was too tired for him to burden tonight. But if anyone could find Juliette's hiding place for the Paring Rod, it was him. Damn, but Strider should have thought of that before. "I need a favor."

Haidee gulped back her beer. "You and everyone else in the world."

"Damn, girl. Learn to share."

She rolled her eyes. "That's hilarious, coming from you."

"No, it's ironic. Learn the difference. But, honestly? I'm a lost cause, too set in my ways. You, however, have a fighting chance."

She laughed and said something in reply, but a piercing shriek in the background drowned out her words. Oh, shit. Strider's eardrums knew that shriek intimately.

He wheeled around—just as a red blur flew past him, aiming for Haidee.

CHAPTER SIXTEEN

WIND RUFFLED STRIDER'S HAIR as he reached out and grabbed Kaia by the waist. He was fast, but not fast enough, and by the time he had the woman anchored over his shoulder fireman-style, both of Haidee's cheeks were claw-slashed and bleeding.

Haidee appeared too shocked to react, much less defend herself. Which wasn't like her. No one had self-protective instincts like Haidee. Either she was slipping or being without Hate had slowed her down.

"You do not touch him. You do not speak to him. Ever!" Kaia snarled in a voice layered with another being's screams, her own fury, and plumes of darkness.

"Damn it, Kaia." Strider smacked her ass. She didn't notice. She tried to twist around and accidentally kneed him in the stomach. Hard. Air gushed from his mouth, and he hunched over, almost losing her. He readjusted his grip, one hand on the back of her legs, the other on the small of her back. And damn, she was hot! Literally. Heat seeped from her, burning him.

Win?

And, there was his demon, making another appearance. Freaking great. At least the bastard wasn't quite sure how to proceed with the Harpy. *I've got her, don't I? What more do you want?*

"Kaia," Strider said. "If you don't settle down, you're going to hurt me."

To his surprise, that worked, penetrating the fog of her fury. In a blink, she settled, remaining draped over him, her palms pressed into his back, her heated breaths wafting over his shirt and slithering past the material, caressing him with molten deliciousness.

Hello again, Stridey-Monster. Thank gods the fall of her legs hid the evidence of his arousal.

Won. Defeat sighed with pleasure and that pleasure shot through him, increasing his enjoyment. An enjoyment far stronger than anything he'd experienced with Haidee.

There were several humans in the bar, watching them. He smiled sheepishly. "Women."

They nodded in understanding.

A frowning Amun rushed to Haidee's side. Haidee said, "It's nothing, baby. I swear." Still, he cupped her cheeks and the frown became a scowl. A scowl he leveled at Strider.

As the keeper of Secrets, Amun could read the thoughts of everyone around him. So Strider opened up his mind and allowed his friend inside. *Don't even think about getting back at her. This could have been a lot worse and you know it. Kaia merely scratched her up, nothing more.*

You protect what's yours and I protect what's mine, Amun signed angrily.

Kaia. His. He didn't want to analyze the thrill of delight that joined the pleasure. And he didn't need to. She *was* his. Just for a little while—another reminder.

Haidee wrapped her fingers around her man's forearm, leaving a smear of blood on his mocha-colored skin. "It's fine. I'm fine."

Kaia traced something on Strider's back, distracting him. A heart, he thought, wanting to smile.

Amun's hands began another furious bout of signing directed at him. *You think this is funny?*

"Yeah. I do. If you'll excuse us, we have a little business to attend to." Strider carted Kaia to the dance floor.

Sabin had yet to arrive, which meant there was no reason to resist. With a shrug of his shoulders, he bounced Kaia up and slid her forward. Her body pressed against his as it descended. Only, instead of placing her feet on the wooden slats, she wrapped her legs around his waist and held on tight, fitting her core against his erection.

He bit off a groan. At least her temperature had cooled, so he didn't have to worry about his cock catching on fire. He peered deeply into her eyes and the world around him faded. There was only Kaia, desire and a need to soothe the temper he had unintentionally roused in her.

He anchored his hands on the back of her thighs to keep her from falling and to prevent his friends from seeing anything they shouldn't. Anything of *his*. Her ass was definitely his.

"Let me go," she said, though her tone lacked any kind of admonishment. He didn't point out that she had a tighter hold on him than he had on her. "I'm going to kill that bitch."

"No, baby doll, you won't."

"Yes, I will." But the black faded from her eyes, leaving the decadent silver-gold he so loved.

Whoa, whoa there. Loved? Hell, no. He *liked* the color, that was all. "Where's Miss Agreeable? The girl I chauffeured over here." That small taste of Miss Agreeable should have been a slice of heaven, too, since that's what he'd always claimed to want from her. Surprisingly, he realized he preferred her this way. On edge and wild.

Maybe because his blood roared at the alluring prospect of taming her.

Another flicker of black. "Miss Agreeable is dead. You killed her when you flirted with another woman."

"If you haven't heard, dead doesn't have to mean gone forever," he teased. "Maybe she can rise from the grave."

A gasp left her. "I knew you'd like me that way." She pounded a fist into his shoulder. "I knew it!"

He laughed, unable to trap his amusement inside.

Frowning sulkily, she stilled and glared at him. "What's so funny?"

"You." Just then she was illogical and adorable, and jealous as hell. Of Haidee, and even of herself. "I just want to eat you up."

Her mouth fell open, pearly whites bared in what could only be a mix of shock and hope. "What?"

Now that he had her attention... He moved his hands just under her thighs, lifting and balancing her on the tip of his straining erection. "You want to tell me what just happened? With Haidee?"

Expression closing off, she stared just over his shoulder. And yet, she nibbled on her bottom lip as he arched his hips forward, rubbing against her. "No. I don't."

"Do it anyway."

He rubbed again. She nibbled harder. Too much, he thought. Too much for this crowded room. He held her steady.

"Tell me," he said.

There was a pause. Then a pouty, "You like her more than you like me."

She'd faced a clan of vengeful Harpies without a single complaint, but the thought of him with someone else was more than she could tolerate. That stroked his ego, yeah, but he didn't like that he'd hurt her. "No, baby doll, I don't."

"Yes, you do. You told me so."

"Then I was delusional. And really, really dumb. I'm very sorry for that." The truth, all of it. He'd only *thought* he'd wanted Haidee in a romantic sense, had gotten snagged by the challenge of winning the heart of an enemy.

After he'd won her, he would have walked away from her without any regrets. Easy. Kaia, though, he'd treated abominably—maybe because he'd sensed, deep down, that he would not be able to walk away from her so easily.

"I like you. A lot."

Her chin lifted, that too-delightful stubborn streak kicking in. "But I slept with Paris and you can never forget that."

He *had* pushed that fact in her face over and over again, hadn't he? Stupid of him. While the knowledge had bothered him before—because yeah, he'd been a little jealous and hurt himself since she'd picked Paris first—it seemed insignificant right now.

How many women had Strider been with over the years? How many after Kaia had declared herself to him? Any one of those women could have been a friend of hers.

"News flash," he said, hoping to soothe the hurt he'd caused, "half the people in this room have slept with Paris."

Hope bloomed, the gold consuming her eyes, overshadowing even the silver, only to swiftly wither and die. "You'll never be able to get over it. Not really. Not with me."

Okay, a little damage control was in order. "Allow me to iron this out completely. Am I jealous? Yes. Are you going to do it again? Hell, no. Not if you like him breathing. Am I worried about *our* first time because of him? Yes. What if I'm not as good? But do I cast stones about what happened? No. You're talking to a borderline manwhore, Kaia. Like I really have room to judge."

"You're jealous?" The lustrous gleam of her skin suddenly peeked past her makeup as her body temperature rose.

His heart galloped into an unsteady rhythm and his mouth watered. A taste, soon, very soon. He had to have one. "Yes. And here's another news flash." His words were slightly slurred, as if he were drunk on desire. "I'm possessive. That's not going to change."

"I don't want that to change. I like that about you."

"Good." The few times he'd tried the relationship thing, that possessiveness of his had gotten old, fast.

"And I—" She frowned, the gleam dimming just as her hope had. "You're just saying all of this because you expect me to win the Paring Rod for you."

Wrong as she was, he deserved the doubt, he really did. Plus, he couldn't stop a wave of guilt from sweeping through him. No matter what he next said, no matter whether she believed him now, she would think he'd lied when he actually did steal that damn Rod.

Worry later. "Does the Rod have sexy red hair and a body that wraps around me just right?"

Her sexy lips puckered. "No."

So kissable… "Then I'm pretty sure I like you for being you. I mean, what's not to like?"

"True," she said, but she didn't relax against him. "I *am* pretty awesome."

"Better than pretty."

"I know. And no one can ever convince me otherwise. No matter how hard he tries." A direct hit, reminding him of all the times he'd pricked at her pride to save himself from craving her.

Not that it had ever worked.

Defeat perked up and Strider gave him a mental shove into a darkened corner. He didn't want the demon's interference right now. This was between him and Kaia.

"I'm sorry I ever said otherwise," he added sincerely. "Clearly I was suffering from some kind of brain injury."

"I suspected." Her expression softened, but still she

didn't cave. "So what do you like about me besides my amazing hair and body? Because last time we talked about this, you said I was too much trouble. You said I challenged you at every turn and you didn't want the hassle of dealing with me."

"Are you going to throw everything I've ever said in my face each time we argue?"

"Absolutely." She admitted it freely, with no hesitation.

"Okay. Just checking." And here was a shocker. He liked that. You had to use every weapon at your disposal to win a fight, and she wielded his past stupidity like a razor. She cut him with it, at the same time teaching him how to soothe *her* wounds.

"Well?"

"You *are* a challenge at every turn, there's no denying that." She stiffened, and he hurried on. "But I'm finding that I don't mind."

Anger flashed, a stormy silver with no hint of gold. "You don't *mind?* Well, aren't I a lucky girl? If one of your past girlfriends ever told you that you have a way with words, she was lying."

Kaia unhooked her ankles and dropped her legs. He didn't release her, though. He hefted her back up, forcing her to remain in place. Flush against him, rubbing just right without stimulating too much.

"Look," he said. "You amuse the hell out of me. You excite me. And I'm finding that what I thought I wouldn't like about you is actually my favorite part. Besides, I know I'm no picnic in the park, either."

She'd begun to soften. At the last little bit, she flashed her pearly whites in a grimace. "You're just digging a deeper hole, you big moron."

"Come on, baby doll." He spread his fingers, covering more ground as he angled toward the greatest rollercoaster ride on earth. "I'm new at being a consort. Give me some wiggle room."

Yeah, he knew it was funny that he was asking for emotional wiggle room when he wouldn't let her move physically, but come on. He was a guy. This was par for the course. But then she realized what he said and froze, not even seeming to breathe.

Suddenly utter vulnerability radiated from her. "Is that an admission that you're mine?" she asked.

Was it? "Yes," he said as realization struck. "For the next few weeks I'll be the best damn consort you've ever had the pleasure of meeting. After that, I can't promise. I've never done the long haul, forever thing. We'll have to reevaluate, see how we feel."

A thought short-circuited his brain. What if she *couldn't* forgive him for stealing the Rod? What if that act proved to be more than "almost anything"? There would be no reevaluation because she wouldn't want anything to do with him. They would be over, done.

A sense of urgency overtook him. He had to get her to agree to have him, all of him, now. That way, later, she would have a harder time shoving him out of her life.

Not that he would want to stick around. As he'd told her, he'd never done the long haul thing before. A few months, but never more than that. And yet, just then he couldn't imagine *not* wanting Kaia. Just then he despised the thought of being without her. So, yeah, he had to get her to agree.

"Give me a chance," he beseeched. "Please."

Win? Defeat said.

Go back to your corner.

In the back of his mind, he acknowledged that the music had changed, the tempo harder, faster, but he refused to accelerate the slow grind he had going with Kaia.

Her shoulders sagged, but rather than stomp away in

disappointment because he hadn't agreed to stay forever, she flattened her hands on his chest and whispered, "That's not good enough. I wish it were, but…"

"For now, it's all I can offer." He cupped her jaw, forcing her attention to remain on his face. "I do know that I hate the thought of you with anyone else. I know you're the only woman I desire."

She started nibbling on her bottom lip again, and he almost, *almost,* replaced her teeth with his own. But not yet. Not until she agreed.

"What changed your mind?" she asked. "I mean, it certainly wasn't my mad street fighting skills since I crashed and burned at Tag."

His stomach churned as an image of her blazed through his mind. Her body limp and covered with blood. Her face swollen, her limbs mangled. Never again, he thought darkly. He would protect her.

Win?

No trying to shove Defeat away. In that regard, yes. He would accept any challenge.

Before he could respond to Kaia's question, she looked down and added, "I threw a fight for you once. Do you remember? That night with the Hunters? I challenged you to kill more than I did, and I totally could have won, but I gave you my targets."

His chest constricted, a pang of some unknown emotion lancing through him. "I remember, baby doll, and I never thanked you. I'm sorry for that."

"Well, thank-you or not, I'm not doing that again. I'm not throwing a fight for you." So gently said.

"I'm glad." Her sense of pride was as intense as his own. She hated losing, and while she didn't experience physical pain when she failed, she did experience a shitload of mental anguish.

Her own people called her Kaia the Disappointment,

for gods' sake. Because of that, she always strove to prove herself worthy. He realized that now. Knew it was the reason she'd challenged him to begin with. She'd wanted to prove she was good enough for him. And the fact that she'd purposely lost demonstrated just how deeply she desired him. He realized that, too.

As if she had anything to prove.

Still. How had he repaid her? He'd dumped on her, time and time again. Shame exploded through him, a bomb he'd built all by himself. Well, no more dumping. As long as they were together, he would treat her with the care and concern she deserved.

"You're glad?" She blinked at him, her warm, sweet breath trekking over his neck. His pulse leapt up to meet every exhalation. "But if I beat you at anything, you'll hurt."

"So you'll kiss me and make me better. Right?"

Her nails dug past his shirt and into skin. "I—I—don't know what to say."

"Say you won't purposely challenge me to something I can't hope to win."

A moment passed in silence as she considered his words. "I'll try not to, but I can't promise. Sometimes you bring out the worst in me."

Ha! He brought out the best in her. No ego check necessary. The truth was the truth, no matter how you sliced it. "Either way, we'll work it out."

"Yes, we'll work—" Slowly her eyes narrowed, her nails sinking deeper into his flesh. "Well, well. Finally I meet *Mr.* Agreeable. Are you buttering me up like a breakfast muffin just so I won't hurt Haidee?"

So suspicious, but that was the nature of the beast. They were very similar in that respect. "You can hurt her if you still want to hurt her, but then Amun will be pissed and he'll attack me. I'll have to hurt *him.*"

"Fine," she said on a sigh. "I like Amun, so I won't hurt Haidee."

"Thank you," he said through gritted teeth. She liked Amun?

She retracted one set of claws and flicked her hair over one shoulder. "So what do you like about me? You never said. Feel free to get wildly descriptive and maybe throw in some poetry. Or one of those limericks you mentioned."

Gonna make him work for it, huh? Even though she'd already decided to give him what he wanted. All the privileges of a consort, the uncertain future be damned. Oh, she hadn't said so yet, but then, she didn't have to. He knew. She was here, in his arms, demanding he romance her.

Typical Kaia. Never a dull moment, but a ton of fun. More than that, she had very nearly mastered the art of pleasing Defeat, offering little challenges here and there to feed him. Challenges Strider could win, no problem.

Win.

See? She'd done it again; she'd challenged him at something easy. But would he take this victory home with poetry? Gods, no. "Well, let's see," he began huskily. "I like your smart mouth. I like your pouty mouth. I like your potty mouth. I like your whiny mouth. I like your shrieking mouth. I like—"

"My mouth," she said dryly, rolling her eyes. Eyes bright with arousal. She wiggled against his shaft, rubbing him perfectly, just the way he liked. "Tell me why."

"No. I'll *show* you why." He moved one of his hands to her nape and urged her the rest of the way forward. Their lips met, opened, and their tongues thrust together. She tasted like mint and cherry, and he decided that was his new favorite flavor.

Her fingers tangled in his hair, her claws digging into his scalp. Desire pumped through his veins, pure, undiluted, blinding him to everything else. To the people around them, the circumstances, the consequences. He held fire in his arms and he desperately wanted to be burned.

And he wanted to burn her. Burn his essence into every part of her, reshaping her into his woman. Everyone who looked at her, neared her, would know who she belonged to.

Mine, she's mine. Damn, she excited him. Their tongues dueled, even that a battle. Such a delicious battle. He dominated, claiming her mouth as his territory. He felt her nipples harden against his chest and wanted to tweak them. Wanted his fingers between her legs, deep inside her, thrusting over and over again.

"Strider," she rasped.

"Baby doll."

"Don't stop."

Won, Defeat said on a sigh, shooting more of that pleasure through him and driving his need even higher.

Strider walked her forward, every jarring step rubbing her more firmly against him. When he reached the nearest table, he leaned down, swiped his arm across the beer bottles littering the surface and distantly heard them shatter on the floor. He pressed Kaia against the wood.

He wanted to do things to her. Bad things. No, good things, he told himself. He had to do good things to her. Had to be her best. But maybe he'd push her for a few of those bad things, make her take everything he had to give, make her beg, need him, crave him like a drug.

"Woohoo! Yeah, baby, yeah!" Anya, the minor goddess of Anarchy, called, her voice dragging him kicking and screaming from the fog of desire. "Rip his clothes off, Kaia. Show us what he's got!"

Strider straightened with a snarl, his gaze scanning, his mind buzzing. Destroy the crowd, return his mouth to Kaia's. As he realized every single person in the bar was watching them, the heat inside him cooled. Some were watching with grins, some with exasperation, some—namely the humans—with lust.

The heat returned, but for an entirely different reason. Fury, so much fury, overshadowed his own lust. He didn't like *anyone* seeing Kaia like this, lost and needy, eager for him. He couldn't allow it. Wouldn't allow it.

He grabbed her arm and jerked her to her feet, smoothing her dress for her. His motions were stiff, jerky. How could he have forgotten their audience, even for a second? Someone could have attacked him. Defeated him. How could he have forgotten what would happen to him if he failed to be Kaia's best? Her best kiss. Her best lay. He'd be ruined, too weak to be effective and no use to her during the coming confrontations.

Although…he wasn't on his knees, overcome by pain, so he'd clearly been her best kiss. Again. The knowledge puffed his chest with pride. Of course he'd been the best, and—*ego check.*

He had better things to do than praise his own magnificence. Like let the guys train her for the next battle the way they'd promised to do, and then haul her back to the motel.

Won, won, won, Defeat said on a sigh, more of that pleasure consuming him.

I never doubted it. He scowled at his friends. "Enough playing around," he snapped, then returned his attention to Kaia. "Get the boys and go out back. Do what I brought you here to do."

Thick red lashes lifted, a curtain rising over a screen of surprise. "You're not coming with me?"

"No." He gave her a little push. "Now go."

CHAPTER SEVENTEEN

To STRIDER'S CONSTERNATION, they never made it outside.

As his friends downed their drinks in a hurry—no drop left behind and all that—the front doors swung open and a black-haired beauty strutted into the bar. Lavender eyes searched the bar…and landed on Kaia. Red lips curled into a satisfied grin.

Strider stiffened. Shit. Wasn't that just his luck. Sabin's mission was now superfluous, which meant there'd be no hunting, no stealing tonight. The Eagleshields had landed.

Kaia cursed under her breath. "Just my luck. Juliette the Nag You Until You Kill Yourself Eradicator is here."

The woman's consort wasn't far behind. Strider hadn't seen him at Tag, had just assumed the guy was off somewhere guarding the Paring Rod, and now he experienced a beat of surprise as the bastard stepped into the bar, expression smug and superior, as if he owned all he surveyed. There was no sign of the artifact. What did he have? Multiple, heavily armed Harpies flanking him. His guards?

During orientation, the hulking giant had sported chains. Now Strider noticed that he sported tattoos. Links had been etched into the flesh around his neck and wrists. Most likely, if he removed his boots, Strider would see ink around his ankles, too.

The tattoos looked red, swollen and fresh, and Strider would have bet his left nut they'd been added only this morning.

Why keep so dangerous a guy around, huh? Kaia had said Harpies could forgive their consorts for almost anything, but come on. The man had murdered other Harpies. Surely that was worse than, say, stealing a priceless artifact from an enemy.

Within seconds, Strider's friends had lined up beside him, forming a wall of menace. They had no idea what was going on—except, maybe, for Amun—but they knew him well. Knew when he was gearing up to fight. Hell, they knew an enemy when they spotted one.

Win!

No combative words had yet been spoken, but even Defeat had sensed the threat. *Consider it done.* With pleasure.

The man—or whatever he was—caught sight of Kaia. Obsidian eyes swirled hypnotically. He was bare-chested, and his pectorals jumped. Because he was imagining Kaia's hands on him?

Strider tensed. *Mine. And I don't share. Ever.*

"Let's kidnap Juliette's followers and threaten to release them if she doesn't do what we want," Kaia whispered to him.

"Wait. What? Threaten to *release* them?"

"They're so horrible, getting them back would be the punishment."

He fought a grin.

"Now, let's zip this convo up and let momma work." She cleared her throat, straightened her shoulders. "Well, well," Kaia said, casual yet loud enough to be heard by one and all this time. "Is it my birthday already?"

"No," Juliette said. "It's mine."

Speaking of, "When *is* your birthday?" Strider asked Kaia. His friends would assume he wanted to know now of all times simply to irritate the newcomers, to show them just how little they mattered. And that was partly true. But

Strider found he really, *really* wanted to know anyway. For himself.

Wide silver-gold eyes swung to him. "You don't know?"

"No."

Pouting, she twirled a strand of her hair. "How can you not know?"

"Do you know mine?" he asked.

"Of course I do. It's the day you met me."

As good a day as any. "No, it's not, because that was a trick question, baby doll. I don't actually have a birthday. I was created fully formed, not born." True story.

"You can be *such* a moron." She threw up her arms, exasperated. "Don't argue with me about this kind of thing. I'll always be right. Seriously. You were dead until you met me and we both know it. Which means I brought you to life. So, happy belated birthday."

Amun laughed, which was a shock. The serious warrior *never* laughed. Anya nodded as if she'd never heard a more solid argument and Gideon snickered behind his hand. Scarlet slapped him in the back of the head.

"You're right," Strider said, wanting to laugh himself. "So when's yours?"

"Shut up," Juliette suddenly snarled. "I thought we were going to trade insults."

He turned back to her, as if surprised to find she was still there. Fury colored her cheeks a bright pink and even thinned her lips. Excellent. Emotion would make her stupid. The consort, though, looked amused. And impressed, even a little wistful.

Make a play for Kaia, dude. I dare you, Strider projected at him.

As if sensing the new hazard, the man moved his gaze to Strider. For several seconds, they simply glared at each other. There was no way in hell Strider would look away first and the guy must have sensed that, because after flashing his teeth in a show of aggression, he returned his attention to Kaia—and licked his lips.

Oh, you will pay for that. Why Defeat didn't pipe in with a "Win," Strider didn't know. Like that would stop him from doing a wee bit of bitch-slapping, though.

"So how'd you find her?" Strider demanded with more force than he'd intended.

"Please. As if tracking you was hard," Juliette replied, deigning only to speak to Kaia.

Finally, Defeat perked up.

Not a challenge, you bastard. And where were you when I wanted you?

No response. Of course.

Kaia grinned slowly. "As if I didn't know you were following me. As if I didn't leave bread crumbs for you to find. And look who ate those crumbs like a mouse and landed herself in a nice little cheese trap."

Score. Juliette shifted uncomfortably from one booted foot to another. Her gaze panned the demon-possessed warriors in front of her and she paled.

Defeat chuckled, surprising Strider further. The demon had had a similar reaction during the games, when Kaia had been kicking major ass. At the time, Strider had been positive he'd misheard. That the noise of the crowd had somehow invaded his head. Now...

What did it mean?

Ponder it later. His demon's amusement wasn't going to slice through his jugular. If he wasn't careful, Juliette might. He had to stay focused.

"So, would you like to tell us why you were tracking me before or after we clean the floor with your faces?" Kaia asked casually. "And by *clean,* I mean coat with your blood."

"While you decide," Strider added, "maybe I should introduce you to Kaia's friends. The guy holding the ax is Gideon. He's possessed by the demon of Lies. The girl next to him, the one tossing and catching the daggers, is Scarlet. She's possessed by the demon of Nightmares. The rocking blonde is the goddess of Anarchy." No reason to mention the "minor" thing. Didn't sound as impressive.

Anya gave a pinkie wave. "Hey, ya'll. Welcome to the party. A few facts about me before you're too dead to ask. I like long walks on the beach, snuggling with my man and murdering people who offend me." Offered in the sweetest voice, the threat was all kinds of frightening.

Strider opened his mouth to continue, but Juliette snapped, "I don't care about any of you. We didn't come here to fight. No reason to. That's what the games are for."

Oh, really? He would have placed good money on the opposite being true—and he would have won, no question.

"You sure?" Kaia asked. "I don't mind making an exception and pretending this is an event. I'll even let you take the first swing without retaliating. Although I can't promise my demon-possessed friends here will behave."

Mutely, Juliette pivoted on a booted heel and stalked to the bar. Her consort and clan followed her.

Won, Defeat said on a happy sigh.

Strider mentally high-fived him, delighting as yet another bout of pleasure spun through him. Only problem was, Kaia couldn't start training now. She couldn't leave, either. Leaving would smack of cowardice. So they were stuck, their marathon makeout session on hold, as well.

"Kaia!" a female voice shouted excitedly. Once again the front door swung open. This time, Bianka raced inside, dark hair flying behind her and slapping Lysander in the face as he followed. Another warrior angel strode in behind him. This one had dark hair, piercing green eyes and features so emotionless they resembled a deep, dark void.

Zacharel. Strider had met the winged warrior weeks ago, when the being was sent to the fortress to prevent Amun from leaving. He'd had a hard time facing the guy, his body reacting every time they'd neared each other.

Strider had never swung that way, but he couldn't be blamed. There was no being more physically perfect than Zacharel. Well, except for Kaia. This time, however, the reaction was muted. Maybe because, as strongly as he reacted to Kaia, nothing else could compare.

Sabin and Gwen strutted in next, moving to flank the angels. Even though Strider hadn't texted his leader to tell him the Eagleshields were here, the warrior didn't look surprised to see them. He must have watched them from the heavens, then, as planned.

Any luck finding the Rod?

"Bianka," Kaia said with a laugh as she launched herself to meet her sister in the middle of the room. The twins hugged and danced as if they hadn't seen each other in years.

"I would have been here sooner but Lysander held me prisoner in our cloud," Bianka said with a grin. "He wouldn't relent until Sabin gave the okay. Which I still don't understand and will continue to punish him for until he spills. Secrets or guts, I don't care which."

That would explain the black eye the warrior currently possessed, Strider thought with a grin of his own.

"You're so lucky," Kaia said. "You can harm your consort."

"I know. And feel free to harm him yourself. Although, maybe don't hurt him too badly. There's all kinds of trouble in the heavens nowadays, something about losing a piece of love, whatever that means, and my pookybear is stressed."

That was the last thing Strider understood as the sisters began talking over each other.

"—because you look amazing and—"

"—wouldn't believe the balls on—"

"—next time I want video feed of—"

"—cut just right, flesh makes the cutest purse—"

"—*she* doing here?"

In unison, they faced the bar, leveling Juliette with glares of abject disgust. Juliette pretended not to notice. Not her consort, though. He smiled at the twins as if they were the Christmas present he'd always wanted.

Blood...heating...

Strider would have volleyed himself like an H-bomb if a hard hand hadn't settled on his shoulder. "I wouldn't," Lysander said.

"You wouldn't. I would." His gaze remained locked on the male he desperately wanted to slay.

An equally hard hand settled on his other shoulder. "Perhaps you should rethink your strategy," Zacharel said in his cold, toneless voice.

Yeah, well, perhaps the humans disagreed with Strider's "physically perfect" description, because they still loitered inside the bar, paying the angels no heed. And hell, they had wings and wore girly robes. Two other reasons to stare right there.

"They cannot see Lysander or me," Zacharel explained. "You were correct. If they could, they would stare."

Strider's jaw clenched. "Stay out of my head."

"Stop projecting your thoughts."

He didn't mind when Amun read him, but Zacharel? An angel? Freaking irritating. "The consort. What is he?"

Lysander didn't ask for clarification. "His name is Lazarus, and he is the only son of Typhon."

Oh, shit. He'd been right—guy was far from human. Strider wanted to shake his head, to deny, to do anything but accept. But when an angel spoke, there was no doubting him. Ever. Truth layered every nuance of Lysander's voice and every cell in Strider's body believed what he'd just been told.

As an elite guard to Zeus, Strider had fought many monsters. None had ever compared to Typhon. Bastard was a giant with the head of a dragon and the body of a snake. His wings spanned the entire length of a football field and a never-ending abyss had waited in his eyes.

Typhon had challenged Zeus, and he would have won, had been winning, until Strider and friends arrived on the scene, causing the giant to flee. *You're welcome,* he thought dryly, recalling how Zeus had blamed them for distracting him, claiming he would have pulled through without them. Strider hadn't heard a shred of gossip about Typhon since, and now he had to wonder what had happened to the guy.

"Who's his mother?" Strider asked.

"I do not know her name, only that she is a Gorgon."

"This just gets better by the second," he muttered dryly. Gorgons could turn a man to stone with only a glance. They had snakes on their heads rather than hair—snakes that poisoned their victims when they bit. Medusa was the most famous of them, and so legendary even humans told tales of her evil prowess.

Mortals. So gullible. If they only knew Medusa was the cream of the crop and a real sweetheart compared to others of her race.

"Clearly, he wants a piece of Kaia."

"Who doesn't?" Zacharel asked, deadpan. As always. "She is a beautiful woman and I have seen how happy a Harpy can make an angel."

Strider had his nose pressed into the angel's a second later, breath sawing in and out. "You better stay away from her."

Win.

No problem.

"I will," the angel said easily. "Stay away from her, that is."

Strider blinked, confused, and backed a step away. "But you just—"

"I just agreed with you. Yes. Every unmated man in this building wants a piece of her."

He was back in the guy's face a second later. "And you?" Damn it. He had to get himself under control. He'd vowed not to let himself be challenged majorly for the next few weeks, yet he kept reacting to everyone who so much as glanced in Kaia's direction.

"I was merely ensuring you desire her, rather than… someone else."

Someone, like an angel. Once again, he stepped backward. Faster this time, his cheeks heating with mortification. So. The bastard had picked up on the earlier fascination.

"You look all innocent and shit, but you're really a devil in disguise, aren't you?"

Zacharel merely shrugged, his expression unchanging. *Win?*

Yeah. We won that round. The angel hadn't made a play for Kaia, and that was all that mattered.

Defeat might have agreed, but there were no accompanying sparks of pleasure. Nor were there spurts of pain.

"What are you doing here, anyway?" he grumbled.

"Bianka competes in the next game. Lysander wishes me to—"

"Lysander can speak for himself," the warrior interjected. "I wished for a supporting arm to either hold me back or help me, should I be inclined to punish Bianka's opponents."

Aw. True love. How sickening.

Both Lysander and Zacharel could create swords of fire from nothing but air. A few Harpy heads would probably roll by the time the second game ended if any harm came to Kaia's twin.

"You do know you'll embarrass Bianka if you—"

"Who are you talking to, Strider?" Though Haidee had closed most of the distance between them, she asked the question from behind her beer bottle, not daring to glance in his direction. He knew she didn't fear Kaia, though she should, but merely thought to prevent another attack while the enemy was nearby.

And damn it. The angels had warned him. No one else could see them. Well, Sabin and Gwen could, he was sure, since they were smothering their laughter behind beers of their own.

"No one," he muttered. *No one important.* He refocused on Kaia and Bianka, the Twin Troublemakers.

"—no better time," Bianka was saying.

"Then let's do it," Kaia responded with an evil grin. "Juliette will never know what hit her."

Shit. Do what? With those two, "it" always involved bloodshed, grand theft auto or a five-alarm blaze. Or, on special days, a combination of all three. He watched, dread coursing through him, ready to pounce at a moment's notice, as the girls moved forward.

Then the worst of his fears were confirmed when they climbed onto the dais.

To karaoke.

CHAPTER EIGHTEEN

PARIS PRESSED INTO A SHADOWED corner of the heavenly harem. Mindless chatter and the sound of playful splashing coasted on the over-warm air. The scent of jasmine oil and sandalwood drifted to his nose and he tried not to inhale. Ambrosia layered both, a waft of coconut that lured and seduced, and he couldn't yet afford to get high. No matter how much his body shook, desperate for a fix.

After his back-alley brawl, he'd taken the first female he'd stumbled upon. Sex had ensured her willingness, despite Paris's ragged appearance, and he'd healed quickly afterward.

Unfortunately, the vital encounter had made him an hour late to his meeting with Mina, the goddess of weaponry, and he'd had to pay extra for the crystal blades.

She liked her pleasure with a bit of bite, and he'd had to do things to her that might haunt him for years. But he had the daggers now and had crossed item one off his To Do list.

He rubbed the hilts as he scanned his surroundings, hating the cobalt wisps of fabric that fell from the ceiling and draped the entire enclosure. Hating the beaded lounge pillows, the naked, glistening bodies strolling this way and that.

Time to cross off item number two. Arca, the messenger goddess. Surely she would know where Sienna was being held, as one of his many partners had led him to believe. Pillow talk—his best friend, and everyone else's worst enemy.

If she wasn't here, he had no idea where to go next. Or who to do.

Don't think like that. No one here had sensed him. Yet. That would change all too soon. Sex craved today's dose. Already the scents of chocolate and champagne drifted from him. Soon mortals and immortals alike, all brought here to service Cronus, would find themselves consumed by hunger.

The god king had given up keeping a single mistress. Now he was keeping thirty…three. Yes, thirty-three, Paris counted. The twenty-seven others standing around the pool ledge were bodyguards, not sexual conquests.

Paris doubted Cronus had slept with everyone here, or that the bastard even planned to nail them all in the future. But Cronus would do anything to piss off Rhea, his traitor of a wife, and nothing hurt a woman's pride quite like infidelity. A fact Paris knew very well.

He'd never been faithful. Could never be faithful. No matter how much he wanted to be. No matter how much his many conquests screamed and ranted at him, desperate for something he couldn't give them. Something… more. His lovers were his demon's food, that was all. He couldn't let them be anything else. And really, he didn't want them to be anything else.

He just wanted Sienna.

If he could find her, if he could touch her, if she no longer despised him—which didn't seem likely, especially after the things, *people,* he'd done up here—would she give herself to him?

So many ifs.

He'd been up here off and on ever since her disappearance, and he'd kept his ear to the ground—aka he'd screwed the information out of anyone close to Cronus.

See? Unfaithful. He was here for one woman, but had slept with another. And another. And another.

Buck up. Otherwise, he'd start wanting that ambrosia. Hell, maybe he should just give in.

Or maybe he should leave. Cronus was going to pop a vessel when he discovered Paris's whereabouts. Would definitely punish him. Because…to hide his activities, Paris had to wear a necklace—a manlace, as Torin called it—the god king had given him. A manlace he was only supposed to wear to hide himself from *Rhea*. Using it to conceal himself from Cronus as well was a small crime, sure, but couple that with Paris's intentions…

You're close. Closer than you've ever been. No matter what happened, he wouldn't give up. So, no ambrosia and no leaving.

"I'm so hot," one woman said. She lay on a velvet recliner, naked and glistening, arching her back as she traced her fingertips between her large, tawny-tipped breasts. "So needy."

"Me, too," another said. She licked her lips as she searched for a partner.

Oh, yes. They had sensed Paris at last.

His friends were used to him, used to his scent and the need it caused, and were mostly immune. Plus, he'd over-indulged Sex, so the demon had rarely acted out like this. Paris wasn't yet used to it.

"I've never been this aroused," another female said.

Then, it was on. Moans of pleasure resounded as an orgy broke out. Multiple writhing bodies, hands stroking, legs spreading. The sight failed to arouse even the barest flicker of need. Been there, gotten tired of that.

They were distracted, at least. He studied them, searching for the telltale "long, braided white hair" he'd been told Arca possessed. Another tidbit he'd learned: she was responsible for the children's story about Rapunzel.

Once, when she'd delivered a godly message to a human king, he'd become captivated by her beauty and thought to keep her. And he had very nearly succeeded. Not just because he'd used black magic, but because his timing had been impeccable. The Greeks had gained control of the heavens, locking the Titans away. Arca had been forgotten.

Paris didn't know if the rest of the story held true. If she had been rescued by a mortal prince. If the mortal had been killed in front of her when the Greeks at last remembered her and dragged her up to the heavens, locking her in another, stronger prison. And he wouldn't let himself care.

What he did know? Arca had been grabbed right off a golden street and tossed here. Paris could work that to his advantage. She had to despise the king, had to crave revenge.

Also, she wasn't in this section of the palace. *Please be in another.*

He slinked along the wall. He could have stripped and presented himself as a slave, or a new addition to the harem, but he refused to relinquish his new weapons. No doubt he'd need them.

He reached a corner, paused, listened, looked. Heard no footsteps. Saw no shadows moving along the marble floor. He inched forward, leaving the bathing area completely. Curtained doorway after curtained doorway greeted him, and he gnashed his teeth. If he had to screw someone just to find out which room belonged to Arca—

A slave strode from the room at the far end of the hallway, a silver tray balanced in his hands. He spotted Paris, but didn't issue an alarm. No, his tanned, naked body reacted instantly, his belly quivering. He set the tray on the floor and practically skipped over, as if in a trance.

He probably was. Paris hadn't fed his demon for twenty-three hours. He wouldn't start weakening for another hour, yet Sex's pheromones—or whatever it was the bastard released from Paris's pores—would continue to strengthen until they'd come inside someone.

A few times, Paris had let himself become so weak he couldn't move. Yet those pheromones had drifted from him, so damn potent that humans had fallen on him, unable to help themselves, lost to lust. A few times, before Paris had reached the point of total weakness, he had lost control of *himself* and fallen on *humans*.

The slave reached him. "Who are you, beautiful?" Callused, overworked hands whisked along his chest, caressing.

Maybe he wasn't as close to finding Sienna as he'd thought. First time he'd neared her, his demon had begun *repelling* others. This slave was far from repelled. But he wouldn't change course, Paris thought. He couldn't. If not here, he had no idea where to go.

"Do you know where Arca is?" he asked, ignoring the question asked of him.

A pink tongue emerged, tracing over already moistened lips. "Yes."

Relief flooded him. "Tell me. Please," he added as an afterthought.

Those questing hands slid lower...lower still... "For you, anything."

He waited, forcing himself to remain still. When no other response was forthcoming, he said, "Tell me."

"Yes, yes, of course, but first I must...have to... please..." Every word caused the slave's voice to dip lower, huskier, absolute yearning in the undertones.

Lost, Paris thought. The slave was already lost to his body's needs. Paris would get no answers until that need was assuaged. He leaned against the wall and stared up at the domed ceiling.

"Drop to your knees," he commanded, pulling Sienna's delicate face, dark hair and adorably freckled skin to the forefront of his mind.

WILLIAM PACED THE CONFINES of his prison cell. After the blonde bitch had dropped her bombshell about Kane, he had erupted, shouting and fighting for freedom. She'd soon realized there would be no calming him down and had had his gurney wheeled here.

About an hour ago, he'd regained enough of his strength to break out of the metal restraints. Not so with the cage. Four walls, all bars, and he couldn't bend or manipulate a single one.

The prison had been built for immortals.

He had to get out of here. Had to get to Kane. Had to stop the warrior from reaching hell. The horsemen. The danger...

"So. You've calmed down."

The blonde. Fury rising inside him, William turned on his heel, following the sound of her voice. And there she was. Ponytail, wire rims, delicate features, lab coat.

"Are you ready to chat now?" she asked.

Don't erupt again. Much as he currently wanted to rip her throat out, he needed her.

He was at a disadvantage, though. Patches of his skin were still charred, his pants—the only article of clothing currently remaining on his body—were bloodstained and ripped, and his hair was sticking out in spikes.

He was still a babe, though. Surely.

He pasted a seductive smile on his face. "Absolutely I'm ready. What's your name, darling?"

She arched a brow two shades darker than her hair. "I thought you didn't care about my name."

Great. She was one of *those.* Stubborn and determined not to let a man soften her. Otherwise she would have melted already. And yes, he usually worked *that* quickly. "That was the pain talking, I promise."

"Okay. I'll pretend that I believe you. My name is Skye."

"I'll call you Dr. Love Button."

"And I'll have you castrated." There was no heat in her tone.

"Kinky. So you work for Galen, do you?" Gods, William hated the bastard. Not for the sake of the Lords, though that didn't help the keeper of Hope's cause, but because William simply couldn't stand people who were deceitful about their evil. Reminded him too much of his brother. And they didn't get more deceitful than Galen, who masqueraded as an angel so he could manipulate a bunch of feeble-minded humans into doing his dark bidding.

Skye, if that was her real name, laughed. "Kinda sorta, though mostly no."

Of all the nonanswers she could have given, that topped the list. "Mind explaining that a little better, pet?"

"Not really, but I'll give it a shot." She shook her head and stuffed her hands into the pockets of her lab coat. "I'm not a Hunter. Or a doctor, for that matter. I never finished med school."

"Then why did you bomb me, nearly kill me, help heal me and what? Lock me away as if you despise me. Oh, yeah. And I can't forget that you also carted my demon-possessed friend into hell." Something humans wouldn't have known how to do—or how to navigate through if by some miracle they did manage to reach it. Which meant a god—or a goddess—had to be involved. And the only divine pain in the ass currently helping mortals was Rhea, the heavenly queen. "Also, how do you know about Galen and Hunters if you're not part of their brainwashed masses?"

A rosy flush colored her cheeks. "First, I didn't bomb

you. Hunters did, yes. And, okay, so my husband is a Hunter, and that's why I'm so knowledgeable, but I'm working with him on that, trying to get him out. As for the other, I only locked you away because you were a danger to yourself and everyone around you."

He placed a hand over his heart, as if she'd mortally wounded him. "As if I'd ever hurt you."

"Whatever."

What would it take to charm her? "Let's backtrack just a bit. Hunters decided to take me out, your husband among them, and you thought you'd try to save little ole me, even though you don't yet have your medical degree and even though saving me might piss off your man? I'm touched, truly."

She fiddled with something plastic in her pocket. "They brought you here, asked me to help."

"And even though you want your man out of their ranks, you decided to aid them yourself." He edged toward her, so minutely she wouldn't realize he was close enough to reach through the bars until it was too late.

"I decided to aid *you*."

Another inch. "But you're not working for them."

"No."

"Shall I tell you all my secrets, then?" Another inch.

Her eyes narrowed, obscuring her pretty irises. "Keep your secrets. I'm not interested." She withdrew a sucker from her pocket, the wrapper gone, and stuffed the thing in her mouth.

Well, he was definitely interested in hers. "If you don't work for Hunters, who *do* you work for? How did you know how to save me? And why don't you set me free now? As you can see, I'm not a danger to anyone."

Out popped the candy. "First, I'm currently unemployed. And as for my saving know-how, trial and error. Some races can regenerate limbs, some can't. Some have wings, most don't. Some respond to human medicine positively, some negatively. As for the Hunters and your release, I'm sad to say they get you back the moment I decide you're well enough."

Yet another inch. Almost there… "But you still claim not to work for them."

She shrugged. "My husband made the agreement with them. He decides."

"And you won't defy him? Or change his mind?" he asked, using his huskiest tone.

"No." Softly spoken, yet firm, unbending. "I can't. I wish, but I can't."

Finally William reached her. He grinned. "Too bad." His arm shot through the bars, his fingers wrapping around her fragile neck.

CHAPTER NINETEEN

THE NEXT MORNING, STRIDER'S ears were bleeding and his mind was echoing the lyrics from Naughty By Nature's "O.P.P." Didn't help that Kaia and Bianka were *still* singing. Badly. So damn badly. Not that he'd ever admit that last part aloud. Kaia looked so happy squawking her heart out and he didn't want to taint an activity that gave her enjoyment. But seriously. He was willing to bet a cat being skinned had better pitch. And yeah, he'd put good money on that bet, not to mention his body and his demon.

Once the girls had started, they hadn't stopped. Tragically, though hours had passed, neither of them had developed laryngitis.

Besides the humans, who had all taken off at closing, the lucky bastards, no one had dared leave the bar. Not the Lords, the Skyhawks, the angels, nor the Eagleshields.

To the Harpies, this was another type of contest, plain and simple. Who could outlast the other? For once, Strider was willing to lose. He would have left, writhed in (grateful) pain for a few days, but damn it all to hell, he had to protect his little Harpy.

A few times, one of the Eagleshields attempted to head up onstage, take over and put everyone out of their misery. Strider jumped up, ready for action, but Lysander and Zacharel, who still couldn't be seen by anyone but Strider and Sabin, immediately formed an impenetrable wall of muscle no one was able to pass.

And the Harpies had tried, hitting, kicking and clawing, until finally giving up in frustration. Of course, Kaia and Bianka were blamed, and he'd heard murmurs of wonderment. What type of strange powers did the twins wield?

Good. Let them wonder.

Knowing the angels had Kaia's back allowed Strider to switch his focus to Juliette and her boy toy Lazarus, who kept their focus centered on Kaia. He didn't like that. Didn't like that *at all*. And he wasn't going to stand for it.

Just behave, he told Defeat, *and we'll be fine. I'll handle this.*

Despite the noise that had left the demon whimpering and begging for a one-way ticket back to hell, Pandora's box, *anything* to escape, Defeat snorted.

So. No cooperation today. That wasn't gonna stop him, however.

Before he could talk himself into waiting, planning, Strider closed the distance and kicked a chair over to Juliette's table, the back slats pressing into its surface edge. He eased down backward and propped his elbows on the tabletop.

Immediately he felt the tension in the room escalate, thicken, and he didn't need to look to know Amun and Sabin had just taken up posts behind him. They had his back, always.

Juliette finally deigned to study him, her soft lavender eyes sweeping over his face and body unhurriedly, languidly, lingering in places they shouldn't. "Wish and I shall receive. I wanted you to approach me, and so you did. But I must admit, I expected you to do it sooner."

If she'd truly wanted his attention, by fair means or foul, she would have tried harder to get it. She wouldn't have waited for him to make a move. Well, if she'd had a pair of balls, she would have. Kaia went after what she wanted, no hesitation. And that, he decided, was exactly how a woman should be. Determined, eager. Sexy.

This one craved revenge, though, her every move designed to help her achieve it. So his approach meant something, he just didn't know what.

"Why?" he asked, genuinely curious.

She was momentarily taken aback, as if she'd expected him to wax poetic about her beauty, beg for lenience for Kaia, or even grab her up and screw her brainless right here on the table.

"I have something you crave, do I not?"

"Like?"

"The Paring Rod. Yes," she added at his start of surprise. "I know all about you Lords and your quest for Pandora's box. I know you need four artifacts to find it, and the Rod is one. Why else do you think I offered it?"

Rather than answer, he asked a question of his own. "How'd you get it?"

A smile bloomed, smug and patronizing. "I never share my secrets."

Oh, really. He glanced back at Amun. The big, dark warrior was frowning, his features tense. When he caught Strider's gaze, he gave an abrupt shake of his head. Huh. Could he not read her mind?

That was rare.

For that matter, why hadn't Sabin used Doubt against her? Or had he tried and, like Amun, failed?

Strider returned his attention to Juliette, keeping Lazarus in his peripheral vision. The fucker hadn't spared Strider a glance, was still watching Kaia. "Well, to backtrack a bit, *the winner* will have something I want," he lied. He *would* get his hands on the artifact before that final game. He wouldn't allow himself to believe otherwise.

"Same thing," she said with a shrug. "Because, either way, Kaia will win nothing."

Defeat growled.

Good boy.

Gideon had recently told Strider that it was possible for the demons to escape their bodies and enter others—not permanently and not for long, but just long enough to destroy the person's mind. Strider would love for Defeat to ravage Juliette, to convince her of her weakness, that she could never hope to win *anything*.

They'd have to try it. Later. *Always later.* He dared not risk messing with the unknown now.

"When Kaia loses," Juliette went on, "I'll expect you to come to me. And maybe, after you beg, I'll allow you to please me. And maybe, after you please me, if you can, I'll let you use my Rod."

Use my Rod. "That's what he said," Strider snickered.

She blinked at him. "That's what who said?" When he offered no response, she demanded, "What did he say?"

Kaia would have understood the joke. Probably Kaia would have pretended a beer bottle was the Rod and jacked it off while laughing. Gods, he dug her sense of humor.

"Well?" Juliette prompted.

"Nothing," he said on a sigh. One thing he knew. No matter what happened, he would beg this female for nothing. Were he to seduce her, even to distract her, Kaia would be hurt. Feel rejected all over again. Which was exactly what this vengeful female desired, and that was not a game he would play.

"Well, I don't care who he is or what he said." She tossed her hair over one shoulder. "I'm far more beautiful than that redheaded harlot and you *will* beg for me."

Anger? No, that was too mild a word for the emotion suddenly sizzling inside his chest. Even Defeat snarled. "Actually, you're not. There's *no one* more beautiful than Kaia. And by the way, she's not a harlot. She's mine. And no, I won't be begging you for anything but your departure."

Her nostrils flared at the insult. "Is that so? Well, let me ask you a question, Strider, keeper of the demon of Defeat. You are one of the fabled Lords of the Underworld and I have researched you meticulously. You prize victory above all things. So why would you of all warriors choose to be the consort of Kaia the Disappointment?"

That. Was. It. His wee Harpy was getting a new name, pronto. "Kaia is many things to me, but a disappointment isn't one of them. But riddle me this." *You coldhearted bitch.* "Did your consort *choose* to be with you?" He motioned to the tattooed chains with a tilt of his chin. "'Cause I'm betting he'd shave your head from your neck without a second's hesitation."

At last Lazarus attended to those at his table. "You are correct," he said, and a minute amount of Strider's hate dulled. *Minute* being the key word. Strider would still, gladly, shove a dagger through the guy's heart.

"You just shut your mouth," Juliette snapped at her consort.

Though glaring, his expression one of molten rage, Lazarus obeyed.

Juliette's narrowed eyes remained on Strider. "He's honored to be with me, I tell you."

Really? "Defensive much?"

Already sharp nails lengthened into claws and black bled into her eyes. Oh, goody. Her Harpy was about to come out and play.

Strider struck while he still could. "Well, *I* really am honored to be with Kaia, and if you try another stunt like you did at the first game, siccing everyone on her at the same time, I will take it as a personal challenge. In your research, did you discover what happens to those who challenge me?"

More black, the whites of her eyes nearly completely gone. Until Lazarus reached over and patted her hand. That was it. A single pat. The black gradually receded and her nails retracted.

Strider had watched Sabin calm Gwen multiple times, but for the first time he was floored by the power a consort truly had over his Harpy. Floored by how much a Harpy *needed* that consort.

But Lazarus was clearly a slave, here by force. So why had he calmed the very woman who had enslaved him? Shouldn't he revel in her upset? And furthermore, *how* had Juliette captured him? Not once, but twice? The man had once cut his way through a Harpy village and come out the winner. Hell, he was the son of Typhon and a Gorgon, which meant he had powers beyond imagining.

Had he *allowed* her to capture him? That seemed like the only explanation that made sense. But why would he have done such a thing?

So many questions and none of them could be answered. Strider made a mental note to call Torin and ask the keeper of Disease to work some computer magic, see what he could dig up. Beyond a doubt, something was going on here.

"You can't do anything to me, warrior." In control of herself once more, Juliette smiled that smug smile. "Not without casting blame on Kaia. Everyone will see her as the weak loser she really is." A dramatic pause before she continued in a singsong voice, "Again."

Exactly what Kaia had once told him. He had believed her, but had discarded the importance of her feelings in light of his own goals. He still did—life and death trumped bruised emotions every time. But now, he was *pissed*.

Win, Defeat said on a low snarl.

Strider knew what his demon wanted. *My pleasure.* Before the games ended, Strider was going to "do anything" to Juliette, without having blame cast on Kaia. Challenge issued, challenge accepted.

That was the very reason he'd needed to stay away from the woman, but he wasn't sorry he'd approached. He was glad. The bitch would pay for everything she'd said today, as well as everything she'd done in the past.

"We'll see," he said with a grin of his own. His list of accepted challenges was adding up. Protecting Kaia from other Harpies—a challenge he'd nearly lost, would have lost, if she hadn't recovered from her injuries. Because she had, *because of his blood,* he was still in the running. Acquiring the Paring Rod—a work in progress. And now this, destroying Juliette.

"Yes, we will see," Juliette replied. "Oh, and warrior. You should know something. If the Rod is stolen from me, or if I'm injured before the games end, Kaia will be killed. My clan is *very* eager to act."

Trying to tie his hands, and damn, she was doing a good job. How could he keep Kaia safe from an entire Harpy army? A cold sweat broke out over his skin at the thought.

The singing stopped, at last.

Absolute silence suddenly reigned, as if everyone was too afraid to even breathe for fear the noise would jump-start another tune. But, no. Footsteps echoed, and then Kaia was tugging a chair to the table.

"Strider," she said tightly.

"Baby doll," he replied, hoping his fear was masked.

"Thank the gods," Juliette said, amusement never wavering. "Your singing was terrible. My eardrums needed a break."

Strider cupped Kaia's nape and massaged. *Steady.* "I thought she sounded lovely."

Kaia's chin lifted. "Thank you."

"Seriously, baby doll. I could listen to you for hours more." *But please don't make me.*

Defeat might have whimpered.

"That's because you're a man of good taste." She leaned over and kissed his cheek.

The imprint her mouth left behind burned deliciously and he barely restrained the urge to reach up and stroke the mark. When she began to pull away, he tightened his grip on her and held her in place. He liked having her nearby. Especially now, with Juliette's threat ringing in his already suffering ears.

Kaia watched him for a moment, confusion curtaining her delicate features. Then she schooled her expression to reveal only bored expectancy and turned back to her nemeses. He was happy to note Juliette had watched the tender exchange, fury building in her lavender eyes.

"I second the motion. Listening to that was pure pleasure," Lazarus said, speaking up for only the second time. Before, his voice had been deep, almost unremarkable. Now it was hypnotic. Sexual. "Kaia the...Strongest, isn't it?"

Strider gripped the hilt of the dagger sheathed at his side. Bye-bye, minute dulling. Hello, renewed, even more powerful hate. *Talk to her like that again. I dare you.*

Juliette laughed. "Is that what she called herself? The *Strongest?*"

Twin spots of pink painted Kaia's cheeks. "And you're Lazarus the Tampon, aren't you?"

Juliette sputtered.

Lazarus merely blinked. "I had heard that is how you and your sisters speak of me, and for so very long I have wanted to ask why you refer to me as a woman's hygiene product. Because I made you bleed?"

Now Kaia was the one to sputter. "Just...you...learn to take an insult the right way, damn it!"

He inclined his head in agreement. "I will endeavor to please you, of course."

Strider and Juliette experienced the same reaction to the bastard's words. Irritation. As evidenced by the fact that they both jumped to their feet. Her chair skidded out behind her. His remained between his legs. Amun and Sabin drew closer to him. Kaia—still perched in her chair—shoved them backward, clearly intent on being Strider's shield. And sword.

Lazarus rose, too. "So. This is go time, as the humans say?" No concern had entered his tone.

"This—" Juliette began harshly.

"I've been meaning to chat with you about something important, Julie," Kaia said, cutting her off.

"Juliette." Lavender eyes darkened to a deep violet. "My name is Juliette the Eradicator. You will address me with the proper respect."

"Whatever. It's a shame you can't fight in the games. One would almost think you accepted the leadership position because you feared competing."

A gasp of outrage. Black bleeding in that gaze, removing any hint of color. "I accepted the leadership position so that I could finally—"

"No," Lazarus said with so much force the bar's walls actually shook. "Enough."

Finally. A glimpse of his power. And oh, yes. Something was definitely up there.

Juliette paled, cleared her throat. "What I meant to say was that something can be arranged. You want to fight me, we'll fight. But really, even if you don't want to, you'll end up doing so. You challenged me all those years ago, but I was never allowed to respond."

"Because you were too chicken?"

"First," the bitch growled, "we had to recover from the damage you caused."

"Me? What about him?" She jerked her thumb at Lazarus.

"You know the answer to that. He acted only because of *your* actions. Now zip your mouth and listen. Second, we had to replenish our numbers, so killing another Harpy outside the games was forbidden. Third, your mother would have declared war against my people." Fury faded, replaced by more of that smug superiority. "But none of those things stand in our way anymore."

Kaia flinched at the reminder of her mother's denunciation.

Juliette pulled a necklace from her shirt and fingering the wooden medallion hanging on the chain. "Pretty, isn't it?"

There was no hiding the trembling of Kaia's chin as she eyed the medallion. "I've seen better."

That's my girl. Clearly, seeing the necklace hurt her and Juliette knew why. Now *he* wanted to know why. Still, that was his baby doll. Always had to have the last word, no matter what. He couldn't fault her for that, was actually proud of her. Aroused by her.

He'd always thought this aspect of her personality was dangerous to him, and it was—but damn, when she turned it on other people, he wanted to pound on his chest like a Neanderthal. Maybe carry her back to his cave and have his wicked way with her.

Maybe? Ha! He wanted to dominate this female no one else could control. The female who scratched everyone else, but treated him to the tenderest of caresses.

Before Juliette could work up a stinging response, every Harpy in the building, even Kaia, stopped what she was doing and frowned.

"What?" Strider asked, concerned.

No answer was forthcoming. In unison, the females withdrew their cell phones. Kaia read the backlit screen and stiffened.

"The next location has been revealed," she said, her

tone devoid of emotion. "We have twenty-four hours to get there."

Juliette chuckled. Though she was leader, she'd checked her phone, too. Shouldn't she already know where they were headed? "Poor Kaia has a very tough decision to make, doesn't she?" she murmured, and then called, "Let's move out, team."

At long last, the Eagleshields and their consorts, Lazarus included, stomped out of the bar. Juliette lingered in the doorway, smiling over at Kaia. "Too bad you won't be able to hide behind your men this time, huh?" With that, she slipped into the sunlight.

"What's going on?" Strider demanded, forcing her to face him. Why did Juliette seem to think he couldn't go?

"We have to leave," she whispered, agonized.

We. Good. "I'll get my things."

"No." She shook her head, hair gliding over her shoulders, his hands, her gaze never quite meeting his. "We. Meaning me and my sisters. Juliette was right. You and your friends can't come."

Like hell. "Why? Where are you—we—going?"

A sigh shuddered from her. "The *Odynia*. Better known as Hera's Garden of Goodbyes, since she used the place to get rid of her opposition without ever having to raise a hand against them. Of course, Rhea's in charge of it now, so I guess *she'll* be our hostess there."

Rhea, the Titan god queen and true leader of the Hunters. Far more dangerous, far more powerful, than Galen could ever hope to be. If Strider attended this portion of the games he'd most likely walk right into a trap. If he stayed behind, Kaia could be hurt, and he'd be unable to reach her and help her heal.

No way in hell, he thought.

CHAPTER TWENTY

THE STUPID MAN WOULDN'T stop following her!

Getting away from Strider had been easy. Letting his demon "win" hadn't. After dropping the Rhea bombshell, Kaia had requested a private moment to talk with him. And by talk, she'd let him assume she meant to kiss him senseless.

They'd stepped outside the bar, the cool air wrapping around her and freezing her already chilled blood. Then, before Strider could utter a word, she'd planted a swift kiss on his gorgeous lips—unfortunately *not* leaving him senseless—and challenged him to stay put for one hour. Oh, and he had to keep Sabin and Lysander by his side.

The savage fury he had radiated as she collected Bianka and Gwen and walked away...the way he'd tackled Sabin and Lysander when the two tried to follow...the feral way he'd fought them...

She would never forget. She'd almost turned around a thousand times, wanting so badly to beg his forgiveness and plead with him to join her. She'd used his demon against him, something she'd never wanted to do. And to do so after they'd kissed so spectacularly, when they'd finally turned onto the right road, headed in the right direction, gods. Only thoughts of Rhea and the goddess's vicious nature stopped her. Kaia couldn't keep her mind on the prize and protect Strider at the same time. Hunters could be lying in wait at the *Odynia* even then, ready to take his head.

At all costs, she had to protect Strider. She needed him more than she needed air to breathe. And he'd been softening toward her. Wanting more from her. He'd kissed her in full view of everyone. Kissed her down and dirty, like they were about to make love. Like he couldn't get enough of her. Like she was a drug he'd been denied for too long. Then he'd called her baby doll and petted her like a treasured companion.

She had ruined everything by challenging him rather than talking to him, and the knowledge made her stomach cramp. But there'd been no time to explain or convince him of the merits of her plan. Team Kaia only had twenty-four hours—nineteen now—to reach Rhea's garden in the heavens, but to do so, they had to first reach the portal the god queen had opened.

With Taliyah and Neeka scouting ahead, Kaia and the rest of her ladies made their way to the wintry wonderland of Alaska. Alaska, the homeland of the Skyhawks, and the location of the makeshift portal—a location chosen in honor of the first contest winner.

Their destination? A forgotten stretch of land between two specific mountains. They left no footprints, disguised their scents and stayed completely out of sight. Just in case another team thought to hamper their progress.

However, *nothing* hampered the determined men on their trail.

"We're going to have to hobble them," Gwen said, mist forming in front of her face. She hopped from the top of one ice-covered tree to another, strawberry-blond locks blowing behind her.

A suggestion from Gwennie, the nice one. "No," Kaia said, jumping to a new tree herself, her wings fluttering beneath her white faux fur coat. That would cause Strider to lose and she couldn't bear the thought of him being laid low, writhing in pain for days, and weakened as a result. It would make him an easy target for Juliette. "The portal will close at 8:01 tomorrow morning. We'll dive through just before it closes, and then they won't be able to follow us."

"That's risky," Bianka said from directly behind her. The limb swayed under their combined weight. Slight though it still was. "We might be too late to enter ourselves and we can't afford to be disqualified from a competition. If we are, we'll be out for good with no hope of winning third place, much less first prize."

Damn it. Consorts were supposed to make life easier, not more complicated. Kaia paused, scrubbed a hand down her chilled face, suddenly so weary she just wanted to collapse. She hadn't slept in days, not really. First she'd been too busy healing, and then she'd been too busy worrying about possible sneak attacks. "Can you think of any other way to pull this off *without* hurting our men?"

There was a whistle of air, unnatural, causing her ears to twitch. It was a sound Kaia recognized very well, and dread washed through her.

They were about to be ambushed.

"Duck!" she shouted, tugging Bianka down with her. The branch shook, but just over their heads, an arrow embedded in the trunk. The scent of avocado and salt hit her nose and she cringed.

"I broke a goddamn nail!" Gwen shouted, more pissed than Kaia had heard her since her bridezilla days.

Kaia sniffed the air, discovered remnants of sweat and fear. Harpies had not loosed that arrow; humans had. Though she would bet big money Harpies had paid the humans to do so. How else would they have known to use arrowheads carved from the pit of an avocado and dipped in salt rather than bullets? How would they have known that combined, the substances weakened a Harpy's heart for weeks, no matter where she was hit?

Or, if not hired by Harpies, they'd been hired by Rhea herself, since Kaia and company were friends of the Lords. As one of the humans drew the string on his bow taut, Kaia caught sight of the figure eight tattooed on the inside of his wrist. The symbol of Infinity. The symbol of the Hunters.

With Strider, Sabin and Lysander nearby... Damn it. She didn't want Strider anywhere near these sick bastards. And maybe that's why the Hunters had been sent. Either to take out the boys, or to take out the girls dating them.

Not that they'd succeed.

"They were lying in wait, and you know how I hate when people lie in wait," Bianka growled, dropping her bag of clothes and supplies. There was a *puff* as the heavy nylon landed in the snow. "Gotta do a little punishing."

"Yeah." In quick succession, six more arrows slammed into her tree, each closer than the last. She withdrew two daggers, found her targets, tossed one, then the other. There was a grunt, a scream. "Save me one, will you?" she asked, dropping her bag beside her twin's.

"Hell, no. It's your turn to save one for *me*."

"Do it anyway and I'll stop calling you the Heavenly Hills Ho." Kaia blew her a kiss before dropping...falling... landing in a crouch with only the slightest jarring. Little snowflakes floated around her as she swiftly scanned her surroundings. She counted fifty-three Hunters, most still on the ground, bows cocked and ready.

"You fight dirty, Kye," Bianka called from just behind her. "But you've got yourself a deal."

She chuckled, happy she wouldn't have to control herself. More arrows peppered the trees, still far too close for comfort. Her Harpy squawked for release. Kaia didn't even try to hold the little sweetie back. Her sisters knew what to do, knew how to stay out of harm's way. Instantly her vision tunneled to black, little dots of red becoming her focus. Body heat.

Her mouth watered for a taste of blood.

These men would hurt Strider if given a chance, and so these men would die. Painfully. She grinned as she unfolded herself, climbing to her feet.

"There, she's there!" someone shouted.

"I see her!"

A second later, arrows soared toward her. She watched them—six of them, moving so slowly. One by one, she caught them, looked them over and threw them down. They weren't very fun toys.

"Well, did you see that? Impossible!"

Kaia leapt into action. One blink, and she was in the midst of the humans. She danced through them, claws slashing, fangs ripping. The sweet taste of blood slid down her throat. Soon, screams of pain and pleas for mercy echoed all around her.

Mercy? What was mercy? She knew not the word. The only word she knew was *more*. She needed more. More screams, more blood. She slashed with more fervor, bit with more enthusiasm. La la la, this was so much fun. Oh, look. She knew other words. *So much fun.* Bones made the most delightful sound when they broke. And when skin ripped, the most magnificent lullaby was created. Scream, scream, plea. Scream, scream, plea. La la la.

All too soon, the bodies stopped rising. The screams and pleas died. There were no more bones to break, no more skin to tear. No more lullabies. Kaia stilled, frowned. But…but…she wanted more. Why couldn't she have more?

In, out she breathed—and caught the scent of cinnamon. Cinnamon equaled Strider.

Strider.

Her Strider.

Her sexy, irreverent consort who called her baby doll.

The Harpy squawked and, sated, calmed by Strider, retreated to the back of her mind.

Kaia blinked into focus. She was panting, she realized, sweat coating her skin. No, not sweat. Blood. Blood and... other things.

"Nice to have you back, sister dear," Bianka said, slapping her on the shoulder in a job well done. "As promised, I pulled one aside and saved him for you."

Kaia turned, saw the crimson snow, the motionless bodies—or rather, what was left of them. Humans had a saying. Mess with the bull and get the horns. Well, Harpies had a saying, too. Mess with a Harpy and die.

The only remaining—and living—human was pinned to a tree. He had an arrow protruding from each shoulder and ankle, and he quaked as Kaia neared him. Each step hurt her and she paused midway to glance down at herself. When she saw nothing out of the ordinary, save for the blood, she removed her now red coat. She had cuts on her arms, stomach and legs—and the tip of an arrowhead in her side. Shit.

"Shit," Bianka echoed as she, too, noticed. "Let's get that out before any more damage is done." Her twin grabbed her bag, withdrew a pair of pliers, pushed Kaia into a sit and went to work, digging out every single shard.

The burn...Kaia wanted to yell and *really* wanted to bat her sister's hands away, but she didn't. She forced herself to concentrate on something else. Her team. She studied Gwen, who was pale but unharmed. There were two team members beside her. Juno and Tedra. One was scratched up, but the other was riddled with puncture wounds and swaying on her feet. She wouldn't be fighting in the next competition. *Damn it!*

And hadn't Kaia smelled cinnamon just a little while ago? Wasn't that how she'd calmed? So where was Strider now?

"All done," Bianka said, straightening. Worry layered her tone. They both knew Kaia needed Strider's blood, or she'd be in bad shape later.

"Thank you." Kaia stood and closed the rest of the distance between her and the Hunter. He was taller than her by at least five inches and probably outweighed her by a hundred pounds, yet the scent of fear wafted from him, acrid and potent. He'd had a front row seat to the show, after all.

"Please...don't kill me..." he cried. "Not like that. Not like them."

"I won't," she promised with a cold smile. "And in return, you're going to do me a favor. Yes?"

"Yes." Tears of relief tracked down his cheeks. "Please, yes."

"Good. That's good. Now, listen closely because I won't repeat myself." She unsheathed the dagger from her ankle holster and ripped a strip of furred cloth from her fallen coat.

"Wh-what are you doing? You said you weren't going to hurt me."

"No, I said I wasn't going to kill you and I'm not." Moving swiftly, she worked the crimson strip around his neck. "Are you listening? Good. Here's what you're going to do..."

STRIDER SCENTED THE BLOOD long before he saw the pools of it.

He'd been on Kaia's trail for hours, his demon going crazy inside his head. *Win, win, win.* If he heard the word one more time, he was going to kill someone. Namely himself. Then Kaia. Seemed impossible, but he'd find a way to do it. He was that determined and she was *that* much to blame for this mess.

Except, as he sniffed to make sure he'd identified the

notes correctly, he forgot about his irritation with Defeat, forgot about his anger with Kaia and thought only of her safety. Definitely blood.

He and Sabin shared an oh-shit glance and burst into rapid-fire movement, shoving past ice-laden branches and being slapped in the face for their efforts. Strider had his Sig in one hand and a dagger in the other, ready for anything—except to see Kaia hurt. Or worse.

Win, win, win.

Find her? Yeah, he would. Save her? Yeah, he'd do that, too. Lysander and Zacharel flew overhead and they must have scented the odor of death as well, because those long, graceful wings began flapping frantically, and they began a quick descent.

All four men hit the scene at the same time.

Bodies littered the ground. All male. Blood soaked the snow, evidence the humans had not died easily—but by the end, they had probably begged for that death.

Lysander walked the scene, sniffing, touching. "A few of the Harpies were injured."

"Kaia?" he croaked, his heart skidding to a stop.

A terrible pause. "Yes, but she walked away. They all did."

Thank the gods. His heart eked back into a semblance of a beat.

"These humans were tainted by the demon of Strife," Lysander added. "Their minds were locked only on dissension."

Rhea was possessed by the demon of Strife. And Rhea had opened her Garden of Goodbyes to all Harpies. To better destroy the women of her enemies? "Not the demon of Hope?" he asked, hopeful himself.

"No. This was Strife's doing, no question."

Shit. Strider's job—protecting Kaia—was now ten thousands times more difficult. Not that he cared. He'd do what he had to do, even go up against the queen of the gods. "How can you tell?"

"Each demon emits a certain scent." The words were said with disgust. "And the pungent stench of discord seeps from these men even still."

"Our girls are in danger, then," Sabin growled.

"We know." But that was Sabin for you, Captain Jack-ass of the *USS Obvious*. Strider scrubbed a hand down his face. Now he was just being testy. Something else to blame on Kaia. Who was injured, without his blood to heal her.

"I will summon my angels to clean the mess," Zacharel said.

His angels? "Not yet." Amid the death, he, too, caught the hint of a scent. Kaia's, to be exact. His sense of smell might not be as highly developed as Lysander's, but when it came to Kaia, Strider was attuned to the littlest things.

Sniff. He followed the coppery odor and Sabin followed him. *Sniff.* Strider crouched and lifted a broken arrowhead. Blood coated the tip. He brought that tip to his nose and gave another sniff, this one deeper. Sure enough, Kaia's scent was there. As Lysander had said, she'd been injured.

Having the evidence right in front of him did something to him. A red haze of fury dotted his vision. The thin shaft snapped in his hand. *I need to hold her. Make sure she's okay. And I need to hurt the one who hurt her.*

"She's fine," Sabin said. "She walked away. The angel can't lie."

He heard a muffled whimper and every muscle in his body stiffened. Someone lived. He and Sabin broke apart, winding around a thick tree stump. A man—human, a Hunter, his arms pinned at his sides and turned to display his tattooed wrist—was trapped there, wearing nothing but a blood-coated bow around his neck. Furred, like Kaia's coat.

A gift, then.

When the Hunter spotted the warriors, he began crying in earnest.

Strider stomped to him and gripped his chin, his dagger pressed against the man's cheek. "You're alive for a reason. What is it?" Wait. Precautions first. "If you dare try and utter a word of challenge, I'll cut your throat before you can finish. Understand?" He wouldn't put something like that past his Harpy. She was a wily little thing, determined to leave him behind.

Well, too bad. Rhea would strike at him the moment she spotted him, but he didn't give a shit. He wasn't supposed to hurt her, because hurting her would hurt Cronus—literally—and Cronus would then eat him for lunch. Neither thought bothered him. He was going to be there for Kaia. Was going to shelter her from the god queen at all costs.

For the Paring Rod, yeah. For his demon, yeah, that, too. But mostly because he was desperate to finish what they'd started inside the bar. If he didn't get that lithe little body under him, and soon, he would implode.

What happened to waiting until after the competition? Stupid plan's been ditched. I want her now.

"Yo-you are the one named St-Strider?" the human asked.

He gave a stiff nod.

"I'm—I'm supposed to tell you n-not to worry. The g-girls have everything under c-control."

Sabin moved to Strider's side. "That's all?"

The human flinched. "N-no. If you follow them, if they catch sight of you, they'll let themselves be d-disqualified."

Strider and Sabin shared another look, far past oh-shit and now entering oh-fuck territory. If anyone was willing to cut off her nose to spite her beautiful face, it was Kaia.

"Thanks for relaying the message," he told the Hunter—just before finishing him off.

He expected the angels to admonish him, but they remained silent as the human's head lolled forward, his worthless life now expunged.

Sometimes, Strider let his enemy walk away, hoping they'd learned a lesson about the shades of gray between good and evil. This time, no, that wouldn't be happening. The man had attacked Kaia. His fate had been sealed already.

The victory was mild and Defeat barely reacted.

"Come on," Strider said, cleaning his blade on his jeans and jabbing it back into its sheath. "We're not too far behind them."

Zacharel tilted his head to the side in thought. "You are willing to risk—"

Strider shut him up with a glare. "We're going. We're just gonna have to make sure we aren't seen."

CHAPTER TWENTY-ONE

THE PORTAL TO THE HEAVENS rested exactly where the text had promised, a shimmery pocket of air between two iced-over, moonlit mountains. Kaia's team was crouched on a cliff high above, watching, waiting. Dreading.

Kaia lay on a slippery ledge, the cold seeping all the way to her bones. Normally, such frigid temperatures did not affect her. This time, she shivered, her teeth chattering. Her wound might be infected, her body slightly feverish, but at least there was no pain. The cold had numbed the stupid, still-gaping injury.

To heal from this kind of injury, she needed Strider's blood.

Actually, she just needed Strider. She wasn't sure how she'd ever gotten along without him. Naughty girl that she was, she wouldn't get him. Not anytime soon—and maybe not even after that. Hopefully, he'd gotten the message she had left him and had charted a course to Buda. His well-being came before her understandably great need for him. But only a little!

She twisted the dial on her binoculars for a closer look at the surrounding area. White, white and more white, but so far, she'd spotted no other Harpies. No misty air to reveal the telltale sigh of heated breath. No bright colors slinking down the rocks, inching ever closer to safety. No clicks in the breeze as arrows were notched. Even still, she expected foul play. At least until they reached the bottom of the mountain. The moment her team stepped through the portal, they would be on neutral territory. No one would be able to strike at them.

The problem, however, would be reaching bottom.

"I think we're good," Taliyah said, confiscating the binoculars and panning the higher peaks. "And really, we can't wait much longer. You and Tedra need to be tended, and we can't do that here."

Bianka confiscated the binoculars from Taliyah and peered down at the flatlands. "If Lysander were here, he could fly above and—"

"*Again* with this crap?" Kaia reclaimed the binoculars and tossed them over her shoulder. For the past hour, Bianka had recited all the reasons they'd be better off if the men were here. As if Kaia didn't already know, damn it.

"Hey!" Neeka gasped. "That hurt."

Kaia twisted, grimaced at the twinge in her side. The beautiful girl was scowling and rubbing at the lump now sprouting below her left eye. "I'd say sorry, but it was totally Bianka's fault because she—"

"Shh!" Bianka clamped a hand over her mouth, silencing her. Her twin pointed to the shimmering portal with her free hand. "Look."

She looked. The Falconways and the Songbirds had just crested the far hillside and were sprinting toward the portal, fast…faster…mere blurs now. No one attempted to stop them, and one by one, they whisked through that dazzling air pocket, disappearing from view.

If Hunters waited, determined to strike, they would have at least peeked from the shadows to see who approached. Right?

"Okay," Kaia said with a nod. "We've got a direct shot to the portal, so here's what we're gonna do. Two of us are too injured to run and we'll slow whoever tries to carry us, and I don't want us separated, so we're all going to slide over this ledge and ride our backpacks to the bottom. Like sleds. Then *boom,* we'll be in the heavens, healthy and whole, before we know it."

Murmurs of agreement met her words.

Within minutes, they were lined up and ready to go. Kaia had the lead. She perched on her backpack, her legs already dangling over the side of the ledge. Her heart drummed in her chest. She'd jumped from this very mountain a thousand times before, playing Who Can Break the Least Amount of Bones with Bianka. She usually won—Bianka always covered her face and let her body just kind of flop on the ice. Not that it mattered now, she thought. *Concentrate.* It was just, if one of her girls was hurt…

She gritted her teeth. Not gonna happen, not again.

As she exhaled, mist formed in front of her. "Here—" she scooted "—we—" she teetered… "Go!" She slid. Wind slapped at her as she descended, faster and faster, just as the other teams had done. The outside of her backpack was shredding quickly, and her coat would be next to go, then her skin. Almost there…

An arrowhead sank into her thigh muscle. Before she could react, another nailed her. She yelped in pain. Damn it! How? Where were— There. Hunters had stepped through miniature air pockets of their own, as if they'd been there, hovering between one realm and the other, watching and waiting. She wanted to fly off her pack and rip through them, one by one, but…she whizzed through the portal, and they disappeared from view.

A rush of dizziness. A wink of too-bright light. Then her backpack skidded to a stop, catching on thick ropes of tree roots. She blinked, clearing her head and reaching for the arrow still protruding from her leg. Gwen slammed into her with a breathy *hmph,* accidentally dislodging her hand.

Another yelp left her, another lance of pain shooting through her entire body.

"You okay?" Gwen demanded, already on her feet and dragging Kaia out of the path of the others.

"Sure, sure." She scanned for the Falconways and the Songbirds. No sign of them, thank the gods. Well, thanks to all but Rhea, the bitch. Kaia would not be thanking her for anything, even in her own head. "You?"

"Yeah, but I think they got Bianka. I heard her shout."

No! She would rather receive a thousand injuries than allow Bianka to receive even one. "I will murder—". The threat died in her throat. One of the tree limbs was reaching out, down, moving stealthily, purposely, the leaves—two of them, a top and a bottom—surprisingly jagged at the edges and clamping open and closed like teeth.

Alive. The trees were alive. Eyes wide, Kaia slapped at the huge, mouthy leaves and rolled out of the way. Yet another lance of pain. "Did you see that?" she panted.

The limb wrenched backward, away from them.

"Yeah, and I'm still reeling. Be careful." Gwen spun this way and that, a dagger in each hand, watching the trees, daring them to try that move again.

Suddenly Bianka appeared, gliding to a bumpy stop. She had arrows in her shoulder, forearm and stomach. Blood soaked her already. "Shit! They got me."

Seeing her, Kaia had to swallow a whimper.

Rhea really hadn't wanted them to make it this far, she thought darkly. Well, Rhea would be in for a nasty surprise. "I'll help you in a sec, sis. Just have to take care of something first." Rage gave Kaia strength as she yanked the arrowhead out of her leg. That done, she limped to her sister and tugged her out of the line of fire—and more of those chomping tree limbs.

Gwen helped, kicking and slashing until they once again flew backward.

"Those bastards!" Bianka rasped, paling from blood loss and pain.

"We'll have to worry about the Hunters later." And their payback. "I think the trees are freaking vampires." Shaking, Kaia kneeled and gently—well, as gently as she was able—removed the arrowheads from her twin.

Bianka complained the entire time, yelling at Kaia, then Taliyah, Neeka and the others when they arrived. Neeka was the only other member hurt this round and Taliyah doctored her. Not a peep did either make.

"What if the boys come through the portal, huh?" Kaia asked. "They won't be prepared."

"If they're dumb enough to cross over, they deserve what they get. Now come on," Taliyah said. "We may be on neutral ground right now, but we've still got an hourlong hike before we reach our destination. We can't be late."

Yeah, and a lot could happen in an hour. "You're just jealous because you don't have a white knight racing to your rescue."

Taliyah rolled her baby-blues. "Your injuries have made you delusional. When I find my consort, I plan to stab him in the heart before he can cause me a moment's unease."

"I understand. Your consort can't compare to mine, no one's can, so you'd rather go without."

"Mine's better than yours," Bianka said.

"No way."

"Way."

"Girls." Taliyah clapped her hands to gain their attention. Just as she'd done when they were children, arguing over a toy. "Both of your consorts suck. Now shut up and move out."

Bianka stuck her tongue out at Kaia. "Mine sucks less than yours," she muttered.

"Yeah, well mine sucks *better* than yours." Kaia kept

her eye on the portal as they limped away, both relieved and worried when the men failed to walk through.

THREE CHEERS. NOT. EVERY team arrived on time. Of course, Team Kaia was the last to cross the battleground threshold, but whatever. They'd sustained a few bumps and bruises along the way, but there'd been no more ambushes, so Kaia wouldn't complain (as Bianka was still doing).

The worst "bruise" belonged to her. One of the man-eating trees had taken a bite out of her, reaching her before she could frighten it away. Sharp, leafy teeth had snapped onto her wrist and sunk to the bone. As she'd yelped, the tree had seemed to, well, gag, shuddering and swaying, and then that tree had withered right before her eyes, turning black, ceasing all movement and allowing Bianka to remove the limb with a single strike of her dagger.

After that, the trees had left them alone. Maybe her fever had poisoned the one that had bitten her and the rest were sentient enough to fear the same. Yeah, she definitely had a fever and there was nothing slight about it now. Gods, no ice around here, but she was still trembling from cold.

Toughen up. This is for Strider.

The competing Harpies crowded the only clearing, with thick (non-biting?) plants surrounding them. The air was warm, the sun golden and bright, little flickers of purple, blue and pink in the undertones. There were no consorts or slaves present and Kaia wondered why these other girls had left their men behind. Certainly not for the same reasons she had.

Rhea was nowhere to be seen. Juliette, however, stood on an outstretched tree limb overlooking the masses, black hair streaming behind her in a perfect breeze neither too light nor too strong.

"Welcome, fellow Harpies," she announced. "I'm happy

to inform you that each of the competing teams has met the deadline." Her lavender gaze leveled on Kaia. Having used a compact to check her reflection—yes, appearances counted, even out here—Kaia knew what Juliette saw. Dark half moons under her eyes, skin pallid, except for her over-bright cheeks. "Thankfully, no one was waylaid."

Bitch knew about the Hunters. How? Only one reason made sense. Was she...could she be working with Rhea? Kaia's stomach twisted, acid churning, frothing.

Juliette continued gleefully, "As you probably suspected, you're here to fight," and cheers abounded. When they faded a few moments later, she added, "The time has come for the second game, Death Drop."

Now "oohs" and "ahhs" echoed.

Juliette held up her hands for silence. "First, a little about the game. You will choose four members to compete. Those four must fight here in the trees and in the air, all at the same time. Your only goal is to knock the opposition to the ground. Once a Harpy touches the ground, she's out for good. And you'll be thrilled to know that there are no rules restricting the methods that you use, so feel free to hit below the belt, as humans are fond of saying."

Eager cackling, fists bumping together. Kaia remained in place, unmoving, heart hammering.

"The first team to lose all four members is disqualified," Juliette said. "To bring home today's victory, one member of your team must be the very last to hit the ground. It's that simple and that easy."

Yeah. Right. Nothing was simple or easy with Juliette.

A toothy, white grin flashed. "Oh, and before you ask. There's no time limit. This contest will last as long as it needs to last. *But* you only have five minutes to decide who fights and who remains on the ground, waiting to administer much-needed medical aid." She glanced at the timer hooked around her neck, right beside her Skyhawk warrior medallion. A medallion Tabitha must have given her—Kaia's medallion—even though they were part of different clans. "Those five minutes start...now."

Within seconds, the teams were sectioned off in huddles, feminine murmurs blending in the daylight.

"I want this," Kaia said to kick them off. She had a lot to prove.

Bianka kissed her cheek. "I love you, Kye, you know that, and you know I think you're Grade A at brute force and vengeance, but flying, well, after everything that was done to you last time, isn't wise. Not to mention the fact that you're still injured!"

"Yeah," she replied dryly. "Thanks for not mentioning. Just for the record, Heavenly Hills, you were just shot up, too."

"Hey! You promised never to call me by that ridiculous name again."

"Like that's a promise I can really keep."

"Bee's right," Taliyah said, ignoring them. "Everyone's already out for our blood. They're going to gang up on us big-time, so we have to have our fastest players in the air."

Kaia sputtered. "I know you're not suggesting what I think you're suggesting. I'm fast. Like, bullet fast."

"Yeah, but Gwen's faster. So am I, for that matter. So is Neeka. So is Bianka. Hell, Juno and Tedra are faster than all of us combined," Taliyah added, motioning to their other members. "That's why I recruited them. Plus, Juno hasn't played yet, and Tedra's already healed from the arrows."

Everyone but Kaia nodded. She pressed her tongue into the roof of her mouth. This almost seemed rehearsed. What was clear, though, was that they didn't want her fighting. Didn't think she could help, only hinder.

Gods, the hurt she experienced...the humiliation...

both nearly knocked her down. Made her want to curl into Strider's lap and cry. His strong arms would band around her and he would coo at her, comfort her, then tell her how capable she was.

Or not.

Last time they were together, he'd wanted her to train with his friends. Even he doubted her skill.

Stomach...clenching...again...

She could have fought her sisters on this. Could have pulled rank and insisted. Instead, she nodded as if she agreed with them. Just as she'd done with Strider. One, they would have argued with her and she had no solid legs to stand on. Just wound-ridden ones. Two, as they'd so rudely pointed out, she wasn't at her best. And three, victory was priority one, not her pride.

"All right," she said, forcing a confident tone. "Bianka, Juno and Tedra. You're up. *If* you're okay, Bee. You were shot up pretty badly."

"I'm fine." She offered Kaia a relieved yet sad smile. She knew the thoughts pouring through Kaia's mind. "I was carrying a vial of Lysander's blood with me and drained the contents on the way here."

Smart. And hell, why hadn't she thought to ask Strider for a vial of *his* blood? Not that he would have agreed to give her one. Not after everything she'd done to him. Plus, to do so, he would have to care for her. Would have to be more concerned for her health than with remaining at her side.

"You guys can decide on the fourth member," she said, knowing they would anyway.

They accepted the decree without a token argument, surprise, surprise, and it was swiftly decided that Gwen would join the fray. Sabin's blood had healed her after Tag and she hadn't been hit by an arrow. Neeka's deafness could be used against her and Taliyah wasn't quite as equipped for airplay as the youngest Skyhawk.

A shrill whistle blasted and the groups quieted.

"Time's up," Juliette announced. "Take your places, everyone."

Footsteps shuffled. While chosen team members climbed to the top of the trees, Kaia remained on the ground, watching, a painful vise-grip on her heart. A grip that tightened when she caught Juliette's eye and the Harpy grinned with her patented smug satisfaction.

Knew you couldn't cut it, that smile seemed to say.

Kaia tried not to flush or tear up.

"Don't pay any attention to that hag," Taliyah said, slapping her on the shoulder. "You're better in every way."

"Thanks, Tal."

Neeka dug the hopefully unneeded medical supplies from their backpacks and joined them. None too soon, either.

Juliette raised a gun high in the air, held steady while everyone tensed, waiting, expectant, then squeezed the trigger.

Boom!

High above was an explosion of movement. Leaves rustled and bodies slammed together. Grunts of might, groans of pain and screams of rage rang out, tolling bells of injury and satisfaction. Kaia tried to keep track of her sisters, but the girls were too high up, moving too quickly, disappearing behind leaves and clouds and she soon gave up. She watched the ground, waiting for bodies to fall.

Within minutes, she felt a whoosh of air, tensed when she heard a splat. Tensed even more when she spied a motionless…Songbird a few feet away. Blood pooled around the girl as one of her teammates rushed to administer aid.

Thank the gods. Kaia's stomach unclenched, though

the burn of acid didn't recede. Would Gwen end up that way? Bianka?

Hands fisting, body trembling, she tore her gaze from the huddle of Songbirds. At the far edge of the clearing, she spotted a shake of leaves and a flash of dark hair. An innocent Harpy, just needing a moment alone? A malicious Harpy bent on attacking someone, even though they stood on neutral ground? A Hunter, who wouldn't care about anything but destroying his target? Or maybe Rhea herself?

Hell, for all Kaia knew, that dark hair belonged to Sabin. Or even Lazarus. The way he'd watched her at the bar, the way he'd taunted her…he wasn't done with her. That, she knew all too well.

Taking no chances, she leaned over to Taliyah and whispered, "Saw something. Gonna check it out."

Her oldest sister didn't switch her attention from the fight. "Be careful. Shout if you need me."

She knew her sister well enough to know Taliyah was merely humoring her. If she'd thought there was an actual threat, Taliyah the Cold-Hearted would have insisted on coming with her. There was another stab of hurt in Kaia's chest, but she shook it off.

She melted into the thick, green foliage. The trees and plants actually seemed to turn away from her now, as if word had spread and they were all afraid of her. Too bad the same couldn't be said for her fellow Harpies.

Staying low, a dagger in each hand, she worked her way around the clearing. Her legs were a bit rubbery, causing her feet to drag. She was louder than she'd intended, but there was no help for it. If the intruder didn't notice the clomp of her boots, he'd definitely hear the beat of her heart, drumming like a jackhammer set to its fastest setting and slamming against her ribs.

Finally she spotted footprints that didn't belong to a

Harpy. These were big, thick and pressed deeply enough that whoever had made them weighed at least two hundred pounds of solid muscle.

That narrowed things down a bit. She was dealing with either a Hunter, Sabin or Lazarus. Her mind buzzed, quickly eliminating suspects. If this were a Hunter, there would be other footprints. After all, Hunters were like cockroaches. Where one hid, a thousand others did, as well. If this were Sabin, she would scent Strider. The two were never far apart.

That left Lazarus the Tampon.

Well, well. Maybe they'd have their knock-down drag-out at last. And wouldn't you know it? They'd have that knock-down drag-out while she lacked full throttle. Wasn't that just peachy?

A hard weight crashed into her back, throwing her face-first to the ground. That same weight pressed against her so forcefully her wings were smashed into their slits, hindering their movements and decreasing her strength even more. Oxygen gushed from her suddenly dirt-coated mouth, an explosion that left her reeling.

She'd been so determined to sneak up on her prey, she'd failed to guard her back properly. She knew better! Damn it, what was wrong with her?

Here was more proof of her weakness. No wonder her sisters hadn't wanted her in the air.

Nothing would prevent her from fighting, though. Her claws emerged, and her fangs sprouted. But just as she attempted to twist and wedge her knee between their bodies, a male voice whispered, "Don't. I won, and that's that." Satisfaction and pleasure layered that familiar—beloved—voice.

Strider. Unlike Juliette's satisfaction, his didn't bother her. She actually reveled in it. He was here. He was with her, alive and well. He was also in danger, but at the moment she couldn't make that matter. He was here!

"We good?" he asked in that same silky whisper. His warm breath caressed her ear and absolute relief washed through her. Until he added, "Wait, don't answer. That bastard Lazarus is just ahead, waiting for you. He set a trap."

When she caught her breath, she rasped out, "What kind of trap?"

"The kind with flowers, candlelight and a bejeweled goblet filled with his probably diseased blood."

Her eyes widened. Lazarus was going to try and…seduce her? Why? "I don't know about diseased, but that blood is probably poisoned." Right? A trick meant to lure her into softening before the bastard went in for the kill.

"If we're lucky, he'll die of disappointment when you fail to show."

"Actually, if *he's* lucky."

"Good point. Now I have to decide whether to kill him now or kill him later."

"Option two?" she asked hopefully.

"My thinking exactly. Right now, I have something better to do." Strider eased back a little and she finally twisted, lying on her back. His legs straddled her waist, and his navy eyes glared down at her. Dirt smudged his sun-kissed skin and his pale hair was pink with dried blood and plastered to his face. "Don't worry, though. He'll get his."

"Are you hurt?" If someone had hurt him, she would unleash her Harpy. She wouldn't be able to help herself. She would—

"I'm fine." His expression softened, and gods, he was beautiful. "Remember the Hunters who last attacked you? Well, they suffered afterward. You're welcome."

Her relief intensified, mixing with a sense of pride.

This was her man, her warrior. No one was stronger. No one was as vengeful or as capable. "Thank you. Now, you have to go," she told him, giving him a little push. "Rhea could be nearby, and you are—"

"Nope." He didn't budge. "Sabin and the angels are looking for her. So far, they haven't found any hint of her presence."

"That doesn't mean—"

"Shut it, Kaia," he said, cutting her off a second time. "You're in trouble and only digging the hole deeper." He pushed to his feet only to bend down and grab her wrist, tugging her to her feet in turn, spinning them both around and leading her away from Lazarus.

Leaves and branches slapped at her, and insects buzzed, some daring to bite her.

"I can't go too far," she said, huffing from exertion already. Damn. Her side and leg throbbed, the wounds having opened when she fell. Now, blood trickled from each, catching in her boots.

"You'll go as far as I tell you," he snapped, unaware of her pain.

"Strider, listen to me. My sisters are fighting. I have to—"

"I don't care what they're doing. You and I are going to talk. Now keep it down while I find a place for us. If you don't, I'll gag you. And Kaia? I really hope I get to gag you."

She pressed her lips together, silent as he urged her deeper and deeper into the forest.

CHAPTER TWENTY-TWO

STRIDER HAULED KAIA through thickening mist and across a rushing river. When he'd first come here, the trees had tried to eat him alive and he'd had to hack his way to safety every few minutes. Now, those same trees remained perfectly still, not a single leaf dancing in the swirling breeze. What was *that* about?

The question ceased to matter when he reached the cave he'd discovered while tracking Kaia. Would serve her right to be thrown inside, a boulder shoved in front of the only exit. She could spend a few years in solitary confinement, thinking about her mistakes.

He meant to yell at her, he really did—for leaving him behind, for almost walking into that bastard Lazarus's seductive trap, which Strider would punish him for setting, by the way—but as he backed her against the crystal wall, he was given his first full-length glimpse of her since tackling her fine ass to the ground. Her gorgeous red hair was damp at the ends and dripping little water beads onto her bare stomach.

The river had washed away the makeup that always coated her skin, leaving her glimmering like a diamond in blazing sunlight. Not as brightly as before, though. And she was shivering. He frowned. Why was she shivering? It was as hot as hell in here.

That did nothing to diminish her appeal. Nothing could. Maybe because she wore a tiny half top and a pair of shorts. Both were white, now see-through, and he *saw*. Blushing, beaded nipples, and then, between the long, lithe length of her legs, a delicious patch of red in the center, and if he didn't look away soon his erection would bust through the zipper on his pants.

He studied the rest of her. She was injured, he realized. The angry wounds in her side and on her thigh caused fury to well inside him, replacing the lust. No wonder her skin lacked its most brilliant sheen and her body couldn't stop trembling.

He bit into his wrist and held the wound to her mouth. "Drink."

Moaning in ecstasy, she obeyed. Such exquisite suction, he thought, such warmth. Her eyes closed in surrender. When he saw the torn muscle and then the flesh weaving back together, he nodded in satisfaction and removed his arm.

He was the one to groan this time. Of course, lack of injury left her beautiful skin bare and unmarred, allowing him to eat her back up with his eyes. The lust returned full force.

Gaze...up... Her lips were pouty, moist. *Higher*. Because, damn. He was throbbing. Her silver-gold eyes were luminous with all kinds of emotion. Upset, relief, arousal of her own, hurt. He wanted to wipe away the bad and magnify the good. And the only way to do that, he told himself, was to have her. Finally. All the way, nothing held back.

Yeah, baby. He liked the thought of that. Felt as if he were thinking clearly for the first time in his life. He needed what she offered. Wanted to stake his claim, warn every other man away.

There would be consequences, he was sure, but he couldn't make that matter. Not here, not now. She'd left him and struck out on her own, and the separation had nearly driven him to the brink of insanity.

He pressed his body against hers and she gasped. Such a lovely sound, needy and wanton.

"Thank you," she said, her voice low and sultry. "You have no idea how much I needed that."

"Welcome."

"Do you still want to gag me? Because I recommend using a racket ball and duct tape if you do."

"No need for a gag. I can handle you." If he couldn't, well, there was no better way to go.

Her breath hitched. "Really?" Now her tone was verging on the edge of hope.

He nodded. "Really. So let's figure out what I need to do to hit this one out of the park."

"O-okay."

"You once told me Paris had given you a bazillion orgasms. Your words, not mine. So exactly how many is a *bazillion?*"

Her cheeks pinkened and she was adorable, all the sexier, in her embarrassment. "I don't know. I didn't count. And I don't want to talk about him."

"Think back. Count. And you're going to talk about him, once and only once. After this conversation you will forget him. Forever."

"Why?" She flattened her palms on his chest. "Why make me think back, I mean, when I only want to think about you?"

"My demon. Why else?" He traced a fingertip along her jaw. "So do it. Please."

Win.

Shocking, he thought dryly. *I will.* He hoped.

Understanding dawned in her expression, and with it, fear. She'd just realized Strider had to give her more orgasms than Paris had. That even sex was to be a challenge to him. Was she wondering if they'd ever have any peace? If there'd ever be a moment just for them, no games, no winner, no loser?

"You knew that's how it would be before you accepted me as your consort," he said stiffly. "Don't even consider tossing me aside now. So do it. Think back and tell me."

"I don't want to toss you aside. I don't want you hurt, either." She chewed on her bottom lip, a nervous action he recognized. "He gave me f-four, I think."

That stutter... "You think or you know?"

A pause. More chewing. "I, uh, know. Yes, I know. Four. It was four. For sure."

Win.

Shut it. I will. He would give her (at least) five orgasms before he came. And he would blow her mind with every single one of them. But he'd have to deliver them while she was still clothed. Moment he stripped her, he would be inside her, filling her up, losing the control he needed.

"I have to say, I'm a little surprised you consider four a bazillion, but to each his own. Just prepare yourself for a quadrillion." He reached between their bodies and unsnapped her shorts.

Her eyes widened. "We're having sex *now?*"

"Yes." *Unziiip.* He arched a brow. "After your assembly line of orgasms. Is that a problem?"

"No. It's just...do you remember when I said I didn't want you hurt? Well, I meant, I didn't want to accidentally hurt you. So you'll just...damn it, you'll need a safe word." Her chest heaved with the force of her breathing. "I'm sorry."

Baffled, he paused. "Me? *I'll* need a safe word?" And she hadn't been afraid he'd fail, only that she'd injure him. He nearly grinned. Already this was the best sexual experience of his life.

She nodded, unsure. "Are you okay with that?"

Delectable female. His gaze lowered to the gap in her shorts. White panties. Lace. Nice. "How about a safe phrase? Mine will be 'someone's out there.'" He didn't wait for her reply, but dropped to his knees.

"Oh, gods." Her belly quivered. "Okay, yes, okay. Gods, I'm repeating myself, but that works."

His gaze locked on the shadow of red beneath the lace and his mouth watered. He leaned in and nuzzled her with his nose, inhaling the sweet scent of female.

"Oh, gods," she said again. "You—you'll be the best, Strider, you don't have to worry. Okay? I know it."

Just then he wasn't worried about anything; his mind was locked on her and only her. On learning her taste, hearing her beg for more, feeling her clutching at him, maybe pulling at his hair.

He forced her legs to part as far as they could with the shorts restricting her movements. Unmindful of her panties, he pressed the tip of his tongue against the heart of her, the heat. Pressed harder. Gods, he could already taste her and he'd never liked anything more.

The ache in his cock intensified, nearly unbearable. Damn. How good would it feel if he reached down, curled his fingers around his shaft, stroked up and down while burying his face between her legs?

He was reaching down before he realized he'd moved. Damn it. He gripped her thighs. He'd have to blank his mind, perform but remain distanced. Only when he'd beaten Paris could he consider his own pleasure.

Strider flicked his tongue over the tight bud of her clitoris.

"Oh, gods, yes," she gasped out.

No need to force his mind to blank. Her pleasured cry short-circuited his thoughts. Satisfied, he wanted her satisfied. Damp, her panties were damp, but he wanted them soaking.

Next his tongue traced lazy circles around her heated center, swiped back and forth, up and down, hitting her from every possible angle. When she began arching her hips to meet him, he caressed his hands up and down her calves, her thighs, then under her shorts. Such soft, smooth skin...so damn warm.

Though he wanted to tunnel his hands up, higher, thrust his fingers inside her, he merely teased her with the possibility, his tongue never ceasing its assault, and finally, sweetly, she gripped the back of his head and held his mouth firmly against her. She was panting, sheened with perspiration.

"I need...I have to have..." She ground him where she needed him most. "Strider!" she screamed as she came.

One down, four to go.

He stood to shaky legs. Without a word, he spun her, forcing her to face the wall. His cock rubbed against her ass and he sucked in a ragged breath. His fingers glided around, sliding under her shorts, inside her panties. Contact. Skin to hot, wet female core, and oh, sweet heaven, she felt exquisite.

A groan slipped from her. Her back arched. Her arms lifted and then her nails were scraping through his hair. He rubbed her swollen little clitoris before inserting one finger deep inside her inner sheath, moving it in and out, in and out, inserting a second finger, moving them in and out, in and out, until she once again writhed against him, desperate for release.

"Strider, I need, I need..."

"I know, baby doll." He gave her a third finger, stretching her. With his free hand, he reached up and cupped one of her breasts. A perfect handful. Her nipple was beaded, probably aching. He pinched. She gasped. The sound affected him, drove his own need higher. "How am I doing?"

"The best. No one better. *Please*."

He couldn't help himself, had to have concentrated contact. He jerked her hips backward, slamming the crease of her ass against his erection, the perfect cradle, and as she moaned, he slowed the thrust of his fingers. Within seconds, her hips began pumping harder, faster, urging him to keep the rhythm. He didn't. He slowed a bit more.

Soon she couldn't quite catch her breath, was panting shallowly, raggedly. Her skin heated another degree, almost burning through his clothes. It hurt, but damn, it hurt so good. Especially when her nails sank deep into his scalp, drawing blood. Then every muscle in her body clamped down, her bones vibrating. Again she screamed his name. This time, a second voice was layered over hers, raspier, almost purring, and he knew her Harpy was right there with her, enjoying.

Two down, three to go.

"Strider, let me…suck on you…you have to be…hurting."

Damn, but he wanted to take her up on the decadent offer. He bit his tongue until he tasted blood. Yeah, he was hurting, but he'd hurt a hell of a lot more if he failed to do this right. "Not yet."

"Please…"

Gods, she was going to kill him.

HE WAS GOING TO KILL HER.

Kaia's legs were trembling, barely able to hold her up. Her blood had reached the point of boiling and she'd long since melted inside. And yet, she couldn't get enough of Strider. He'd given her an orgasm and she'd immediately craved another. He'd given her another, and still she craved.

If she felt that way, how must he be feeling? On fire? Ready to burst? Damn it, she wanted him to enjoy their time together, not suffer through it.

Dizziness consumed her when he spun her back around. He didn't give her a chance to speak or recover; he simply meshed their mouths together, his tongue thrusting inside the way she wanted his cock to do. When he cupped her ass and lifted her, she had to wind her legs around his waist for balance. The moment she did, he pressed, hard, and the long, thick length of his erection hit her dead center.

She moaned. He groaned.

He never stopped feeding her that kiss. It was sweet, it was torture; it was wonderfully debauched and erotic and affected her all the way to her soul, and oh, gods above she was coming, again, before she could work her hand between them and fist his erection.

"You're beautiful when you climax," he said fiercely, his voice strained. "Two more times, baby doll, okay?"

He didn't understand. How could she make him understand? The number of orgasms didn't matter. Not with him. The fact that *Strider* was kissing her, *Strider* was touching her, *Strider* was pleasing her, was enough. No experience would ever be better than this.

She had to make him understand.

Kaia's legs were boneless as she forced them to the ground. He pressed her back into the crystal wall—so cold—and cupped her breasts, squeezing. Lines of tension branched from his mouth. His swollen, still moist mouth.

She wrapped her fingers around his wrists, applying so much pressure he would not be able to move without experiencing a twinge of pain. His gaze shot up, meeting hers. Those navy blues were glazed, hungry.

Now that she had his attention, she flung him to the side and danced in front of him, switching their positions. Her claws ripped at his jeans. The material was damp where she'd rubbed against him.

"What are—" The question ended on a hoarse moan when her fingers whispered along his flesh. His hot, needy flesh. "Kaia, don't…you can't—damn it, baby! Do it, please."

She'd already moved to her knees. Now, she sucked him deep, all the way to the back of her throat. His fingers tangled in her hair. Maybe he'd meant to jerk her away from him, but as she lifted her head, sucking harder, laving her tongue over the thick vein riding the length of him, he merely massaged her scalp, gentle, tender, as if afraid to tug the strands.

"Baby…sweetheart…*please*." He was pumping his hips in tune with her mouth, in and out, in and out, still trying to be gentle and slow when his body clearly craved hard and fast.

Even though she enjoyed pleasuring him like this as much as he enjoyed being on the receiving end, his earlier doubts played through her mind, taking root inside her. What if the number of orgasms did, in fact, matter to his demon? Strider would be her best, hands down, no question, no matter what, but if the number mattered and she failed to have more than four before he had one, Strider would hurt. If he was hurt, he wouldn't bed her again.

He'd remember the pain rather than the pleasure.

Oh…damn. Her point would have to be proven later.

She stopped abruptly and he groaned as if agonized. He probably was. Two more, she thought. She had to have two more climaxes before she could give him one. She felt selfish and greedy, but she couldn't risk this. Along with proving her point, she would make this up to him later. Would give him so many orgasms he wouldn't be able to walk for a week.

Trembling more intensely, she stood, tugged his hand from her hair and moved it down her shorts, between her legs, where she was hot and drenched. At the moment of contact, a moan parted her lips.

"Kaia, please—you have to…I need…" His voice was

strained, his features so taut he reminded her of a rubber band, ready to snap at any second. And his eyes…his eyes glowed with a mix of blue and red, Strider and his demon vying for dominance.

"I surrender," she whispered, arching against him, sliding those fingers deep. "I'm yours and we'll do this your way. However you want."

"No, I want…need…"

"I know, darling, I know, but keep touching me like this, okay? Touch me like this until I say stop. Then, you're going to bury this beautiful cock so deep inside me…I'll never…be the…same." The last emerged on another moan. The pressure…building again…taking over…

"Yes," he growled.

"Oh, yes." She moved his thumb to her clit and pressed. A fourth orgasm shot through her quickly, causing her to tense and spasm. She rode the waves of it, not allowing his fingers to slow their ruthless, relentless friction. Her blood, boiling before, became an inferno. Steam actually seeped from her pores, creating a mist around them. She didn't understand, knew it was weird, wrong, but wasn't going to worry about it now. This was too important.

"Kaia…hurry…" Sweat beaded his brow, dripped from his temples. Breath rasped in and out of his nose. "I can't hold out much longer. Dying…"

Her undulations never ceased and the pressure built once again, coiling through her. "Just a little more…" Her nipples scraped again his chest, creating more of that decadent friction. "Please, just a little more."

"I'm going to come the moment I'm inside you."

"Want you to."

"Gods, Kaia. I've never been this ready."

Good, that was good. As much as he needed to be her best, she wanted to be *his* best. To drive away thoughts of all his others. To be his one and only. Forever.

"You're mine," she said.

"Yours. Never should have resisted you." Predatory growls sprang from low in his throat. His free hand slammed into the wall behind him, right beside his thigh, cracking the crystal. He hit again. Split. Again. Shatter.

All that intensity…all for her… The steam thickened around them and she found herself climbing him as if he were another mountain, hiking her legs around his waist. He shoved his fingers deep, so deep, and finally, blessedly, she shot off. A scream ripped from her, so intense she saw silver stars winking behind her eyelids.

In the next instant, she was flying backward. She hit the floor with a *thwack* and lost her breath. There was no time to recover. Her clothing was ripped away. Her eyelids popped open just in time to see Strider, his expression frenzied, his control gone, looming over her. He'd just removed the last of his own clothing. He spread her legs as far as they would go and thrust deep inside her, all the way.

He roared. But he didn't come, not yet, and she cried out as she arched up to meet him. Those predatory growls of his become savage as he pumped, stretching her. He wasn't human or immortal, she mused. He was animal and she loved it. And really, she should have been past the point of responding. Should have simply become a receptacle for his pleasure. But as he drilled into her, consuming her, she, too, became lost to sensation, an animal herself.

Then he stopped. Stopped. He stared down at her, beads of his sweat dripping onto her. "Baby doll?" he gritted, voice rough and gravelly.

"Yes, I am. Now move!"

"No. Get you…pregnant?"

"No. I'm not fertile right now."

He was moving an instant later and she was lost again. This was her consort, her man, and they were joined. One.

The knowledge was sultry, intoxicating to her. Her claws sliced at his back, flaying his flesh. Her fangs bit at his lips, tasting his blood, and then he was kissing her, too, his tongue thrusting like his cock, branding his taste inside the hollow of her mouth. This was everything she'd ever secretly wanted and she gave herself up to Strider's possession.

Yes, possession, she realized. His demon was a part of him, but Strider was a part of her, essential to her survival.

"Strider," she gasped. "My Strider."

Perhaps his name on her kiss-swollen lips pushed him over the edge, because he released another roar, the crazed sound echoing off the walls. His entire body tensed over hers. Absolute pleasure consumed his face and he pumped inside her a final time, coming…coming…shooting her straight into another climax.

CHAPTER TWENTY-THREE

SHE'D BURNED HIM. *LITERALLY* burned him. Strider had blisters all over his body. Or at least, he'd *had* them. The moment he'd climaxed, jetting inside her, his demon had climaxed, as well. Kaia, a strong, capable Harpy, had surrendered to them, utterly and completely, giving them everything, all that she was, and the unending pleasure that knowledge had wrought in him had given way to shocking strength. The blisters had begun healing mere seconds after forming.

He'd never experienced anything like it. And now he felt…invincible. Yeah, that was the word. He could do anything. Could topple an army, find Pandora's box, whatever. His demon felt the same, was even then moaning with abandon, still lost to the sensations.

Somewhere during the time Strider had spent on his knees, feasting between Kaia's legs, and the time she'd spent on *her* knees, feasting between *his* legs, being her best had ceased to matter. He'd wanted only to be with her. Her, *Kaia*. No one else.

She'd become his sickness and his cure, shooting him to heights he hadn't known existed.

Now he rolled to his side, keeping her tucked against him. He didn't want to let her go. Not now, not ever.

She buried her head in the hollow of his neck, her silky hair tickling his skin. They were both sweat-soaked, and her body temperature had cooled only slightly. His favorite, though: she glowed. Damn, did she glow, all the colors of the rainbow shining from her skin. She made his mouth water for another taste, when arousal should have been impossible. For a year, at least.

Her fingers traced along the edges of his azure butterfly tattoo, the ink seeming to rise up to meet her, as if craving more of that heat. A deeper burn. He'd never before allowed a female to fondle the mark. That's where Defeat had entered his body, a constant reminder of Strider's stupidity. Sometimes he looked at the jagged ink and felt ashamed. Just then, he liked that it was there. He liked Kaia's attention to the details.

"You're not…hurt, are you?" she asked in a voice full of gravel.

When he wanted to bang his chest and whoop with pride? "Opposite of hurt."

"Really?"

"Really." She asked that a lot, as if she didn't dare believe his words. "Didn't even need my safe phrase."

She chuckled, but her amusement quickly washed away. She stiffened, getting serious. "So you had a good time, then?"

He flattened his chin against his sternum, looking down at her. She had her own face angled down, so he saw only that crest of red hair. "Are you serious?"

Clearly offended, she huffed out, "Would I have asked otherwise?"

"Did you not hear me roar? Twice?"

"Yes," she admitted softly. "I did."

"And you still want to know if I had a good time?"

"Well, you're not in pain, as you said, so you know you were my best. But there's no way for me to know about you unless you tell me."

Ah. He opened his mouth to respond, but she'd only

just warmed up to her subject. "And really," she continued, "you resisted me for so long. You never wanted to be with me. You made sure I knew we were only temporary."

Temporary. The word settled inside his head like a bomb seconds away from detonation. The thought of this woman with another man, naked like this, sated like this, sharing like this... Every cell in his body screamed in protest. *Mine.*

If he committed, she would expect forever.

Usually the word *forever* made him cringe. Just then, forever didn't seem like enough time with her. There were too many things to talk about, to do, too many ways to have her, and still practice the old stuff.

Did that mean he...loved her?

That thought didn't make him cringe, either. But loving her would mean putting her needs above his own, above his mission, above everything. If he did that, and then later lost her...losing her would mean losing everything. More than that, she would challenge him constantly, whether she meant to do so or not. She would demand his attention and she wouldn't let him get away with shit.

But—and that was a BIG but—he'd thought he would hate living that way. In fact, he'd thought he needed a break from the challenge of simply being who and what he was, which was why he'd gone on that vacation with Paris and William. A vacation that hadn't lasted long. He'd been bored out of his freaking mind within a day. Bored and more restless than ever, searching for...something.

Which might explain why he'd gone rushing to Kaia's side the day she'd called him from jail. Which might explain his decision to act as her consort, without wanting to sign on for double occupancy. But that didn't explain what he felt now. Possessive on a bone-deep level, protective and exhilarated.

Bottom line, he needed to be challenged to survive. Not only because the victories from those challenges fed his demon, keeping the little shit happy rather than frothing inside his mind, but also because he felt so *alive*. And when he was with Kaia, he wasn't just alive, he was sizzling. Inside and out.

He recalled how desperately he'd craved her one night when he'd found her in the hallway of the fortress, dressed only in a purple robe, her hair in disarray around her shoulders, her nipples hard and peeking through the thin material, her feet bare. She'd looked well-pleasured and aroused at the same time and he'd wanted to sate that arousal in a way previous lovers had failed to do.

Thank the gods Paris had stuck his head out his bedroom door and tossed Kaia her slippers before Defeat locked on the challenge of having her. Or so Strider had thought at the time. He'd walked away from Kaia and blocked all images of her from his head. Since that moment, however, he'd been grumpy, no one able to satisfy him. Even his reluctant crush on Haidee hadn't helped distract him from the Harpy. Now...

His satisfaction was unparalleled. So was his desire to keep this woman with him. To never again let her go. To never again walk away from her.

Yeah. He loved her.

He wasn't shocked by the revelation. He'd probably known on some deep, primal level all along, he just hadn't wanted to admit it. Had fought it. *No more fighting*.

Kaia was it for him. The one he wanted, needed, had to have. She was the beginning and the end. His. His in every way. His other half, his needed half. He'd resisted her appeal far too long, convinced himself she would be like all the others. But how could she be like all the others when she was so much more, in every possible way?

To tell her or not to tell her? Would a declaration from him distract her from the games?

"Strider?" Her tone was hesitant, as if she feared she'd scared him.

When you looked on the surface, she was cocky, confident and unmanageable. When you looked deeper, you saw how vulnerable she truly was. He hated himself for not seeing those vulnerabilities sooner. How many times and in how many ways had he hurt her over the past few weeks?

He squeezed her tight. "You know I won't lie to you, right?"

And he'd thought her stiff before. "Right." So much dread layered that single word, all hope disintegrated.

Even as he ached for her, he tried not to grin. "Then here it is, flat out. You were... Shit, there aren't even words to describe how good you were. I've never experienced anything like it, like you, and I loved every damn moment of it."

"Really?" she asked again.

"Oh, yeah. Really."

"Well." She kissed his chest, and she sounded self-assured when she added, "That's because I'm made of awesome."

"And dipped in awesome."

"And sprinkled with awesome."

"Gods, I love the taste of awesome."

Another chuckle escaped her, warm and rich as wine. "Thank you."

"My pleasure. And I mean that. You're a goddess, Kaia."

Another kiss, soft and sweet. "Nah. That's just a rumor one of my old boyfriends started."

A grin quirked the corners of his lips. "So." He traced

his fingertips up and down the ridges of her spine. "When will you be fertile?"

"Why? Do you want a baby?"

"Hell, no. Are you kidding? I'm scared enough about the day when Maddox and Ashlyn's little Strider and Stridette are running around." Although, he almost…liked the idea of a little redheaded brat wrecking havoc on the fortress, driving him insane, challenging him every minute of every day. That "like" sort of panicked him. "I asked about fertile-time because I'm trying to figure out when I need to buy stock in Trojans."

She scraped his nipple with her teeth. "Smart-ass. Harpies are only fertile about once a year and I don't hit that part of my cycle for another eight months. Plus, you only have, like, a one in a million chance of making an immortal with me anyway."

"Actually, I have a one in ten chance of making a felon."

A laugh bubbled from her, and he relished the carefree sound.

Pride filled him. *I did that.* "Why such low odds?" he asked, curious. If she thought him lacking in that department, well, he'd haul her ass to a specialist, do the cup thing and prove just how exceptional his little swimmers were.

Ego check.

Well, they were.

"Because of my paternal heritage," she said, a bit hesitant. "The Phoenix have never made children easily. That's why they're nearing extinction."

"If it's so hard for them to procreate, how'd your mother have twins with one?"

Her glow dimmed. "She's an overachiever."

"So are you." Speaking of kids, though… "When you were little, what did you want to be when you grew up?"

He found that he was desperate to learn about her, her past. Her hopes and dreams.

A sigh of longing. "To be honest, I wanted to be ruler of the entire world. Or the ruler's trophy wife."

He was the one to laugh this time.

She lifted her head long enough to glare at him. "What?"

"I like your goals, that's all. They're cute. Like you."

"Cute." She rolled her eyes. "Exactly what every girl wants to be in the eyes of the man she, you know, is riding like a carnival pony."

Now who was the smart-ass? "Hey, there's nothing wrong with cute. I'm cute as a button."

Another roll of her eyes and she settled back into his side. "I've mentioned your humbleness before, I'm sure. It's touching, really. So what did you want to be when you grew up?" Her fingers traced little circles over his chest.

He clasped her hand and brought those fingers to his mouth, kissing the digits before returning them to his chest. "I was never a kid, so I never thought about it."

"Oh, yeah. I keep forgetting. So why do you have a birthmark on your ass?"

An eyebrow arched up. "Noticed that, did you?"

"I'm very observant," she said gravely. "Had nothing to do with checking you out all the time or following you with stalkerlike focus."

Adorable girl. "It's not a birthmark. It's a tattoo. Or what remains of one." And something he never discussed, but this was Kaia. "A woman challenged me to have her name inked into my skin. I did, but I had Sabin there to tattoo over it if the stupid thing couldn't be removed."

"You killed the woman, of course."

So bloodthirsty, his Kaia, but then, that was one of the

things he loved about her. "I killed her dreams of happily ever after with me."

She nodded in understanding. "Now she suffers eternally. Good job. But, man, that's sad, about your lack of a childhood, I mean."

His shoulders lifted in a shrug. "Not really. You can't miss what you don't know about."

"Well, one day very soon, we're going to take a bath together and I'm going to show you how to play rubber ducky." Her hand glided down his stomach, swirled around his navel and finally cupped him.

He jolted in exquisite reflex. "I think I'll like that game."

"Good. And guess what else? You finally earned your nickname."

"Oh, yeah?"

Her tongue flicked out, laving his nipple into a tight little bead. "Yeah. Bonin' the Barbarian."

An unexpected snort left him. "I like it. Way better than the Sexorcist."

"*Way* better."

"Well, you've earned a new nickname yourself, Kaia darling." When her hand remained on his sac, he reached down and moved her fingers around his ever-hardening cock. Oh, yeah. That was the stuff.

The location change distracted her from their topic, but only for a few seconds. She tensed. Nicknames were painful for her. He got that. He also got that while she hated her title, she felt like she deserved it. But everyone made mistakes and she'd been blamed for hers long enough. For gods' sake, she'd been a child. Strider couldn't even imagine the trouble he would have gotten himself into if he'd grown from child to man, rather than springing to life fully formed.

Look what he'd done *without* a childhood. Stolen Pandora's box. Unleashed demons upon an unsuspecting world. Given away the Cloak of Invisibility to wicked, amoral creatures.

Enough of that. He rolled on top of Kaia, pinning her with his muscled weight. Automatically her arms looped around his neck—damn, he hated that her fingers were no longer squeezing his length. Oh, well. This was for the greater good. Her legs parted to create a cradle for him.

He cupped her chin, forcing her gaze to remain on his face. "I want to talk to you about something," he said.

In the back of his mind, Defeat ceased moaning with pleasure. Perhaps he sensed Strider's unease and feared a fight with the Harpy.

"I know what you want to discuss." Kaia licked her lips, and the sight of that pink tongue caused his cock to twitch. "Paris, right? Well, you have to—"

He shook his head. "We're done with that subject. He's wiped from your memory now."

"For sure! But what happens when I bump into him? If I hang with you, I will. You'll see us talking and remember that you can never forgive me for—"

Another shake of his head silenced her. "There's nothing to forgive, baby doll. You and I weren't dating then. We weren't even flirting."

Luminous eyes pierced his soul. "But...but...that's why you resisted me. That's why you said we couldn't be together. Not that I think we're together right now," she rushed to add.

"We're together," he growled, and his hard tone left no room for doubt. *Just try and leave. See what happens.*

Her mouth fell open, revealing those lovely white teeth, minus the fangs. "We are?"

"We are."

"All the way?"

"All the way. I'm your consort and you're my woman. Just mine. Do I need to wear a ring or something? Do you?" He recalled the medallions her mother and a few other Harpies had been wearing. Recalled, too, that he'd wanted to talk to her about them. "Or maybe a medallion?"

"No," she croaked. "No rings, no medallions. Those are for warriors and mine was taken from me after…you know."

No wonder she'd been so upset at the sight of Juliette wearing one. Well, Kaia would get her own and hers would be *the best.* Like her consort. *Ego check.* "So we're officially going steady?"

Disappointment clouded her delicate features and damn if tears didn't pool in her eyes. "Yes. Until the end of the games, I know."

Whether his admission would distract her or not, he had to tell her. He couldn't let her wallow like this. "After the games, too. And if anyone needs forgiveness, it's me, for pushing you away as long and as harshly as I did." As he spoke, those eyes got bigger and bigger, wetter and wetter. "I'm sorry for that, I am." He traced her mouth with his thumb. "Believe me, I will regret that forever. Because… damn it, Kaia, I love you."

Defeat seemed to freeze inside his head, not daring to move as he listened to the conversation. If Kaia didn't say those words back, the demon would…what?

Don't care. "You don't have to say anything," Strider went on. *I'll win her heart.* And he wanted to do it *without* the demon's influence. Otherwise, Kaia would never believe the feelings were his own and not born from his need for victory. "In fact, I don't want you to say anything right now. We'll huddle up about this after the games."

She blinked, but gave no other indication that she'd

heard what he'd said. "Huddle up? As if we're playing a few rounds of football?"

See? She would never let him get away with anything. "You're allowed to show a little joy about what I said, you know," he grumbled.

Her lips pursed before quickly smoothing, as if she didn't want to reveal a single hint of what she felt. "I can't."

"You *can't?*"

Defeat growled, liking her response even less than Strider did.

Finally emotion peeked through Kaia's expressionless mask and he saw a mix of fear and hope. "I love you, too, I think. I mean, I've never let myself consider feeling something deeper then lust, but I've never burned for anyone the way I burn for you. But what if I fail you? I won't deserve you and I'll have to let you go. You'll *want* me to let you go. What if—"

He kissed her, long and hard, filling her mouth with his tongue and his taste, and demanding a response. She gave it to him, gripping his head and stealing his breath. Hearing the words *I love you,* even with her uncertainty accompanying them…damn. He was more revved now then he'd been seconds before getting inside her.

She. Loved. Him. No question. She might not have worked it out in her mind yet, but she loved him and the knowledge slayed him. *Slayed. Him.* He hadn't realized how much he'd longed for her love until that moment.

He was king of the freaking world, man.

Defeat got his moan on.

Strider forced himself to end the kiss and rolled to his side. Kaia tried to crawl up his body, tried to finish what they'd started, but a tight grip on her waist locked her at his side. Sex, yeah, they'd go again, but apparently they had to get a few things straight first.

"You are not Kaia the Disappointment. Do you hear me? That's what I was trying to tell you earlier. You are Kaia the Mighty. How many Harpies out there do you think could have brought down the most badass Lord of the Underworld? The same Lord who also happens to be the strongest, sexiest and smartest. And by the way, in case there's any doubt, I'm describing me."

"I know." Tears leaked from her eyes and onto his chest, so hot they left little welts on his skin. "Only me?"

"That's right. Only you. Now, challenge me to stay with you."

She arched like a bow against him, taut fury making her stiff. "No!"

"Kaia—"

"No. I won't do it. I don't care what you say. You have to stay of your own free will. Not because you don't want to be struck with that god-awful pain from your demon."

He didn't want her afraid he'd leave her at any moment, though. "Do it and I'll give you another orgasm."

Slowly she relaxed. "Well…"

Her cell phone beeped, startling them both. Then *his* cell phone beeped. One they could have ignored. But both? Something had happened. They jolted up in unison.

"I bet the competition is over. My gods, my sisters. How could I have forgotten about them?" She scrambled to her discarded clothing and rifled through her shorts pockets.

He found his cell and they popped the screens at the same time. She gasped. He grunted. Then they peered over at each other, silent.

"Tell me your news first," he said.

"They won." She sounded dazed and unsure. "They won first place this round. They're injured, but alive and healing. They also managed to disqualify the Skyhawks. Meaning we're now on equal footing with my mother."

"That's great." He frowned when he saw the new flood of tears tracking down her cheeks. "Right?"

"Right." A firm nod. "My family is alive and they brought home the victory we needed. I'm so happy I could burst."

"But?"

Her shoulders sagged. "But they did it without me," she whispered, clearly agonized. "I didn't help. They don't need me. I'm a hindrance. They lose when I help, but win when I don't."

His chest constricted. "Baby doll, just because they won without you doesn't mean you're a hindrance. That just means they were better prepared this go-round."

Silent, she dressed. He sighed and joined her, tugging on his own clothing.

"Sabin and the angels found Rhea," he said, even though she hadn't asked. "Or rather, they found where the goddess was supposed to be. She left in a hurry, they think, and she left days, maybe even weeks ago. Her clothes were thrown all over the place, there were white feathers on the floor and dust on everything."

"Feathers. Galen?"

He nodded. "Sabin said there are no tracks, so it'll be impossible to hunt either one of them from here. They must have flashed somewhere."

"But…why host one of the competitions here if she couldn't watch?"

"Maybe her absence was unexpected. Maybe she'd planned to be here, but something stopped her."

"And the Hunters?"

"Maybe she issued orders to kill you before she took off, or maybe someone else was leading them."

Kaia straightened, peered at him, head tilting to the side as she pondered. "There's only one person I know who hates me enough to—" She frowned. She'd taken two steps toward him but now stopped abruptly and looked down at her feet. "I'm stuck. Strider, I'm stuck!"

He tried to move toward her—but couldn't. Just like hers, his feet were glued in place. He, too, looked down and frowned. The cave floor was…thinning? Yes, that's exactly what it was doing. Thinning, losing its rigidity, turning to…mist.

In a desperate bid to hold on to his woman, he reached out. Just before contact, they fell in unison, whooshing down…down…

Down.

CHAPTER TWENTY-FOUR

KANE AWOKE SLOWLY, THOUGH he gave no indication the synapses in his brain were kinda, maybe firing again. He'd gone to sleep in pain, drugged, and sadly, that had happened many times before in the past few...days? Weeks? He'd trained himself to come out of a stupor and take stock before moving a muscle or uttering a word.

He ached like a boxer who'd just lost the big match after going eighteen rounds. Though many of his injuries had already begun to heal, the deepest of them still etched his name in the May Not Recover book of regrets. And wouldn't you know? His demon loved it, every bit of it, giggling inside his head, soaking up the effects of the catastrophe—then and now.

Kane had a beefy guard on each arm, holding him up, dragging him down a long, winding cave that smelled of sulfur and decay, human feces and acrid fear. He tried not to gag. He knew the scents well, his demon having cohabited with them for centuries.

There was also a guard in front of him and five behind him. None of them gave any sign they knew he'd awoken.

As he planned an escape—picturing angels swooping in (not gonna happen), his friends busting through caves walls (again, a no-go) and him turning green and hulking (only in his dreams)—fury flash flooded him. He wouldn't have to do anything. In the end, his demon would destroy these humans. Disaster lived for moments such as this. And if Kane died in the process, so what?

He remembered the explosion, remembered William being wheeled away from him and tossed into a different vehicle. William. Was the immortal alive? Being tortured? Probably. The fury intensified. These men would pay. No matter what.

You hear me, Disaster? They need to pay.

The giggling became a gleeful laugh that razed the entire circumference of his skull.

Wait for my signal. None of the guards had any idea about the devastation they were soon to face. And they wouldn't. Until it was too late.

When his leader, Sabin, took off to battle Hunters, Kane was often left behind. Too many little disasters ruined their efforts, even sabotaged them. But sometimes...sometimes Kane was sent in alone. When that happened, no one walked away.

"—too heavy," one of the guards was panting. "Let's just leave him here."

"Can't. Doctor's orders. We transport him to the gate, or we don't come back."

"I'm sweating like a pig."

"You *are* a pig. BBQ much, you fat bastard? The walk is doing your tub of lard body some good."

"Eat shit and die, asshole. I have a glandular condition."

"I'm with Duane. He sweats any more," someone else said, "and he's liable to burst a vessel or something. He won't make it back, gate or not."

The temperature *was* a bit uncomfortable, the humidity so thick you practically needed a knife to cut through it. They were clearly hauling him deeper into the earth, closing in on the gate to...hell? But how would Hunters know how to do that? *Why* would they do that? That wasn't their usual M.O.

Capture, torture and now kill to steal the demon from inside him, *that* was what they lived for. This made no sense. Made him uneasy, as if he might not be dealing with who he thought he was dealing with.

He wasn't going to take time to question them. They'd proven their intentions when they'd pulled their little "look at my pretty bomb" routine. He just had to figure out the best place for his demon to work. Their final destination, most likely—in more ways than one. The "gate." The deeper they were, the less likely innocents were to be in the way.

In the distance, he heard the click of a hammer being cocked. No one around him seemed to notice. The guards continued chattering. Was someone about to shoot Kane? Or the guards? His demon prowled through his skull, ready to act, to destroy something, someone.

Not yet. Not yet.

The laughter grew in volume. Pretty soon, Disaster would strike, no matter what Kane did or said.

If the gunshot *was* meant for him, he'd survive. But he didn't want to act just in case his friends were here to rescue him. Hope blasted him.

When the *crack* reverberated, his guard grunted. Kane's left side was released, sagging toward the ground. The guard on his right cursed. The chatter ceased.

"What the—"

"Who was—"

Another *crack.*

Kane's right side was released as well and he smacked into the dirt-laden floor. He lay still, even when a heavy weight slammed into him, pushing the air from his lungs in one mighty heave. One of his guards, he thought, was now unconscious, probably dead.

Yep. Warm liquid pooled on his back, dripping down his sides.

Crack, crack, crack. There was no time for the men around him to prepare or hide. They fell, lifeblood gushing from the bullet holes in their chests, ending them. The entire gunfight lasted less than a minute, over and done without any resistance.

A rescue, yes, but still he didn't move or speak. He simply waited. Cautious...

Footsteps pounded. He recognized the heavy thud of boots.

"You see him?" someone called. A male, unfamiliar.

Shit! Hope withered, died. Not his friends. So who the hell did that leave?

"I got him! He's here."

The guard was rolled off him.

"He alive?"

A rustle of clothing, then hard fingers were digging into his neck. "Yep, sure is. Maybe not for long. His pulse is thready, so we'll have to act fast."

"That doctor is one lucky bitch. If he'd died before we got here..." Rage and hate layered the man's voice. "I might knock her around, anyway, for disobeying her orders."

"No, you won't. She's not one of us, and besides, her hubby would have your head. Let's just take the guy to Stefano and let *him* decide what to do."

Stefano. Galen's right-hand man, a Hunter top dog, and an all around pain in the ass. Too bad the bastard wasn't here. But just like that, Kane began to understand. Hunters had blown up the house. Hunters had taken him to that female doctor, who was not a Hunter but married to one, ensuring he survived. Hunters had not had him carried down here. The female had, against her husband's orders.

The husband must have found out and killed her accomplices.

"Demon animal," the guy who'd checked his pulse

muttered as he straightened. A booted foot slammed into Kane's stomach, rubbing a few of his organs against his spine.

Kane willed his eyelids to remain shut. Willed his muscles to remain lax. Meanwhile, Disaster churned in his head, now a seething cauldron. *Not yet,* he repeated. If they planned to cart him to Stefano, he could finally, at long last, destroy the bastard, taking out as many of his enemy as possible—even if it meant taking out himself, t. That's what he'd planned to do here, anyway. A change of , ation hardly mattered on that score.

Of course, when Kane kicked it, his body would no longer be able to contain the evil inside him and his demon would be unleashed upon an unsuspecting world. Disaster would escape, crazed, hungry, desperate to create tragedy after tragedy.

That had happened to Kane's friend, Baden. He'd died—beheaded by Hunters—and his demon, Distrust, had roamed the earth unfettered. Perhaps that was why nations had fought each other for so long. They always suspected the other of foul deeds and even fouler intentions. Perhaps that was why so many marriages had failed over the years.

Then, not long ago, the Hunters had somehow managed to find Distrust and pair the demon with a new host, one of their choosing. A female. She had yet to challenge the Lords, probably still too lost to the evil inside her to do more than moan and writhe and beg for relief.

"Diego?" someone muttered.

"Yeah," a man with a slight Spanish accent replied.

"You ready?"

"Yes, sir." There was a nervous tremor to the words.

"Markov, Sanders, hold his arms. Just in case he wakes up before he dies. Billy, cut deep and cut fast. There's no room for error."

"I'm not stupid. We've gone over this a thousand times," was the belligerent reply from the man who'd kicked Kane.

"Yes, we have, but this is go time, our one and only chance. If we aren't careful, his demon will escape the cave before Diego can absorb it."

O-kay. There would be no waiting, no reaching Stefano, Kane decided. They were going to murder him and try and pair his demon with a Hunter, thinking to control Disaster and use the demon to fight for their cause. To destroy his friends. To rule the world.

Cue evil overlord laugh, Kane thought dryly, then sobered. This was serious business.

Get ready, he told his demon.

The churning quickened, quickened, and the entire cave shook. Just a little. Just enough to cause dust to plume in the air and pebbles to fall from the ceiling, thudding on the ground.

"What's that?"

"Doesn't matter. Just hurry. Let's get this done. Knife?"

"Here."

Strong hands suddenly gripped Kane's arms and flipped him over so that he was lying on his back. Those same hands pushed, hard, pinning him in place. Kane didn't wait a second longer.

Now!

The shaking increased swiftly, the falling pebbles becoming falling boulders. *Boom, boom. Boom!* Someone screamed in pain. Kane was released. There was another scream, a round of curses.

Finally, Kane opened his eyes. Just in time, too. A boulder was heading straight for him. He rolled out of the way, coughing as his mouth filled with dirt and debris. The abrupt movement tore the stitches riding the curve of a rib.

His gaze panned his surroundings in one swoop. He was in a cave, just as he'd suspected, though it was more spacious than he would have believed possible, branching in several different directions. No wonder the Hunters had so easily overpowered his original captors. Not even an army could protect itself from ambush here. There were too many places to hide.

The Hunters scrambled for cover. The shaking continued and the rocks rained down. Another scream, a grunt. The crunch of breaking bone.

Kane lumbered to his feet. *That's the way, buddy. Keep at it.*

"Don't let him escape," someone shouted.

"Got him in my sights!"

Crack.

A sharp pain lanced through his leg. A dark curse left him. Someone had shot him. He hurried to one of the darkened enclaves, dodging the boulders along the way. More shaking, more boulders. Soon he would be trapped. If he wasn't already. But there was no way to stop a disaster of this magnitude once it had started.

He honestly didn't mind the prospect of dying. He'd almost died a thousand times before and had long ago prepared himself for the eventuality. At least he was taking these Hunters with him. Not that Kane would give up without *trying* to save himself. His warrior instinct would allow nothing less.

He searched the shadows for a way out...saw the barest crack of light to the right. Not stopping to think, he dove for it, jerking at the rocks, widening the airy space, ignoring the twinges of pain shooting through him.

"Kane!"

William? He stilled, stiffened. Shit. Shit! If he killed his friend...

Crack.

"Human!" William shouted angrily. Someone must have shot at him. "You're gonna hurt for that."

Boom, boom, boom.

"Get out of here," Kane shouted. "Run!"

"Kane, damn it! Where are you? I didn't knock Nurse Ratchet out and travel all the way down here to my least favorite place just to play hide-and-seek with you. Get your ass over here!"

Kane pushed to his feet, inhaling more dust. He raced out of the safety of the enclosure—just in time to see William grab a Hunter by the throat. He wasn't paying attention and didn't see the massive rock descending on him.

And because Kane was watching William, *he* didn't see the massive rock descending on *him.*

"SWEET SUNRISE, THAT was amazing."

Paris rolled away from the grinning, panting female and her glistening sweat-sheened body to peer up at the ceiling. As he'd hoped, Arca hated Cronus and hadn't minded betraying the god king. As he'd dreaded, she'd had a price— Paris's body, his demon's scent arousing her the moment he stepped inside her chamber.

He'd just spent the past hour pleasuring her in a way he was sure she'd never been pleasured. She had enjoyed every second of his attention, while he had loathed himself, his actions.

You do what you have to do.

He hadn't had to worry about interruptions. The spacious bedroom was hidden in the back of the harem. A bedroom Arca couldn't leave. Cronus had actually cursed her so that she would experience utter, absolute agony if she stepped outside the spacious boundaries of her "home." And having learned from the mortals and their mistakes, the king had ensured there were no windows for the goddess to utilize.

Clearly, the king had thought it was better to deprive

Arca of sunlight and fresh air than to chop off her long, silky hair.

She propped herself up on her elbow and stared down at him, white braids draped over her shoulder. "Well?"

"Yes, that was indeed amazing," he said automatically, as he'd said to a thousand others.

Her smile slowly waned. "You could at least *try* to sound convincing."

Sighing, he studied her. He'd been with countless others over the centuries, and she was by far the loveliest. But appearances mattered little to him. What was a beautiful face when a monster could very well lurk beneath? All that mattered was how the other person made you feel, inside and out.

He doubted Arca was a monster inside. She had spent so many years in captivity, both on earth and here in the heavens, that she *should* have been warped, a shrew at the very least, but when he'd strolled inside, she hadn't yelled at him. Hadn't fought him. She had peered at him with wide blue eyes, clasped his hands and smiled, so lonely and desperate for attention, any attention, that she'd caused his chest to constrict.

And when he'd tried to question her about Sienna, when she had shaken her head and said, "After," already lost to the lust-haze his demon created, Paris had given in without protest.

"I'm sorry," he said, letting his voice dip with husky promise. Another skill he'd perfected over the years. "It's just, you wore me out, sweetheart. I have no energy left."

She chuckled and fell beside him, snuggling into his side. "Cronus won't find out, I promise. So if you want to return to me…"

He remained silent. He couldn't sleep with her again. His demon wouldn't let him. Even if he spent hours kissing and touching her, his cock would remain flaccid and useless. Always did around anyone he'd already bedded, and really, Paris wouldn't have wanted a repeat, anyway. He felt guilty enough, sleeping with anyone other than Sienna.

He'd had her and he *could* have her again. He could get hard just thinking about her. Which was why everyone he'd nailed after her was like a slap in her beautiful face. Like she wasn't good enough for him. Like she couldn't satisfy him. But he couldn't save her if he died and he really would die if he remained celibate.

Plus, he felt guilty for another reason. These lovers of his…they didn't want him, not really. If not for his demon, they might not have ever slept with him, might have turned him down flat, found him unattractive, whatever. So, in a way, he was forcing them to be with him.

As always, his mind cringed away from the thought.

"What's wrong?" Arca asked. "You tensed up."

He forced himself to relax and rubbed her arm up and down, a gentle caress. "Earlier I mentioned a woman. A slave, killed and in soul form, and now possessed by a demon. Wrath. Her soul is invisible to the naked eye." He tried not to reveal his own sense of desperation. "Do you know of whom I speak?"

She twirled a braid around one of her fingers. "Yes. I remember. You want to know where Cronus is keeping her."

Easy, steady. "Do you know the answer?"

"I haven't heard anything, no."

He closed his eyes, fighting a rush of disappointment and regret. He'd thought…he'd hoped…he'd been so sure…

"But," she went on, "I do know where he kept prisoners he couldn't control, people he didn't want anyone to find, before his imprisonment in Tartarus."

"Tell me." The words rang out with more force than he'd intended.

"I'll do better than that." Her arms tightened around him, and she trembled. "I'll show you."

His stomach churned. *Can't alienate her.* "You know that isn't possible, sweetheart," he croaked. "You have to stay here."

"But…" She sat up again, expression tight as her braids fell around them, framing them. "*Please.* I have to leave. I can't stay here any longer. I hate it, and I'm slowly going insane. *Please.*"

He cupped her cheeks, trying to be gentle. "Tell me where to find this secret place and once my mission is done, I'll come back for you. I'll find a way to save you."

Tears pooled in her eyes. "That could take forever. You could die."

"I know and I'm sorry, but that's all I can offer." He couldn't save her now. He couldn't try and free her now. That would alert Cronus. The god king would come gunning for him and Sienna would be lost to him forever.

If Paris lost his head, if that was his destiny, he first wanted to move Sienna somewhere safe. She'd died because of him. She'd been paired with a demon because of him. Because he'd brought her to the god king's attention. Paris owed her.

"I could aid you," Arca said. "Not just find the place for you, but help you navigate the secret corridors."

"I know, sweetheart, but that doesn't change my mind."

"Please…"

He didn't tell her that feminine pleas held little sway with him. How many had begged him to remain in bed with them? How many had cried as he walked away? "I'm sorry, but this is the best I can offer."

And if she wouldn't tell him what he wanted to know, if she continued to refuse him, he *would* hurt her. *Hurt… kill…* anyone who got in his way. Anyone. He'd come so far. She wouldn't stop him from going further.

For a long while, she sobbed silently. Then she bucked up on her own, squaring her shoulders and lifting her chin, the stubborn expression reminding him of Kaia.

How was Strider handling the female determined to bring him to his knees? Either the possessive warrior was fighting his attraction or he'd finally given into it— otherwise he would have been here, right beside Paris, meeting the terms of their "challenge."

"Do you swear you'll come back for me after you find her?" Arca asked.

"Yes. I swear. When she's truly safe, I will come." The moment he spoke the words, he was bound to them. He knew it, felt the strength of the ties. To break your word to a god or goddess was to suffer eternally. If you survived.

She wiped at her tears. "All right. I'll tell you what you wish to know. If Cronus has remained true to his old ways, and believe me, I know that he has, you will find your woman in one of two places. If she's in the first, she's lost to you forever. If she's in the second, and you venture there, you won't emerge unscathed."

Sienna was *not* in the first and that was that. "The name of the second place?"

As the words left her lips, his blood chilled. Breath abandoned him. He'd known Cronus would punish her for running to Paris, but he hadn't known the god king planned to torture her eternally.

Paris unfolded himself from the bed and dressed as swiftly as possible.

"Will you still go after her?" Arca asked.

"Yes," he replied without a moment of hesitation. He was more determined now than ever.

CHAPTER TWENTY-FIVE

KICKED OUT OF HEAVEN and straight into hell, Kaia thought darkly. Or rather, her version of hell. And she hadn't even gotten to enjoy her afterglow!

A campfire crackled in front of her, orange flames twined with blue. Heat licked over her. She'd never truly cooled down after making love with Strider—remembering, a shiver slid the length of her spine and she had to cut off a moan—and she was glad. She liked the heat. Mostly because of the lingering hum of satisfaction her...consort had provided.

Consort.

Currently Strider was "scouting the area for Hunters." Didn't take two hours to scout a small stretch of land. He was looking for the Paring Rod, no question. He wouldn't find it. Not here. Juliette wasn't foolish enough to hide the thing under her makeshift mattress.

So badly Kaia had wanted him to acknowledge the link between them. So badly she'd wanted to touch and taste him. Wanted to be touched and tasted by him. That she had, that he had...gods, she was now scared to death. Because...

He loved her. That still shocked her. They were a couple. A real couple. He would have her back, and she would have his. More than that, he came first now. That's just how it had to be. Whether he was being a pain in the ass or a romantic mattress god, he was hers. She had to protect him. Had to see to his future. And bottom line? He wanted, *needed,* the Paring Rod. Needed it to survive.

Therefore, she had to get it for him.

Right now her team was on the road to acquiring the artifact fair and square. But what if that changed? Juliette would then expect Kaia to make a play for it and the odds of actually getting her hands on it would cease to lean in her favor.

Therefore, there was no better time to strike.

Of course, that would take Kaia out of the competition and prove once and for all that she was unworthy, weak, but better her pride suffered than Strider died. She couldn't live without him. She needed his blood, yes, but she also needed him. His smile, his laughter, his wit, his strength.

So, no contest and no more thought necessary. She would steal the Rod. Boom, done. She wouldn't involve her sisters, though. She wouldn't risk their lives. Not again. Especially now, when they were injured from the second game.

Had to happen tonight, she thought, her hands fisting. Most everyone would be intoxicated, healing or passed out. She'd make love to Strider—if he wanted and he had better want—and let the heat fill her once again. That heat energized her, a combination of lust and rage that swirled inside her, wanting so badly to escape. To consume.

Tonight she'd let it.

Soon…soon… Her narrowed gaze found Juliette. The brunette danced around the flickering fire, right alongside Kaia's mother. Despite their recent loss, they were jubilant, carefree. As if they knew something she did not.

Juliette must have sensed her scrutiny; she met Kaia's eye and grinned slowly, and, as always, smugly. Oh, yes. Tonight.

Kaia and Strider had fallen from Rhea's forest and landed here, in Alaska, between the two mountains, right where the mystical portal had been. They'd opened their eyes and found themselves here—along with all the other Harpies participating in the games and their consorts.

At first, confusion reigned. Then anger that they'd been ejected from the heavens—anger they'd hoped to take out on each other. A fight would have broken out if Kaia's mother hadn't declared this neutral ground. Apparently whatever Tabitha the Vicious wanted, Tabitha the Vicious got. So, instead of attacking, instead of going their separate ways and awaiting the third competition, the Harpies had decided to stay and party.

Stolen beer abounded, hard rock blasted through the night and vehicles commandeered from the nearest town shot bright headlights into the ice-laden valley. Many of the combatants were still bruised and bloody from the earlier battle, and some were still unconscious, but that didn't discourage the revelers.

A few hours earlier, someone had stolen Kaia's coat and she had no doubts as to the culprit. Juliette probably expected her to issue a private challenge over it, ruining everyone's good time. Well, Juliette could suck it. The thing had been dirty as hell anyway.

"Hey, baby doll," a sexy male voice said.

Strider. Her Strider. He smelled like cinnamon and looked like paradise, his cheeks pink and his hair disheveled, framing his face in a vivid halo.

Did she love him? She hungered for him, was amused by him and delighted in his attention. But love? Trusting him with all that she was? Her sisters were the only members in her Faith Circle and she'd never thought to welcome another. Especially someone who did indeed have an agenda different than her own.

He plopped beside her and held out a frosted glass. "This is mine. Not yours. Don't touch."

Maybe trusting him wasn't so bad. She took the glass

from him with a muttered, "Thanks," and sipped. Despite the coolness of the drink, her body temperature continued to rise.

"I talked to Sabin and Lysander. They've set up camp about a mile away and are doctoring Bianka and Gwen."

So he hadn't been searching for the Rod? Wonder of wonders. "What about Taliyah, Neeka and the others?"

"They took off without a word."

"They're always doing that," she grumbled.

"Well, this time I followed them."

Her gaze swung to him. His navy eyes were bright, his lips curled seductively. Her heart skipped a beat. He wore a leather jacket, jeans, boots. Typical Strider attire. The man was always ready to give an ass-kicking.

"Really?" she asked. "And they didn't sense you?"

"I didn't say that."

She considered him anew. There were fresh cuts on his palms, nicks on his fingers. "What happened? Did they hurt you? Because if they hurt you, I will personally—"

"Easy, Red." Those lips curled farther until he was grinning. "They just warned me away. Anyway, they had no idea I was behind them at first. They snuck through a few of the tents of warring teams."

"Searching for the Rod?" But why would *they* do so?

"I don't think so." He stroked his chin in thought. "In the woods back there," he hiked his thumb behind him, "they met a group of guys I didn't recognize. Warriors, though. Immortal. Taliyah scented me out before I could get close enough to listen to their conversation."

Taliyah. With men. Interesting. And unusual. Her older sister usually kept her distance from the opposite sex, never wanting to chance finding her consort. Not that Taliyah was a man-hater. She wasn't. She just liked her space, liked doing her own thing. Liked having no ties, able to leave anyplace, anytime with no hindrances.

"Something's up," Kaia said.

"True, but I don't think it concerns us or the games. The men were mostly interested in Neeka. Almost…proprietary toward her. So. Speaking of the Rod," he went on, "I've been thinking. What if Juliette doesn't have it? What if she's got a fake?"

A possibility, though a dim one; Kaia recalled the power she'd felt emanating from the spear when Lazarus had walked on stage with it. One way or another, though, she would discover the truth.

Drunken feminine laughter cut off any reply she might have made. Good thing, too. There were too many possible eavesdroppers for them to have this conversation here. "We'll talk about it later."

"Nope. Now. We'll just be more circumspect." Strider wound his arm around her shoulders and tugged her closer. He didn't release her, but whispered straight into her ear, his warm breath caressing her. "Couple questions are plaguing me. We didn't know where the Paring Rod was. How did she? And how'd she get her hands on it without alerting anyone in our world? And why hasn't she used it? Why would she give it away? Okay, that's more than a couple."

Kaia's nipples had hardened at the contact and moisture had pooled between her legs. *This* was circumspect? Didn't matter. She'd play. "Rhea could have given it to her, I suppose," she whispered straight into *his* ear. Then she couldn't help herself and had to lick the shell.

He pushed out a breath. Tempted to eat him alive, Kaia returned her attention to the dancers. Juliette and her mother were gone, she noted distantly.

"But why would she?" He saw her lick and raised her a warm puff of air. "There's no reason good enough. Rhea hates my kind, wants us dead. She wouldn't want us to get our hands on such a prized possession. She would have given it to the Hunters. To Galen."

Goose bumps broke out over Kaia's entire body. "Maybe Juliette stole it from her. Rhea's missing, after all, and no one's heard from her. Maybe Juliette killed her and assumed control of the Hunters." She nibbled on his lobe before showing him her profile, eager for him to have his next turn.

He didn't disappoint. He kissed along her cheekbone while his fingers caressed their way to the underside of her breast. "If that were the case, Cronus would be dead. The two are bound, so when one dies, the other will, as well. And Cronus is very much alive. Amun has been meeting with him."

She leaned into his touch, her nerve endings sparking to dazzling life. "Juliette could have her locked up, then." To find the Rod, Kaia knew she'd have to snatch up Juliette and torture her for information. She'd already considered and accepted the necessity. Now, she'd ask about Rhea and the Hunters, too.

Strider circled her nipple once, twice. "If so, she's more powerful than we realized."

Sweet fire, that felt good. She flattened her palm on his thigh, not surprised to find her claws sharpened, ready to dig into his flesh. "Don't worry. I'll handle her. Besides, I owe her."

No matter the answers Kaia might force from Juliette, it was clear the bitch had somehow orchestrated this whole thing. To steal Strider, perhaps, as she'd first suspected. Not that Juliette had made much of an effort on that front, but she'd definitely wanted to taunt Kaia with what she could never have. Victory. Respect from her fellow Harpies. But also from Strider, if she failed him?

And if she *did* fail him, would he still love her?

She didn't want to contemplate the answer, was already chilled to the marrow by the mere possibility.

"For future reference," she said, no longer whispering, "you should know that I don't get mad. I get even."

"Good." He placed a soft kiss at the edge of her mouth. "'Cause that's how I like my candy and my women. Hot and spicy."

The comment roused an unexpected chuckle from her. "Anyway, like I said, we shouldn't discuss this here." No matter how much she enjoyed the exchange of information.

He sighed. "You're right."

"Of course I am."

He reached up and ruffled her hair. "Braggart."

"Just being honest. So what happened to your hands?" she asked, changing the subject before she launched herself onto his lap and had her way with him right here, right now.

"Nothing." There was a note of finality in his voice. A note that dared her to press—and lose.

A lie. She knew it, but still she let it slide. Now wasn't the time to argue with him. They needed to display a united front.

"Lucky me," another sexy male voice said, this time from behind her. "If it isn't my favorite Harpy."

Strider stiffened and they turned in unison—united, yay—and pushed to their feet. Lazarus stood before them, thick arms crossed over his middle. Like Strider, he wore a jacket and jeans. Unlike Strider, he did not make her heartbeat quicken.

"Hey, there, Tampon. Where's your master?" Kaia asked him.

The obsidian in his eyes swirled menacingly. What? No more amusement for his pet name? "She's having a private meeting with your mother about all the ways they plan to destroy you. I'm supposed to keep you occupied—a task that is no hardship. Would you like to go someplace private with *me*? I could at last meet all your needs."

Strider growled low in his throat and the sound reminded her of a countdown clock. *Tick, tock, tick, tock, someone's about to die.*

"Thanks," Kaia said, "but I'd rather be on an island, a millionaire hunting me so he can kill me and drape my skin in front of his fireplace."

"You and I will play that game later, baby doll," Strider said. "You, on the other hand," he threw at Lazarus, "can go someplace private with me now."

Cold fingers of dread ran down Kaia's spine. *Please, please, please don't challenge him.*

"Thanks," Lazarus replied, "but you're not my type. So, if you won't leave with me, sweet Kaia, why don't we stay here and chat?"

The words earned another savage growl from Strider.

Oh, gods. The two were going to come to blows and there would be no stopping them.

She knew how powerful the immortal in front of her was. He'd ripped through a camp of Harpies, escaped unscathed and remained hidden for…well, she didn't know how long, just that he had. Strider was powerful, too, but he had a handicap. His demon.

Like that'll slow him.

The thought was immediately followed by another. *You can use this.* She needed to know what her mother and Juliette were planning and a fight between Strider and Lazarus would serve as the perfect distraction, allowing her to slip away unnoticed to accidentally on purpose overhear something.

Strider must have considered the same thing—and his demon must have accepted the challenge of finding out—because he launched himself at the warrior without another word. The two flew to the ground in a tangle of limbs. And knives. The silver tips glinted in the moonlight.

Yeah, Strider wanted to kill the warrior, but that wasn't why he'd started the fight and she knew it. He'd given her the cover she needed to find the women in question, but damn it! She hated to leave him.

As the warriors grunted in pain, dashed and ducked, threw punches, kicked and slashed, the Harpies around the campfire noticed. A second later, the cheering and betting began.

Kaia worked her way through the throng, her gaze remaining on Strider until the last possible second. He and Lazarus were now rolling in the snow, leaving pools of blood in their wake. Her stomach clenched.

Don't worry. He can take care of himself.

That didn't stop her from trembling as she crouched on the fringes of the crowd and sniffed, searching for her mother's familiar scent. Nothing. She inched forward. Still nothing. To the right. Nothing. To the left—there!

She propelled in that direction, staying in the shadows as much as possible. All too soon the mountain's incline stopped her forward progress. She glanced upward. Ice, jagged rocks. A ledge.

A ledge that most likely led to a cavern.

How cliché. Harpies could jump higher than humans, and even hover in the air for short periods of time, but because their wings were so small, they couldn't fly. She had to do this the hard way and climb. She placed her hands and feet precisely, lest a pebble or ice chunk fall. If the women were up there—and she thought that they were, the unimaginative villains—the slightest noise could alert them. Oh, she didn't doubt that they heard the chaos below, but that was something they'd expected.

The clenching in her stomach worsened when a voice she recognized as belonging to an Eagleshield whooped and shouted from below, "That's the way, cowboy. Beat his face in!"

Who was the cowboy? Strider or Lazarus? Her money was on Lazarus because Juliette was an Eagleshield, which meant her clan would prefer him to Strider. Even though Strider was a delicious Lord of the Underworld. Idiots. They made her ashamed to call herself a Harpy.

"Holy hell, I think you broke his nose. Sweetest punch ever. Do it again! Do it again," someone else chanted.

"Gut him!"

"I get to nail the winner!"

"No way. I do."

You can't afford to look.

Up she continued to climb, not pausing until she reached the ledge. Her arms shook and her thighs burned, but she held herself steady, listening. There was a murmur of voices, yes, but they were whispered and she couldn't tell if they were male or female. Couldn't even guess how many were speaking.

To find out, she'd have to go in.

If they spotted her, they'd fight her. But a fight was better than a secret meeting, where plans were made and enacted. At the very least, she'd prevent the attendees from solidifying any goals.

She inhaled a measured breath, reached down, dangling from the ledge by one hand and palmed a dagger. Then she did the same with the other hand, until she was two-fisting weapons and ice. *Then* she hauled herself over.

A mistake. One she knew she would regret forever.

She'd been set up, she immediately realized with dread.

There was no time to act. Manacles shot out from the bottom sides of the cavern and latched around her ankles, metal teeth digging so deep they hit bone. She stifled her cry of pain, even as her knees buckled. *Can't distract Strider.*

Her mother and Juliette hadn't met in private. They hadn't met at all. They'd simply assembled a group of murder-minded Hunters. And those Hunters were staring at her, smiling, as if they'd been waiting for her all along.

CHAPTER TWENTY-SIX

WIN, WIN, WIN.

As Strider fought the strongest immortal he'd ever encountered, his demon chanted excitedly, nervously. That wouldn't have been so bad, or so distracting, if there hadn't been *another* voice inside his head. Tabitha's. Prodding him toward a raging darkness he'd never felt before.

They want to kill her. They will *kill her.*

He damn well *knew* the Harpies wanted to kill her. Would they succeed, though? Hell, no. But if Tabitha was talking to him, she couldn't be meeting with Juliette. And if she wasn't meeting with Juliette, why the hell had he accepted a challenge he might not be able to win, just to distract the ranks, giving Kaia time to infiltrate her enemy's camp?

WIN!

You aren't helping. Hard knuckles connected with his mouth, his teeth shredding the bastard's skin. Not quite the silver lining of his dreams. His brain banged against his skull and for a moment, he saw stars. He hated stars. Blood coated his tongue, slid down his throat. Lazarus rolled on top of him, pinning his shoulders with firm, bony knees. Punch, punch, punch.

Bone cracked. Broke. Shattered.

WIN!

I damn well know, he mentally sneered. And he *would* win this. Just as soon as he found his knives in the bloodstained snow. Bastard was going to lose his head. Maybe. Hopefully.

Surely.

At the very least, Lazarus was going to spill his guts. He was a threat to Kaia. Threats to Kaia were not allowed to live.

She will die. Tonight. There is nothing you can do to save her. Tabitha again.

Punch, punch, punch.

More stars, riding the coattails of pain. Rage stormed through him, lightning caged too long, finally released. He bucked with all his strength, sending Lazarus crashing behind him.

Strider was on his feet in an instant. Through swollen eyes, he saw Lazarus smile with delight as he, too, stood. In the back of Strider's mind, he knew Lazarus could have done a lot worse to him. Could have sliced and diced him. Could have gone for his man-business. Instead, the child of a god and a nightmarish monster had used his fists. What was up with that?

As the Harpies cheered, the warriors circled each other.

"How predictable you are," Lazarus *tsk*ed under his tongue. And wasn't that weird. He'd spoken in the language of the gods, used so long ago. A language the Harpies probably didn't understand.

Strider replied using the same harsh tones and nearly forgotten words. "How pathetic *you* are. Lazarus the Lapdog, Juliette's bitch."

Bye-bye smile. Gold star for Strider—and suddenly, he really liked stars. Go figure. Defeat chuckled.

"You think you'll be any different? Juliette will enslave you the same way she has enslaved me. What else do you think this competition is about? Not the idiotic games these females like to play. This is simply about punishing the redhead."

"For what *you* did, the way I hear it."

Lazarus shrugged, unconcerned. "She freed me. The blame falls on her."

"She was a child."

Another shrug of those wide shoulders. "And I was worked into a fury over my circumstances. I cannot control myself when the fury hits."

Which meant he wasn't worked into a fury right now. Or, if he was, the chains tattooed around his neck and wrists prevented him from doing anything about it.

"Start fighting again already," a Harpy called.

"Seriously. *Bor-ing!*" This speaker tossed an empty beer bottle at him and the glass slammed against his stomach.

WIN!

Stupid Defeat.

You talk. She dies. And there was Tabitha yet again.

He gnashed his molars. He knew the bitch was simply taunting him, trying to distract him, to work him into a lather, convincing him to walk away from this altercation and purposely lose. Then he'd be out for the count and Kaia vulnerable.

"If Juliette's so powerful, why hasn't she tried to enslave me yet?" Strider demanded. Answers first, ass kicking second. "Tit for tat."

Lazarus's gaze was pitying. "Haven't you learned anything? The Harpies enjoy drama and theatrics more than any other race."

No denying that. "How'd she do it, then? You're a pretty tough guy. For a pussy. How'd she enslave you?"

Swollen lips twitched. With amusement? "As are you. All I can tell you is to beware of first prize."

The Rod? *The Rod* had enslaved Lazarus? "So it's the real deal?" There went his theory that Juliette had been faking. A theory he'd wished to the gods had proven to be true. No hands were better than the wrong hands.

"I can't say."

"Won't, you mean."

Those onyx eyes glittered with a thousand secrets. "No. Can't. I'm skirting the edge of obedience even saying that much."

"And what happens when you disobey?"

"Pain. Death. The usual suspects. And now, I'm sorry to say, I must continue distracting you."

Strider cocked a brow. "You're sorry to say?"

A confident nod. "You're not really a bad sort and I actually like the redhead. She's feisty."

"She's mine."

A grin as slow and thick as dripping honey. "You have to survive first." That was the only warning Strider had. Lazarus sprinted forward, a blur the naked eye couldn't see.

Fists once again hammered into him, the impact throwing him in a tailspin of pain. He rotated when he hit, uncaring that he could no longer breathe as long as he could protect his face.

Win!

At least the demon wasn't screaming anymore. Strider scanned the snow and bodies for weapons, darting left and right as he did so, moving around the Harpies, hoping the warrior wouldn't punch them just to reach him. Dude reminded Strider of Sabin, who thought men and women were equals in battle and didn't discriminate when it came to killing. But Juliette was his mistress and she'd probably forbidden him from hurting her sisters.

Finally. He spotted broadswords. Not his own, but a Harpy's. He slid them from their sheathes at her back.

"Hey," she squawked when she realized what he'd done. He darted away before she could claw him for the theft.

His boots slipped on the ice. Finding his balance proved difficult, but he kept moving, listening for any telltale sounds that might give away Lazarus's location.

Feminine huffs—directly behind him. That meant Harpies were being shoved aside, rather than danced around. Such an obvious mistake, he thought. Lazarus was too good a fighter for that. Did he *want* to lose?

Damn it, Strider didn't want to like him.

Spinning when he reached an unoccupied stretch, Strider went low. He stretched out his arms, the blades extended. Contact. Lazarus jumped, but he was too late. The metal sliced into his ankles, hobbling him. He fell and fell hard, the ice offering no cushion from impact.

With Defeat cheering inside Strider's head—*won, won, won*—he pinned the warrior exactly as he had been pinned, knees to shoulders. Lazarus didn't resist.

"That *hurt*."

"Sorry." Strider slammed the sword tips beside the man's temples. "And thank you," he said, fighting the wave of pleasure victory had brought. It would distract him.

Eyes bright with surprise peered up at him.

"What, you didn't think I'd realize you'd thrown the fight? Give me some credit, at least." Once again, he used the ancient language of the gods.

Then that wave of winning-induced pleasure blasted free of his restraints. He couldn't hold it back a second longer. He shivered and moaned right along with Defeat.

Sparks of ecstasy ignited in his veins, heating him up. Not to the same degree that making love with Kaia had, but enough to cause him to spring instant, embarrassing, wood.

Before Lazarus could reply, the man's surprise gave way to amusement and the warrior winged a brow in question.

"Not for you," Strider said, flushing.

"Thank the gods for that."

"So." *Let's get the rest of this over with.* "You heal quickly?"

"Yeah."

"I'm sorry for this, but I need five minutes alone and I can't have you coming after me." He reclaimed the swords, jerked them from the ice, then slammed them into Lazarus's shoulders. "Do me a solid and stay down."

A grunt, a stiffening of that big body. Boos all around him.

Strider pushed to his feet and moved out of striking distance, already scanning the vista. Harpies gaped at him, even backed away. A few of the braver ones offered him pinkie waves and seductive grins, open invitations to bed them.

He caught Sabin's gaze. Lysander was beside him, golden wings arching over his shoulders. Despite the cold, the two were sweating. They must have heard the commotion and rushed here.

He motioned to the mountain at his left with a tilt of his chin and they nodded. While Lazarus had been pounding his face in, he'd kept an eye on Kaia. She'd climbed that mountain and disappeared inside a cavern.

He stalked forward, determined. Within a few steps, the consorts were flanking his sides. Along the way, he thought he smelled smoke. And burning flesh. Panic suddenly infused him and he looked up. The panic mixed with dread. Dark smoke wafted from the cavern.

Shit! No time to climb. "Get me up there," he demanded. "Now."

Lysander caught his urgency. He gripped Strider under the arms, wings extending, legs bending to push. They shot into the air and the angel dropped him onto the ledge before heading down to repeat the process with Sabin.

"Kaia!" Strider rushed inside, coughing as the smoke

thickened and burned his throat. He waved his hand in front of his stinging eyes, trying to see. Then he was in the center of the destruction, and there was no reason to wave away the darkness. He could see just fine.

At least twenty-five bodies were on fire, flames still crackling from them, illuminating the area. They were so charred, he couldn't tell if they were male or female. His heart nearly burst from his chest, his blood heating with more of that panic. She couldn't be one of the dead. She just couldn't.

He would have failed her. He couldn't have failed her. He needed her. Loved her. "Kaia," he said past the lump growing in his throat. "Kaia, baby doll. Where are you, love?"

"What the hell?" Sabin demanded behind him.

"Great Deity," Lysander breathed.

Strider ignored them, bending to study the bodies closest to him. He was shaking as he reached out and removed the dagger clutched in that blackened hand. The hilt was so hot his skin immediately blistered, but he didn't release it. He didn't recognize it, either. Okay. Okay, then. This one wasn't her.

A whimper echoed a few feet ahead of him. Female. Pain-filled. Familiar. No sweeter sound. He was on his feet in an instant, racing toward it. Then he saw her, and ground to an abrupt halt. His stomach twisted into a hundred sharp knots, each one cutting at him.

They'd staked her to the wall.

As relieved as he was that she lived, *he* wanted to die. Swords were anchored into her shoulders, pinning her to the rocky wall. Blood dripped down her naked body, covering her with crimson streaks of pain. If they had raped her...

With only the thought, Strider felt ready to open himself

up to his demon completely, to let his wicked half reign, to beat every citizen in the world to pulp.

Rage later. See to her now. One stomping step, two.

Flames crackled on his shirt, burning the material, singeing his skin. He stopped and patted himself down. When that didn't help, he ripped the fabric over his head and tossed it aside. Only then did the fire die.

"What happened—"

"Get out," Strider growled, and Sabin shut his mouth. "Both of you. Now." She would not want anyone to see her like this.

Silence. Reluctant footsteps. Strider studied his woman all the while. Her eyes were black, the whites completely gone, but interspersed throughout that midnight canvas were the same flames that had singed him. They crackled angrily.

"Kaia," he said gently.

She struggled against the swords, gave another whimper.

"Be still, baby doll. Okay?" He dared another step closer. A mistake. His jeans caught fire next. Again he stopped. This time he didn't bother patting himself down, he just cut the offending material from his body, leaving him in underwear and boots.

"Baby doll, listen to me. Okay?" he said, trying again. He dropped the blade, lest she think he meant to hurt her. "Please listen to me. I want to help you. I'm going to help you, whether you want me to or not. Please don't kill me until I get you out of here."

He expected Defeat to kick up a few protests about that litany of "pleases." Maybe consider it a challenge. The demon remained silent, however. Still afraid of Kaia? Or mourning what had been done to her after the pleasure they'd experienced in her arms?

"Here I come." Strider inhaled the thickened air…

held…held…and strode forward. His skin continued to heat, but he didn't catch fire again, and finally he reached her. Gently, so gently, he cupped her cheeks, his thumbs tracing the fine bones beneath her silken skin. He was surprised to see his own claws had emerged. The demon's claws. Yet he didn't cut her, was oh, so careful.

"Oh, baby," he groaned, his chest aching. "I'm so sorry."

Tears leaked from the corners of those midnight eyes, and he knew he was reaching the woman inside. He hadn't protected her from this and he wasn't sure why he wasn't in pain as a result of his failure. Because she would heal? *Please let her heal.* Because someone other than Harpies had done the damage? If that was the case, who had done it? Hunters again?

Desperately he wanted to slice open his jugular and give her all the healing blood she needed. But he couldn't. Not yet. He couldn't risk her bones and flesh healing around the metal that caged her in place.

"I'm going to remove the swords, okay?" He couldn't allow this to happen to her again. Ever. He couldn't bear it. *That is a challenge,* he told Defeat. *A challenge you will accept. She is ours to protect and if we fail her again, we will suffer, even if she will later heal. Understand?*

A pause. Then, a faint, *Win.*

Though Strider didn't want to release her, he did, and gripped the swords. They were hotter than the dagger he'd used to cut his pants and his already blistered hands throbbed in pain. He didn't care. His pain mattered little. What did matter? *Her* pain. That small movement tormented her, he knew, because her tears fell more quickly.

Unwilling to prolong the agony, he jerked with all of his strength. For several seconds, the metal caught on bone. He had to jerk harder. She didn't make a sound. Finally, though, she was free and sagged forward. He dropped the swords and caught her, easing her to the ground. There were also wounds on her ankles, but they weren't bound, so he ignored them.

Again he wanted to hold her. Again he didn't allow himself the luxury. He used his claw to slice deep into his neck, leaned down and placed the wound just above her mouth.

"Drink, baby doll. You'll feel better, I swear. And then you'll tell me what happened and I'll punish everyone involved. That I swear, as well."

At first, she gave no response. Then her tongue licked, a flick of fire, as hot as the sword hilts. He had to pant through it, but he didn't pull away. Then her mouth latched on, branding him now and forever, and she sucked and sucked and sucked, and oh, yeah, did he like that.

"That's the way," he praised. "Good, good girl. Take all you need. Take everything."

She took him at his word and drank her fill. When she finished, dizziness swam through his head, but he didn't care. He was only glad Defeat hadn't viewed that as a challenge, either. He straightened and peered down at her.

Her eyes were closed, her breathing harsh, shallow. Her temperature had cooled a little and her face wasn't quite so pallid. That meant she was healing. Right?

He needed to get her out of this smoke-infested cave. His holey shirt rested a few inches away. He grabbed it up and wrapped what was left of the material around Kaia's body. As tenderly as he was able, he lifted her in his arms. He wobbled on his feet, but didn't let that deter him.

At the mouth of the cave, he called for Lysander. The angel appeared a second later, hovering just in front of him, wings gliding gracefully through the air.

"Take us to our tent," he croaked. He couldn't lose this woman.

CHAPTER TWENTY-SEVEN

"COME ON, BABY DOLL. I've let you sleep long enough. Now you're just being lazy."

Strider, Kaia thought dazedly, her entire body sparking to life. He was here, next to her. He had to be. His voice, so close, so sweet. Soft fingertips smoothed the hair from her brow. She knew that touch. Loved that touch and she leaned into it.

"Come on. That's the way."

His husky baritone proved to be a lifeline and she clung desperately. Inch by inch, she pulled herself from the thick, cloying darkness surrounding her. Even though every movement *hurt*. Strider, she had to reach Strider. That had been her last thought, she recalled. Her last thought before—

She'd heard so many screams. Of terror, of pain. Hers, so many others. The scent of melting skin had hit her nose and she'd gagged. Gagged now, remembering. Released the lifeline. Down, down she fell, back into the darkness.

"Kaia! I'm not going to tell you again. Wake the hell up. Now!"

Strider. She grabbed the lifeline once again. Again she tugged her way up…up… A bright light waited at the surface. She had only to reach out…grab it…almost there… another tug…

Her eyelids popped open as a gasp of shock and lingering outrage lodged in her throat. She was panting and sweating, muscles locked onto bone. She tried to sit up, but hard hands held her down.

"No. You're still healing, so I don't want you moving."

Suddenly Strider's beautiful face loomed over her. His deep blue eyes were glassy, feverish. Concern etched deep lines around his mouth and his normally tanned skin was nearly as colorless as his hair. No, not true. There were spots of color, but they were bright red welts and blisters.

He was naked. Seeing him, something sizzled inside her. Knowledge, power, connection. Yes, a connection more prevailing even than what she felt with Bianka. More than binding them, that connection wove them together, until she couldn't tell who was who. They were simply one.

"Are you all right?" Gods, even speaking hurt. Her throat was raw, agonized, as if someone had scraped the insides with jagged glass and then, just for funsies, painted the bleeding flesh with acid.

"I'm fine, so don't worry about me. Worry about you. You've been out for three days."

Three days? Her eyes widened. "The third game—"

"Starts two days from now. Bianka has kept me informed."

Thank the gods. *Still.* Three days. "I must look terrible," she muttered. She would have finger-combed her hair, but decided lifting her arm would require too much effort.

"You look alive, and that's goddamn beautiful to me."

Darling man. Her heart skipped a beat as she soaked up his praise.

"Besides," he said, "we're both clean. Lysander gave me robes. Angel robes. A stack of them. Every time I put a new one on, it was like taking a bath. You, too. Everything from your hair to the bottom of your feet was—is—washed. And let me tell you, that was *weird.*"

Why tell her that? Unless…oh. Oh. He wanted her.

Okay, she would put the effort into *that*. Arousal warmed her up and her nipples tightened.

Her gaze swept over her body to catalog the damage she'd have to work around.

She was naked, her shoulders discolored and scabbed. Stomach, fine. Legs, fine. Ankles, bruised. Not bad.

She was lying on a faux fur rug her twin must have delivered, inside a nearly barren white tent, the air around her heated even though the air by the flapping entrance was almost crystallized from cold.

Leaning his weight into one arm, Strider was careful not to brush the long, thick length of his erection—and oh, yes, he had one—against her. Warm heat instantly pooled between her legs. She craved his touch, his mouth. Wanted to explore this new, deeper connection thing. She licked her lips.

"You move fast," she said with a grin.

"Damn it, Kaia. Get your mind out of the gutter and talk to me. I've been waiting patiently for *days*."

His *pet name* for her brought her gaze back to his face. The concern was back full force and she recalled why she was here, in the condition she was in—and the danger she had become to this man. She didn't have to push her sexual need aside. It vanished on its own.

"Okay. Yes. What do you want me to talk about?"

His eyes glinted down at her. "First, if you ever had any doubts that I'm your consort, you can put them to rest. You slept next to me."

Not the terrible topic she'd expected and she relaxed against the fur. "Sorry, darling, but that's not how the consort sleeping thing works."

He gave her a fierce frown. "How does it work, then?"

"Naps don't count if the Harpy falls asleep while injured. I have to sleep next to you when I'm healed and that hasn't happened yet."

"It will." Determination radiated from him and she knew he saw this as a challenge. A challenge he clearly accepted.

She didn't let it bother her, though. She wanted to sleep next to him, cuddled into his side, something she'd never done with another man. How or why that occurred didn't matter.

"Now tell me what the hell happened," he continued, each word gruffer than the last. "Did those men...are you...?" Okay. Blisters weren't the only thing coloring his face now. Fury did. So much fury.

Fury over her mistreatment? "Did they what? Pin me to the wall? Yes. Did they catch fire and burn to death? Yep, that, too." Once more the screams and the flames flashed through her mind. Rather than torment her as they had in the dark, dark void, she experienced a surge of satisfaction.

Victory belonged to her.

"No, baby doll." His expression softened, became tender and seeking. He traced a gentle fingertip along the slope of her nose. "Did they...rape you?"

"No." She shivered from the succulent contact. "I would have killed them deader if they had."

Relief joined the fury and the tenderness. "I won't piss on their charred remains, then. So how'd you kill them? I mean, I know they burned to death, like you said, but *how* did you manage that? You had to have done it after you were pinned. Otherwise you would have been sliced like a Christmas ham."

Smart man. "I..." As *those* memories surfaced, she frowned, looked away from him. "I don't want to tell you," she whispered. While she was satisfied with the end results, *getting* those results had opened a veritable Pandora's box of complications—and she didn't think Strider would appreciate the irony.

Dark lashes fused together. "Do it anyway. Now. And start from the beginning. I want to hear everything."

So commanding, her warrior. So sexy. She hadn't wanted to tell him, but she would. Had planned to even while uttering the refusal. She would do anything, even this, to keep him from experiencing a moment of pain. "I climbed the ledge and the Hunters were waiting for me. They rushed me and we fought. I would have won, too, but they knew to go for my wings." Probably courtesy of Juliette, even though discussing such a weakness with *anyone* was forbidden and punishable by death. "Once those were broken, pinning me with the swords was easy."

Every word had him tensing. "I didn't hear you scream."

She knew that; she'd made sure he hadn't, holding her cries inside. She hadn't wanted to distract him from his fight with Lazarus. Which he must have won, since he was here and evidently pain-free.

Had she called him sexy? She meant irresistibly ravishing. But why hadn't he heard the Hunters' screams? she wondered. Interesting. Had someone somehow kept the noise inside the cave?

"The rest," he urged on a croak.

Do it. "I was so mad, so…desperate, the heat inside me just kind of spilled out."

"I know that heat," he said huskily.

Her brows knit together in confusion. "You do?"

"Yeah. When we made love, you burned me pretty badly."

"What!" She must not have been paying attention to his body, only her own. Selfish much? "Gods, Strider. I'm so sorry."

"I'm not." His lips twitched in his first true display of humor since she'd woken up. "I liked it."

That didn't calm her. She could have *killed* him. Rather than considering that, however, and perhaps bursting into tears, she hurried on with her story. "I caught fire, but it didn't hurt me. I didn't understand what was happening, just watched as the men around me caught fire, too. And when the others tried to run out of the cavern, I looked at them and the next thing I knew, they were writhing as they burned. My Harpy laughed." To be honest, so had she. "Then I just kind of blacked out."

"I don't understand. How could you catch fire and be okay minutes later?"

The answer was the very reason she hadn't wanted to discuss this. "I should have put the pieces together before this, but I discarded them as silly. Maybe because I was too distracted with the courting of my consort."

He barked out a laugh. "Discarded *what* as silly? And you're saying you courted me? Baby doll, if the past few weeks are your idea of courting, we seriously need to work on your dating skills."

"Shut up. I nabbed you, didn't I?"

"Yeah," he said tenderly, huskily. "You nabbed me."

That mollified (and melted) her. "As I was saying, my father is a Phoenix shape-shifter. I must have inherited a few of his abilities." And she didn't like that she had! Of course she valued her newfound ability to fry her enemies to a smoldering crisp, but the Phoenix were an exclusive, unwelcoming race and anyone who displayed the tiniest bit of pyrokinesis was captured and kept—forcibly—within their territory.

Honestly. She had no idea how her mom and dad had ever hooked up in the first place.

O-kay. *Gross.* She shied away from that thought. *Anyway.* That's why her dad had kidnapped her and Bianka all those centuries ago, to ensure they did not exhibit an affinity for fire. They hadn't and so they'd been set free. Not just set free, but told never to come back.

She should not be exhibiting such an affinity now. Phoenix could withstand intense heat and control fire from birth. Until now, she'd never been able to. So how had this happened? Why now? Latent ability, perhaps? But then, shouldn't it have hit with puberty? Only other thing she could think of was the one thing that had changed in her life. Her need, *her burning desire,* for Strider.

When—if—her dad found out, would he come for her? Demand she live with his people? No need to consider it. Yeah. He would. And she would refuse. Would she be forced to war with him and all his brethren, just to live her life as she wished? Would he make a gamble for Strider in an attempt to force her hand?

"I'm glad you inherited your father's abilities. You're alive and nothing is more important than that," Strider said. "You did a great job."

"Really?" She would never tire of his praise.

"If your goal was to worry me to death, then yes." He was glowering now, his affection morphing into anger. She figured the what-ifs were driving him crazy. "You are never going off on your own again. You will chain yourself to my side and like it. Understand?"

She would not deign to respond to such a ludicrous statement. "Just so you know, you did a good job, too." Maybe if she applauded him, he'd stop letting his concern speak for him and remember *she'd won.*

"Well, you didn't do a great job, and that's the gods' honest truth. You almost died! You didn't scream and I know why. You didn't want to distract me. But guess what? I'd rather you had distracted me! I could have raced to the rescue and helped you do that killing."

He also could have burned to death with the Hunters. "Well...well...you didn't do a good job, either!"

"Nope. You already said I did."

"And then I said you *didn't.*"

"Sorry, no take-backs. You sucked this up because you

let yourself get pinned. Don't do that again. Do you even realize what they could have done to you?"

Yep. The what-ifs were definitely driving him. The indignation drained from her. How could she blame him? Had the situation been reversed, she would have done the same thing. "I won't do it again."

Strider pushed out a labored breath, visibly relaxing more with each molecule of air that escaped him. "So why didn't you want to tell me about the Hunters?"

Well, maybe she still possessed a *little* indignation. Quite primly, she said, "Because telling you about my newfound firepower meant I'd have to tell you something even worse—we can't have sex anymore." And she meant it. She might have forgotten her resolution upon first awakening, but she recalled it now.

"Like hell!" he roared.

"Strider, we can't. I'll burn you." Badly. Perhaps even kill him.

He softened his voice when he said, "You didn't last time." Then he finally, blessedly, turned into her, pressing his cock between her legs, hitting her right where she wanted him most.

Her need exploded back to life and she had to clench her hands in the rug to keep from reaching for him. The heat...she could feel it building again, seething beneath her skin. "Liar. You said I blistered you."

"I also said I liked it."

Don't you dare soften. "Doesn't matter. Last time I'd never set anything on fire. Now that I have, the chances are greater that I will again. And when I'm with you, I apparently lose all hint of common sense. I won't be able to control myself."

"If that's the case, you won't be able to fight in the other two games, either. Your anger most definitely will be ignited and you'll erupt, killing everyone around you."

"Yeah, but I want to kill my opponents." Not really, but she didn't want to admit he had a point.

"Which will endanger your family."

Damn him!

"Just pucker up, buttercup, because this is happening. *If you can take it*," he added thoughtfully. "Your injuries..."

He'd just pricked the hell out of her pride and her chin lifted. "I can take anything."

"Good. I've worried about you for too damn long and I need you. More than that, I deserve a reward for taking care of you. *Don't I?*"

Concern for his safety persisted. He was the most important part of her life. "That's your demon talking. I know it. If you would just think this through, you'd—"

"Baby doll, I haven't thought clearly since I met you. We're having sex. You're gonna like it, I'm gonna like it, and we're gonna come out of this alive." He paused, snickered. "Get it? *Come* out of this."

She rolled her eyes, but his complete disregard for her fears did much to help alleviate them.

Strider wasn't done, though. "My demon likes to dominate you, yes, and being with you sexually is far more satisfying than anything else because he's also afraid of you, making your surrender all the sweeter. But he hasn't accepted a challenge yet. This is just you and me. And need. Hard, raging need."

She nibbled on her bottom lip. "I don't want Defeat to fear me. I want him to like me always."

A slow smile curled his lips. "Good. 'Cause the bastard just purred his approval."

"Really?" Finally she allowed her arms to wind around his neck. He pressed his shaft against her, rubbed back and forth and pulled a groan of pleasure from deep inside her. But the heat intensified, pulsing from her and he began to sweat. That scared her. "Strider."

"I'm your consort. You can't hurt me."

Another good point. "But…that's your arousal talking."

"No, that's my trust in you and your strength talking."

"You said I did a piss-poor job."

"Did not."

"Did, too."

"Zip it, Kaia, and stop stalling. Look at it this way if you want. Your Harpy is one badass chick and she loves me. She's not going to hurt me. Deal with it and let's move on."

"She *tolerates* you," Kaia lied.

"She obviously needs a vocabulary lesson. She loves me. And," he went on before she could comment, "she's stronger than your Phoenix side. She has to be." As he spoke, he thrummed her nipples, giving her more of the sweet, sweet contact she'd craved so badly. "Otherwise you wouldn't have gone this long without setting people on fire. *But.* If it makes you feel any better…"

He lifted her in his arms and carried her to the exit. She felt the drop in temperature the moment Strider stepped outside. Snow poured from the darkened sky, as determined as a rainstorm.

"We're alone out here," he said. "Everyone else left yesterday and Lysander posted guards on the other side of the mountains. No one will be sneaking up on us."

Good to know. What was embarrassing was that she hadn't given the possibility of a sneak attack a moment's thought. Only this man. Only his touch.

"You're going to freeze to death," she warned as he laid her down in the snow. Goose bumps formed over her skin as she cooled.

"Make up your mind. Either I'll burn to death or I'll freeze to death. Which is it?" He spread her legs as far as they would go and crouched in front of her. "So pretty," he said, running a finger through her moist slit.

Her back arched in supplication. "So *good*."

"So mine." He teased her clitoris, ramping up her desire—and touching everywhere but *there*. "Say it."

"I'm yours," she breathed. Always.

A kiss and a lick at the center of her need, making her moan, and then he was once again looming over her. The snow fell around him, hauntingly beautiful. He didn't enter her, not yet, but started that slow, hard rub all over again, teasing, teasing. She gave another needy moan.

"Strider. Please."

"Gods, you taste good. I need another." Back down he went, licking and sucking.

The pleasure slammed through her and her fingers tangled in his hair. The heat blossomed again, despite the chilly winds, spinning through her veins. Though pleasurable dizziness hazed her eyesight, she watched him, determined to stop him at the first sign of danger. Sweat beaded on his temples and dripped onto her thighs. Sweat, but no welts. Good, good, so good.

His tongue never stopped working her, sinking in and out, making love to her, before finally sliding over her clitoris. With one final press, he brought her to a quick orgasm. Satisfaction burst through her, traveling from between her legs into her chest, her arms, her feet, sweeping a tide of sensation through every part of her. Flames erupted from behind her eyelids, but at no time did those flames leave her.

She began to believe. She could never hurt this man. Neither intentionally, nor unintentionally. He was her other half, as indispensable as her heart. Hell, he *was* her heart. He calmed her Harpy and now, apparently, he tamed the Phoenix.

"Open your eyes, baby doll."

She obeyed without question. He was poised over her, hair plastered to his scalp. Sweating still. The tip of his penis brushed her drenched opening and she had to bite her lip as renewed desire sparked.

"Confession time," he said. Another brush. "You burned away the angel robes. From both of us. That's why we were naked. And you did set me on fire. Once. But I got over it." He didn't wait for her reply but slammed into her, sinking as deep as he could go.

Automatically she arched to meet him, to take him, to take everything. "You...bastard," she managed to gasp out. He was so wide, he stretched her. So long he hit her deeper than any other. But she was so wet, the glide was easy. "I could...kill you, doing this." She'd been so sure, after that climax, that she couldn't hurt him. Now, to find out that she *had* hurt him...that she could again...

"Accident," he said on a moan. He surged deep again, pulled out, surged.

"I won't risk you." Could she push him away? *For his own good, for his own good.* "Strider—"

"You don't have to risk me. And I'll prove it."

CHAPTER TWENTY-EIGHT

STRIDER BROUGHT HIS WOMAN to peak after peak, showing her no mercy, bending her body in every position imaginable. He sucked on her nipples, licked her from head to toe, teased her sex with long, sure rubs, pounded inside her, slow and easy, then sped up, fast, faster, strokes becoming quick, shallow, then deep, piercing.

When she lay on her back, nearly unable to catch her breath, he placed her legs on his shoulders. When she reached another peak, he moved her legs to his waist. When she reached yet *another* peak, he flipped her around and took her from behind. Through it all, she writhed and moaned and begged for more.

More. Yeah, he could give her more. He thought he could love her like this forever and still another day, despite his own raging need to climax. A need that was building and building, consuming him, but he'd never been more determined to brand himself into another being. And he would. Until every cell she possessed wept with knowledge of him, unable to deny him in any way.

That way, she would never forget that she belonged to him, never forget what he would do to her if she scared him again. Not that this would be much of a deterrent. Hell, he was giving her a reason to get her ass kicked every goddamn day. Almost die, and she'd get the best sex of her life. No damn ego check required, thank you.

He just...he didn't want this moment to end. He needed this. Needed her.

Keeping him at a distance wasn't an option. Yeah, he'd known how she would react when she found out she had burned him. And yeah, he'd confessed only when she'd been unable to kick up much of a fit about it. Hello. He was *smart*. But like he'd told her, charring him over an open flame had been an accident. What he hadn't told her, but something they would cover later? It had been an accident he'd incited.

She'd been dying, gasping that final breath. He'd seen enough people die to know when the Grim Reaper would be called. And he'd known Lucien would soon be called. Lucien would have heeded the summons, too, no matter how hotly Strider protested. He would have taken Kaia's soul to the afterlife, as his demon, Death, required. Knowing that was about to happen, Strider had fallen straight into bat-shit crazy land and pulled a Gideon.

He'd married his woman.

He'd recalled how Gideon had raved about slicing himself, then slicing Scarlet and combining their blood. The old-school way to get hitched. The action had bound their lives, their souls, and Gideon's strength had become Scarlet's. So Strider had done it. Sliced himself and then Kaia. The moment the blade had sunk into the sensitive flesh between her breasts, she had erupted, thrashing, the fires starting all over again.

A *little* of his skin had melted—like, the top half of his body—but that had been a small price to pay for her life. He'd already been her consort, but he'd added a little... spice to the relationship. Made them equals. Partners. And gods, the knowledge just about felled him.

Mine, he thought now. *My wife. Always.*

With every climax Kaia had, Defeat became a little more confident in his ability to tame her. A little more possessive of her. Like Strider, the bastard had realized she would never purposely hurt him, that winning her—something no other man had ever done—was one of the greatest victories of their existence.

Bastard was also pouring pleasure straight into Strider's veins and it was almost more than he could bear.

"Strider," Kaia moaned, her sweet, curvy ass wiggling as he once again slowed his thrusts. "Please."

The snow continued to fall, an exquisite storm he saw but didn't feel. His woman was too hot. A heat he welcomed, adored, craved…hadn't known he needed. Heat now represented Kaia, pleasure and satisfaction. A potent combination. He'd probably sport an erection all through the summer.

"Have you learned your lesson?" The words were practically ripped from his throat, his need causing his voice box to constrict.

"Yes."

Leaning down, he pressed his chest into her searing back, the ridges of her spine creating the most delicious friction against his flesh. She murmured her approval. But much as he, too, fancied this new, deeper contact, he didn't stay that way. He wound his arms around her and lifted them both so that they were on their knees, hers inside of his.

His aching cock never slid free of her and she hit the root of him. Her head fell to his shoulder, the length of her silky hair tickling him between their bodies. He moved one hand to her breast, the beaded pink nipple peaking from between his fingers. He moved his other hand to her wet, wet core.

"Damn you, move harder!" she commanded, her movements uncoordinated now. "Faster."

"No. Tell me what you've learned first," he demanded,

keeping himself still. He didn't brush her clit, just teased the sensitive, swollen bud with his nearness.

She growled. "That I won't hurt you by losing control during sex. FYI, I learned that about five climaxes ago, you bastard."

"Hadn't realized you were such a quick study."

"So why aren't you moving? I will hurt you if you don't finish this!" That growl was sharper by the second. Her claws sank into his thighs as she said, "I swear, I'll finish myself and leave you to rot."

A rough chuckle left him. So impatient, his woman. *Thank the gods.* He wouldn't have her any other way.

"I love you," Strider told her. Before she could reply, he angled his head and meshed their lips together, his tongue driving against and rolling with hers. He gripped her hips and forced her to ride him, burying his cock as deep as it could go with each downward thrust, impaling her, then almost leaving her with each upward glide.

When that wasn't enough, he pressed his thumb against the sweetest little spot on earth. She was so small, so tight, he knew he was nearly too big for her. Perhaps that should have made him take care, but she was strong and she could take anything he meted out. So he meted out a lot, hitting her hard and fast. The kiss never ended, never slowed, and he loved that they tasted of each other's passion.

One of her hands lifted, those nails next digging into his scalp. "Strider," she gasped, pulling from his lips. "Yes. *Yes.*"

Such a sweet benediction. His muscles quivered with the depths of his need. His bones ached. Had to...needed... would...damn it! He'd held his release back for so long, he couldn't quite breech the resistant wall he'd erected.

He hammered at her, hips pistoning, and when that didn't work, he dropped to his side, the ice barely noticeable, taking her with him, moving her top leg over his and spreading her as wide as he could.

Harder...harder still...but release continued to elude him. He was becoming desperate, sweating so much the ice melted and pooled beneath him. His fingers dug into Kaia's hip with such might he knew bruises would form by morning.

She moaned and groaned and whimpered. And when she cried, "I love you," as she broke apart, shattering, her inner muscles clenching at him, he realized that was exactly what he'd been waiting for, what he'd needed. Her declaration.

He, too, broke, her body practically ripping the seed out of him, the hot jets shooting inside her. Bright lights winked behind his eyelids, his roar echoing through the night.

When he'd emptied himself out long moments later, he collapsed beside her. She was shaking. Not from cold, but from exertion. He was too weak to smile and bang his chest with the force of his pride. His woman—his *wife*—was pleased.

"Did you mean it?" he managed to ask, sleep tugging at him as surely as she had.

She didn't pretend to misunderstand. "Yes." Her voice was delicate, exhausted.

"About damn time."

"Oh, just shut up and afterglow with me."

Okay, so he wasn't too weak to smile after all. "You gonna sleep? For real?"

"Try and stop me." She yawned and burrowed her head into the hollow of his neck.

"You trust me to protect you?"

Several minutes dragged by in silence.

"Kaia?"

"What?" she murmured sleepily.

"Do you. Trust me. To protect you?"

"Of course," she said. Her eyes were closed and within minutes, she was sagged against him, completely lost to the sweet kiss of slumber.

Of course, she'd said. As if she hadn't made him sweat about the answer. He dredged up the strength to carry her back to the tent, where he held her tight, all night, swearing to the gods he would never let go.

KAIA WAS STILL REELING over Strider's absolute possession of her body two days later when they reached her sisters. They had their heads bent over their weapons, sharpening the tips and preparing for the third competition.

She and Strider hadn't made love again and they hadn't discussed their feelings for each other. A courtesy on his part, she knew. She had to remain focused, her eye on the prize. Unfortunately, she hadn't been able to kidnap and torture Juliette for information about the Paring Rod. Which, Strider had told her, was apparently all too real and not the fake they'd been hoping for.

And there was no time to do so now, either. The journey from Alaska to Rome had eaten up her chance. While Juliette was now within her reach, the game would be starting in half an hour.

Bianka noticed Kaia when she glanced up to find her polishing stone. "Kye!" Grinning, she jumped to her feet, her weapon clattering to the floor next to her bucket of water. She rushed over and gathered Kaia in a welcome embrace. "I almost killed Strider when he refused to let me see you, but I knew you'd disapprove if he got so much as a scratch." A long-suffering sigh. "Thankfully, he's been texting me daily reports, so I knew you were on the mend. But seeing you..."

Hot tears stung her eyes. "Yeah, I know. I needed to see you, too." She knew Strider hadn't told her sisters about the fire thing, and neither had their men, who'd witnessed the aftereffects. Not that Strider had explained things to them.

He'd left the decision up to her.

To tell, or not to tell? If she did, her sisters wouldn't want her to fight. *Like they do anyway?* She ignored the harsh inner voice. Their reluctance would be wise. She may or may not be able to start another fire. If the Harpies pissed her off, yeah, she probably would. Like the Hunters, they would die. And that was fine, expected even. Using your abilities was encouraged during these kinds of competitions, every advantage exploited.

But if she lost control, would she harm her family, too?

She wished she had time to practice, to test the limits of her Phoenix side. Was strong emotion the trigger? Or would simply thinking about the flames work? Even now, the heat coiled through her veins, at the ready.

She would have liked to ask someone, but the only other Phoenix she knew was her dad and she would rather spend the rest of eternity wondering about the truth than speak to him for a single minute. His evil, his absolute lack of concern for others, for his own daughters' well-being... she shuddered. He wasn't exactly Father of the Year material.

That was another reason to remain out of the game. If she caught fire, or set someone else on fire, word of her new ability would spread. Daddy Dearest might come for her.

"Damn, girl. Are you feverish?" Bianka was sweating when they parted, though her twin didn't sever all contact, keeping her arm wound around Kaia's waist.

"Nope," she lied. "Flushed. And I know, you don't have to say it. Strider is a lucky man."

"That's the truth."

Quashing a spark of guilt before it could form—she

absolutely hated lying to her twin—Kaia glanced around the room. Taliyah nodded in acknowledgment before returning to her blade-sharpening task. Gwen blew her a loving kiss. Neeka offered her a small smile and the others waved.

"Catch me up," she said.

Bianka pulled her forward. Kaia's other hand was intertwined with Strider's and stayed that way until the last possible second. As she and her twin sat on the floor of the Team Kaia tent, she saw Sabin, Lysander and Strider gather in a corner and put their heads together, chatting, their voices low.

She tried to listen, her ears twitching, but she couldn't make out the words. She tried to read their lips, but they kept their bodies angled away from her, not allowing her a single peek.

She was very close to standing up, stomping over, gripping her man by the shoulders and shaking him. Then she would demand he tell her what was going on, what he didn't want her to know.

You trust him. You know he would never hurt you. And that was true. She did. She trusted him with her life. Obviously. Otherwise, she never would have slept, truly slept, with him.

Gods, that had been amazing. Rousing from seductive dreams and feeling her man beside her. She'd been cocooned, had luxuriated in his strength, his thick arms banded around her. Sleep had still held him in a tight fist and his features had been relaxed, boyish.

Never in her life had she been so content.

"So...what do you think? You in?" Bianka asked, drawing her attention.

Shit. She hadn't heard a single word her sister had said. "In what, exactly? Tell me again, because your explanation was so lame it confused me."

Bianka knew her very well and rolled her eyes. "You are such a bad liar."

Am I? she almost asked with a smug lift of her chin. *You didn't catch my last one.* "You're projecting. Continue."

"I was telling you how we're in Rome, in the Coliseum. And get this. It's the Coliseum of old, exactly the same as it used to be—only *way* different."

Kaia supposed that, when you were as pretty as Bianka, you didn't need to be smart. "Bee, darling. You are so, so exquisite, but you are also highly deranged. Do you have any idea how contradictory that statement was?"

"What are you talking about? I make perfect sense if you don't actually ponder anything I say. Now guess what? The Coliseum is hidden from the mortal eye. *We're* hidden from the mortal eye, in a realm we didn't need a portal to access. Here, but not here."

"And how'd we manage that?"

"Juliette. Somehow."

Just the name had her gritting her teeth. Juliette had set her up, had arranged for mere mortals—and Strider's enemies—to slaughter her. Bitch needed to pay. Soon. "And?"

"And we'll be fighting like Gladiators. Which is what I was trying to tell you before, if only you'd paid attention. So anyway, you're very good with your hands and our team needs you this round. You up for it? You were hit pretty badly in Alaska."

They *needed* her? When they'd brought home their first victory without her? She eyed her sister critically, searching for any sign of duplicity or placation. Only innocence and assurance rested in those lovely amber eyes. Only determination hardened those red lips.

No placation, then. No recrimination over her past defeats, either. Bianka believed in her.

Could she believe in herself?

Her new ability might hurt her sisters, yes, but it would definitely aid her in a second victory. A victory Strider needed her to achieve for his very survival.

She glanced over at him. He was still in that circle with his friends, but he was facing her now. His blond hair was mussed, his cheeks flushed. They were always flushed around her, as if he were constantly aroused. She liked that.

His lashes were so long they curled upward. And wow, were they the perfect frame for those wicked blue eyes. His lips were swollen, delightfully red. They may not have had sex again, but they'd certainly kissed. A lot. At every possible opportunity she had sucked on his tongue.

No question, she was addicted to him.

Her study intensified. There were cuts on his fingers and palms, she noted. He'd borne those same injuries before, but those had healed. Hadn't they? She frowned, hating that he was hurt again. Hating more that she didn't know why or how. Had *she* inflicted the damage?

The thought caused her stomach to cramp. She just, well, she loved him so damn much. She hadn't known for sure until she'd shouted the words, but she did. He was strength personified. He was devilish. He was fun and charming, with a smart-ass mouth she couldn't resist. He made her laugh. He pushed her to the edge, knowing she could take it. He teased her, didn't fear her. He knew her, understood her, was sometimes tender, sometimes harsh. He worried about her, trusted her.

He'd also married them.

The knowledge had shocked the hell out of her. Yeah, he thought that was still his little secret, but she was onto him. She wasn't sure why he hadn't confessed, or even why he'd done it, but she was stubborn enough to wait him out. And she was just devious enough to tease him until he came clean.

After all, she liked his methods.

She also loved the knowledge that she was as much his as he was hers. And that's exactly how she knew he'd done it. She *felt* him. He was a part of her mind, in her blood, her soul, her heart, that bone-deep connection stronger than anything she'd ever experienced.

Since waking up in his arms, she'd known something was different between them and had spent many, many hours puzzling over what it could be. Little flashes of memory had come and gone—the glint of a blade, the drip of crimson, the press of Strider's skin, the whisper of his breath. The words, "You are mine, and I am yours. We are one. From this moment, we are one."

Oh, yes. They were wed and she'd never been happier. She owed this man so very much.

She watched as he pulled a packet of Red Hots from his back pocket and shook the contents into his mouth. He chewed, his strong jaw working. Her chest constricted at the sensuality of him.

He must have felt her gaze because he glanced over at her and winked. Again her chest constricted. She had to keep him safe. Whatever that entailed, she had to keep him safe.

She had to get that Rod.

She turned her attention back to her sister and lifted her chin. "I'll fight," she said.

CHAPTER TWENTY-NINE

ONCE AGAIN STRIDER SAT in the stands to watch his woman—wife!—compete. But the Roman Coliseum was a far cry from the bleachers in "Brew City," Wisconsin. He'd been here a time or two, remembered the travertine, tufa, brick and marble, and had never thought to see such things again. Not in such pristine condition, at least. As if no time had passed, as if the ancient world had somehow blended into the present.

There were four floors. The first three boasted wide, arched entryways fit for nobility, and the fourth, the bottom, had rectangular doorways meant for the common man. Nets rose from the arena to protect the spectators.

And the arena itself, well, he remembered that, too. A wooden floor stained with the blood of thousands covered the entire area, but it was a floor that could be removed, the land then flooded with water to reenact navel battles. Oh, how the Romans had loved their games.

And how the *Harpies* loved their games. The combatants occupied one of the subterranean chambers, waiting to be summoned. Meanwhile, Juliette droned on and on about what was to happen. If ever there'd been a blah, blah, blah moment, this was it. He wanted to stab his own ears more now than when the twins had been singing.

"—toughest match yet," she was saying now. "And with two competitions under our belts, this one might just identify a clear leader."

We know. The teams would fight each other, all at once, with any weapon of their choosing. But they were only allowed one weapon each. They could, however, pick up discarded weapons as the fight progressed.

There would be ten combatants from each team. That was fine, whatever, except Kaia only had seven in her corner—counting herself. Which meant they all had to go in. *If* they wanted to go in. Big surprise, each of them had wanted, even though they were already at a disadvantage.

Around him, females were cheering. "Hit 'em hard, break their backs, that's the way to show 'em what they lack!"

Kaia had nearly died mere days ago and though he'd kept her fed and medicated, she wasn't yet at top strength. But he'd known better than to ask her to bow out. Her pride was important to her, and what was important to her was now important to him.

Even if that meant losing the Paring Rod.

He could always steal it from whoever won it.

Win.

Yeah, yeah. Defeat was on edge. Kaia was a part of them now. She was theirs, and Strider assumed her victory was as important to the demon as his own. He didn't know if he would experience gut-wrenching pain if she lost. He hadn't last time, despite the challenge he'd accepted to protect her from other Harpies—and he figured that was because there was a fine line between protecting and punishing to a demon and he could still do the punishing—but then, they hadn't been married last time. He prayed he did not learn differently today. Actually, he knew he wouldn't. She wouldn't lose. Despite her continued weakness, despite the fact that every single member of every single team was going to turn on her first, she had this one in the bag.

Not five minutes ago, he'd held her in his arms, hugging her tight before she abandoned him here.

"Any tips for winning?" she'd asked.

"Yeah. Do what you gotta do to survive."

"That's it? Wow. You suck at pep talks."

He'd gripped her shoulders and peered down at her. "All right, how about this? You're so emotionally invested in this, you let those emotions color your every move. Normally I'd say that's dumb, but I like my balls where they are. That's why I'll just tell you that you can't turn your feelings off, but you *can* use them."

"How?" she'd gritted out.

"Well, part of you loves the women you're up against, no matter how badly they've treated you, and you can't deny it."

She didn't try.

He continued, "You have to remember that, despite the love you feel, they'll turn on you in an instant."

"Okay."

"Also, you're easily distracted and—"

"There's *more?*"

"Listen. While you're down there, don't think about me. Don't think about what I'm doing or whether I'm okay."

She snapped her teeth at him. "You'll be looking for the Paring Rod. How can I not—"

"*Don't think about what I'm doing.* Okay? That includes right now, this moment."

A stiff nod.

"Also, if you don't defeat them, Kaia, I'm going to kill them far more cruelly than you would have. Defeat issued a challenge to protect you from other Harpies before I came here, but this one is all me."

Her jaw dropped.

"There. Now you're properly motivated to do what needs doing. So go kick some ass."

Beside him, Sabin and Lysander shifted restlessly, bringing him back to the present. Zacharel hadn't yet made an appearance.

"I hate this Gladiator shit," Sabin muttered.

"Yes, well, where do you think the Romans learned this kind of behavior?" the angel asked.

Sabin sputtered for a minute. "You're trying to tell me *Harpies* are responsible for this? That the Romans learned from them?"

"I must try only if you're lacking intelligence."

Sabin opened his mouth to snap a reply, but a trumpet blew, signaling the start of the third game, and the crowd quieted. A second later, several of the iron doors groaned and creaked as they were raised. The combatants spilled out, sprinting into the arena.

Strider straightened, focused. Several more iron doors opened. Lions, tigers and bears—oh, my—joined the race. All were agitated, their mouths foaming.

He searched...searched...there. A glimpse of that bright red hair, bound tight in a ponytail. Kaia wore scarlet, like the rest of her team. Unlike the others, she did not clutch a weapon. He frowned.

The women at last reached the middle of the grounds, and without pause, the match began in a tangle of teeth, claws and metal. Grunts and shrieks instantly abounded. Blood sprayed.

Damn it, Kaia, he cursed as realization set in. She was going to use her fire—her new, as yet untested fire—and she hadn't wanted anyone to accuse her of using two weapons.

If she burned a fellow Harpy to death, she would hate herself afterward. Or worse, if she couldn't summon the fire, they would kill her and he would hate them, punish them, destroy them as promised. For him, though, for the Rod, she'd decided to risk it. Damn her!

He'd thought he'd motivated her to victory. He'd merely incited her to craziness.

"What the hell is she doing bare-handed?" Sabin asked conversationally. "Even Gwen has a weapon."

He didn't answer, couldn't. There was a knot in his throat, cutting off sound, air. The other teams turned on her, just as he'd expected. What he hadn't—the animals charged her as if she wore a bull's-eye and he could guess why. Someone had worked them into a frenzy using Kaia's scent.

Which they'd most likely gotten from her stolen coat.

Strider was on his feet and shoving his way through the crowd in seconds. Until something hard slammed into his back, knocking him down. There wasn't time to catch himself. His forehead hit rock, a sharp pain exploding through his head. Oxygen abandoned his lungs. His vision blurred.

Nothing stopped him from bucking off the weight and standing, running forward, not caring to look behind him to see who'd tried to stop him.

Win...her, Defeat said.

Yes. I'll win her, save her. I will.

Through a haze, he zeroed in on Kaia. She was darting around the arena, throwing her competition at the frothing animals. The beasts were all too happy to tear into their new toys as they followed her.

The hard weight slammed into him a second time, tossing him back on the ground like a rag doll. Roaring, Strider swung around, intending to do a little killing before he resumed his journey.

Win. A new challenge.

Yes, he thought again. *I'll win this one, too.*

"Your woman will be disqualified if you aid her." Lazarus unfurled from him and stood. He was weaponless, shirtless, pants unfastened and clearly hastily tugged on. The dark chain tattooed around his neck was pulsing, slithering around his neck like a snake, the inky links actually clanking together.

Strider stood and took stock. "I'd rather she were disqualified than killed. Now, then. You and I have a bit of business to attend to before I go."

Lazarus quirked a brow. "Good luck with that."

Win.

On it. Eyes narrowing, he stalked forward—only to stop when he saw Sabin and Lysander barreling toward him, calling his name. They were looking at him, but not actually seeing him. In fact, they raced *through* him before he could jump out of the way.

Shocked, he peered down at himself. They had run through him as if he were no more substantial than mist.

"No one can see us," Lazarus said easily. "Not even the angels."

Red dotted his vision. "What did you do to me?"

Boos and hisses from the crowd had him swinging around and peering below. The combatants had thinned out somewhat, but most of Team Kaia still fought. Including Kaia herself.

She was coated with blood and he wasn't sure if it came from her or the others, but her movements hadn't slowed. She was still throwing punches, kicking and flinging females at the—no, not the animals. At Bianka, who finished them off with a long, curved blade. The animals were now fully fed and satisfied, sitting off to the side and watching the rest of the battle through slumberous eyes.

The panic inside him eased. Kaia hadn't resorted to fire. Or maybe, as he'd supposed, she didn't know how to summon it. But either way, she was kicking ass and taking names. Even better, the teams were no longer able to converge on her en masse. She moved through them too quickly.

"I only have a few moments," Lazarus said, now at his side. "If Juliette notices I'm gone…"

Win.

Reminded of the challenge that had been accepted, Strider said, "I'm sorry, but I have to do this." Lightning fast, he threw his own punch, knuckles crunching into the warrior's nose. Cartilage snapped. Blood leaked from his nostrils.

Defeat sighed with satisfaction, pouring pleasure through his veins.

Lazarus straightened and wiped the crimson away with the back of his wrist. "I doubt I will be the first person to tell you how annoying you are."

"You might be the thousandth." He walked the rest of the way through the balcony, until he was poised over the edge. The warrior followed him, returning to his side. "So how are we here but not here?"

"Juliette has been forced to grant me more and more powers in order to see these games through as she wishes."

"She can give you powers? Just like that?" He snapped his fingers.

A stiff nod.

"Like what?"

"The ability to cast illusions no being can penetrate." Another nod, and their surroundings changed in an instant.

Strider blinked, one moment seeing the stands as they'd once been, the next seeing them as they were: crumbling, eroded by time and harsh elements. Not to mention the humans touring through the designated sections, snapping pictures. Then, after another blink, the stands were brand-new again.

"Plus the ability to hide our immortal world from the mortal one?" Strider asked.

"Yes. That, too."

"And you're sharing this with me because…" 'Cause

yeah, Strider knew damn good and well this could be a trick. That the bastard could mean to lull him into a false sense of security before striking. Hell, as distracted as he was, Lazarus could attack him at any moment without much resistance.

"I am a slave and I no longer wish to be."

He could dig, but... "I don't trust you. I'm not going to trust you." He watched as Kaia and Bianka clasped hands. Bianka swung her around, Kaia's legs slamming into the three females gunning for her. When her twin released her, she went flying like a bowling ball, knocking others down like pins.

What a woman.

He had a present for her and it was burning a hole in his pocket. Why hadn't he given it to her yet? He didn't know. Wasn't sure she'd like it. Was kind of embarrassed that he had it. To be honest, it was ugly as hell, and it proved how much of a pansy he'd become since meeting her.

For that alone, she'd love it, he thought, grinning.

"What?" Lazarus demanded.

"Kaia," was all he said.

"Yes, she's strong. She's also honorable, in her way. You have no idea how I envy you."

"As long as that's all you do, you'll be fine. Maybe."

"Which brings us back to the reason we are here. I do not need you to trust me," Lazarus said, his tone all the more urgent. "I need you to listen. Do you know what the Paring Rod can do?"

That captured his attention completely. He gripped the balcony rail tightly, knuckles leaching of color. "Tell me."

"The Rod steals from the living. Their souls, their abilities, their life forces, whatever. It strips a body of *everything,* trapping what it steals inside itself."

"Paring it down to nothing but a shell," Strider croaked

as comprehension dawned. That made sense. Scary, scary sense.

"Yes. But when you wield the Rod, you cannot take the powers inside yourself. You have to give them to another. Or, if you want them yourself, you have to entrust the Rod to someone else and have that person grant you the powers."

"And Juliette has done that for you. Granted you powers." Like the illusion thing he'd mentioned.

"Yes," the warrior repeated. "Nothing that matters, nothing that could hurt her, just little things that I am to use to impress her sisters."

"How do these powers impress them?"

"You have to ask?" Offense layered the big man's voice. "Never have the games been held in such exotic locales."

"Like I'd know. I've never been to the games before."

Lazarus huffed. "Your ignorance is forgiven, then. Barely."

"Thanks," he replied dryly. "I feel so much better."

"As I said—annoying."

"So how did Juliette get her hands on the Rod?"

"Like the rest of her race, she is a mercenary. She will do anything if the price is right, and Cronus's wife used that information to her advantage. She knew Juliette had been searching for me for many centuries. And she, in turn, had been searching for a way to secure the Paring Rod for herself and her Hunters. That's why, a few months ago, the queen promised to hand me over if Juliette could steal the Rod from my mother, the Gorgon tasked with its protection. Juliette jumped at the chance.

"But greedy witch that she is, when she learned exactly what the Rod could do, she decided she wanted it *and* me. So she killed my mother, intending to have a replica of the Rod made and trade the fake for me. But Rhea and most of her army disappeared just before their meeting, allowing

Juliette to simply grab me out of my cell, no trade necessary. No resistance."

"Why were you locked away?"

There was a flicker of shame in his eyes. "Hera, the former god queen, enjoyed keeping a menagerie of males. I had heard my father, who was made to sleep the sleep of the dead, was kept there, and so I allowed my own capture in the hopes that I could somehow rescue him. But I never found him, and then I could not escape."

The sleep of the dead. That meant Typhon was alive, aware, but unable to rise from his bed. So that was what had happened to the creature. "I'm sorry," Strider found himself saying. He had his own sob stories, but nothing compared to Lazarus's suffering.

He had known that the Paring Rod would be destructive in the wrong hands, but he hadn't known how dangerous it could truly be. And now he also knew why the Hunters had sought out Kaia and her sisters. With Rhea's disappearance, Juliette had taken more than the Paring Rod; she taken control of the Hunters. "What happened to Galen, Rhea's right-hand man?" Surely he would have something to say about that.

"Galen is the keeper of Hope?" At Strider's nod, he said, "The warrior took off just before Juliette's arrival. I'm not sure about his destination."

So. Galen was out there. Somewhere. "And where is the Rod now?"

"I have it."

In a whirl of determined movement, Strider faced him. The warrior's earlier urgency finally infected him. "Where is it?"

Lazarus looked bored. "I now have the ability to hide objects in the space around me. It is here. Here."

Eyes wide, Strider glanced around him, then patted the air around the warrior's shoulders. He encountered only body heat, but he knew. It *was* here. So close he'd probably brushed against it during their conversation. His heart hammered against his ribs.

"Give it to me. Now," he said. Then he recalled what Kaia had said to him, not so long ago, and he paused.

If he stole the Rod, she would be humiliated in front of her people. Except, while she'd been passed out and sick, writhing in pain from her injuries, she had babbled about stealing it herself. So he suspected she'd been planning to do so. For him. He should walk away—for her—but he couldn't. Too many lives were at stake. He would find a way to make it up to her, he told himself. He would.

Black eyes became flat. "I...can't."

"Like hell. Pull it out of the goddamn air. Like you did that first night, during orientation."

"I can't," Lazarus repeated.

"Why?" His voice lashed like lightning.

"Part of my soul is trapped inside the Rod. Physically I cannot do anything Juliette has forbidden me to do. I just can't, no matter how hard I try. Believe me, I *have* tried. That is the only reason she entrusted me with the Rod's care. And so I am to die before I allow the Rod to be taken from me."

Strider withdrew a dagger from his ankle sheath. "I don't want to fight you."

A stubborn chin rose, reminding him of Kaia. "And I do not wish to fight you. I have considered this so many times I've lost count, and always the solution is the same. Juliette controls the Rod, and therefore controls me. She will never willingly part with either. I am her consort, and as I am sure you have learned, the Harpies do whatever is necessary to keep their consorts by their sides. Even if the impossible occurred and I managed to escape her a second time, she would never cease searching for me. I have decided I would rather die than help her in any way.

I would rather die than make her happy. A decision you should support, since she wants me to seduce and *hurt* your woman."

Dude was so not doing the seduction/hurting thing. "Just to be clear. You're saying..."

"I am saying I have been used as a sex slave before. I will not be so used again. I am saying your woman once set me free, and I hurt her for it. I will not hurt her again. I am saying Juliette killed my mother. Now I will kill her dreams."

Shock pounded through him. "You—"

"Want you to slay me. Yes. More than destroying Juliette, I cannot live as a slave any longer. I've spent too many centuries inside a cell, and now I'm supposed to while away the rest of eternity with a woman I despise? No! I crave freedom, even if I can find it only in death." Lazarus dropped to his knees and tilted his head to the side, exposing the length of his vulnerable neck. "Do it. Before I change my mind."

In that moment Strider realized he had never admired a being more. Self-sacrifice had never been a big part of his life, but here was Lazarus, giving up everything. Not for love, but for revenge, and that motive was a hell of a lot better.

If anyone deserved a second chance to live a long and happy life, he thought suddenly, it was this man.

Strider had done a lot of despicable things in the name of victory, done even worse as a consequence of the war with the Hunters, but this—putting a good man down— would top them all. In another life, they might have been friends.

"Death doesn't have to be the end," he said to make himself feel better.

He saw a spark of regret in the other man's expression. "For me it will be. Much like you Lords would be incomplete without your demons, I am incomplete without the part of my soul that is trapped inside the Rod. When I die, the best I can hope for is that that part of me will wither and die, as well. As I've been led to understand, it is improbable to hope for the two pieces of my soul to unite and journey to heaven."

"So basically what you're saying is that you don't know what will happen to you?"

A blink of bafflement. "Is that what you need to believe to do this deed? That there's a chance for me to be happy in the afterlife? Because I must admit I am confused by your reluctance to end my life. I expected more from a fearsome Lord of the Underworld. Don't make me challenge you for this, Lord of Defeat. Just do it. Set me free."

He raised the blade higher, watched that pulse batter. His wrist twitched, but he remained exactly as he was.

Damn it. He couldn't do it. He couldn't end this creature forever.

Lazarus must have sensed his waning determination. "Should I live, I will find a way to get your woman into my bed. Should Juliette live, she will kill your woman when I'm done with her. And that is only if she's feeling generous, which she never is.

"The plan now, as I know it, is to finish the games, humiliating your woman with her many failures. And then, when she tires of the ridicule, Juliette will take Kaia's free will, just as she has done to me. Kaia will be unable to stop herself from joining the Hunters under Juliette's command. Oh, did I not tell you that part? Juliette will force Kaia to destroy you and all that you love. Do you understand what that means? You will be at war with your woman."

Just like that, the decision to act solidified. Not because Kaia would come after him, but simply because Kaia's happiness was everything to him, and she, too, deserved a second chance.

He would not let Juliette humiliate her. He would not let the bitch play with her mind, her emotions. And allowing Juliette to further screw with Lazarus, a guy who was noble enough to jump ship to save someone else? A guy who'd been hurt enough? Not going to happen.

"Thank you for your sacrifice. It will not be in vain. Juliette will be punished," he vowed. "You have my word."

"Thank you...friend."

Strider struck.

CHAPTER THIRTY

A few minutes earlier...

HER TEAM MIGHT HAVE STARTED out at a disadvantage, Kaia thought, panting from exertion, but they'd certainly evened the odds. And quickly, too. Right now, only members of the Eagleshields and Skyhawks were still conscious.

At first, insults had been hurled at her. "Weak." "Stupid." "Bitch." For once, they hadn't distracted her. Maybe because she'd been locked on a single thought: save Strider from pain.

The man who hated being challenged had challenged himself. For her. If she'd harbored any doubts about his love, that would have convinced her.

She had to win this. For him. He'd threatened to kill anyone she did not defeat, but she knew he wouldn't follow through with that one. He loved her too much to hurt a member of her race. So, if she failed, and then he failed to deliver punishment, would he experience twice the pain?

Win, win, win.

Oh, yes. Her strategy? Beat and run. She hadn't let herself engage a single person. Well, no longer than it took to punch once—okay, sometimes twice. She'd struck, and then she'd moved on, never allowing herself to be surrounded. When more than one Harpy had converged on her, she'd simply moved out of the way and let them slam into each other. That had, of course, sent them into a fight of their own, effectively doing the work for her.

Their determination to end her, and her alone, was going to be their downfall. Fitting, she mused, swinging around to face her next opponent. When she spotted the Harpy, her anticipation withered.

Her mother.

Kaia's throat dried. For the first time this round, sparks of heat lit up inside her. She'd been so careful.

Tabitha dropped the motionless body she held by the hair and faced off with her forgotten daughter. Around them, the battle continued to rage. Bianka noticed what was happening, though, and alerted the others. Soon Team Kaia was moving the rest of the females outward, giving Kaia and her mom a wide berth.

"At long last, the daughter I once spent an entire morning praising, telling my competitors that you would one day be stronger even than me, only to find you'd nearly ruined us all," Tabitha said. *Her* anticipation was palpable. "Finally you will be punished for that. I will put you in your place for the humiliation you caused."

She'd spent an entire morning *praising* Kaia? Had claimed Kaia would be stronger? *Don't soften. That's what she wants.*

"And where is my place?" She had to be cold. This fight was necessary, and centuries in the making. *Use might, not fire.*

One seemingly delicate shoulder lifted in a shrug. "At my feet. Of course."

At one time, that would have destroyed Kaia. Today, however, she experienced only the mildest twinge. She was loved, and by a man who didn't love easily. He considered her worthy. That was enough. "You can try."

"Oh, I'll do more than that."

Talk, talk, talk. Kaia waved her fingers, the fire beaten back. "We just gonna stand here or are we gonna do this?"

Surprisingly, Tabitha remained where she stood and arched a dark brow. "I'll give you five seconds to run away, a chance I've never offered another. For old time's sake, you could say. And Kaia, that's the only handicap I'll give you. After that, I will take your head." She tossed a dagger in the air. A dagger already coated with blood.

"One," Kaia said.

If she wasn't mistaken—and she had to be mistaken—pride flickered in her mother's amber eyes. "You're weaponless. Do you really expect to win?"

"Two."

Another flicker. "Trying to impress your man? Too bad he's not up there. He disappeared several minutes ago."

No reaction. She wouldn't fall for such tactics. Wouldn't be distracted from her purpose. "Three."

The corners of Tabitha's mouth quirked. "Do you recall when you were a girl and I spent hours training with you? I had you laid flat every time."

No damn reaction. "Four."

"All right. No more conversation." Tabitha threw her gaze at the crowd. "No one is to interrupt us. Is that clear?" With that, she assumed a battle stance, her legs apart, her knees bent and her arms at the ready. "It's just you and me now, daughter."

Her heart skipped a beat. "Five."

They flew at each other.

Tabitha hadn't earned the name "Vicious" for nothing, and slashed at Kaia the moment they were within striking distance. They were too close for her to avoid being hit and Kaia knew it, cursing herself for expecting her mother to try and get her on the ground first. So she did the only thing she could. She lifted her arms, allowing the blade to slash at her forearms rather than her neck or her chest. As the sharp pain tore through her, skin splitting open, her mother struck again, lightning fast, aiming for her stomach this time.

Kaia counterattacked. She caught Tabitha's hand midway, gripping her wrist in her elbow and twisting up, using the momentum to her advantage. When their arms reached shoulder level, she pressed Tabitha's wrist and the blade against herself and punched her mother in the temple with her free hand. She could have used the flat of her other hand to bat at the dagger and send it flying, but better to strike now, while she had the chance, than to remove the weapon from her mother's possession.

Why fight as if they had forever when she could do something to end things now?

Tabitha stumbled from the impact and dizzily dropped to her knees. Of course, she regained her footing in the few seconds it took Kaia to close the distance between them. Before she could strike, Tabitha spun, avoiding contact. Then, within a blink, Kaia was struck from behind. In the skull. She staggered, thinking fast. Knowing her mother as she did, she was sure the woman would fly at her, try to push her to the ground, cutting her neck while her weight smashed her wings. Only one way to combat that. Kaia used those staggering steps to push off and back flip.

Below her, for less than a blink, she saw the top of Tabitha's dark head. Saw that she'd been right. Saw Tabitha stop, realizing she wouldn't be winning so easily. Then Kaia landed and kicked out, aiming for her mother's kidney. Score.

Grunting, Tabitha fell to her knees. Kaia kicked again—no mercy—aiming for those fluttering wings. *Boom.* Her mother's body was flung forward, the cartilage in the right wing snapping on impact. Again, the entire action happened so quickly, anyone watching would have missed it if they'd blinked.

That should have slowed her mother down, but Tabitha had about a million years on her and had fought with a broken wing before. Seemingly impervious to the pain she must be feeling, the woman rolled, stood, turned.

"That all you got, baby?" Tabitha was smiling, but there was blood on her teeth.

Cold. Merciless. "Let's find out."

Once again they launched at each other, meeting in the middle. There was a flurry of punching and blocking. *Cold, stay cold.* With every shot of her mother's left arm, the dagger she held made a play for Kaia's jugular. Kaia was nicked a few times, but the blade never sank deep enough to do much damage. And that wasn't because her mother pulled her blows! Kaia had skills even she hadn't known about.

Tabitha currently had the lead, pushing Kaia backward. She held her own—cold, cold, so cold, tamping down any new flickers of heat that tried to spring from her—until she tripped over an unconscious body. Down, down she fell. Tabitha was on her in an instant.

When the dagger arced toward her, she knew there was only one way to save her neck. And her life. That dagger needed a target. She met the metal with the palm of her hand, allowing the tip to spear her flesh all the way through, going in one side and coming out the other. Hurt like a son of a bitch, but it was totally worth it. Even though her bone was splintered, the dagger was stuck between the pieces and Tabitha drew back an empty hand.

That didn't stop her. Fist after fist battered at Kaia's face so swiftly she couldn't avoid them and she was almost knocked senseless. Still she remained cold and finally gathered the strength to roll backward, to her shoulder blades, scooting her mother off her stomach and allowing Kaia to swing her legs.

She locked her ankles around Tabitha's neck and jerked

down. The woman fell to her back and lost a lungful of oxygen. Or would have, if Kaia hadn't jammed the heels of her boots into her mother's throat, crushing her windpipe and preventing the air from escaping.

Without a pause, Kaia stood, her field of vision shit as blood dripped into her swollen eyes. *End this.* With all of her might, she jerked the dagger from her palm— and damn, it hurt worse coming out than going in!—then tossed the weapon out of the circle. Now they were both unarmed.

She stalked forward, hoping she would be on her mother before the practiced soldier had time to heal or strategize. That didn't work out for her. Tabitha was on her feet in an instant and they were facing off for the third time, circling each other.

"Bravo for you," Tabitha rasped, voice broken thanks to her still-healing trachea. "I expected you to fold long before now."

"That's because you think too highly of yourself and too little of those around you."

"With good reason." Emotionless.

I will make her feel something. Kaia licked her lips, tasted copper. "Mother of the Year Award, meet Tabitha the Vicious. Or not. But don't feel bad. I took Father's away, too."

Tabitha stilled, blinking, those lids hiding and revealing distress. "I'm a good mother."

Uh, what? *That* had struck a nerve? "If by *good* you mean you're the world's worst, then yeah, you're at the top of the list."

Amber eyes narrowed, the distress vanishing. "When you're dead, another Harpy will take possession of your man. You know that, don't you? And as your conqueror, I'll have first rights."

Ouch. Going for the jugular with words now, too, trying to elicit an emotional response. As Strider had said, Kaia was all about her emotions. She could feel the fire springing back to life inside her, heating…heating…

She could release the flames, end things now. They'd fought. There'd be no crying foul now. Kaia had held her own, but though there was no love lost between mother and daughter, she didn't want to burn the woman to death.

What she wanted didn't matter, however. Not now. *Do what you gotta do to survive,* Strider had told her.

It was time.

Finally she opened her mind to the heat, welcoming it, letting it grow, spread—consume.

Hotter…hotter… She didn't know what to expect. Last time, the change had come over her so unexpectedly, she hadn't had a second to stop and think about what was happening. What would she do if the flames refused to come?

Shock clouded her mother's expression. There was a roar in Kaia's ears, her body hotter, hotter, then all she could see was a cerulean haze. In less than a heartbeat, the flames had coiled from her pores, catching every inch of her in a raging inferno. Even her clothes burned away.

"Sorry about this, Mom," she said. She leapt, closing the distance between them. Contact. They fell to the ground. Flames jumped from Kaia to Tabitha. She paused, waiting.

Where were her mother's screams?

"You really think I would have slept with a Phoenix if I wasn't protected against his fire? But I'm impressed. You fooled me. I had no idea you were capable of this."

"I—I—" Had no response. Was too stunned.

Tabitha went on, "I can't summon the flames, but I *can* withstand them. So, fight *on*."

Once again Kaia was rolled to her back and punched over and over again. This she allowed, more from her own sense of astonishment than an inability to fend her mother off.

When her senses crystallized back into focus, she stopped trying to protect her face and neck. There was only one way to end this.

The punches continued to descend. As sharp pain exploded through her, her eyesight soon obliterated, her throat soon crushed—and knowing claws were coming next, and with them, the loss of her head—the heat was replaced by a return of her cold determination.

Do whatever it takes.

Kaia arched up, still taking the blows. Her mother suspected nothing, too lost in the rhythm of her fists, expecting Kaia to slip into unconsciousness at any moment. Kaia reached around her mother's back and ripped. A shriek echoed through the air as warm blood coated her hands. Those fists finally stopped raining. The weight lifted from her shoulders.

Kaia brought her hands to her mouth and licked. Anything to survive, she told herself again. Blood, any blood, was medicine and she needed to heal. Her mother's life force slid down her decimated throat and into her stomach. The effect wasn't as powerful as when she drank from Strider, but her vision cleared somewhat and she sat up the rest of the way.

Her mother lay a few feet away from her, unconscious and naked from the blaze. She might have withstood a broken wing, but she couldn't withstand a total loss of them. Her back was a mess, her wings completely gone. Kaia's chest constricted. In sorrow that their feud had come to this, in pride that she had won.

She considered her surroundings. The rest of the fight had ended, as well. To her disappointment, she saw that the Eagleshields had defeated her sisters, who had in turn defeated the Skyhawks. Those who were still standing regarded her with stunned expressions. She only cared about her team.

Thankfully, every beloved member was alive. Held at bay by sword-point, but alive. One at a time, she met each of their gazes. They nodded in apology and appreciation. She didn't care that they'd lost—only that they lived.

They would have a chance at vindication during the next competition. And perhaps she could have validation now. Unconcerned by her nakedness, she lumbered to her feet. No matter what happened next, there were now only three contenders for first place in round four. And whoever won there would win *everything*. Bragging rights and the Paring Rod.

Had Strider realized how close they were to ultimate victory?

Strider. Her sisters might be alive, but she had lost. By defeating her team, the Eagleshields had defeated her. Strider had just lost his own challenge.

No, she assured herself in the next instant. He'd only sworn to kill those who defeated her. Or was it hurt her? Either way, there'd been no time limit for his death-blow deliveries. Right?

She searched the cheering crowd, but caught no sight of him. There were Sabin and Lysander, who'd disappeared for a while, too, but had now returned. Both were tense, pale and agitated, clearly wanting to grab their women and leave.

Was Strider okay? Where had he gone?

Was he currently in pain?

She could have challenged the Eagleshields and continued the fight. But she couldn't disable all of them at the same time. One of her team members would be harmed, maybe killed. So she had to decide. Save them, or save Strider agonizing pain.

Praying he would understand, she knelt, admitting defeat.

Three things happened at once. Their surroundings changed, the Coliseum no longer new and fresh but old and crumbling, man-made blockades and humans suddenly materializing around them. Juliette's scream of rage and disbelief echoed from the walls. And, worst of all, Strider's agonized shout cut through her soul.

CHAPTER THIRTY-ONE

ABSOLUTE, UTTER CHAOS surrounded him.

Winded, stricken to his knees by debilitating pain, Strider gripped the Paring Rod. Harpies, consorts and slaves raced in every direction, trying to get away before the cops arrived. And they would, bringing reporters with them. Countless laws had been broken and a national treasure desecrated. Even now, blood soaked the ground, pooling around Strider's feet.

What the hell should he do? And why was his demon so agonized, moaning and writhing inside his head? They'd won. Hadn't they?

The moment Lazarus lost his head, the artifact had appeared. Something shimmery had risen from his body and been sucked into the tip of the Rod as if a vacuum switch had been thrown. The warrior's soul, probably, the rest joining the piece inside.

No longer able to hold the illusion, the world had returned to normal. Strider hadn't thought of that little complication, and therefore hadn't prepared for it. Had only considered at last acquiring the Rod. Now he had it, but few options for successfully hiding it.

Juliette knew her man was dead, knew he wouldn't have disobeyed her otherwise. That scream… She would be searching for the body. Would learn who was responsible. There'd be no covering up the truth. Not now. Too many people had seen Strider hovering over the lifeless body, a bloody sword in hand. Not that he would have tried to cover up the truth. He'd done the crime, the consequences his to bear.

Now, though, he'd brought evil to Kaia's door. Juliette would no longer be content to humiliate her. Juliette would want to punish her. Hurt her. Destroy her.

The truth struck him and he wanted to vomit. What the hell had he done?

Strider lumbered to his feet, his head swimming. He swayed, comprehension a bitch slap of truth. He had challenged Kaia to win the game; she must have lost. Shit. Shit! Was she okay?

Someone slammed into him and he stumbled, his pain intensifying. His grip tightened on the Rod. He had to keep it safe; he also had to reach Kaia. Sabin and Lysander were probably looking for their women, so they would be no help.

With his free hand, Strider jerked his cell phone out of his pocket. He needed Lucien.

His vision was too blurry to see the numbers. He tried to call the keeper of Death, anyway. The warrior was on speed dial, so all Strider had to do was press three numbers—just three—then utter one word—*help*—and his friend would appear.

Someone else bumped into him and he stumbled more forcefully. The phone fell from his hand, clattering to the pavement. *Shit!* He bent down, his bones and joints protesting as he patted the area around him. Finally his fingers closed around the plastic.

Multiple pairs of booted feet stomped all over his hand, crushing the bone—and the cell. Those same feet dug into his back, breaking his ribs and stabbing the jagged shards into his lungs, deflating them. Next, his face was shoved into the dirt.

Stampeded, he thought, dazed. How humiliating. He

jerked the Rod underneath his body, hoping to shelter it. He doubted anything could break it, despite its fragile appearance. There was an hourglass on each end, the staff itself thin and wooden, but the thing had been made by the gods. And he was living proof that the gods didn't make inferior products. But the Rod *could* be stolen and that he wouldn't allow.

He almost couldn't believe that he was holding the fourth artifact. After all this time, the final piece of the puzzle had fallen straight into his lap. At a terrible price, yes, but he had it.

Eventually the footsteps let up and Strider forced his battered body to stand. He wheezed, swayed. A few more Harpies ran into him as they raced past, but they failed to knock him down. Maybe because they weren't trying. They were just in a hurry.

Another feminine scream rent the air, closer this time. The agony in that scream...agony and rage, blending together in a vicious harmony.

"I. Will. Kill. You." Juliette's words reverberated, each one a lash of hatred.

Even though he couldn't see shit, he turned and let the momentum of the thinning crowd lead him away. A few times, his knees threatened to buckle, but he used the Rod as a walking stick and kept going.

How close was Juliette on his heels?

Kaia! he mentally shouted. They'd never spoken telepathically, but he'd never been this desperate to reach her before. He could only hope their marriage had enhanced their connection. *Where are you?*

"I'm here." A familiar fragrance filled his nose a split second before a warm arm snaked around his waist, jerking him to the left. "Is that what I think it is?"

Thank the gods. She was alive, she was here, and they *could* speak telepathically. An advantage he would explore when they were safe. Right now, he could feel her heart beating against his side, fast, but hell, it was beating, it was beating and that was enough. "Yes. I'm sorry, baby doll. I had to take it. Couldn't let the opportunity pass. And don't touch it, okay?" He didn't know how the Rod worked, how to pass the souls and abilities trapped inside to another person, or how to steal souls and abilities from the living, and he didn't want to risk doing irreparable harm to Kaia. "Are you okay?"

"You can't see for yourself?"

"Nope. Corneas busted."

"That explains why you were about to smash into the wall," she said dryly. "Listen. Even though I want to bash your head in—seriously, you think I'll take the Rod from you?—I'm sorry I lost. I'm sorry you're in pain. I could have won, could have killed everyone, but my sisters would have died, too, and I couldn't—"

"You don't have to explain. I'm just glad you're here. And no, I don't think you'll take the Rod from me. But it's dangerous and I don't know how to work it properly." Should have explained that.

She tugged him to the right. "All right, then. I forgive you for snapping at me, but back to the subject at hand. You hate losing. Honestly, I think you would kill your own mother to win a battle. If you had one. And you put your faith in my ability, but I—"

"Kaia," he said, cutting her off again. "You are too stubborn for your own good. Nothing matters but the fact that you're alive, I swear. And to be honest, you aren't even the one who needs to apologize. You told me not to take the Rod, to let you win it, but I took it anyway."

"I had changed my mind about that."

A tug to the left. "I know. That doesn't change the fact that I—"

"You knew? How? Never mind. We'll discuss it later. Now who's the stubborn one?"

Despite his pain, he found himself grinning.

"Damn," she suddenly cursed. "Juliette's still on our tail and I can't seem to lose her."

His amusement vanished.

Kaia ushered him down a flight of stairs, around a corner. "She's closing in, and if I don't do something, she's gonna reach us." Without a pause for breath, she pushed him against a hard, cool wall. "Stay here."

There was no time to question her. She released him and a second later, a sizzling blast of heat wafted over him. She'd just set herself on fire, he realized.

Female shrieks erupted.

"You will pay—" Juliette began, only to be cut off by a grunt of agony.

He wished he could see what was happening.

Sweat rolled down his body. His pain hadn't lessened and without Kaia there to distract him, to move him, he experienced each lance full force. He hunched over, vomited. He should be fighting alongside Kaia, yet here she was, doing everything on her own. He was a hindrance. If not for him, she could have escaped already, with no problem.

"That should hold the bitch up for a while," she said with satisfaction, once again winding an arm around his waist and jerking him forward. Though she wasn't currently on fire, her body temperature had risen substantially.

"You're getting good at that," he said, gritting his teeth to help withstand the burn of her.

"Maybe because she keeps me in a constant state of white-hot fury."

The scent of burning cotton filled his nose. His shirt, he realized. And then another thought hit him. She'd caught fire. Completely. Her clothing would have already burned away.

"You're naked, aren't you?" He hated the idea of anyone but him seeing her like that, but he was amused by the picture the two of them must make.

"Yeah." No shame accompanied the affirmation. "I have been for a while. So how'd you get the Rod?"

A wave of guilt slammed through him as he explained about Lazarus, Juliette and the kind of power at stake. All the while, Kaia piloted him around corners, down steps, up steps.

"So Lazarus is dead?"

A cool, welcome breeze slapped at him. "Yeah. He wasn't such a bad guy. I wish there'd been another way." And maybe there was. Lazarus had said *As I've been led to understand*—which meant he could have been wrong. He could possibly survive what Strider had done to him. His soul, anyway. He could be trapped in the Rod right now.

"Yeah, he was growing on me, too. Perhaps—crap. Let's talk about this later." She released him. "Gotta get my things and dress. Hold on."

So they were in the tent they'd occupied earlier, he thought as he swayed. His ears perked as he listened for her sisters, but only the sound of her movements greeted him. Then she was gripping him and ushering him through the maze. He could picture their surroundings now, and knew a fence loomed in front of them.

"Climb," she said, confirming the layout in his head.

His already damaged body protested the entire way over, but he made it. Continued forward.

"Now jump."

Another fence, though this one was barely more than a hurdle. He landed with a grunt of pain.

"Boulder," she said, jerking him to the side.

Soon as they rounded it, they ran. Just ran. Through labored breaths, he inhaled the fragrance of pine, dirt and car exhaust. His boots pounded into rocks and grass, then pavement. A few times, he heard the surprised—and perhaps horrified—murmurs of humans.

Kaia slowed, stopped, then pulled away from him again. "Stay here." Several minutes ticked by. He hated standing there, helpless, the Rod out in the open. "Cash," she muttered when she returned to his side.

"Smart girl."

A haze of gold broke past the darkness of his sight and he blinked. Another blink. No change. Just that dim little light, but that was enough. He was already healing.

What seemed an eternity later, Kaia rented a motel room and secured them inside. She helped him to the bed and he collapsed atop the mattress, taking the Rod with him.

"FYI, you look like shit, Bonin'." She eased beside him and smoothed the hair from his brow with a gentle touch.

He leaned into the caress. "Thanks, Red. Must say, I've felt better, too."

"Is there anything I can do for you?"

"Nah. All's I need is time."

"So what does that thing do? You mentioned the soul thing, yeah, but I'm confused."

"You got a cell phone?" he asked, rather than answer. First things first. He had to get the artifact out of Rome and away from Juliette.

"Yep. Grabbed it when I got dressed."

"Call Lucien and ask him to come here."

As she obeyed, the light he saw expanded, his vision clearing a little more. He began to notice little details. Overhead, the ceiling was a mix of white and yellow. The walls were white stucco. There was a window draped by thick red material. Beside him was a scarred nightstand, a blue lamp resting on top. His gaze moved to Kaia, who paced as she spoke into the phone. That ended and she went silent. She jabbed at the keypad, agitated.

Another couple minutes passed before he could see her clearly. Bruises colored her left eye and jaw, and her upper lip was cut and swollen. Her hair lay in tangles around her shoulders. She wore a clean T-shirt and jeans, but no shoes. She'd run through the streets with bare feet, and it showed. Her toes were blackened from dirt and each step she took left a smudge of blood on the tiled floor.

Not once had she complained or even uttered a squeak of pain. She was a warrior to her core, and his heart swelled with love and pride for her. She hadn't cared that he'd taken the Rod. No, she'd praised him. Even though he'd caused her nothing but trouble.

One of a kind, his Kaia.

She deserved the best. Therefore, he was going to be a better man. For her.

Frowning, she shoved her cell phone in her back pocket. "Lucien will be here in a few, he said. Also, I texted my sisters and told them where we are. Taliyah and Neeka are nearby and they'll be here in a few minutes, too. I haven't heard back from anyone else."

Before the last word left her mouth, there was a knock at the door. Taliyah didn't wait for Kaia to answer; she just strode inside, Neeka right behind her. The sisters embraced.

"Sorry about the loss," Taliyah said, patting her on the head.

Kaia shrugged. "Like I haven't caused my fair share of them lately."

"So you're a Phoenix, huh," Neeka said.

"I know." Crimson-streaked fingers scrubbed at her face, highlighting her fatigue. "I was surprised, too."

Taliyah shook her head, a study of femininity as her

pale hair danced around her shoulders. "Oh, Neeka and I weren't surprised."

Kaia's brows knitted together. "Why not?"

"You've been exhibiting signs for several weeks now. Plus, you burst into flames the day you were born. Mother wanted to protect you from your father, so she gave you something to ensure you wouldn't do so again for centuries and would even react to the Phoenix toxin if you were scratched or bitten." Another pat, then Taliyah padded to Neeka's side. "I knew it was only a matter of time before your ability resurfaced."

Strider could actually hear Kaia's thoughts; they were so forceful, they rode the threads of the connection between them, jolting him. *What a freaking shocker. Mother actually acted motherly and helped me out. I want to hug the woman, then shake her. Can't soften, though. This is war.* "Well, you should have told me!" she fumed aloud.

"Seriously," Strider said. He would have sat up, glared, something, but damn, the pain inside him continued to intensify, his demon moaning and groaning.

Taliyah paid him no heed. "And cause you pointless worry? Hardly. Now that it's happened, you still have nothing to worry about. Okay? Your father will not try and take you, I promise."

"You really think?" Vulnerability wove through each of the syllables.

He wanted to call her over, hold her tight. If her dad— his father-in-law, he realized with a start—proved to be a problem, her dad would feel the wrath of a demon-possessed warrior.

"I really know," Taliyah assured her. "He's dead. I killed him myself. And I know, I know. His people would have wanted you the moment they heard you could withstand their fire, since there aren't many females who can."

"*Would have* wanted?" Kaia and Strider asked in unison. He noticed she gave no indication that her father's death bothered her. No sorrow wafted through their connection, her mind calm.

A stiff nod, as if their surprise offended her. "I'm sure Strider told you about Neeka and I sneaking off and meeting a group of men. Anyway, Neeka owes me a big-time favor and agreed to wed a Phoenix warrior in your place."

That must be some favor, if wedding a stranger was appropriate payback. And what the hell had she meant? "In her *place?*" Strider hadn't intended to yell, but damn. "They think she'll marry someone besides me? They can damn well think again! She's mine."

"I don't understand," Kaia said softly. "And he's right. I'm his."

Hearing her confession heated him up as surely as her internal fire always did, but at the same time it soothed him, as she'd probably intended.

Taliyah said, "They would have come after you, and they would have killed him. I knew that would upset you, so I made other arrangements."

Just like that? "Now they'll just try to take both of them."

"No," Taliyah assured him. "I won't give you specifics about the deal—that's up to Neeka—but they won't come for Kaia."

"Neeka," he said, his gaze landing on the gorgeous black girl.

She was watching the sisters, expression a little sad, so she didn't realize he'd spoken to her. Kaia looked at her, too, and the Harpy nodded.

"Why?" Kaia asked her.

"I saved her life," Taliyah answered for the Eagleshield. "Like I said, she owed me."

"Can she withstand their fire?" Strider asked. If not, the warriors would come after Kaia, anyway.

"Not yet," Neeka replied.

His gaze returned to her and he saw that she was watching him now. "Then what you're doing is—"

"I will. One day, I will. But right now, I have something else they prize just as much."

"And now we really do have to go," Taliyah said, tugging her friend back to the door before Neeka could expand on that statement. Not that she would have. She'd zipped her lips pretty damn tight. "We're tracking Tabitha, making sure her people get her to safety. You messed her up pretty damn good. I was so impressed, baby girl."

"Thank you." A tendril of guilt drifted from her.

Taliyah gave the most fleeting of smiles. "Soon as I know she's taken care of, I'll come back."

The door shut and the pair was gone.

Strider watched as remorse washed over Kaia's pale features.

"For your mother?" Strider asked.

"Yeah," she answered, knowing what he meant. "I wish our relationship hadn't reached such a terrible point, but—"

Lucien chose that moment to materialize and Kaia pressed her lips together. The big warrior took in the scene in an instant and cursed. "What the hell happened to you two?"

Strider focused on his friend. Black hair, mismatched eyes—one blue, one brown—and a face as scarred as the nightstand. "What happened doesn't matter. Only the end result. This," he said, holding out the Paring Rod with a grimace, "is the fourth artifact."

Lucien's eyes widened as he assumed ownership. "You're kidding me, right?" His gaze raked over the item in question.

"Nope. There's a very angry Harpy out there who wants it back and she will do anything to get it."

The keeper of Death popped his jaw, every inch the dedicated soldier. "How'd she get it in the first place?"

"That's a story for another day." Strider's voice...so weak, so distant. Again he tried to sit up, anything to keep himself focused and *there*. The gut-wrenching pain and exertion of the day began to drain what little strength he had left. He lay there, fighting for breath, and pressed on. "At least we finally know what this artifact can do. Somehow, it can trap souls and supernatural abilities inside its tip. That tip can also *impart* those souls and abilities to others."

Tense, heavy silence as Lucien absorbed the news.

Then a *beep* echoed around them.

"A text." Kaia whipped out her phone, stared down at the screen and sighed in relief. "Gwen and Sabin are safe. I told them where we are and they're on their way."

Strider experienced a wave of his own relief and hurried on, wanting to get the rest of the deets out before he slipped into unconsciousness. "I don't know how to use the damn thing. I only know that whoever is holding it can't ever take what's inside. They can only give the powers to others."

Beep.

A pause. "Lysander can't find Bianka," Kaia said now, traces of panic in her voice. "He's worried, and asks if anyone has seen her."

"I'm sure she's—" Lucien began.

Another *beep.*

Another pause. "Oh, my gods." Kaia choked on a cry of rage. "No, no, no. No!"

At last Strider found the strength to sit up, concern rocking him. Her upset fueled his own. "What is it, baby doll?"

The rage glassed her eyes as she showed him the screen. Her hand shook as he read, Want sis 2 live? Let's trade.

His throat constricted when he saw the symbol for an attachment. "What's the attachment?"

"Attachment? I didn't notice one." Her trembling increased as she studied the phone. She pressed a few buttons and choked on another cry. "A video. I see Bianka. She's tied up. Bleeding."

After a few seconds' static, he heard Bianka shout, "Tell her to go fuck herself, Kye!" Then Juliette was speaking over her. "You bring me the Paring Rod in one hour, or I swear to the gods I will remove your twin's head the same way your bastard of a consort removed Lazarus's. And if you dare—*dare!*—think to do your fire thing..."

A screech of rage. "You know what? Bring your consort, too. Either your sister dies or he does. You pick. For every minute you're late, your precious sister will suffer." A pause. "Oh, and Kaia. I hope you're late. Good luck finding us."

CHAPTER THIRTY-TWO

JULIETTE HAD MESSED WITH the wrong girl.

Kaia had used her entire allotted hour to gather her trusted loved ones and friends. They hadn't hesitated to rush to help and for that she would be forever grateful. All the while, Strider, who was still in obvious pain, kept her calm, assuring her all would be well.

Sweet, darling man. He was directly behind her, his cinnamon scent enveloping her, and she chose to believe him. Plus, she'd realized they were more deeply connected than ever, and he kept feeding her support, uplifting her.

She had defeated her own mother. She could do this, too.

Finding Juliette hadn't been difficult. Not with Lucien doing his flashy thing. He'd followed her spiritual trail until he'd located her, checked on Bianka (she was injured but holding her own), informed Kaia where to go and then returned to guard Bee, invisible, and no one the wiser.

Lucien's stealthy presence was the only reason Kaia had yet to rain a world of hurt on Juliette. Same was true for Lysander. Well, that, and Zacharel's firm hand holding him back.

Anything changed, Lucien would tell them and they'd alter their current plan. A plan to ensure the Eagleshields never tried something like this again.

Taliyah and Gwen at her sides, Kaia marched with her head held high. Strider and his brothers by circumstance were behind them. Lysander and his army of warrior angels were in the air, circling the area, their white-and-gold wings gracefully outstretched. Kaia had been told they were needed in the heavens, some kind of angelic war brewing, but Lysander had brought them all here, instead.

His woman was the most important thing to him.

So, actually, Juliette had messed with the wrong *family.* For that's what the people surrounding her were, Kaia thought. Her family. Not a single one of them would rest until Bianka was safe. In fact, they would die for her. Would die for Kaia.

Just as she would die for them.

Won't come to that. She squared her shoulders, deliberated her surroundings. Juliette had chosen a lovely location. The beach, on this moonlit night, was a deceptively tranquil sight. Across the way, ancient Roman ruins stretched toward the darkened sky and boulders glinted silver. Water washed into sand, creating a soothing lullaby.

Too bad blood was about to spatter and screams were about to erupt.

"Juliette," Kaia shouted. No more waiting. She wanted this over and done.

A seething, soot-covered Juliette stepped into a golden moonbeam, her hatred so strong it actually vibrated in the air. Her clan formed a menacing line behind her.

Kaia stopped a few feet away, barely out of striking distance, and her posse followed suit.

Juliette seethed, "I'm surprised your half-wit self managed to find me, but I'm very glad you did. We finish this now. Where's the Rod?"

Rather than answer, Kaia said, "I'm sorry about your consort, I really am, and I wish things could have ended differently, but I can't change the past. I can only embrace the future. So I'm giving you one chance—only one—to walk away from this. Release my sister and I'm gone. The end."

Juliette's reply was instantaneous. "Oh, no. You will not leave this land unscathed." She snapped her fingers and two Eagleshields dragged a fuming and bloody Bianka to the front of the line. "I believe you had a choice to make, Kaia the Disappointment. Your sister or your man."

Lysander's roar of outrage echoed from the sky. Juliette was lucky Zacharel was here to stop him from rampaging.

After Bianka gave a thumbs-up to her man, she met Kaia's gaze and grinned wickedly. Kaia almost collapsed from relief. Hearing on the video that her sister was well was not the same as seeing for herself, live and in person.

"Told you," a raspy male voice whispered. Trembling fingers traced the length of her spine. Strider. Despite his pain, he was still showing his support.

And suddenly Kaia could see the humor in the situation. Bianka would forever use this experience to bend Kaia to her will.

You remember the time your enemy kidnapped me? her twin would say. *Me, too. That's why you have to do this one little thing for me.*

"Actually," she said, tossing Juliette a wicked grin of her own, "*you* have a choice. Surrender or die. Lysander," she shouted. "You're up."

The angels arrowed from the sky. In less than a second, the Eagleshields were on their knees, heads bowed, winged warriors holding swords of fire at their necks.

"Wow, that was easy," she said. Hopefully, the Harpies would not realize the angels—who lived by a code of conduct Kaia didn't pretend to understand—were not actually allowed to hurt them without "just cause." Whatever that was.

Lysander swooped Bianka into his arms, cooing at her, demanding to know what had been done to her.

Bianka kissed her man, then glowered back at a stunned Juliette. Though kneeling, the leader of the Eagleshields didn't look properly cowed. "Told you that you were dumb to mess with an angel's consort."

"But...but..."

"Yeah," Kaia said as she watched the realization finally sink in. "You were defeated *that* fast." She snapped her fingers in a parody of the gesture Juliette had used to summon Bianka. "And now that that's taken care of, let's discuss a little business. Lysander, will you tell your flunky to nix the fire sword on the brunette and only the brunette, please?"

A moment passed in heavy silence. Then Lysander gave a stiff nod and the dark-haired angel who had Juliette corralled backed away, the flickering sword soon disappearing altogether.

Juliette popped to a stand but didn't try to run. Wise of her. Kaia would naturally have followed her and the end result would not have been pretty.

"There are only three clans left who can take first prize," Kaia said. "Mine, yours and the Skyhawks."

"Not true," a female said weakly.

Kaia's mother limped from the shadows to stand beside the angels.

She met Tabitha's emotionless gaze, trying not to panic. Tabitha had yet to heal. There were smudges of fatigue under her eyes, her shoulders were hunched and her legs shook, as if nearing collapse.

"What are you doing here? Planning to protest my place in the finals?" Kaia lifted her chin, proud of herself. There'd been no hint of her own emotions in her voice. No tremor to give her away. "Well, you can—"

"No," Tabitha said, shocking her further. "Taliyah told me what was happening. That is why I'm here. I choose to withdraw my team from the competition."

"What?" Kaia and Juliette gasped at the same time.

Tabitha nodded, the movement almost toppling her. "I simply wanted you to have a chance to prove yourself to the clans, without any aid from me. And so you have. I am no longer needed. And as you can see, I am no threat at the moment."

Kaia was utterly speechless.

"If that's true, why did you taunt me?" Strider demanded, speaking up for the first time. His fury lent strength to the words.

"She taunted you?" Kaia gritted out, anger helping her find her own voice. "When?"

It started at orientation, she heard him say inside her mind. *Before Tag.* He could speak into her mind? She'd known some couples could do so, but she'd never expected to be one of the lucky. Bonus!

Tabitha's chin rose, a mirror of Kaia's own stance. *So that's where I got it. Huh.*

"I didn't taunt you, you stupid man." Amber eyes shimmered with rage. "I *warned* you of her enemy's intentions. You're welcome, by the way. You gave me nothing but grief for my generosity."

"Don't call him stupid," Kaia snapped. Only she had the right. But, uh, her mother had tried to *aid* her? "And why should he believe you? You hate me."

I'm fine, baby doll. Don't worry about me.

There was the slightest softening of Tabitha's expression as she returned her attention to Kaia. "You're my daughter…Kaia the Wing-Shredder. *That* is why he should believe me."

Kaia the Wing-Shredder. The name echoed through her mind, a dream come true and so much better than the one she'd once given herself. "I—" Didn't know what to say. Never in a million years—or fifteen hundred—had she expected to hear those words leave this woman's mouth.

"Just so you know, I do not hate you. Yes, I was genuinely angry that you disobeyed me all those centuries ago. Yes, your actions were disappointing. You were supposed to redeem yourself, but you never did and I tired of waiting. When I realized you'd found your consort, I knew you would either lose yourself completely or at last discover the warrior you were always meant to be. And yes, that means I've been keeping tabs on you all this time. That means I also helped ambush you—for your own good. I was quite proud that you fought off the Hunters and figured out our plan."

That wasn't a confession of love, either, Kaia noted. But then again, abrupt, harsh and unchangeable, that was Tabitha. Was she a liar, though? No. Never. Tabitha stated her thoughts and that was that. Always. Knowing it, Kaia felt her chest swell with emotion she could no longer hide. Her mother did not hate her!

Did this mean they were getting together for Christmas? She doubted it, but hell, this was more than she'd had in years. She'd take it. 'Cause really. Her mom didn't hate her. She would never get tired of thinking that. Rock on!

"I can't say I'm grateful for the tough love," Kaia replied, "but I'm happy with my life."

Strider's satisfaction slipped around her like a cloak.

"Now you're strong enough to keep what's yours. Of course you're happy." Tabitha limped forward to close the distance between them and extended her arm. "Here."

Frowning, Kaia accepted…a Skyhawk medallion for warriors. A new one. A nicer one than Juliette's. Her eyes were wide as she slid the leather band around her neck. The wooden disk was light, cool to the touch, and yet managed to burn her deep.

"Visit me soon, and we'll…talk." With that, Tabitha faced Juliette. "I have long enjoyed your company, as you have enjoyed mine. I knew you and Kaia would one day come to blows, and that was justified. She took your consort. My only hope was that she would be somewhat prepared for your attack. Now she is.

"But you should have struck at *her* consort rather than Bianka. After all the years I spent training you, I would have hoped you'd have learned that the punishment should always fit the crime. And so, for your actions this day, I leave you to the fate you have brought upon yourself. An ass-kicking from my daughter." Having said her piece, she turned and stumbled away.

She truly doesn't hate me. Kaia sniffled, trying not to cry from joy. Her mother hadn't exactly defended her, and had called her only "somewhat" prepared, but still. No hatred!

And now to keep what's mine... "Looks like it's just you and me now," she said to Juliette. "We're gonna battle this out."

Satisfaction spread over her enemy's face. "Oh, really? You won't let your slaves jump in and save you?"

"The angels and Lords are my friends, not my slaves, though I realize that concept is foreign to you. And why would I allow them to take over? I'm going to soak the ground with your blood. Fair and square."

Juliette's gaze shifted to Strider, narrowed, and Kaia halfway expected her to challenge the warrior instead. "Winner leaves with your consort."

Bitch. "No way in—"

"Do it, baby doll," Strider broke in, speaking out loud this time. He kissed her cheek. "There's no doubt in my mind who'll win this thing."

She had failed him last time, but he still trusted her. She could feel it. Determination rose inside her, an unstoppable tidal wave. Juliette would suffer for issuing that particular demand.

"With *no* interference from *anyone,*" Juliette growled, not liking the complete disregard for her skills.

"Done," Kaia replied. "Weapons? I'll let you pick. I'm sweet like that."

"Hand-to-hand. And no fires, bitch."

"Can't handle a little heat?" She was too coldly resolute to resort to the flames, anyway. "Very well. But the way I hear it, you're out of practice with the hand-to-hand thing. Isn't *that* the real reason you didn't enter the games yourself?"

Juliette's nostrils flared. "You'll find out."

Strider looked as if he wanted to argue the fire thing; instead, he gave her another kiss. Still trusting her. The tidal wave became a tsunami.

"When I'm done with you, there'll be nothing left," Juliette added as she discarded multiple daggers and a gun.

"You're so deluded I feel sorry for you." Kaia discarded her own arsenal. She watched as the angels forced the Eagleshields to crawl away, preventing them from helping Juliette in any way. The Lords went with them. Strider brushed his fingers along her spine one last time before limping away from her.

Just like that, she and Juliette squared off, circling each other, hatred pulsing off the woman and vibrating in the air. *You made a critical mistake, Julie girl,* she projected. Throwing Strider into the mix had guaranteed that Kaia wouldn't mess around. This was serious and she would act without any hint of mercy.

Wait for it...wait...

"You think you're invincible, now that you've defeated your mother," Juliette snapped. "Well, clearly she didn't give the fight her all."

"Whatever you need to tell yourself." *Wait...*

Circle...circle...

"I've watched during each of the competitions." The

smugness had returned to Juliette's tone. "Know what I noticed?"

Wait... "That you're inferior in every way?" *Wait...*

Eyes narrowing... "That you lack control."

How ironic. Right now Juliette's emotions were driving her every move. She thought Kaia was distracted. Kaia wasn't; she was simply prepared.

A shriek echoed. Juliette's body tensing...flinging toward her...

Now!

Just before the other Harpy reached her, Kaia leapt into the air, wings working overtime, backflipped behind Juliette. Having witnessed what Kaia had done to Tabitha, Juliette had suspected the move and quickly spun. But Kaia had suspected *that* move and quickly performed another flip. Once again, she was behind Juliette.

Before the Harpy realized Kaia had changed locations, Kaia grabbed her wings, claws sinking past skin and into tendon, and ripped with every bit of her strength. Exactly as she'd done to her mother.

A patented Kaia the Wing-Shredder move, and as easy as licking the bowl of her favorite ice cream during Fertile Week—aka Hell Week—but then, what did you expect from a woman with a name like hers?

Strider whooped. "That's my girl."

Juliette grunted as she fell face-first against the sand. She tried to pull herself to her knees, but she no longer had the strength, and simply collapsed. Blood pooled around her, as promised, the stark crimson nearly obscene against the purity of the white granules.

The Eagleshields were silent for several heartbeats, their shock palpable. Then, gasps sounded.

Grinning, Kaia crouched beside her nemesis. Juliette's pain-filled eyes looked past her. "We've both hurt the other. Let that be enough. I'll even say I'm sorry it came to this. But, and hear me well, if you come after anyone I love, I will ruin you. And you know I can do it now. I have the Paring Rod and I will take your soul without remorse. Plus, I've got those goody-goody angels on my side. You shouldn't have pissed them off. Enough said."

She didn't wait for a reply. Juliette might taunt her about not truly knowing how to utilize the Rod or might even push her to do something she didn't want to do. Namely, take the woman's head. So she stood and walked toward Strider.

Grinning, he met her halfway.

KAIA SPENT THE REST OF THE DAY making love to her man, in her bedroom, of all places. Being in her Alaskan house, the very house where he'd once broken her heart, was surreal. Anyway, he'd gotten an infusion of strength after her victory against Juliette. An infusion he'd put to very good use.

Now, she lay in his arms, sated beyond compare. She owed this man *so much*. Her current state of happiness, yes, but also her confidence in herself. She was strong, but he'd made her stronger. Because he trusted her, saw deeper than the surface, never caring what other people thought of her, never caring about her mistakes. And he wasn't afraid to love her for who and what she was, changing her the furthest thing from his mind.

"I love you," she told him.

"That's because you're smart. Further proof—look who you ended up with. Me, rather than that shithead Paris."

She chuckled. Did her good to hear him discuss his friend with amusement rather than resentment or jealousy. "Didn't you have something else to tell me?"

"Yes." He sighed. "Here goes. Speaking of Paris, I have to head up to the heavens to help him find his not-so-dead girlfriend. I promised him. I told you that before, right?"

"You did."

"Good. I want you to go with me."

As if she had to think about it. And her willingness didn't just spring from a desire to remain by Strider's side. She wanted Paris happy. "Of course."

"Thank you. And I love you, too. Not only do you make me happy, you make my demon happy. You feed him in a way I hadn't known he needed, making me stronger than ever. That's why I'm challenging myself to make sure you're blissed out for the rest of your days."

She groaned. "You have to stop doing that." If he was hurt—again—because of her...

"Don't worry. I'll let you convince me of the merits of not challenging myself, baby doll."

"And just how will you let me convince you, hmm?"

"Don't be silly. With your body, of course."

She planted little kisses all over his face. "And I will. But didn't you have something *else* to tell me?"

"Yes, but how do you know that?"

She tapped a finger against her temple. "Smart, remember?"

He sat up, reached down and dug into his discarded pants' pocket. When he straightened, he held out his hand, a chain dangling from his fingers. "Here."

"What's this?" she asked, sitting up beside him as she claimed it. A thin wooden disk hung from the links. In the center was an intricate, if lopsided, blue butterfly, matching the one tattooed across his stomach and hip.

A flush colored his cheeks. "It's a necklace. Well, a medallion. It's not the same as your mom's or the one she gave you, but—"

"The cuts on your hands," she gasped out. "You carved this yourself."

He nodded.

Her eyes filled with tears as she removed the one Tabitha had given her, placed it on the nightstand and

donned the new one. "This is *better* than my mother's."
She threw her arms around his neck. "I love you, Strider.
I was just kidding before, but now I mean it."

He gave a warm, husky chuckle. "Actually, I prefer
Bonin'. And I seriously love you, too, Red. More than I
can ever say."

"All Sabin did was tattoo Gwen's name on several parts
of his body after they got married, the loser," she said, fingering the medallion's surface. "I'm so lucky."

He stiffened. "Uh, yeah, speaking of married…"

"Finally," she said on a laugh. "But if you've got something to confess, there's a better time. Like, when you're
about to be inside me."

"You know we're hitched," he said, studying her in-
tently, and she nodded. He relaxed. "How?"

"Some people make bad secret-keepers and would be
better served spilling everything to their doting wife."

"Kaia."

"Fine. I felt the connection."

"Because of the mind-speak, I'm betting. I should have
known." He grinned at that. "And you don't mind?"

"Mind? I want to be your wife. You remember my goals
as a young girl, don't you?" She nibbled on her bottom lip.
"But…maybe you *should* get my name tattooed all over
you. I mean, I adore the medallion so the ink would just
be icing on the cake, proving we're a better couple than
Sabin and Gwen."

"Consider it done."

As she straddled his waist, he reached up and cupped
her jaw. "Now, I'm not doubting you, you understand, but
I'm gonna need you to prove your love. You do remember
promising to do so, don't you?"

"I do. Just tell me how," she whispered, breathless,
knowing exactly where he was headed with this. "I mean,
I love you for your mind, of course, so I guess I could sit

here for hours, describing how I delight in your every ge-
nius idea. And then I could—"

"Just for today, we're going to pretend you love me for
my body." He lay back down, pulling her with him. "So,
you can start up top and work your way down. Okay, okay.
You can also show me how grateful you are for my bril-
liance while you're at it. I mean, your sister is safe because
of me. It's the least you can do."

She barely cut off her laugh. "You're not afraid I'll challenge you?"

Those navy eyes gleamed. "Baby doll, I'd be disappointed if you didn't."

EPILOGUE

Kane came awake in an instant, jolting upright. Panic swam through him, perhaps left over from the falling boulders—and deepened when he saw the iron bars around him.

Bars? A cage? He was in a damned *cage?* What... why...? Before the thought could fully form, he saw that William, unconscious and bleeding, was outside the cage and being carted away.

Dread slapped at Kane, cold and hard and stinging. He reached out, his hand shaky, and tried to shout for his friend. *Wake up. Fight.* But no words emerged.

Kane swallowed, his throat filled with sawdust. And damn it, his head throbbed like a son of a bitch. His stomach threatened to heave at any moment, his body jostling left and right, left and right.

The cage was being wheeled through a cavernous hallway, he realized. Then dizziness flooded him and he closed his eyes. He measured his breaths, hoping the spinning would stop. The air was hot, humid and layered with the scents of rot and sulfur.

Rot. Sulfur. They could mean only one thing. Hell. He was being taken deeper into hell.

His demon roared.

Kane cracked open his lids and glanced at his surroundings, slow and easy this time. He spotted horned, winged monsters beside his cage. They had scales rather than skin, and glowing red eyes.

Demons. Minions.

The roaring in his head turned to laughter. His demon was genuinely amused. That was not a good sign.

He must have groaned. One of the creatures glanced in his direction and scowled, flashing long, white saber teeth. A moment later, a clawed hand reached inside the cage and batted at his cheek, splitting skin.

Once more, Kane slipped into oblivion.

ONE ITEM LEFT ON HIS LIST, and then he could go after Sienna, Paris thought. All he had to do was find Viola, the minor goddess of the Afterlife and discover how a man like him could see the souls of the dead.

Word was, she frequented a bar in the heavens. He was headed there now. As he stomped along the streets, he withdrew his phone and sent his man Strider a text.

I release U from UR vow

He pressed Send and pocketed the phone. After what he'd learned from Arca about the dangers of the two realms he'd have to enter—and the possibility of never leaving one of them—he wasn't willing to risk his friend's life. Especially since the guy had just married his Harpy. Yeah, he'd gotten a text from Strider with the happy news.

I'll never have that, he thought hollowly. Rather than wallow in despair, however, he opened himself back up to the darkness now constantly frothing inside him. So much darkness. A mist, sweeping through him, turning him into a cold, hard bastard.

Hurt...kill...

Good. He needed that coldness, now more than ever.

No matter what, he would save Sienna—even at the expense of his own life.

* * * * *

Don't miss Paris's long-awaited story,
THE DARKEST SEDUCTION,
coming soon from Gena Showalter and HQN Books.
For an exclusive early sneak peek,
pick up your copy of DATING THE UNDEAD
by Gena Showalter and Jill Monroe,
on sale from Harlequin Nonfiction
in January 2012!

Glossary of Characters and Terms

Aeron—Former keeper of Wrath

All-Seeing Eye—Godly artifact with the power to see into heaven and hell

Amun—Keeper of Secrets

Anya—(Minor) Goddess of Anarchy

Arca—Messenger goddess

Ashlyn Darrow—Human female with supernatural ability

Atropos—One of the Three Fates; snipper of threads

Baden—Keeper of Distrust (deceased)

Bait—Human females, Hunters' accomplices

Bianka Skyhawk—Harpy; twin sister of Kaia

Cage of Compulsion—Godly artifact with the power to enslave anyone trapped inside

Cameo—Keeper of Misery

Cloak of Invisibility—Godly artifact with the power to shield its wearer from prying eyes

Cronus—King of the Titans, keeper of Greed

Danika Ford—Human female; All-Seeing Eye

Dean Stefano—Hunter; right-hand man of Galen

dimOuniak—Pandora's box

Galen—Keeper of Hope

Gideon—Keeper of Lies

Gilly—Human female

Gorgon—Immortal with snakes for hair and the power to turn man to stone with only a glance

Greeks—Former rulers of Olympus, now imprisoned in Tartarus

Gwen Skyhawk—Half-Harpy, half-angel; daughter of Galen

Hades—One of the rulers of hell

Haidee—Immortal; former Hunter

Hate—A demigod and keeper of the demon of Hate

Hera—Queen of the Greeks

Hunters—Mortal enemies of the Lords of the Underworld

Juliette Eagleshield—Harpy; enemy of Kaia

Juno—Harpy; ally of Kaia

Kaia Skyhawk—Harpy; sister of Bianka, Taliyah and Gwen

Kane—Keeper of Disaster

Klotho—One of the Three Fates; spinner of threads

Lachesis—One of the Three Fates; weaver of threads

Land of Cinder—Home of the Phoenix race

Lazarus—Imprisoned immortal consort of Juliette; son of Typhon

Legion—Demon minion; friend of Aeron

Lords of the Underworld—Exiled warriors to the Greek gods who now house demons inside them

Lucien—Keeper of Death; leader of the Budapest warriors

Lucifer—Prince of darkness; ruler of hell

Lysander—Elite warrior angel and consort of Bianka Skyhawk

Maddox—Keeper of Violence

Medusa—Most famed of the Gorgons

Mina—Goddess of Weaponry

Moirai—AKA The Three Fates; three immortal females who weave destiny

Neeka the Unwanted—Harpy; ally of Kaia

The Odynia—also known as "the Garden of Goodbyes"; Rhea's heavenly realm

Olivia—An angel

One, True Deity—Ruler of the angels

Pandora—Immortal warrior, once guardian of dimOuniak (deceased)

Paring Rod—Godly artifact, container of souls and granter of abilities

Paris—Keeper of Promiscuity

Phoenix—An immortal with the power of fire and the ability to raise the dead from its ashes

Reyes—Keeper of Pain

Rhea—Queen of the Titans; estranged wife of Cronus; keeper of Strife

Sabin—Keeper of Doubt; leader of the Greek warriors

Scarlet—Keeper of Nightmares

Sienna Blackstone—Deceased female Hunter; new keeper of Wrath

Skye—A pseudodoctor; wife of a Hunter

Strider—Keeper of Defeat

Tabitha Skyhawk—Harpy; mother of Taliyah, Bianka, Kaia and Gwen

Taliyah Skyhawk—Harpy; elder sister of Bianka, Kaia and Gwen

Tartarus—Greek god of Confinement; also the immortal prison on Mount Olympus

Tedra—Harpy; ally of Kaia

Titans—Current rulers of Olympus

Torin—Keeper of Disease

Typhon—Father of Lazarus; immortal with the head of a dragon and the body of a snake

Unspoken Ones—Reviled gods; prisoners of Cronus

Viola—Minor goddess of the Afterlife

Warrior Angels—Heavenly demon assassins

William—Immortal warrior (and god among gods—or so he says)

Zacharel—A warrior angel

Zeus—King of the Greeks

GENA SHOWALTER